SWORDS OVER FIRESHORE

PATI NAGLE

Evennight

Evennight Books
Cedar Crest, New Mexico

Swords Over Fireshore
copyright © 2012 by Pati Nagle

ISBN: 978-1-61138-166-5

Published by Evennight Books, Cedar Crest, New Mexico, an affiliate of Book View Café

Cover art by Lynne Whitehorn, based on a photo by Vasiliy Koval *for my brother, Darragh*

Acknowledgments

Thanks to:

~ *Chris Krohn (as always), my beloved partner and first reader*

~ *Plotbusters*

~ *Lynne Whitehorn for improving the cover*

~ *Peggy Whitmore, Pari Noskin, and Debbie Smith, for believing in me*

~ *My wonderful colleagues in Book View Café*

Map of the Ælven Lands

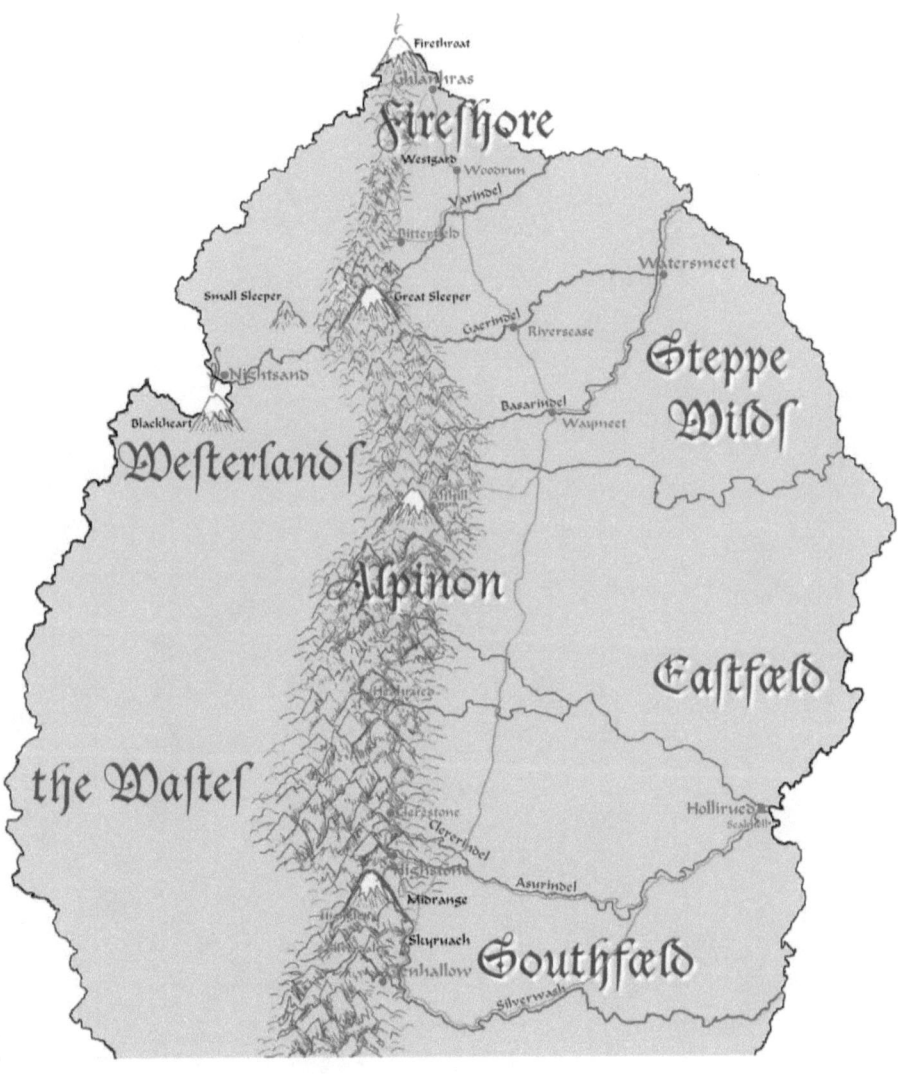

Let all your actions enhance the well-being of others

Khi is a gift to be honored, respected, and served

Guard the world's creatures, for they are the hope of your future

All living beings are kindred, deserving your care

—Creed of the Ælven, third stave

❀ Fireshore ❀

Eliani paced back and forth across the road, gazing ever northward past the bridge she would soon cross, as if she could see all the way to Ghlanhras. She could not, for the darkwood forest, dense and high enough to obscure much of the sky, blocked her view. In her mind, though, she saw the city as she had fled it earlier that night: torn by sudden chaos; black-clad, snow-haired alben atop the stone wall that surrounded its graceful structures.

Come daylight, when the alben hid from the sun, she and her escort would return to the city to rescue her cousin Luruthin and Governor Othanin. Those two she felt certain would be held in Darkwood Hall. Any other ælven in the city must wait for aid until the army arrived from the south. She hoped they would not suffer too severely.

"My lady?"

Eliani turned to see Vanorin, the stern-faced captain of her escort, holding out a set of leather armor. "If you will."

The leather was finely worked, traced with leaves and vines in ornate detail. Nothing like her own comparatively simple leathers, which she had left behind in her escape.

She frowned. "Whose are these?"

One of the escort—Revani, a fair-haired Greenglen female—stepped forward, dressed in only her soft tunic and legs. "Mine, my lady. Pray do me the honor of wearing them."

"But—"

"Revani will remain by the gate, to carry word to Woodrun if we should fail."

Revani smiled shyly. "May I assist you?"

Resigned, Eliani allowed the guardian to help her don the leathers. "Lovely work."

"Thank you, my lady. It is my own."

"Is it?"

"My family are leather workers."

"Well, I shall have a commission for you when we get back to Glenhallow."

"I would be honored to serve you, my lady."

"Eliani, please. If we are sharing clothing, we need not be formal."

Eliani offered an arm to Revani, who clasped it with a grateful smile. "Spirits watch over you, my lady. Eliani."

"And over you."

Eliani watched her walk away, then turned to Vanorin. "Thank you for reminding me that I am not indestructible."

Vanorin grimaced. "If I thought I could convince you to stay behind, I would try."

"You cannot."

"Still, I ask that you not be at the fore when we reach Ghlanhras. Your gift must be preserved for the good of all ælvenkind."

Eliani drew a sharp breath. Luruthin had said something much the same as he urged her to flee the alben. Now he was captive, all for the sake of her safety, her gift of mindspeech.

"I will take care."

"Thank you, my lady."

"*Eliani*, Vanorin. You have been forgetting of late."

"I forget nothing."

An unfamiliar tone in his voice made her glance up at him, but he was turning away. Eliani frowned, wondering if he was angry with her. She had thought she had set him at ease enough to make him treat her with friendliness. Lately, though, he had reverted to formality.

Perhaps the burden of commanding her escort had told on him. She was not easy company, she knew.

Not until the first flush of dawn had strengthened into full brightness would Vanorin allow the party to start northward. Eliani was dancing with impatience by the time he agreed to let them cross the bridge.

She carried her sword against her shoulder, for she had no sheath to it. The sword was the only possession she had brought out of Ghlanhras. As she walked, she turned her thoughts toward the challenge ahead.

Darkwood Hall was not as vast as the Southfæld governor's palace in Glenhallow, but it was much larger than her own home of Felisanin Hall, from which her father governed Alpinon. To find Othanin and Luruthin within its sprawling structure was her first concern, and she worried how to do this without alerting the alben to their presence. She had raised the question with Vanorin, and all they had been able to decide was to wait for daylight, then go quietly and listen in the hope of hearing something that would lead them to the captives.

That did not satisfy her. She frowned, pondering how else she might locate her cousin, and was startled by a sudden bloom of warmth upon her brow: her partner Turisan, signaling that he wished to speak with her.

We are moving, love. May I speak to you later?

Eliani, I beg you to reconsider this—

My escort will protect me.

Will you not wait until I can consult with Ehranan at Midrange?

For all you know Ehranan is still fighting. And I cannot afford to wait even one day. In that time the alben will consolidate their hold on Ghlanhras. They might move their captives.

She stepped on an unseen pebble and stumbled, twisting her ankle slightly. Next to her, Vanorin flung out an arm to prevent her falling. She glanced at him, embarrassed and grateful.

"May we pause for a moment?"

A flicker darkened Vanorin's eyes, then he nodded and turned away. Eliani leaned against a tree at the side of the road, rubbing her ankle, while her escort moved to the opposite side. They talked in quiet voices and cast curious glances at her, even as they gave her distance. After all their journeys together, they were still fascinated by her gift. She closed her eyes, the only means of privacy she had.

My love, we discussed this. I thought we had agreed.

Yes, but I am worried for you. She sensed Turisan's desire for her, and it sharpened her own. A fleeting memory of their one night together in the Star Tower smote her. She suppressed an urge to moan.

Then ask the spirits of your elders to watch over me.

I do. Every day, even as I pray that we shall be reunited.

Eliani drew a sharp breath. She had lost count of the days since their parting, but with all that had passed it must be close to Midwinter. She had hoped to be back in Glenhallow by now, not marching northward again.

We shall. She swallowed, hoping the longing she felt was not obvious to Turisan. *I must go, love.*

Speak to me when you reach Ghlanhras. Before...

Yes.

She sent a flood of love toward him, then withdrew. Opening her eyes, she blinked at the brightness of the day. The sun was not visible overhead—that would not occur until midday—but already its heat washed through the forest. Her guardians glanced at her, then gathered to move once more.

Strange, she thought as she started forward, to be in so warm a place at Midwinter. Her own realm would be deep in snow by now.

An old Midwinter song came into her mind, a tune she had learned as a child. A song of snow and cold, of hope for the return of light. She laughed under her breath. Fireshore had no lack of light. No doubt the folk who dwelt here did not sing such songs.

A tingle poured through her veins. That was it! Would that she could sing, but her voice was fit only for bawdy guardian's camp songs, at best.

"Vanorin?"

The captain, who had fallen into step beside her, glanced her way. "My lady?"

"Do they sing 'The Winter Star' in Southfæld?"

"Yes."

"Do you know it? Well enough to sing it?"

"I believe so. Why?"

"You may need to."

Eliani hummed softly. Snow and the hope of light. A good tune to carry into the enemy's holding.

"Your pardon, Bright Lady. You asked to be brought the escaped female's things."

Shalár nodded to Torith, one of her better hunters, to come into her new chamber. New as hers; it had been her father's many centuries ago.

She scarcely remembered that time. She glanced at the walls, at the minimal ornaments placed there by the ælven governor, who was now her captive.

The hunter stepped into the front room and paused uncertainly. He carried a leather saddle pack, a pale green cloak, and a set of leather armor, blue in color.

"Put them on the table."

She watched him lay them down, noting the suppleness of his movements. He seemed unwearied by the night's work. Capturing Ghlanhras had been surprisingly easy. Shalár flipped open the saddle pack and began to explore its contents.

"It is time we all fed. You will organize a hunt, Torith. Take twenty hunters and bring back at least fifty kobalen." She glanced up at him. "You may have to cross the mountains."

Torith's eyes brightened with interest. He was hungry, no doubt, and would probably be happier on a hunt than idle in Ghlanhras.

"Yes, Bright Lady."

"Have the Stonereach sent in to me before you go."

Torith bowed and departed. Shalár watched him out, then reached for the leather armor that had been found in the escaped female's room. That one, too, was a Stonereach, according to Othanin. The daughter of Alpinon's governor. Kin to the male now being held under guard.

Shalár ran a hand along the armor. Blue, a Stonereach color, and there was a leather belt stained violet. She could smell the dye. No adornments, other than the color. Alpinon was a young realm, and had fewer artisans than the older realms of Southfæld and Eastfæld. Even the Steppes were older than Alpinon and had their own specialized crafts. Only Fireshore was newer.

Shalár picked up the cloak, a fine light wool dyed pale green and lined with silver silk. Greenglen colors. Othanin had said the female Stonereach was handfasted to a Greenglen, so that would now be her clan.

Holding the cloak in her hands, Shalár felt the tingle of khi in it. Mage-blessed, she realized with delight. Such a cloak would protect its wearer well. Hers now.

She put it down and returned to the saddle pack, which contained little of interest. A small packet of dried meat and another of dried sunfruit. A spare tunic and legs, in need of washing. A comb and other grooming tools. A small reed flute.

Shalár took the flute up and felt a whisper of khi in it as well; not the strong, laid-in khi of mage-work, but the resonant khi of an object long used and well loved. It was the only item among the Stonereach female's possessions that was not strictly necessary for travel.

A knock on the door made her turn, flute in hand. "Come."

The door opened and the Stonereach male was brought in, his hands bound behind him, his gaze lowered. The three hunters who brought him watched him warily. Shalár thanked them and indicated they should leave.

"He is not to be trusted, Bright Lady. He tried to flee us."

"Ah, is that how he got this?" She touched the ælven's cheek just beneath a cut. He flinched away.

"We had to knock him down. He is dangerous."

"Not to me."

She smiled and sent a pulse of khi toward the hunters, a warning and a reminder. One of them winced slightly. All started toward the door.

"Stay a moment. Take these." Shalár indicated the cloak and the armor. "Have them dyed black, with the good dye that was found at the crafthall. These, too." She tossed the Stonereach female's spare clothing to one of the hunters.

"Yes, Bright Lady."

They gathered up the escaped female's things, and Shalár saw that the Stonereach male watched them furtively, looking dismayed. The hunters hastened to leave, closing the door behind them.

Shalár strolled toward the ælven, looking him over with interest. His features were classic Stonereach, russet hair and green eyes, which flicked to the flute in her hands, then away.

"Your friend will not get far."

He said nothing, but she saw the eyes narrow, the lines of the face tense. He was preparing to strike. Shalár smiled, then summoned her khi and wrapped it around his.

A small grunt of surprise was all the sound he made, but in silence he struggled. He was strong. Shalár had to use all her own strength to subdue him, and it cost her.

The hunger that whispered in her flesh sharpened. She ignored it, concentrating her will on the ælven, who slowly sank to his knees on the thick carpet of the governor's chamber.

His breath came in labored gasps, yet still he resisted. Losing patience, she gave that part of his khi under her control a twist, a technique she had developed herself, one that caused pain. She took no particular pleasure in giving pain, but it was useful.

The ælven let out a small groan. She released him suddenly and he dropped forward, gasping for breath.

"You look uncomfortable. Perhaps you should get up."

He glanced at her, green eyes full of outrage, shadowed with fear. She smiled.

"You would do well to comply. You will spare yourself much unpleasantness."

He looked away again and made no answer. Shalár felt a stab of annoyance.

"Get up."

He gave no sign of having heard, merely stayed there on his knees, head down, staring at the floor. Shalár pushed him onto his back with a bare foot, then straddled him. Alarm filled his eyes and flashed through his khi.

Shalár's smile widened as she made herself comfortable. Clothing still separated them, but that was easily amended. She wanted to enjoy his discomfort first, as he realized the use she would make of him — though it would not be for pleasure, but for her people's future.

She wished for a child, and though the ælven were her enemies, she knew that they also represented the best hope of conception. Capturing Ghlanhras had meant that she had also captured new breeding stock for her people. She would waste no time making use of it.

She took hold of the Stonereach's khi again, and this time he was distracted enough that she got a firm grip on him. He closed his eyes and turned his face away, small and futile gestures.

"This must be uncomfortable for you, with your arms bound so. It really would be better if we moved to the bed."

She got up and stepped back to give him room to rise. When he failed to move, she sent him a warning with khi. He made a small, strangled sound, then slowly rolled onto his knees once more.

"Good. Now stand up."

It took two more warnings to make him obey. By then his eyes had gone dull with the knowledge that she could make him do absolutely anything she wished. Shalár smiled.

She nudged him through the doorway into the bedchamber behind the front room, and made him climb onto the bed and recline against the extravagant heap of pillows. She left his hands bound, not because she feared he would overpower her, but to remind him of his position.

He wore the clothes he had been taken in, an undertunic and legs of good silk, feet bare. Shalár pulled off the legs, marveling again that the ælven all seemed to have silk. True, it was the most durable and comfortable fabric to wear beneath leather. Clan Darkshore had to make do with fleececod, having failed to find silkworms anywhere west of the Ebon Mountains.

She touched him and he flinched, then squeezed his eyes shut. Shalár laughed softly as she began lazily caressing his flesh into arousal.

"I want a child, my Stonereach friend. If you are lucky enough to oblige me, you shall be rewarded. Tell me, have you ever conceived?"

His eyes opened in a glance of startled surprise, then he shut them again and turned his head away. Shalár's heart leapt with excitement.

"Show me!"

She took hold of his khi, searching it for his memories. She could sense such from one who was willing, but from this resistant Stonereach she felt only hints, enough to know that he had indeed conceived, and recently.

Her closest attempts had been with Yaras, while he had openly shared with her his own memories of conception. His child had been conceived and born almost fifty years ago, though, and was nearly grown, now. This Stonereach had memories that were far more fresh.

Shalár straddled him again, lifting her silk robe to bring them flesh to flesh. He made a small sound of distress, then was still. Thrilled not by this but by the chance of conception—a better chance than she had known in centuries, perhaps ever—Shalár mounted him. She inhaled with pleasure as she sank onto his flesh, feeling it push against her inner self, the self that must open for her to conceive.

"Show me!"

"No."

His whisper was a plea, not a denial. He could not deny her. No one could. Shalár smiled as she reached deeper into his thoughts.

Luruthin tried to hide, tried to curl himself into a small, hard ball of anger. It was no use. The alben's khi filled him, tainted with a strange tang, like metal on the tongue.

She was older than he, much older, and powerful. Revulsion and despair went through him in waves, even as she beat herself against him, even as his flesh responded against his wish.

He tried not to think of Jhinani, of the moment when their son to be had greeted them, a moment of joyous surprise. The alben clawed her way into the memory, defiling it. That roused more wrath in him than he had ever felt, and in hurt and anger he tried to strike back.

Using his khi as he had never done before, as the creed of the ælven forbade, he tried deliberately to hurt her. She cried out, but not because of his clumsy attempt to fight. With horror he felt her flesh open to receive him, to welcome his seed.

He tried to withhold it, but that too was futile. Her rapturous excitement carried him along and he felt himself emptying into her even as her flesh clamped around him.

He turned his head, letting grief slip from beneath his clenched eyelids. She had stolen from him, and he had allowed it.

Stolen like a thieving kobalen. That was the sort of creature she was, a low creature, without precepts. She was not ælven.

A brilliance filled his mind, a new presence. The soul of the child to be, come to greet them. He had never expected to be a father once, let alone twice, for it was a rare occurrence among his people. Yet no joy came to him now, despite the radiance that filled him.

Conception was the only time in many an ælven's life that mindspeech was possible. Luruthin held himself away from the contact, even as he heard the alben's thought.

Thank you! Thank you!

She was delirious with joy. Luruthin only felt sickened. He tried to empty his mind, think of nothing, build a gray wall between him and the others. The child penetrated it as if it did not exist.

Thank you, my father, for opening my path.

A shudder went through him. He answered.

This was done without my consent. Why have you chosen such a path into the world of flesh?

A shimmer of emotion enveloped him, of happiness blended with sympathy, with regret. Despite himself, he felt eased by it.

We take the paths that are offered. I accept the accompanying challenges.

You have chosen a dark way.

And my khi will bear the mark of it. I am not the first.

Luruthin made no reply. The alben leader did not share the conversation; he sensed that the child had excluded her, which gave him a small measure of satisfaction.

All lives are woven of both dark and light. A life is a complicated plan, inevitably filled with shifts and adaptations. I welcome the opportunity to learn.

You come into a bitter time.

Yes. I will do what I can to lighten it.

A flicker of something—hope, or pride—rose in Luruthin's heart. He tried to suppress it. He wanted nothing of this child or her mother.

I understand your concerns. We will meet again, in time. My name is Shiláni.

A shock went through him at the name. Taken from her mother's, the alben leader's, with only the tiniest part of his own name. How appropriate.

They were bound now, he and the alben, in a way that could never be broken. They would always be joined through this child. What should only be a joyous experience had been forced on him through pain and fear.

The alben—with a grimace he made himself acknowledge her name: Shalár—had violated his person and his thoughts, and had broken the cup-bond he had made with Jhinani. He would hate her forever, a realization that filled him with both anger and sorrow. Hatred was difficult to atone for; the atonement must be to oneself.

He felt Shiláni withdraw, adding her strength to the barrier he had made. Beyond it he knew that she remained, speaking with her mother.

While their flesh was bound together in conception, he and the alben would remain joined in thought, though Shiláni had shielded him from direct contact. Luruthin sensed Shalár gloating, though. He withdrew as far as he could beyond the gray wall, trying to ignore what he knew he could never forget.

He lay silent, becoming aware of discomfort in his flesh. His arms ached from the weight on them; his weight and hers, for the alben had sprawled over his chest in sated bliss. Disgusted, he lay wishing for her flesh to release him. At long last it did so, and the alben gave a deep sigh as she slowly slid away, leaving him exposed, the air cold on his wet and shrunken flesh.

The child was still present, he was dimly aware. She would remain near her mother until the body she had claimed was ready to receive her.

The alben moved off him, the absence of her weight a slight relief. Luruthin kept his eyes closed, determined not to respond to her.

"Well." Her voice was strangely soft. A long moment passed before she spoke again. "I am grateful to you, Stonereach. What reward would you have?"

He did not move, scarcely breathed. He felt her shifting on the bed, then felt her hands on him, pushing him onto his side and then tugging at the cords that bound his hands. It hurt, but he made no protest.

His hands tingled as blood flowed back into them. He had to move, then, to sit up and rub his aching wrists. Shalár placed herself in front of him but he would not look at her. His anger swelled at a glimpse of her bare thigh, at the bitter, musky scent of her, but he knew if he tried to attack her she would quickly subdue him with khi. Also, he realized with dismay, he could not endanger the child.

"I am in earnest, Stonereach. I wish to reward you. Name your pleasure."

"I want only one thing, and that you will not give me." His voice sounded strangled. Like his heart.

She laughed. "Do not be so certain. I can be generous."

He met her gaze then—those awful, black eyes—and let her feel his resentment. "Release me."

Her eyes widened as her smile faded. "Ah, no. That I cannot do."

Luruthin looked down, unsurprised and freshly angered. At least she would not trouble him again until after the child was born. Perhaps he would find a way to escape before then.

"But I can give you some kinds of freedom."

He moved away, to the edge of the bed. He sought his borrowed silk legs among the bedding, found them and pulled them on.

"You may dwell here, if you wish. In this chamber." Her voice was caressing, which sickened him. Could she not guess that nothing would be farther from his wishes?

She came to stand in front of him. He shut his eyes, unwilling to see her.

"What is your name?"

He held his breath. If she wanted that from him—anything from him—she must take it by force, as before.

"Ghlanhras is mine now." Her voice was sharper on the words. "Fireshore is mine. That, Stonereach, is something to which you must resign yourself."

He said nothing, made no move. After a moment he heard her step away and open a drawer. One of Othanin's drawers; this was the governor's chamber. Or had been.

She returned, and Luruthin flinched as she reached toward him. Something soft and cool fell around his shoulders.

"Wear this, and you may have your freedom within Darkwood Hall."

He looked down at the red silken cord that draped around his neck and hung to his chest, ending in an elaborate knot. A symbolic bondage. He wanted to refuse it, but knew that to do so would be foolish. Walking free within the hall was a step toward actual freedom.

He would not thank her, though. He remained silent.

She moved away again, and he heard the sound of liquid pouring. Keeping his face averted, not wanting the slightest glimpse of her, he bolted through the outer chamber and into the corridor.

He was halfway to the audience hall when he realized she had not pursued him. He forced himself to walk, to behave as if he had the right of freedom she had promised him.

He was shaking. He paused to steady himself, drawing deep, gasping breaths. Grief brought fresh tears, but he blinked them back.

He must get away, out of Darkwood Hall. Out of Ghlanhras. Somehow he would do it. He must.

Jhinani. He would return to Glenhallow and beg her forgiveness. She had healed him once; perhaps she could do so again. The hope of it steadied him enough to walk on.

The guards in the audience hall glanced up as he entered. Their eyes went to the red cord he wore. He felt his face begin to burn but would not acknowledge it. Watching the guards, who watched him in turn but made no move to detain him, he crossed through the chamber and into the main corridor of Darkwood Hall.

Here he hesitated, at a loss what to do next. He would not be permitted to leave the Hall, he was certain. The alben leader had not achieved her place through carelessness.

For lack of a better plan, he walked toward the entrance, and passed through one of the two sets of double doors that flanked the stone wall of the hearthroom. A place of welcome in every ælven home; this hearthroom had already changed. The hearth was cold and dark; the outer doors closed.

Six alben guards stood before those doors, two of them bearing swords. They all moved their hands to their weapons at Luruthin's approach, and it was all he could do to keep from flinching away. It was not the swords that aroused his dread, it was the nets.

He felt the blood drain from his face at the memory of those nets. Dozens of them, tripping him, dragging him down, their leaf-shaped metal weights biting at him....

He shook himself, and made himself face the alben guards. All of them wore black leathers, all were black-eyed and white-haired like their leader. Two were female, and Luruthin felt a stab of anxious dread at being in their presence.

The alben stared back at him, suspicious. One of the males spoke.

"Begone from here, Stonereach. These doors are ever closed to you."

Luruthin made no reply, though he was oddly heartened by the claim. If these doors were closed, he must simply find another. Or a different path altogether.

He left, meaning to walk back down the vast, empty central corridor. Outside the hearthroom, though, an alben guard stood waiting. Luruthin frowned as their gazes met.

His heart filled with sudden rage, so vivid he had to close his eyes. Not so generous after all, his captor. He might have a measure of freedom, but apparently it did not include privacy. It should not have surprised him.

Swallowing, he composed himself and walked past the guard, ignoring his presence as if the alben did not exist. He set a leisurely pace down the corridor, noting the footfalls of the guard who shadowed him. This intrusion only made him more determined to escape.

He must choose his moment carefully. Daylight would be greatly to his advantage.

In the meantime he would go to Othanin, still being held in the room where they had both been thrown. If he could free the governor, then when daylight came, they could escape together.

A flicker of hope kindled in his heart and quickened his step. Hope was almost painful, but he held to it as his only beacon through this dark night.

Eliani paused as they came in sight of the darkwood gates of Ghlanhras. The wall that surrounded the city, built of black volcanic rock, was a massive darkness looming beyond the myriad greens and shadows of the forest.

Vanorin halted the party with a gesture. As one, they drew to the side of the road, their backs against the dense forest. For a long moment they waited, listening.

Eliani strained her ears, but heard only the creatures of the woodland. She had seen large, colorful birds with raucous voices on their journey hither, but none of those were evident today. A smaller bird's mournful, falling cry was all that broke the stillness.

Catching Vanorin's eye, she nodded to the right. The plan they had agreed upon was to circle eastward from the gates, along the cleared pathway outside the wall. The gates would be guarded, but Eliani guessed that the alben would not be able to guard the entire wall. She had escaped the city by climbing the wall at the eastern side. She meant to return the same way.

A stab of dread went through her at the thought of going back into Ghlanhras. She looked up at the sky overhead, seeking confidence in the height of the sun.

Vanorin moved ahead slowly, followed by two other guardians. Eliani had agreed to be placed in their midst, though she fretted at being so coddled.

Belatedly, she sent a query signal to Turisan. He answered at once, and she could feel anxiety in his khi.

We have reached Ghlanhras.

Stay in contact with me.

That may not be wise—

I will not distract you, I swear. Please, love.

She knew his reason for asking. He feared, as she did, that this might be her last deed—or worse, that she would be captured. She had already decided to end her life if that occurred, though she had not shared this decision even with Turisan.

Very well.

They were at the gates. The guardian ahead of her turned right, following the path around the wall. Eliani paused for a moment and stared hard at the gates, as if expecting the enemy to come rushing out of them. Impossible, she knew, but the tingle of fear between her shoulders persisted as she followed the guardian down the curving path.

With dark forest on her right and the blacker stone wall to her left, she felt hemmed in. She knew the woods here were too dense to traverse. They would have to return this way, pass those gates again, to get back to the road and their path homeward.

The guardian ahead of her slowed. Eliani craned to see Vanorin, who had paused and was crouched, looking at something on the ground. She moved forward to join him.

She recognized the shattered fragment of a water gourd in the captain's hand. This was where she had fought the alben whose boots and weapons she had taken. Eliani had left her here, unconscious, but apparently the alben had recovered.

She should have killed her. The thought was cold, but Eliani knew that any mercy they showed the alben now would only mean another, harder fight ahead. For her soul's sake, she had not wanted to atone for taking the helpless alben's life. As a warrior, she knew it had been a mistake.

Vanorin glanced up at her, question in his eyes. She nodded. She had told him of this encounter. He dropped the gourd fragment and stood, looking up at the wall.

Eliani gestured that they should continue along the path. They were still too close to the gates for her liking. She had crossed the wall farther to the east.

They resumed their silent march, listening all the while for any sound of alarm from the city. Eliani expected none. The wall was solid; the alben would be in hiding. She and her escort would steal into the city like beams of sunlight.

When Vanorin halted once more, she nodded. They were almost due east of the city; this place would do.

Vanorin gestured to Birani, who was small and lithe, to climb the wall. Birani gripped the rough rocks with gloved hands and booted feet, pulling herself up the wall with cautious movements. Slowly she raised her head above the edge. Eliani knew she would see little thus, nor be seen; the wall was wider than an armspan.

Vanorin tensed beside her as Birani hauled herself atop the wall. Eliani swallowed, listening. No sound came from within the city; no cry of alarm or clash of weapons. Birani lay still for a long moment, then shifted to whisper down to Vanorin.

"I see no one. The houses are all shuttered."

Eliani nodded. "They are empty."

Vanorin gave her a sharp glance, then turned to Revani. "Wait here. If you hear any sound of trouble, start for Woodrun at once."

The guardian acknowledged this, and stepped back against the forest, into the shadow of a darkwood sapling. Vanorin and two others climbed atop the wall. Birani was no longer in sight; she must have descended into the city.

Four guardians awaited Eliani. Two of them climbed beside her as she set her hands to the rock, grateful for Revani's gloves. Her first climb over this wall had cut her bare hands and feet.

She paused atop the wall. She could see Darkwood Hall, its terraced rooftops rising above the other structures. Ghlanhras was silent, more so than any ælven settlement should be. No smoke rose from any chimney, no sound of labor rang from any yard or crafthall. If there were ælven remaining in the city, they were not at liberty.

She lowered herself down the inside of the wall, joining the others in its shadow. When the last two of her escort had followed her, she turned to Vanorin, nodding to the nearest street. She did not know if it was the

street she had taken before, but it did not matter. Ghlanhras was an
ælven city; its straight streets all ran toward the public circle at its center,
crossing the curving avenues, concentric rings that flowed outward from
the city's heart.

She could see the public circle ahead, a vast, open ground where
markets and festivals were held; empty now. Before they reached it,
Vanorin halted and drew the others into the last avenue outside the
circle. The houses here looked more recently inhabited—some of the
windows were open, and one or two hearthroom doors stood ajar—but
there was no sign or sound now of anyone within.

With a gesture, Vanorin sent three of the guardians toward the circle.
They were to go to the stables and ready horses for riding, if the horses
were to be found. Legend said the animals disliked the alben, and Eliani
hoped that the city's invaders had not yet dealt with the horses in
Ghlanhras's stables.

She watched the three guardians hasten to the circle and disappear
from sight. Holding her breath, she listened for a sound of alarm, but
heard none.

She looked at Vanorin and nodded, and the party continued along
the avenue toward the rear of Darkwood Hall. She had only glimpsed
the garden wall in her hasty escape, but thought it might offer the easiest
way onto the roof of the Hall.

As they followed the avenue's curve, a blackness appeared blocking
their way. Vanorin turned to look at Eliani and she nodded; this was the
wall she remembered. It was smaller than the wall around the city, and
made of shaped blocks of stone rather than the rough rocks of the outer
wall.

Vanorin slowed their pace and walked near to the houses on their
left. Eliani's shoulder blades prickled with a sense of danger. Part of her
wished to flee, but she walked on, gritting her teeth.

The avenue ended at the street that ran along the east side of
Darkwood Hall. Vanorin paused and looked to the left, then swiftly
crossed the open space to the garden wall, followed by the others.

Eliani glanced toward the Hall; there had to be windows, but
perhaps the alben had covered them against the daylight. They paused,
clustered beneath the wall. No sign of their having been seen reached
them. Ghlanhras remained silent.

Vanorin summoned Sunahran with a gesture, and after a whispered
consultation, the guardian braced himself against the wall and Vanorin

climbed onto his shoulders.

Eliani bit her lip, watching as Vanorin cautiously looked over the wall. After a moment he pulled himself up onto it, and gestured for the others to climb up.

Two more guardians climbed onto the wall with Vanorin's help. As they moved forward toward the roof of the Hall, Eliani climbed onto Sunahran's shoulders, whispering her thanks. She took Vanorin's hand and he hauled her up, setting her on her feet. She smiled, but he was already reaching down to help the next.

Eliani joined the other guardians on the roof and watched the rest of the escort climb up, Sunahran coming last with Vanorin's assistance. Now they must be especially cautious, and move with absolute silence. Any sound would alert the alben below to their presence.

She swallowed a sudden dryness in her throat. They would do this; reaching this point had been half the battle.

The sun's heat rose up from the roof tiles, making her uncomfortably warm in her borrowed leathers. When the guardians were all gathered, she gestured toward the highest roof in the complex, the large expanse that covered the audience chamber. She had found a way to see into it as she fled, and glimpsed Luruthin below—bound, at the feet of the alben leader—the last she had seen of him. She wished to see what the chamber held now.

Vanorin and three others went ahead, the rest came behind Eliani. They walked with hunters' stealth, crossing the tiled roofs, keeping wide of the ornately filigreed screens that covered the high windows, lest their shadows fall across them and draw the notice of those inside the Hall.

Eliani wondered about those screens. They were designed to bring light into the central areas of the Hall while minimizing the heat that came in. The alben would not care for the light, however.

She reached the corner where she had previously looked through a screen, and knelt to look again. The small hole she had made in the silken gauze covering was still there, but behind it was a darker, heavier cloth. She could not move this aside to see down into the chamber; the fabric eluded her grasp.

She glanced up at Vanorin, standing over her, and shook her head. Carefully she rose again, looking westward toward the wing where she and Luruthin had been given rooms, and whence she had escaped.

She started toward it, going slowly, trying to remember from which window she had crawled onto the roof. The varying levels of the roofs followed the major passages of the Hall; she found the main corridor easily enough, for it adjoined the audience chamber.

Following it toward the front of the Hall, she remembered the turning into the guest quarters, and so reached the passage where she had fled the alben. She stood above the very spot where Luruthin had been taken, and closed her eyes briefly at the memory.

Spirits, guide me now. Help me find my kin.

Drawing a deep breath, she walked slowly along the roof of the passage. She whistled a few notes, quickly and without rhythm. Bird-like.

Beside her, Vanorin frowned. Holding his gaze, she whistled another phrase, and his brows rose. He understood; he had recognized "The Winter Star."

She waited, listening, then walked onward. The passage turned and she followed it. She remembered her desperate search for a way outside from that passage; she had found none. It had rooms to either side, and at its very end, a room without windows.

She whistled again, a few notes at a time, pausing between like a bird waiting for its mate to answer. A few steps, another line of the song.

Murmured voices below made her freeze. The others all did likewise, standing motionless in the hot sun. Eliani held her breath, straining to listen to the muffled voice from below.

"Did you hear it? Do you know what sort of bird that is?"

Eliani inhaled sharply, and looked at Vanorin. Luruthin? She mouthed the name silently, questioning, and the captain shrugged.

She whistled a few more notes. More murmuring came from below, then a hesitant whistled answer—the next phrase of the song.

Her stomach clenched. She had found him.

❀ Darkwood Hall ❀

Luruthin leaned against the door of the room where Othanin was being held. The alben guards frowned, but apparently the red cord he wore bought him a measure of tolerance. He spoke urgently to the door.

"Did you hear it? Othanin?"

"Get back from there."

The alben male put a hand on his sword hilt and took a menacing step toward Luruthin. Though he could not help flinching, he did not move away from the door.

"We are just talking. That has not been forbidden."

"Do as he says, or you will find your privilege curtailed."

Luruthin flashed a resentful glance at the guard who had followed him. No doubt the alben meant to earn reward by reporting to his leader everything Luruthin did.

His pulse sped as he thought of her; he forced the memory away. Someone was here—someone from the south—and he had to make Othanin understand.

A creaking of wood sounded nearby. Luruthin reacted, but managed to keep from looking up. A tingle went through him; hope, dread....

The sound came again, from a little way down the hall. Another creak, small and swift, as of a peg being drawn.

"What was that?" One of the guards.

"Othanin, did you hear that bird?"

Luruthin raised his voice as much as he dared, as if to make himself heard through the door. One of the guards buffeted his shoulder, thrusting him back.

"Get away!"

He glanced upward and thought he saw movement; a tiny breeze stirring the gray cloth that had been hung to block light from the overhead windows. He caught his breath, then a horrendous groan of breaking wood began.

The shouts of the alben guards turned to cries of anguish as five of the overhead windows were staved in and sunlight poured into the passage. Luruthin squinted, looking up into the sudden brightness.

Figures appeared in the open windows, light glowing all around them, burning white in their pale hair. Luruthin gasped in spite of himself.

Not alben. Not outside at midday.

Someone grabbed him roughly. He wrenched away, out of the guard's grasp and into the sunlight. Two ælven dropped down to land beside him, one to either side.

One drew a knife and ran down the passage in pursuit of one of the alben. A second alben lay writhing in the sunlight; the other ælven dispatched him with a quick knife-thrust, then turned to Luruthin.

"Othanin—where is he?"

It was Taharan, one of his own clan. Grateful tears sprang to Luruthin's eyes. He pointed toward the door at the end of the corridor.

The last alben—the one that had been following him—stood against the door, cowering in the small shade remaining at the end of the corridor, menacing with his drawn sword. Taharan glanced upward.

"Sword!"

A blade was lowered hilt first into the guardian's waiting hands. He advanced toward the alben.

"Luruthin!"

Eliani's voice! Gasping, he looked up, but the sun was behind her and he could not see her face.

"Eliani! What are you doing here?"

"What do you think?"

A rope fell out of the sky toward him. He flinched, remembering the nets, then recovered and caught hold of it. A loop had been tied in its end; he set his foot into that and gripped the rope with both hands.

The clash of swords drew his glance as he was lifted—the alben and Taharan, fighting—then he lost sight of them as the rope spun him round. He glimpsed the other ælven returning along the passage, wiping his bloodied knife, then hands caught at Luruthin's arms and shoulders and hauled him onto the roof.

He rolled aside and sat up. At once he was caught in a fierce embrace. Eliani's smell filled his senses and her voice whispered hoarsely in his ear.

"Forgive me! I would not have left you—"

"No." His throat tightened. "There was no choice."

"Your pardon."

Vanorin stood above them. Eliani looked up at the captain, then released her hold on Luruthin, to his relief. Her sudden embrace had set his heart racing with fear. Even from her, his beloved kin and former love....

At Vanorin's gesture, Eliani stood and moved back from the broken windows. Luruthin joined her. Sounds of commotion came from below, though he heard no more swordplay.

Two guardians were on hands and knees by the window nearest the end of the passage. One of them answered a call from below by throwing down the rope once more. They both hauled on it, and a moment later Othanin appeared, looking bedraggled and confused. The guardians pulled him onto the roof, and Eliani went to help him up.

The sword was handed back up. Luruthin stepped toward the guardians.

"The other sword—the alben's. Bring that, too."

Sunahran, one of the Southfælders, looked at him in surprise. Luruthin explained.

"They do not have many swords. Every one we take from them is an advantage."

Sunahran's brows rose, then he turned to call down into the corridor. The second sword appeared, then the two guardians were hauled up with the rope. Sunahran came to Luruthin, offering the alben's sword.

He accepted it; a plain sword, well made, but lacking the virtues of a mountain-forged blade. Luruthin inhaled sharply, realizing where his own sword must be—in the hands of the alben leader. A tremor of wrath went through him, but he mastered it. It was good to have a blade in hand, at least.

Vanorin consulted briefly with the two who had been below, then led the party across the rooftops. He and two others went first, then Eliani with Luruthin and Othanin, the rest coming behind.

They moved as swiftly as they dared, keeping their steps silent. Even so, before they had passed the large, high roof of the audience chamber, a shout was raised below.

Vanorin cast a glance back, then sped his steps, abandoning caution. Terror coursed through Luruthin's veins as he followed.

He would not be taken again. He would die first, on the stranger's blade in his hands if need be.

Eliani kept an anxious eye on Luruthin and Othanin as they followed Vanorin to the rear of the Hall, down onto the wall, and into the street. The party sped down the avenue, away from Darkwood Hall, crossing streets without hesitation. Caution would not serve them now.

They started across a particularly broad street. Recognizing it, Eliani slowed.

"Hai! This is it!"

She turned south along the city's main street, and could see the darkwood gates ahead as she ran. Vanorin and the others followed. She glanced back to assure herself that Luruthin and Othanin were still there.

A shout from ahead drew her notice. Something flew past her, singing as it brushed her face. The next moment Vanorin slammed into her, pushing her into an avenue and against the wall of a house.

She grunted and drew breath to protest, then met the captain's terrified gaze. A stinging started in her cheek. She put her fingers to it, touching blood.

Eliani?

I am all right. A scratch.

Turisan said no more, but she could feel his worry. She wanted to embrace him, accept his comfort, but it was Vanorin's arms around her, not Turisan's.

She struggled free of Vanorin's grasp, and sent Turisan the signal to wait. She could not afford to be distracted just now.

The others gathered, sheltering beside the house. Cærshari, one of the Southfælders, crept forward to glance around the front corner, then ducked back as two arrows sang past. She returned to the party, speaking in a low voice.

"The windows are open in every house between here and the gates."

Vanorin grimaced. "And full of archers, apparently."

Eliani swallowed, her heart still thundering at the nearness of her escape. "So we go around."

She pushed away from the house. Vanorin stepped ahead of her, glaring. She yielded to him. Glancing at Luruthin and Othanin—both pale but determined—she followed Vanorin to the next street, and along it toward the outer wall.

They soon reached a vast darkwood yard near the front of the city. The street they were on ran along the east side of it. Stacks of darkwood boards lay beneath high shed roofs, and several vast, twining, uncut trunks of darkwood lay in the midst of the yard.

Vanorin made the others wait while he took a few steps down the unsheltered street. Eliani held her breath, keeping her eyes on a long crafthall at the far side of the yard. That hall was the only structure between them and the main street, and if she were a conquering alben she would have put archers into it as well.

If archers were there, however, their attention was not on the wood yard. Vanorin stepped behind a stack of cut wood and gestured for the others to join him.

They hurried across the exposed space and clustered together behind the wood. Othanin picked up an arm-length scrap of darkwood and slapped it into his free hand, a passable club.

Vanorin turned to Eliani, gesturing to a line of sheds, some empty, most sheltering stacks of wood. "We can keep out of sight most of the way to the wall. If we do not see the others when we reach it, we go over."

Eliani gave a reluctant nod. She did not wish to leave the three that had gone to the stables to fend for themselves. She wanted them back, with the horses if possible. She wished to leave none of her folk in Ghlanhras.

Following Vanorin, the party darted from shelter to shelter along the width of the darkwood yards. No sign of movement came from the crafthall.

The last stack of cut wood was only shoulder high to Eliani; she and the others crouched behind it. An open space of perhaps two rods lay between them and the outer wall. Vanorin crossed it swiftly and flattened himself against the wall.

Eliani peered around the front corner of the wood, looking toward the gate. She saw what she hoped for; three guardians, with horses behind them, in the street beyond the gate. They were some distance from it, though, and they appeared to be pinned. Arrows flew toward them from the front of the crafthall, falling short or striking the wall.

Eliani grimaced and looked across at Vanorin. He nodded; he had seen. He looked about to speak, then flinched as an arrow struck the wall beside him.

Eliani ducked back, heart pounding. She beckoned to Vanorin, but arrows continued to come at him. He would be hit before long.

Anger drove her to pull at a board from the stack beside her. It was heavy; it tumbled to the ground, nearly striking her foot. With the help of Taharan she lifted it, then turned it upright.

The board was half again her height, and slightly less than her width. She turned to Taharan. "Take it to Vanorin."

Taharan nodded and took the board from her hands, holding it as a shield as he carried it across the open space to the wall. It was poor shelter for both him and Vanorin, but better than none. Sunahran pulled down a second board and carried it across; side by side, the two boards formed an adequate makeshift wall.

Vanorin called to Eliani across the open space. "We go over the wall."

"No! The horses!"

"We cannot get to them."

Stubbornness set in. She could hear her father chiding; knew Turisan would scold. She did not care. She reached to pull down another board.

"We form a shield wall and move to the gates. We can open them."

Othanin came forward to assist her. "It takes three to raise the bar. It is solid darkwood."

"Then three will raise it while the rest hold the shields."

Vanorin frowned. "My lady—"

Luruthin stepped up beside her. "We can do this." He held out his sword to her.

"If you will carry this, I will carry a shield."

Eliani cast him a grateful glance as she took the blade, her throat tightening. Luruthin had already shielded her once. Now he supported her again. How she loved him!

Vanorin offered no more argument, though his lips were a thin line of disapproval. The guardians each took a darkwood board in hand.

Eliani scuttled across the open space behind two boards carried by Sunahran and Birani. Five boards across filled the space that ran along the city wall, three others formed a shield wall at angles with the first, and the whole party moved toward the gates.

Their progress was slow. Arrows began to batter against the darkwood shields like hail in a tempest. Now and then one came through a momentary gap, but the party reached the gate without injury.

The shield-bearers shifted into a single line between the gate and the now-constant rattle of arrows. Eliani laid her two swords at her feet and stepped forward to help Vanorin and Othanin lift the bar.

It was massive, and the three of them strained to raise it clear of the brackets. Behind her she heard a small, sharp cry from one of the guardians.

Dread spilled down her spine. If the shield wall failed now—

She strained, digging in her feet to lift with her shoulders. The bar rose up another handspan, enough to clear the brackets. Together she and the two males stepped back, dropping the bar at their feet. It narrowly missed the swords.

Eliani picked up the blades, shoulder muscles already complaining. Othanin was pulling the left gate open. When the gap was a shoulder's breadth, Vanorin turned to Eliani.

"Go!"

She slipped through the gate and out into the clear, gulping deep breaths of freedom, filled with sudden relief. The road stretched southward before her, leading home.

Othanin joined her, then Luruthin. She moved away from the gate to the side of the road, against the forest.

A loud clap sounded, then two more guardians came through the gate. It was opening wider, now; swinging away. Two darkwood boards lay fallen inside the gate.

Eliani watched as the rest of the shield-bearers shuffled backward through the gate, then dropped their boards along the side that remained closed and hastened to where she stood. Felahran pulled off a glove as he joined the party, revealing a bloodied finger.

Eliani stepped to him. "You are hurt! Let me see it."

"Just a nick."

He showed her his hand. An arrow had sliced through the glove across one knuckle. Eliani took his hand between hers and heat flared at once in her palms, the healing that she still scarce understood. She had little chance to focus on it; a thundering of hooves drew her gaze to the gate.

The horses screamed in terror and pain as they came through the gate, arrows striking the animals and the guardians who rode and led them. Six horses and two riders cleared the gate, but the last rider's horse reared just inside, stumbled on the darkwood boards, and fell.

"Jhathali!"

"Taharan, no!"

Vanorin grabbed at the guardian's arm but failed to catch him. Eliani watched in horror as Taharan ran back through the gate, unprotected.

"Taharan!"

Birani's voice was wild with anguish. Eliani caught the guardian and held her, terrified of losing yet another of her party.

Taharan dropped to his knees beside the fallen horse and rider. Arrows hammered into him, jerking his body with each blow until he fell across the horse and moved no more.

Tears sprang to Eliani's eyes and she gasped with grief. The screams of the last two horses rose from within the wall.

The horses that had escaped had run well down the road before the two riders were able to halt them. Vanorin gave orders in a stern, low voice, moving the party southward to join the horses. They halted still within sight of the gate, which remained open.

Everyone moved to tend the animals and the riders, all of whom had been struck by arrows. Eliani could not help glancing toward the gate now and then, though she knew the alben would not venture out in daylight to close it.

She pulled arrows and bandaged wounds, work she had done often as a guardian, oddly soothing in its familiarity. None of the wounds was serious, though one horse was badly lamed.

As she used her healing gift to ease the riders' pain, she listened to the others around her. Their voices murmured in quiet grief. Someone was sobbing; a female.

Looking up, Eliani saw Birani curled against the base of a tree. Felahran knelt beside the guardian, but she pushed him away.

The healing warmth faded from Eliani's hands. She gave Mihlaran a reassuring smile, then stood and walked over to Birani.

"Stand up. I need you."

Her voice sounded harsher than she intended, though she had not meant to be gentle. Birani looked up at her, blinking, her cheeks mottled with weeping.

"Stand up."

Anger flashed in the guardian's eyes as she obeyed. Eliani led her to the horse that was least injured, caught the reins and held them out to Birani.

"Ride for Woodrun. You will overtake Revani." She collected another mount's reins. "Take this horse for her, and get word to the town as swiftly as you can."

Birani wiped at her face, looking sullen, but she mounted and took the reins. The horses moved forward in response to her command.

Eliani watched them out of sight. Vanorin came to stand beside her.

"That was well done."

The kindness in his voice made Eliani catch her breath on a sob. But for her stubbornness, Birani would have needed no distraction from grief.

She had sent Birani south not only to give the guardian occupation, but to ensure that the sacrifice of Taharan and Jhathali was not wasted. Woodrun would be alerted the faster to the alben threat. Though important, this did not seem worth the loss of two of her escort.

Warmth spread across her brow; Turisan, asking to speak. She returned the signal for "wait." She was not ready to tell him of her folly.

Othanin came to stand with her and Vanorin. Eliani glanced at him, frowning to hold back her grief.

"It is the hardest part of being a leader." Othanin's voice was barely above a whisper, not meant to be heard by the others. "To live with the consequences of one's decisions."

Eliani swallowed, blinking. She must learn to make better decisions, then.

She looked around at the escort, seeking someone who needed help, but all had been cared for. Turning her attention to the horses, she frowned at the one that was lame.

"We cannot burden that horse. It will slow us, but ... I would not abandon it."

"My lady, it might be best to send all the horses to Woodrun." Vanorin looked at Sunahran. "Three can ride, with one leading the lame beast. The rest of us will find another way."

Eliani frowned. "Why?"

"I would have you away from the road, my lady. The alben will send pursuit as soon as darkness falls."

"But the road is the only way through the forest!"

Othanin coughed. "That is not quite true. My lady's people know the ways of this wood, game trails that can be traveled. I would like to contact her in any case."

Eliani caught her breath. He meant the Lost, the folk of Ghlanhras who had fallen victim to the alben's curse and gone into voluntary exile. His lady, Kivhani, had become their leader after becoming afflicted.

"How can we find them? Did you not say that they have no settled home?"

"We exchange messages at a place not far from here."

He said it so calmly, yet Eliani knew that some ælven would consider his maintaining contact with the Lost a betrayal of the creed. She began to feel a greater respect for Othanin, who at first had seemed weak and indecisive. She was beginning to understand just how difficult a governor's choices could be.

She turned back to Vanorin. "Then none of us should take the road. Let us all go to the Lost."

Sunahran came forward, traded a glance with Vanorin, then bowed before her. "Allow us to serve you in this way, Lady Eliani. The horses will have difficulty following game trails, especially the lame one. Allow me to take the road, and the alben will waste their efforts pursuing. If need be I will turn the lame horse loose; they will not bother with it. I will ride to Woodrun."

"And I!" Cærshari hastened to join him.

Vanorin nodded. "One more to ride, then."

Mihlaran stepped forward. "I will."

Eliani misliked this plan, but to continue protesting it would be disrespectful to Vanorin. She yielded, and listened to him give instructions to the riders. She, Luruthin, Vanorin, and three others would go with Othanin.

She stepped aside and signaled Turisan. At once his anxiety filled her.

We are out of Ghlanhras.

Did you find them?

Yes. She looked at Luruthin, sitting at the base of a darkwood, hugging his knees. *I will tell you of it later. We are about to set forth.*

Yes, you should get as far from Ghlanhras as you can.

That is our intent.

She bade Turisan farewell, then went to Luruthin, taking up the sword he had asked her to hold and offering it to him. He did not hear her at first, and when she laid a hand on his shoulder he flinched before looking up at her.

"Are you hurt, cousin?"

He paused too long before answering. "No."

He stood, took the sword, and walked away without a word. Eliani's heart was heavy as she looked after him. He moved to stand by Othanin, as if anxious to be away from Ghlanhras.

Well, and so were they all. Eliani bade farewell to the riders, promised to meet them in Bitterfield if not Woodrun, and followed Othanin southward.

Shalár heard running footsteps and raised her head. Someone was coming along the passage toward the audience chamber where she stood. A hunter; he ran along the aisle toward her and dropped to his knees at her feet.

"Bright Lady, the ælven governor and the Stonereach have escaped."

"What?!"

"The ælven broke through the roof and overwhelmed the guards. They let in the sunlight ..." He drew a gasping breath before continuing. "They took the two ælven out through the roof."

"Search the city." Shalár grimaced; the hunt would be difficult until nightfall.

"Bright Lady, the search was begun at once. There was fighting at the gates. They escaped that way."

Shalár turned away so as not to vent her anger on the hapless messenger. She wanted to go out and search herself, but even if she shielded herself in the heaviest leathers she had, some sun would reach her. She could not risk any harm to her child.

She was angry, but there was nothing to be done now. They were gone. Until the sun set, she could not send pursuit.

She disliked feeling trapped in her own city. That must be amended, somehow.

She thanked the hunter and sent him away to rest. She could tell by his khi that he had been sun-poisoned despite his heavy cloak and hood.

Soon more of her people came to her, reporting that the ælven had let sunlight into other parts of Darkwood Hall, hampering their ability to move through the palace. Annoyed, she ordered that the damaged parts of the roof be repaired, then summoned Torith. He came to her in the audience chamber and knelt before her.

"Choose two hunting parties to leave at sunset. One to pursue the ælven southward, and a smaller party to take the north road and search the shore."

Torith nodded. "As you will, Bright Lady."

He rose, bowed, and went off to do her bidding. Shalár walked across the dais to the large darkwood chair that was plainly the governor's. Hers, now. She sat there, brooding.

She needed a way to move about Ghlanhras even in daylight. She wanted watchers at intervals around the city wall, and they would need shelter. Covered platforms, perhaps. And some way for them to come and go from the hall, otherwise they would be cut off from her during the day.

A covered pathway—or a completely enclosed passage, perhaps—must be made between the hall and each of the watch posts. She needed someone to organize this construction before the ælven returned in force.

How long might that be? Long enough, she hoped, for Yaras to return with more of Clan Darkshore. Her handful of hunters were barely enough to hold the city, not enough for what she wanted to do next, which was to carry the fight forward to Woodrun.

Her lips twisted in a mirthless smile. Woodrun was where the ælven had gone, no doubt. If she could get to them there, she might take back her prizes. She cared little about the spineless usurper who had called himself governor of Fireshore, but the loss of the Stonereach angered her.

He was hers. He was useful. So few of her people conceived, and those who managed to conceive with ælven always had strong children.

Shalár paused, her hand going to her belly, her thoughts to the spirit that would enter the body growing there. The child had long been silent, but she felt its presence nearby. For a moment she was gripped with a strange desire to apologize for the loss of its father.

Folly. The child was hers, and the sire was unimportant to its future. This child would grow to be a leader of Clan Darkshore, and would see them achieve a new prosperity in their homeland.

❈ Midrange ❈

Rephanin's soul was spread across the valley, tied to each spark of ælven khi by the task that had brought him here. Ehranan shone brightest for him, closest in thought though not in flesh.

Rephanin had all but forgotten flesh. His own lay in a guarded tent well south of the battle. The flesh of others, of the hundreds of the ælven in the valley, he tried to ignore, for there was much pain there, and much fear.

Marovon, move twenty of your guardians up that slope to your left.

Ehranan's voice sang in his mind, even as it rang through him to every guardian on the field. This was his gift as he had never before made use of it. He could not speak over great distance, but he could speak to any ælven nearby, and in this war he was the conduit for Ehranan's commands.

He sensed the twenty guardians moving, cutting off a group of kobalen trying to cross the ælven's flank. A small ripple in the seething cauldron of the valley.

Kobalen dead lay everywhere, black-furred corpses piled in the river and along its bank, heaped in ghastly rows across the valley that marked the ebb and flow of the battle over the last few days. Now the ælven were moving, pressing north on both sides of the Silverwash.

In the valley's bowl to the west of the river the ælven's main force pushed steadily forward, forcing the kobalen back toward the pass. Another army hastened through the forest along the eastern bank, gathering within the trees at the outpost near the north ford. Ehranan was with them. Soon he would lead them across to fall upon the kobalen from behind.

So long had he been Ehranan's voice to the ælven warriors that his awareness was spread like a net among them, each individual ælven a knot in the web. They moved as one, obeyed as one the commands of Ehranan, who watched and thought for them all.

A strange elation filled him, a sense of the army's power as his own.

Despite his passive role, he knew none of this would have happened as successfully as it did without his aid. The theory had been proven. Mindspeech was a powerful tool for an embattled army, therefore a powerful weapon.

How strange to think of oneself as a weapon. Rephanin was disturbed by the idea. As one who had tried—not always with success, but always with sincerity—to keep the creed, it seemed ironic that he should now become a tool of widespread destruction of life.

There was no choice, of course. They must fight or be overwhelmed, so they fought.

Make ready.

Ehranan's voice rang in his mind, and through him to all the armies. A tension rose in the khi of the ælven as the hundreds across the river braced to move, took firm grip upon sword or bow, and turned their gaze westward. Their silence was a heavy weight within the wood.

To Rephanin it seemed even the trees watched. Their slow, dull, constant khi—the foundation of the forest—was more alert than usual. All living things awaited the outcome of this conflict.

Among the ælven west of the river, those engaged in fighting the kobalen, the reaction to Ehranan's command was anticipation, hope. If all went well, their ordeal would soon be over.

Forward.

Ælven warriors poured from the wood, streaming across the ford, thigh-deep in water that was cold and fouled with kobalen dead. The army had taken no water from the river since the battle began.

Reaching the western bank they spread across the valley, silent and swift. If any kobalen saw them they raised no alarm.

Swords to the fore, archers behind. Prepare to loose a volley on my signal.

The warriors crossed the river. Ehranan's voice in thought rang out with the force of every ælven's will.

Now!

Arrows vaulted through the air, a chorus of high-pitched voices singing doom to those below. They rose over the heads of the waiting sword-bearers, sailed in a high arc across the battle-littered ground, then fell with deadly effect among the kobalen, who shrieked and turned to see the new threat behind them.

Again! Loose!

A second volley rose and fell, scattering the mass of kobalen. They were fewer than they had been when they had first crossed the mountains, though they still outnumbered the ælven.

Loose!

With the third wave of arrows, kobalen broke from the fight and began to swarm up the steep mountainsides to the west. Some ran into the river and were swept away by the deeper waters below the ford. Some ran north toward their attackers, shrieking their anger, fitting darts to their throwing sticks as they ran.

Charge!

A cry rose from all the ælven as swords were raised and the line of warriors moved to meet the foe. Rephanin had a fleeting sense of his hand gripping a sword hilt, felt an echo of Ehranan's racing heartbeat as he advanced with his army.

Bright sparks of pain or surprise or bewilderment lit across the field as ælven were struck by kobalen weapons, wounded or killed. Rephanin tried to hold himself apart from them, tried to let the points of anguish fade against the greater glow of elation from the ælven armies.

The trap had worked; the kobalen were broken. All that remained was to hunt them down or drive them west into the cold winter grip of the Ebons.

Midrange Pass lay to the north of the northern army, out of the kobalen's reach now, and in any case it was blocked with snow. A cold death would be the fate of kobalen who ran westward and tried to struggle across the unforgiving mountains to their homeland.

Many did so. Many others tried the river. The few that managed to reach the eastern shore were picked off by ælven archers.

A few hundred maddened kobalen persisted in fighting, besieged north and south by the ælven. They fought ferociously, eager to cost the ælven as dearly as they might. A group of them broke through the northern army and scattered, some running across the ford, some escaping into the pass.

They would have to be hunted down, Rephanin agreed with Ehranan's fleeting thought. Highstone, Alpinon's chief city, was less than a day's ride to the north. The folk there were aware of the kobalen threat —indeed, some of the warriors on this field were from Alpinon's Guard —but it would be better to prevent any kobalen from reaching them.

The fighting dwindled as the last few kobalen on the field were slain. Rephanin drifted, waiting for Ehranan to give more commands. As fear and tension drained away, a great weariness overcame him.

Captains to me. Where is Phaniron?

On the field, some warriors began to tend the ælven dead and wounded, seeking out fallen friends and comrades, while the rest gathered around Ehranan. The army made no cry of triumph.

Rephanin let commands of a more mundane nature wash through

him. Companies were sent to harry the kobalen who had run west, to begin clearing the river of kobalen dead, to gather wood for pyres.

Rephanin let it all pass over him. There was an ache within him, and he could not find its cause.

Night was coming on a cold wind. He preferred the night; when at home in the magehall in Glenhallow he was a night-bider, taking his rest by day. It had been so long now since he had rested at all that he had no will to try to find his flesh and ascertain its needs.

He should do so, he knew. The needs of the flesh, the needs of the soul. He wondered, did his soul bear the weight of all these kobalen dead? If so, he could not see that he would ever be able to atone.

Turisan fretted as he rode across another of the valleys south of Midrange. Sunlight had broken through the clouds, turning the snow in the road to slush and then to mud. The sun should have cheered him, but his thoughts were far distant.

Eliani was safe, but something had upset her. Only the conviction that she was not in immediate danger kept him from speaking to her. They would talk when both were resting.

He rubbed at his aching shoulder. The wound, taken a few days since at Midrange, still troubled him. The kobalen's dart had gone deep.

Was the battle still underway? He heard no sound of it on the wind, but they were yet some distance from Midrange.

The sun's warmth was making him uncomfortable. He threw back his cloak from his shoulders, and rubbed a hand across his heated brow. At that moment, his party crossed the ridge into the next valley.

He recognized it; the last valley to the south of Midrange. He had camped on the north side of it the night after being wounded, along with other casualties of the battle.

Some of them had not lived the night. One in particular he remembered—a guardian who had been severely injured, and whose passing he had eased with Eliani's help. Dahlaran had been his name; a young recruit. Too young.

"My lord..."

Turisan shifted his gaze to the ridge, where Gothalan pointed. Beyond it rose a towering pillar of smoke.

He drew a sharp breath. The smoke was thick and black, so the fire must be new. High Holding had burned, but not like this.

"Let us hasten."

The guardians were eager enough to comply. Likely they all had friends on the field at Midrange. To know their fate the sooner, whatever it might be, was easier than waiting.

The horses ran willingly, catching the anxiety of their riders. Even so, it was needful to stop halfway across the valley and rest the animals. Turisan bit back impatience as they slowed to a walk.

The smoke had begun to spread, flattening against the sky. Turisan could smell it now; a foul, unclean fume. He frowned, contemplating his choices.

If they crossed into Midrange Valley and discovered the battle was lost, they must retreat at once. He would like to reach Highstone, less than two days' ride from here, but if the enemy held the valley he would not be able to do so without crossing the Silverwash and swinging far to the east. Even then, he would be risking his life and those of his escort, circling around the enemy.

If the battle was still underway, though ... he would seek out Ehranan and deliver his message, then be sent to safety behind the lines, no doubt. Ehranan might even order him back to Glenhallow. He would have to compose a diplomatic refusal. He meant to continue north, whatever the situation at Midrange.

His gaze remained fixed on the smoke as they progressed. The sun grew warmer, intensifying the smell. Turisan considered getting out a cloth to tie over his mouth and nose, but that would require halting to search in his packs.

At last the horses were rested enough to trot again. The party crossed the valley floor swiftly, then slowed as the road began to climb the southern slope of the next ridge of mountains.

Turisan glanced westward, seeking the campsite, for it had been near a stream running down from the mountains. He spied the stream and called it to Gothalan's attention. Nodding, the guardian led the party off the trail, uphill toward the place where the wounded had camped. They paused to water the horses and fill their own flasks.

Turisan silently acknowledged those who had died in that place, promising anew that they would be remembered with a conce. As he looked up the hillside, his gaze fell upon the blackened patch of ground where the pyres had been lit the next morning.

He drew a sharp breath, and looked northward. The smoke, now half-hidden by the ridge, billowed and roiled as black as ever.

A pyre? His heart quailed at the thought. If so, it was a pyre larger than any he had ever known.

After a brief rest, Gothalan remounted and led them back to the road, which climbed steeply now through the pass that led into

Midrange Valley. The horses labored even at a walk. When they reached the crest, Turisan urged his mount forward, beside Gothalan's, gazing over Midrange Valley.

Scattered all across the north side of the ridge, the southern edge of the valley, were the camps of the ælven forces. There was no clash of battle to be heard, only the tremendous roar and stench of the massive fire half a league away, at the center of what had been the battlefield.

Turisan swallowed, his nostrils contracting at the heavy smell of death. It was indeed a pyre, though not for ælven. Even at this distance he could see that the burning heap was not shaped in the way of his people's custom. Ælven had surely made the pyre, but not for their own. They were burning the enemy's dead.

"It is over." Gothalan sounded oddly disappointed.

Turisan looked away from the fire, scanning the camp. "Where is Ehranan?"

"Those tents?"

There were few tents on the field, and most were makeshift, from blankets. Two large pavilions stood out among the rest, well up the slope. Turisan followed Gothalan toward them, with the rest of his escort coming after.

"Hail, Mindspeaker!"

The shout startled Turisan; he glanced toward the sound, but could not identify the source. Others took up the cry, and suddenly he saw cheer in the faces that had been gloomy a moment before.

If they knew the tidings he brought, they would not be so welcoming. Keeping that thought to himself, he made an effort to smile and wave, returning their greeting as he rode toward the commander's camp.

❈

Voices, real voices of the flesh, intruded on Rephanin's awareness. Someone was near his resting place, and the knowledge brought him back to it.

The vague ache he had felt for so long now came into focus, and it was a hundred aches, complaints of his neglected flesh. He was almost too weary to reclaim it, but he did so, opening caked eyelids just as Ehranan came into the tent.

A cold gust followed before the flap fell again. Rephanin shuddered, and realized that cold was one of the many troubles of his flesh.

Ehranan came over to where he lay, frowning down at him. The ælven commander was from Eastfæld, hailing from Clan Ælvanen as

Rephanin did himself. The warrior's long black hair was caught back from his face in a hunter's braid. His sharp blue eyes sought Rephanin's, dark with concern.

"How long has it been since you have eaten?"

Helpless to answer, Rephanin merely shook his head, the slight movement seeming to require a great effort. Ehranan's frown deepened. He turned away and strode to the tent door again, and for a moment Rephanin feared he would be abandoned.

"Bring some hot liquid. Tea, or broth, and bread. Quickly!"

The cold breeze came again, setting Rephanin shaking this time. Ehranan returned and knelt beside him, pulling Rephanin's dark gold cloak up over him, taking his hand. Khi flooded through his hand into Rephanin's flesh, breathtaking in its brilliance.

"Forgive me." Ehranan's voice was low and pleading. "This is my doing. I should have—"

No blame. You had one or two other concerns.

Ehranan's eyes searched his face. I have demanded too much of you.

Not more than I was willing to give.

Rephanin remembered how to smile, and did so as he gazed wearily at Ehranan. The warrior's frown eased a little. He held Rephanin's hand in both of his, the warmth of his flesh a comfort as much as the light of his khi.

Rephanin felt a small stirring of desire, and willed it away. They had been in close contact for so long it was inevitable that a bond had formed between them. He never had been able to engage in extended mindspeech without being drawn to his partners, male or female, young or old. Ehranan must be aware, but showed no sign of it. Perhaps it was best ignored.

"Lord Ehranan?"

"Come."

The cold breeze came again as a guardian entered bearing a wooden bowl and a half-loaf of bread. Steam rose from the bowl. Rephanin's stomach clenched with sudden need, so sharply he drew a surprised breath.

"Vishani is making some tea." The young guardian cast a frightened glance at Rephanin. "We brought food during the battle, but he did not rouse—"

"Yes, yes." Ehranan summoned him with a gesture. "No blame. Bring it here."

The guardian, a Greenglen, hastened to where Rephanin lay, eyes growing wide as he looked down at the magelord. Rephanin idly wondered what he saw to make him so alarmed, then was distracted by Ehranan's hand beneath his shoulder.

"Can you sit up? Let me help you."

Stiff muscles complained as Ehranan helped him rise a little from the makeshift couch of packs and blankets. Ehranan pushed spare blankets behind him to prop him up while the Greenglen stood watching, pale beside the dark Ælvanen commander.

Ehranan took the bowl and nodded to the guardian to give the bread to Rephanin. The Greenglen leaned forward and gently laid it by Rephanin's hand. Rephanin smiled his thanks and moved his hand to hold the bread, though he doubted he had strength to lift it.

"Thank you. Bring the tea when it is ready."

"Yes, my lord."

The guardian made haste to withdraw. Ehranan held the bowl closer and brought a spoonful of broth to Rephanin's lips.

Rephanin's parched mouth tried to water at the smell of salt and stewed meat. Venison, he thought. He opened his lips to let Ehranan tip the spoonful into his mouth. Its warmth moistened his tongue, then slid down his throat to waken his empty belly. He drew a grateful breath as the small spot of heat began to spread through him.

Another spoonful. He took it, then paused to feel his senses awaken, some painfully. He looked at Ehranan, who patiently offered the spoon again.

"Thank you." Rephanin's voice was a croaking whisper.

"Drink." Ehranan frowned, though his eyes showed concern.

You must have more pressing tasks.

Than keeping you alive? I think not.

Rephanin made no more protest. He was grateful to have Ehranan's help, and took several more spoonfuls of broth before he paused to let his flesh cope with the sudden nourishment.

You were not planning to leave us, I hope.

Ehranan's eyes were sharp with care, dark with a shade of dread. Rephanin managed another smile.

No.

Good. I have more demands to make of you. This is not the end of it.

Rephanin read his meaning in his eyes. More battle. More death.

I know, but I cannot... not now...

No, no. I did not mean now.

Rephanin closed his eyes. A shudder went through him. He heard the click of the spoon against the bowl, then felt Ehranan's hand cover his again.

Forgive me. I did not know it would hurt you so.

None of us knew.

I—sensed an echo of it, I think, while the battle was on. It was too late by then.

Yes.

Rephanin did not want to talk of the battle, or to think of it. He wanted to rest in the strange, odd silence that now enveloped him, silence in the absence of the army's thoughts. He felt alone, now, save for Ehranan's presence. Alone for the first time in many days, and he reveled in it.

The cold gust of the tent door's came again. Rephanin opened his eyes to see two guardians: the one who had brought the broth, and the commander of the twenty guardians posted outside to protect him—a female—some Greenglen whose name Rephanin should remember but could not find just now. She bore a brazier of coals, which she set on the ground near Rephanin's feet. She bowed stiffly.

"I crave pardon, my lords. I have been remiss."

"No." Ehranan shook his head. "You were ordered not to disturb him."

Ehranan's voice was curt from long habit of command, but the Greenglen might not know that. Rephanin tried to comfort her with a smile. Her own lips curved for a fleeting moment, then returned to a grim line.

She glanced at the other guardian, who bore a steaming ewer and a slender pottery cup. He brought them forward and set them at Ehranan's side, then returned to his captain. Both moved to go.

"Thank you." Rephanin's voice was still feeble, and he gave up, resorting to mindspeech.

Thank you for all you have done. For watching over my safety. I am grateful. I could not have done this without your help.

The captain seemed to take heart at this. She made another small, stiff bow, then departed along with the other guardian. Rephanin felt the echo of her relief as she walked away from the tent. Ehranan glanced after her.

You have a good understanding of a warrior's needs.

Of these warriors' needs, yes. I have been in close contact with them for some time now. These few set to guard me feel they have not done all they should, since they were not on the field.

Nonsense. Their task was of vital importance.

Ehranan's frown had returned. Rephanin watched him, knowing the frown betokened concern, not disapproval. So many concerns he had, being in command of two armies, of hundreds of warriors from three ælven realms and a dozen different clans. It was a vast responsibility.

Reclaiming this valley was a feat that would be lauded as much as the first Midrange War. A part of Rephanin was horrified, another found it richly amusing.

"Can you take a little more broth, or do you want the tea?"

"Broth."

Rephanin gripped the bread on his lap and tried to pull off a piece. His hands were too weak, though. They shook with the effort.

Ehranan set down the bowl, tore off a few morsels of the bread and dropped them in the broth, then offered one, sopping, in the spoon. Rephanin took it and slowly chewed. He was relieved to feel his strength returning, and somewhat abashed that he had neglected his flesh so badly. Another time he must take care to be more watchful.

Another time. He closed his eyes and swallowed. How could he bear another battle? He wanted to weep, but the tears would not come.

So many dead.

"Rephanin, you saved lives. Hundreds of ælven lives. This would have been much worse without you."

Would it?

That was a dreadful thought. He had no desire to imagine worse.

"Eat a little more."

Rephanin managed two more bites of broth-soaked bread, then leaned his head back. Ehranan set the bowl aside and poured tea into the pottery cup, wrapped Rephanin's hands around it, then helped him guide it to his lips.

The tea was simple, a blend of gentle flowers, the sort brewed for comfort. The warmth of it spread through his fingers, the fragrance filled his senses.

"Lord Ehranan? "

The commander turned toward the door. "What is it?"

"Lord Turisan is here, and desires a word with you."

"Turisan?" Ehranan glanced at Rephanin. "May I leave you for a little while?"

"Of course." Rephanin was pleased to find that his voice had improved to a hoarse whisper.

"Do you want someone to stay with you?"

Rephanin shook his head and smiled to assure Ehranan that he need not be watched so carefully. He would not slip away. He welcomed solitude.

The commander stood and went out, and his voice sounded at once outside the tent, consulting with Avhlórin, who commanded the forces from Eastfæld. Their voices faded to a murmur as they walked away, leaving Rephanin in silence.

Silence at last. He had never thought he would cherish it so. He closed his eyes and drew a deep breath, letting it out in a sigh of relief.

✿ Fireshore ✿

Eliani was beginning to hate the darkwood forest. It closed in all around them, filled with unfamiliar khi, strange smells, and the calls of birds that never flew in the pine forests of her homeland. Instinct told her that danger dwelt beneath the darkwoods, but she had chosen to follow Othanin and would not now turn back.

They walked close to the stream, from which the undergrowth had been cleared to make a passageway. The Lost kept this way, which began a few rods into the forest from the road. After struggling through that dense growth, Othanin urging them all the while to leave no sign of their passing, this small cleared path had seemed wonderfully spacious, but that feeling had long since given way to a sense of confinement.

Sunlight did not reach the floor of the forest. Instead a greenish glow surrounded them, and steamy heat dulled their senses. Eliani wondered if it was dark enough here that alben would risk coming into the forest during the day. She hoped not.

Luruthin, ahead of her on the path, stopped walking. Eliani held up her hand to signal the halt to those behind her.

Othanin was in the lead, with Vanorin behind him for his protection should they be attacked. Vanorin disliked having the party strung out single file on the path, Eliani knew, but there was no help for it.

Luruthin knelt to scoop water from the stream with his hands. Eliani joined him, glancing anxiously at him. He looked so drawn and weak, and there was a haunted fear in his eyes, but he had made no complaint during the journey.

Whenever they stopped to rest, which was often, he drank from the stream and then sat with eyes closed. Eliani had not spoken to him, sensing his need to conserve his strength for the march. She ached for him, though. He had plainly suffered as a captive of the alben, and she feared his suffering went beyond what could be seen.

She had regretted leaving him behind from the moment she had done so. Now she saw in part what it had cost him, what he had suffered for her sake. She did not think she could ever repay him.

Her brow grew warm. She sat back and closed her eyes.

Yes, love?

Where are you now?

In the forest, west of the road. Othanin is leading us.

Does he know his way?

He seems to.

Turisan's concern crossed the silence. It comforted her, wrapping her like a warm, soft cloak.

We are all right. I do not think we shall be followed.

How is Luruthin?

Weak. I have not had a chance to talk with him.

If he has a message for Jhinani, I can ask Rephanin to pass it to Glenhallow.

Eliani was surprised, struck for a moment at the realization of the power of mindspeech. Among the four of them—herself, Turisan, Rephanin, and his partner Thorian—they could send a message from Fireshore two realms away to the southernmost city on the land, Glenhallow, where winter must now be taking hold.

I think that would be a great comfort to him. I will offer.

She opened her eyes. Luruthin had leaned against a tangled root of darkwood, and a green-winged fly had settled on his brow. Eliani brushed it away, and the movement startled him into looking up at her.

Green eyes, like her own, but sunken now and filled for a moment with fear. Eliani laid a hand on his arm.

"A fly. It is gone now."

Luruthin seemed to relax, and sat blinking at her. Khi leapt to her palm where it touched him, telling her even through his sleeve that he needed healing. She moved to face him and raised both hands.

"May I?"

He hesitated, then nodded. The sharing of khi was an intimacy most ælven avoided except in private.

Healing was a form of this, and from the little she had done so far Eliani had gained a great respect for those who devoted their lives to this kind of service. Jhinani was one of those, and Eliani could not help thinking of the golden-haired, gentle Greenglen lady as she now took Luruthin's hands in hers.

He drew a sharp breath at the contact, then closed his eyes. Eliani did so also, allowing her thoughts to focus on the khi that poured through her palms into his.

Its source was all around, in every living thing and in the very air they breathed. Prime khi, Jhinani had called it. Eliani knew she was only a channel, a focus for this khi. Because she was healing no specific wound, it flowed through her hands to every part of Luruthin's being. The healing humbled her, as always, reminding her that she was only a small part of the living world.

Something troubled her—something was odd. She waited, holding her awareness open, hoping for understanding to come. As the heat of healing finally began to ebb, at last she recognized what bothered her. Luruthin's khi felt strange.

Having once been lovers, they had shared khi as intimately as was possible without mindspeech. She knew the tone of his khi as well as she knew her own father's, yet now it felt different, less smooth than it should. Perhaps Luruthin's distress had caused the shift. She had never heard of such a change, but she knew little of the study of khi. She would have to ask an experienced healer.

She released his hands and opened her eyes to look at him. His face seemed more peaceful than it had, and he sat quietly for a moment before stirring. When he looked back at her she saw a spark of his old spirit in his gaze.

"Thank you." His voice was hoarse. "You *are* good at that!"

Eliani smiled. "Turisan sends you his good wishes. He is with Rephanin, and can pass a message to Glenhallow for you."

"Glenhallow?" Luruthin stared uncomprehending.

"To Jhinani."

A jumble of fleeting emotions passed through his face. Eliani could not read them all, but sensed his confusion and dismay.

"Jhinani." He blinked, frowning. "Yes. Tell her—"

A stirring on the path ahead distracted him. Othanin was standing, preparing to move on.

"Tell her I hope she is well."

Luruthin got to his feet. Eliani watched, troubled by his reaction. His affection for Jhinani could not have changed, could it? She carried his child. Eliani remembered the joy in his face when he had told her of it. Surely that had not changed.

This was not the time to question him about it. The party moved forward again, single-file along the narrow path, making conversation difficult.

For the most part they were silent, with only the murmur of the stream and the small sounds of the forest for company. Judging by the oppressive weight of the heat and moisture, and by the falling-off of activity among the living things dwelling in the forest, she thought it must be mid-afternoon.

Othanin halted again and Eliani suppressed a sigh. They were not making fast progress, but that could not be expected, given Othanin and Luruthin's weakened condition. The governor had been right that they should not travel on the road, for the alben would easily have caught up with them come nightfall, at this pace.

She heard murmuring voices, glanced forward to see Othanin talking with Vanorin, then walking away. Luruthin had already settled himself to rest. Eliani stepped past him and went to Vanorin.

"Where is he going?"

"To his rendezvous. He does not want the rest of us to make his lady wary."

The guard captain frowned as he delivered this news, and Eliani could not help feeling a moment's doubt of Othanin's intentions. Could he have led them into a trap? Could he be planning to abandon them here, where their only choice would be to return to the danger of the road?

She put these suspicions aside. Othanin had no reason to betray them. They had rescued him from captivity, and they wished to return him to his place as governor of Fireshore.

It was he who was taking a risk, bringing them close to his lady and the Lost. It was possible that the Ælven Council would consider the Lost the same as the alben.

How terribly wrong that seemed, but then, Eliani knew that she had a rather different view of Othanin and his lady's plight than most. She must remember to share all her thoughts on this with Turisan, in case she did not get out of this forest alive.

Eliani squatted and drank from the stream, then found a sapling darkwood that would bear her leaning against it, and sat back to await Othanin's return. After a moment, she became aware of a broken sighing. Someone was weeping. Looking down the path behind her, she saw Onami, a Greenglen, crouched forward with her head on her knees, arms wrapped around herself as she stifled her sobs.

Eliani got up and quietly went to her, wishing to comfort her but hesitant to intrude. Onami's head turned slightly as Eliani knelt beside her to whisper.

"What is it?"

"Taharan. He was k-killed at the gates."

"I am sorry." Eliani reached out a hand to touch her shoulder.

Onami was still for a moment, then flung her arms around Eliani and collapsed against her, sobbing. Eliani held her, silently bringing the khi of healing to comfort her. Taharan had been Stonereach, a member of Eliani's clan, a citizen of Alpinon, yet Onami who was a Greenglen grieved for him. Eliani's escort of mixed Stonereaches and Greenglens had become one.

They had also shrunk from twenty down to four: Vanorin; Onami; and two Stonereaches, Birani and Felahran who was a distant cousin of Eliani's, were all that remained. When she had set out on this journey, Eliani had balked at Governor Jharan's insistence that she travel with an armed escort, but she saw now that he had been right. Unforeseen troubles had reduced their number, and she had not expected to be fighting the alben. She wished now that she had brought twice as many.

Ahead on the path, Vanorin rose. Eliani heard the sound of approaching footsteps. She gave Onami, who was calmer now, a gentle hug, then rose and went to join Vanorin.

He glanced at her, but said nothing and returned to watching and listening. In a few moments, Othanin appeared. His face was filled with relief.

"She is here. She was watching for me, as I thought. She has agreed to meet with you, Lady Eliani."

Eliani drew herself up. "Very well."

Vanorin stepped forward. "I will accompany you."

Othanin's brows twitched together in a frown. Eliani turned to Vanorin.

"That is not necessary."

"I am charged with your safety. I will accompany you."

His voice and manner were stiff and formal. Eliani nodded.

"Lead us on, then, Governor Othanin."

Othanin's dark eyes rested on Vanorin for a long moment. At last he glanced at Eliani and a slight smile touched his lips.

"This way."

The path turned away from the stream after a few paces, a change which made Eliani the more uncomfortable. She did not like this looming forest, with its twisted darkwood trees reaching toward a sky that could not been seen.

High among the black branches the broad leaves were dotted with clusters of white flowers. Eliani wondered if her eldermother, Heléri, had ever seen darkwood blossoms, and if she knew of any benefit to be derived from them.

They were approaching a darkwood that was larger than most, older than most by its breadth and height. Its highest branches twined away into the green canopy. Its trunk was broader than two armspans at the base and leaned sharply to one side, making Eliani wish to run up its slope to the first branching of its limbs.

She saw from the polished shine of the smooth, black bark that others had so trod upon it, and realized that this must be Othanin and his lady's rendezvous, the place where they exchanged messages. Eliani could imagine finding a crevice in the branching to leave a scrap of parchment in, just as she had hidden treasures in the highest branching of her favorite oak, back in Alpinon.

As they approached the great tree a solitary figure stepped from behind it. This person wore a heavy hood, but Eliani could see into it. She gasped and took a small step back at the sight of a white-haired, black-eyed female.

Alben, instinct told her as she recoiled. She had first seen such coloring only a few days ago, when the alben had captured Ghlanhras.

The leather clothing the female wore, including the hood and the gloves that covered her hands, was undyed, the light brown of deerskin. Despite her coloring, something about the bones in her face made Eliani think of Clan Steppegard.

Her pale hair was caught back from her face, and a small band of braided deerskin bound her brow. She carried a bow and quiver, and a long knife was slung at her hip.

Othanin stepped between them, raising a hand in formal introduction. "My lady, I bring you greeting from Lady Eliani, daughter of Governor Felisan of Alpinon. Lady Eliani, I am honored to present you to Lady Kivhani."

"Kivhani will do." The lady's voice was deep, quiet. "We are too few to be so formal."

"I am honored to meet you." Eliani bowed slightly, her flesh tingling with fear at speaking to one who appeared alben. "This is Vanorin, captain of my escort."

Vanorin made a formal salute, at which Kivhani's lips twitched slightly. She nodded to him, then gazed at Eliani again.

"Well met. My lord tells me you seek refuge with us."

"We cannot travel quickly enough on the road to avoid pursuit from Ghlanhras. Othanin has told you—?"

"He has told me."

She exchanged a glance with Othanin, and though both were silent, Eliani could see the intensity of feeling they shared. Not all couples needed mindspeech to communicate so.

"Your bringing him out of Ghlanhras is all the claim you need on me. I owe you thanks and all the assistance I can give."

She stepped toward Eliani and offered to clasp arms. Eliani hesitated for the merest instant, then reached out her own arm. Kivhani's khi startled her; it prickled, like the air before a thunderstorm.

Eliani nodded as they let go. "Thank you. Is your camp very far?"

"The main camp is in the mountains, three days' march. A few of us are camped nearby. My loyal folk refused to let me watch here alone."

Kivhani's lips twitched again in the hint of a smile. Eliani smiled back, beginning to feel kinship with this stern lady.

"We need to go south."

"The camp is south and west of here."

Eliani bit her lip. She wanted to go to Woodrun, and she must also warn Bitterfield. She wanted to be far from Ghlanhras, and she wanted rest and healing for Luruthin. She could not have all she wished.

At least she had sent warning to Woodrun. Comforted by this thought, she decided that her next priority must be the safety of her party.

"We would be grateful to shelter with you for a while."

"Bring your people here and I will lead you to the camp. I have sent a message ahead to alert my friends. We have few comforts, but will gladly share what we have."

"Thank you. We shall have to h-hunt." Eliani faltered as it occurred to her that hunting must have a different meaning for Kivhani's people. "Perhaps you can advise us what game is to be had nearby?"

"Small game and hard to catch, in this part of the forest. We have fruit and nuts you are welcome to share."

Eliani nodded, strangely comforted by the thought of the Lost eating fruit and nuts. "I will bring my people. Thank you, Lady Kivhani."

She bowed again, formally, then glanced at Vanorin and nodded to him to come with her. Othanin remained behind, no doubt to share a precious moment alone with his lady. He had talked of her with the pain of longing in his voice, the night Eliani and Luruthin had spent in Darkwood Hall.

That seemed so long ago. Eliani marveled as she returned down the path to the stream. Had it really been only last night? So much had happened.

Ghlanhras attacked and taken by the alben. The rescue, costly but absolutely essential. Impossible to leave the governor of an ælven realm in captivity. She could see that Othanin would be useful in communicating with the Lost.

And Luruthin ... Luruthin.

He was still sitting with eyes closed when she reached him. She was dismayed anew at how unhappy he looked. A dark wish for revenge woke in her heart, a thought she knew was unworthy and against the creed. She tried to forget it as she came to stand beside Luruthin and softly called his name.

He looked up. Eliani smiled and offered a hand to help him stand.

"Othanin's lady will shelter us. Come."

He smiled back and reached up to take her arm. As she pulled him to his feet she felt a shock of recognition.

Luruthin's khi—the khi that had felt so unfamiliar—had the same prickle to it as Kivhani's.

❀ Highstone ❀

Turisan rode into the public circle at Highstone with a weary sense of satisfaction. He had not been here since his first visit, back at Autumn Evennight, and was somewhat surprised to see the city blanketed in snow. The year had turned; Midwinter was upon them now.

Moonlight threw a blue cast over the steep-roofed stone houses of Highstone, making the windows, lit by glowing candles, lanterns, and flickering firelight, look all the warmer. As on the first occasion of his coming here, those warm windows seemed to welcome him.

Rephanin reined in beside him. "How small it is."

Turisan turned to look at the magelord, huddled in his cloak and leaning forward over his saddle. He smiled, remembering that he, too, had been unimpressed with his first sight of Highstone and Felisanin Hall.

Turisan's escort of five Southfæld Guardians looked around with curiosity. Some thirty-odd Stonereaches from Alpinon's Guard had accompanied them from Midrange, and these turned anxious eyes toward the houses of the city. A door opened in one and a female let out a muffled cry of joy as she ran to one of the guardians.

Turisan dismounted, and the others took this as a signal to do likewise. The Stonereaches turned from an orderly column into a chattering mass, laughing with relief and the pleasure of being home, fast melting away down the streets that radiated from the public circle.

The five Southfæld Guardians stayed close to Turisan and Rephanin. Attendants came from Felisan's stables to take charge of their horses. Turisan retrieved his saddle packs, then stood by while Rephanin slowly lowered himself from his own mount.

"Welcome, Lord Turisan! Is the fighting over at Midrange?"

Turisan turned to the attendant holding his horse. "It is over for now."

"That is glad news. How fares Lady Eliani?"

A somewhat impertinent question, but understandable. All Alpinon loved Eliani, and it was natural for her people to feel protective of her.

"She is well. Has Governor Felisan retired for the night, think you?"

"Oh, likely not." The attendant flashed a grin. "Minstrels are here from Clerestone, come to play at the Midwinter feast tomorrow. He is sure to keep them playing as long as there is strength in their fingers."

"Then I will dare to intrude. Thank you."

He glanced at his escort and saw that they were ready. He led the way across the trampled snow of the public circle to the stair that was cut into the hillside and led up to Felisanin Hall, eager to see Eliani's home again.

Her home. He frowned slightly. If Hallowhall was not to be their home together, could Felisanin Hall be so? He could not see himself living here, much as he liked Highstone. He was his father's nextkin, and would one day assume the governorship of Southfæld. It would not be possible to govern from the seat of another realm.

Well, they would know if they came here together and their handfasting ribbons came loose. Until the ribbons, bound by magecraft, loosened, their future home was a mystery.

Dismissing the thought for the present, he led his party through the open front doors of Felisanin Hall and into its spacious hearthroom, where a fire crackled merrily on the welcoming hearth. He rang the visitor's chime and a youth appeared through a curtained doorway.

"Lord Turisan!"

"Good evening, Curunan. Is the governor receiving guests?"

"He will certainly receive you, my lord! Welcome! Let me take your cloak."

"Thank you. This is Lord Rephanin, master of the Magehall at Glenhallow."

Curunan bowed gravely. "Welcome to Highstone, my lord."

Turisan helped the magelord remove his cloak and handed it to Curunan, who disappeared through a side door, then returned and led them with due ceremony into the hall. The room was wide and doubly long, about half the size of Hallowhall's audience chamber. Its ceiling was high and vaulted, its windows of colorful glass depicting scenes of hunting and battle along with more placid images of gardening, woodworking, a scene that must be of Clerestone's crystal mines and an image of the Three Shades, the great waterfall near Highstone.

Turisan had not noticed that picture before, and his breath caught at the sight of it. It had been at the foot of the Shades that he and Eliani had discovered they shared the gift of mindspeech. The rumble of those mighty waters had haunted him during the last part of the journey here. Even now he could hear it, a low whisper of sound to shake the soul.

"Turisan!"

Felisan leapt up from his chair in the center of a long feast table. His face, so like Eliani's, was tense for a moment. Turisan smiled to reassure him that he bore no bad tidings of the governor's daughter. Felisan's eyes lit with relief, then with pleasure as he hurried around the table to clasp Turisan's arm.

"Welcome indeed! I had not thought to see you here. Has the battle concluded?"

"It has, and your guardians accompanied me here. They have gone to their homes."

An outburst of excited talk followed this announcement. Several of the revelers hastily took their leave, and it was some moments before Felisan was free again.

In that time, Turisan noticed Lady Heléri, standing at her place at table beside Felisan's empty chair. Her hands were tightly clasped before her, her dark blue eyes fixed on Rephanin, and though her face was calm Turisan sensed she was concerned for the magelord.

Felisan at last turned to Rephanin. "Lord Rephanin, I am honored to welcome you to Highstone, and to my hall. Will you come and sit beside me?" Felisan glanced at Turisan to indicate he was included in the invitation.

"Thank you."

Turisan followed them to the table and took a chair offered to him by a Stonereach female. He smiled thanks to her, thinking she looked familiar, though of course they all looked familiar. Eliani's eyes gazed at him from a hundred faces in this hall.

Lady Heléri drew up another chair for the magelord. The Southfæld Guardians were made welcome around the table and immediately pelted with eager questions about Midrange. Turisan had the governor's questions to answer. He told Felisan what he knew of the battle's progress, much of it gleaned from his conversation earlier with Lord Ehranan.

"Ehranan is bringing the forces from Southfæld and Eastfæld north. He will keep them on the plains road."

Felisan's brows drew together. "Why do they march north?"

"Because of news from Fireshore."

Felisan's gaze sharpened, an unspoken question in the green eyes that were usually tranquilly lazy. Turisan gave a slight nod but said no more. Some issues were better discussed in private.

Felisan seemed to understand, for he reached for his wine goblet and an ewer from which to fill it. "Tell me of Eliani. Is my daughter well?"

"She is well. She sends you her love."

Felisan's lips twitched in a smile, though the slight frown of worry did not leave his brow. "Give her the same from me, when you speak again."

"Of course."

"What is wrong with your shoulder?"

Turisan realized he had been rubbing it. He had worn the sling while riding, but had taken it off before entering the hall, and the weakened limb was aching.

"A slight wound. Nothing of concern."

Felisan's brows went up. "Wounded? How did this come to pass? Jharan will be furious, you were supposed to stay out of harm's way!"

Turisan chuckled. "He was furious. I met him at Willow Bend."

He told Felisan of his own adventures at Midrange and of leading the column of wounded southward until they met his father coming north. Felisan laughed aloud at his description of Jharan's reaction to his wounded state.

"Gave him a good fright, did you? Well, he cannot keep you under his wing forever."

Turisan glanced at Felisan, surprised at the remark. It had not occurred to him that he was being kept under Jharan's wing. But then, neither had it occurred to him that he might ever dwell anywhere but at Hallowhall. He was only just beginning to consider other possibilities.

Kitchen attendants brought platters of food and fresh ewers of wine which they set before the new arrivals. Felisan raised an ewer, offering to fill Turisan's cup.

"Not as elegant as your father's table, I fear."

"Yet far better than the camp cooking and trail fare we have been eating. Fresh bread!"

Turisan picked up a small loaf and tore it in half. Steam rose from the soft bread and set his mouth watering. He heaped the plate before him with cheeses, meat, and sweet cakes, and ate with zeal.

Before he had finished his meal, Heléri and Rephanin rose and took their leave of Felisan. Rephanin looked somewhat drawn. Turisan watched them away, glad that Heléri was with him. If anyone could bring Rephanin peace and healing, it was she.

The musicians struck up a new tune, one that sounded vaguely familiar. Not until a young female, rather like Eliani but softer of face and of form, stepped forward and began to sing did Turisan recognize the melody.

He glanced at Felisan, wondering if the governor had signaled his wish to hear the Ballad of Turisan and Eliani. Felisan grinned back at him, giving no sign of anything but guileless pleasure.

Turisan took a large swallow of wine and assumed a polite smile while he listened to the tale of his own ride to Skyruach earlier in the year, the ride that had been made to prove his gift of mindspeech. It was strange to hear himself lauded so, like the heroes of ancient lore. He did not feel heroic.

He had never heard the song through, only snippets of it when it was first being composed. Back at Hallowhall, he thought, and closed his eyes, suddenly weary.

The song drew to a close. The last verse, which he had never heard, described his handfasting to Eliani in such poignant terms that he found his throat tightening at the memory of the one night they had shared before parting.

Please the spirits, may it not be our only night together.

Cheering filled the hall at the ballad's conclusion. Turisan smiled and applauded, nodding to the singer whose cheeks colored with pleasure at the gesture. Felisan called her forward.

"Well sung, Kelari. Your voice grows sweeter every season."

"Thank you, my lord governor."

Felisan gave her a small gold ring, which she accepted with another bow and a shy glance at Turisan. Turisan smiled at her, but it quickly faded. The ring reminded him of the gold earrings that the kobalen at Midrange had worn.

Thousands of kobalen, all marked with rings of gold no kobalen could have made, nor had ever worn before. The first time Turisan had seen such an earring had been here, in Alpinon. It had seemed a strange thing then, worthy of concern. How much more alarming the thousands of earrings at Midrange, now melted in the charnel fires that still smouldered.

He and Ehranan had examined a number of those rings on the

kobalen dead. All had been the same—finely wrought, engraved with a single ælven word: "preserve."

No ælven had made those rings, nor set them in kobalen ears. It was the work of the alben. And since so many kobalen at Midrange had worn them, it made sense to conclude that they had been sent there by the alben.

"Are you tired, Turisan? You need not put up with all this noise."

Turisan pushed aside his wine goblet. "The music is most excellent, but I fear I am a little tired. Will you object to my retiring?"

"Of course not. You will stay for Midwinter, yes?"

"I would be delighted."

"You will be my guest in the Hall. I have only Curunan for company now, and he is always off adventuring."

"You honor me." Turisan lowered his voice. "May I have a private word with you, before I retire?"

"Of course."

Felisan led the way to the back of the hall where an arch gave onto the governor's private quarters. A small hallway lit by sconces evoked a cozier feeling than the hall.

Echoes of his earlier visit here flitted through Turisan's mind—a cup of wine shared in Felisan's study, a farewell late at night following a handfasting, the Autumn Evennight celebration—and his chest tightened with a longing for Eliani, who walked through all his memories but was not here.

Rephanin lay in a weary daze, listening to the ringing in his ears. He was someplace quiet now, dark and warm, away from the noise of Felisanin Hall, yet the ringing remained to remind him he was far from well.

I am not ready. I am not ready to go on. Please, I need to rest.

A rustle of fabric nearby made him open his eyes. Soft candlelight filled the room where he lay, and a dark figure moved between him and the light, haloed by its glow. He did not remember coming here.

The figure leaned forward and a cool hand lay briefly on his brow. He smelled sweet herbs, and something warmer and more intimate. It was both strange and familiar, comforting and thrilling.

"Do you feel better?"

Heléri's voice, warm and low. Memories of the evening flooded back to him. He had been so tired, but then he had seen Heléri and known all would be well.

"Yes." His voice cracked on the word. He did feel better, if only for knowing she was close.

Heléri sat beside him on the bed, her weight shifting how he lay, drawing him toward her. He lifted a feeble hand and hers met it, her fingers cool and strong.

"Where are we?"

"The old hall. I live here alone now."

Alone, since her lord had crossed into spirit. Alone here for centuries, yet she did not betray loneliness.

"Do you want tea? I have the kettle on the fire."

"No." He shook his head slightly. Even that small movement made the ringing increase. "Just sit with me, please."

"Of course."

Her hand squeezed his warmly. The other smoothed his brow, and he closed his eyes, sighing as he strove to let the tension seep away. Heléri's hands grew warm, a sign of the healing power in them. He basked in the warmth, and slowly the ringing subsided.

"Oh, Rephanin. How dreadful it must have been. Can you tell me? Can you show me a little?"

He cringed at the thought that she should know anything of Midrange. He wanted to forget it, not share it. He could see no purpose in showing her what would only aggrieve her. The mere thought of it brought moisture to his eyes.

He could not bring himself to voice an answer. It was all he could do just to breathe, and hold the memories at bay.

Heléri seemed to understand. She did not ask again, but sat quietly beside him, her hands warm on his flesh. Slowly he became calm again in the gentle light of her presence.

A part of him looked on in scorn. There was nothing wrong with his flesh. Nothing wrong with his voice. This self-indulgence was as wasteful as any he had known. More so, perhaps, because he was imposing on Heléri, who surely had more important things to do.

Enough!

Startled, Rephanin twitched violently. Heléri's hand tightened on his, even as he realized who had spoken.

Davharin.

Acknowledgment came together with a sharpening of awareness, the tingle of contact with Heléri as well as with Davharin, her lord, who dwelt now in spirit. A moment later Rephanin felt his being flooded with light, a light so bright it should have been painful but was not. It burned into every corner of him, stilling the small chiding voice within him, chasing away the shadows that had clung in his heart.

He yielded, trusting the spirit to know what he could tolerate. The darkness in his heart, the darkness that was Midrange, burned away in the brightness. Rephanin felt suspended in pure light.

Wisps of sensation brushed his awareness: a chord of music, a cool and pungent scent, a warm breeze. He noted them but did not try to hold onto them.

He did not know how long it had been when the light finally receded. He knew only that it was still night, and that the darkness that had troubled him was gone, at least for the moment. He opened his eyes and drew a breath. Heléri sat beside him still, eyes closed and a serene expression on her face.

Thank you, Davharin.

Wordless warmth was the reply. Davharin preferred feelings, images, or symbols to words, and Rephanin had to agree that they conveyed much more, much more simply, when they could be so employed. He had used thoughts in this way at Midrange, time and again.

Remembering Midrange did not hurt this time, not as he had expected. A small ache was there, but only in a distant, quiet way. What had Davharin done?

Healing.

It was Heléri who had spoken. Rephanin shifted his gaze to her face again, and saw that she was now gazing back at him. The tenderness in her eyes reached straight into his heart. He squeezed her hand, then sat up, surprised at how easy it was. His strength was returning.

He raised a hand to Heléri's cheek, feeling warmth leap between their flesh as he held it there. Warmth swelled within him, too. Gratitude and relief, and affection. He leaned forward to kiss her, softly, lips warm together for an instant, then his arms came up around her and he buried his face in her fragrant hair.

She sighed, returning the embrace. *I was afraid for you. I feared you would leave.*

He drank in the smell of her, seeking the heady intoxication of fleshly desire. *No. I am not finished here.* She had said much the same to him, not long ago.

She pulled back to look at him, but voiced no speculation on his meaning. This moment was too sweet, and he sensed she had no more wish than he to dwell upon what he must do in the future.

Abandoning words, he showed her his longing, his deep, unending desire for her. She smiled and kissed him, sharing her own need, so sharp and hot it took his breath away.

He sought for Davharin, who had sometimes shared in their lovemaking, but the spirit had withdrawn. Heléri's hand slid into his sleeve, flesh tingling on flesh, and he forgot all else as their hearts and bodies twined together.

Felisan pulled aside the heavy tapestry that covered the archway and held it for Turisan to pass through. He let it fall behind them, muffling the music and shutting out the bright light of torches. A slight smell of dust followed the fall of the tapestry, giving Turisan a strangely comfortable feeling.

Felisan's quarters were far from pretentious, and casually kept. Turisan remembered the governor's comfortably cluttered study to which Felisan led him. It was rather more cluttered now, books and scrolls scattered on every surface including the floor. Eliani had tried to keep it in some order, he suspected, but she had been gone a while.

Felisan poked at the coals in the hearth and added a log, then invited Turisan with a gesture to sit. "Do you care for more wine?"

"Thank you, no."

"Will you rest in Eliani's chamber, or would you prefer another? Mind, hers is somewhat untidy."

Turisan hid his amusement, though he did smile. "Nothing would please me more than to rest in Eliani's chamber."

"You must miss her." A small, sympathetic frown creased Felisan's brow. "Well, so do I. The Hall is too quiet without her."

Turisan gazed at the new yellow flames. "I will not apologize for her absence."

"Oh, no, no! I never meant that you should." Felisan sighed and shifted his shoulders as he sprawled in his chair. "I knew she would go when you told us of the mindspeech. Suspected before then that she would go to you, at least for a time."

Turisan tilted his head to look at Felisan. "Did you? I did not. It seemed to me I could do nothing to please her."

Felisan chuckled. "Well, you did not know her. She fights her own heart, sometimes."

"Mm."

Felisan's eyes betrayed an unaccustomed worry. "You said she is well?"

Turisan turned his chair more toward Felisan. "She has been to Ghlanhras."

Felisan leaned forward, eyes intent. "And met Othanin? What did he say? Why did he not come to Council?"

"Our messages never reached him. The alben intercepted the first party in the mountains. That was the party Kelevon had met, and he was taken with them."

"Ah!"

"And the second party was slain here in Alpinon. We had word of it a few days ago from Clerestone."

"So the guardians Eliani sent back arrived safely there? Good. She will be glad to hear of it."

"Can you—can you speak to her now?"

Turisan nodded. "I will, but I must first tell you of Fireshore." He looked down at his hands and rubbed them together. "I have no gentle way to say it. Ghlanhras was attacked and captured by the alben shortly after Eliani arrived."

"What?!"

"Eliani escaped, but Luruthin was taken. So was Othanin, and the others dwelling in the city."

"Where is my daughter?" Felisan looked as close to anger as Turisan had ever seen him.

Turisan leaned back in his chair. "She and her escort rode back to Ghlanhras to rescue Luruthin and Othanin."

"No!" Felisan jumped up and began to pace. "I forbid it!"

"It is done, Felisan. They succeeded, although at some cost."

Felisan stopped and met his gaze across a table cluttered with maps and candlesticks. "The cost?"

"Two dead, three wounded, three unaccounted for and presumed captured."

A look of pain crossed Felisan's face. Just as swiftly, it fell into a neutral mask, reminding Turisan of his own father.

"Shall I speak to Eliani now?"

"Wait." Felisan frowned in thought. "I had rather speak to her myself."

Turisan's brows rose. "Would that you could."

"I can, with Rephanin's help. And yours, of course." He glanced at Turisan, a self-conscious smile curving his lips. "Rephanin has done me the favor before. He helped me and Jharan achieve our lifelong wish."

A small tingle ran through Turisan's flesh. He knew his father and Felisan had sought mindspeech together in their younger days—had entreated the spirits to be blessed with the gift. It had occurred to him that the mindspeech he shared with Eliani might be the spirits' answer to their fathers' plea.

"Rephanin helped you share mindspeech."

Felisan smiled as he returned to his chair. "Yes. At long last. It was a great gift."

"My father did not mention it to me."

"You were in the field, I believe." Felisan laced his fingers and tapped his thumbs against his chin. "I think Rephanin would help you and me to speak together, if you are willing. That way I could tell Eliani my concerns directly."

And share a moment's closeness, in case she does not return. Turisan did not voice the thought. Instead he shifted in his chair.

"Rephanin is weary. He was scarcely recovered from the battle when we came here, and the journey told on him."

Felisan nodded. "I could see that. A day's rest may help. I will not trouble him tonight. Tomorrow, perhaps. Before the feast?"

Turisan hesitated. His contacts with Rephanin had been few, mostly in the field where he was but one of hundreds who heard the magelord's voice. More intimate mindspeech would be uncomfortable—he still felt a shadow of mistrust, an echo of his upbringing—but for Felisan's sake he was willing. He nodded.

"Thank you. Thank you, my son."

Turisan smiled, touched by the endearment. "I will inform Eliani tonight. What more shall I say to her from you in the meantime?"

"In the meantime, give her my love."

Turisan sighed. He became aware that his right hand was rubbing at the polished wood of his chair's arm. He stopped and folded his hands in his lap.

"How many alben are in Ghlanhras?"

"At least a hundred. Probably more."

A look of disbelief crossed Felisan's face. "So few captured the city?"

"There were few ælven in residence. That is the other news Eliani sends." Turisan drew himself up, misliking the task of bringing bad tidings. "Ghlanhras is dying. Most of the ælven have left it. There were only a hundred or so before the alben attacked."

"The city is dying? Why?"

"The hunger has returned there."

Felisan looked aghast. "The alben's curse."

"So it is believed by many of Fireshore's people. Eliani tells me few of them will go as far as Ghlanhras any more. Most of the darkwood trade is now conducted out of Woodrun."

"Poor Othanin."

"His own lady was afflicted, and sought voluntary exile west of the mountains with a group of others who were likewise stricken. Othanin is deeply saddened. Eliani said he seemed hopeless."

Felisan closed his eyes. "Fireshore has ever been a source of woe to us. Would that we had never gone there."

"We would not have darkwood, in that case."

"Darkwood." Felisan shook his head. "It is not worth the cost."

Turisan tried to imagine a world without darkwood, the hardest, strongest wood known. So many things were made of it—bridges, buildings, furniture. The roof beams of this very hall were of darkwood, hauled along the trade road from Fireshore.

"Have you told Jharan of this?"

Turisan nodded, saddened by the concern writ on Felisan's face. Felisan, who was always merry, no longer merry now and it was Turisan's doing. How he disliked being the bearer of bad tidings.

"Eliani has sent word of the fall of Ghlanhras to the Steppes. They may be expected to respond with action."

Felisan let out a wry huff of laughter. "Battle on her doorstep? Oh, yes, Pashari will respond." He shifted forward in his chair, leaning his elbows on his knees and dropping his head into his hands. "Another war."

Turisan nodded though he knew Felisan could not see it. "I fear so."

"All this is happening too swiftly."

Turisan made no answer. They sat in silence for a while. Turisan watched the dancing flames and listened to the fire's gentle murmur.

Felisan sighed, his face wrought with trouble. "Ehranan marches north."

"Rephanin and I are to join him there and ride to Fireshore."

Felisan had been staring at the fire as he listened, but he glanced sharply up at this. "You are going to Fireshore?"

"To join Eliani."

"But how will we know..."

"What is happening in Fireshore? Rephanin has found a distance partner, Thorian, a guardian. He will keep my father informed of events in the north."

"Another mindspeaker!"

"Yes."

"Then you will bring Eliani home?"

"I mean to, yes."

"Well, that is good news at least! Come, I will show you to her chamber."

They rose and left the study, going down the small hallway to a door at its end. Felisan took a taper from a small shelf and lit it from the nearest sconce.

"If you find this room uncomfortable take one of the others. Any on this side of the hall. A guest house has been provided for your companions." Felisan pushed open the door, smiled slightly, and stepped into the chamber, beckoning Turisan to follow.

The candle's light glinted off metal and glass, a shelf filled with keepsakes. Felisan moved to a low table beside a bedstead draped in violet, its headboard carved with stag's heads. He lit an oil lamp, then set the taper into a candlestick beside the lamp. Light from both flames danced on a cruet of blue glass and a small matching cup beside it on the table.

Turisan looked around at the chamber, much smaller and simpler than his own at Hallowhall. He moved to the shelf and stood gazing at the clutter of trinkets, small boxes, carvings and curiosities, wondering what their stories might be, and which of them Eliani treasured most. They reminded him of how little he knew about her.

He wanted to ask what each was, to entreat her to share the memories that went along with them. They were part of her, and he wanted to know them, as if that would sharpen her image in his heart.

Felisan stepped to a washstand and glanced into the pitcher that stood upon it, then gestured to a tasseled bell pull of blue and violet broidered with golden flowers. "If anything is wanting for your comfort, ring and Curunan will attend you."

"Thank you." Turisan smiled as he offered his arm.

Felisan clasped it with both of his own, smiled briefly, and let go. "I am glad you are come. Thank you, Turisan, for the tidings you bring."

"I only wish they were better."

"Some are joyous. Eliani is alive and well."

Sunlight invaded the room where Rephanin lay, and he flinched. A door closed quietly and the light was banished. He lay still, breathing deeply, remembering the night. He was alone; Heléri had gone some time since, he thought. Why then the door opening now?

Low voices in the next room served as answer. A visitor. Rephanin heard his name spoken, the voice familiar. An echo of the weariness he had felt remained, clouding memory. He sat up, listening, striving to identify the voice.

"—if he is not too tired."

Felisan. The governor of Alpinon, seeking some favor. Had Jharan been in Highstone he could have guessed what it might be.

"We can return later if he is still resting." A second voice; Turisan's.

Rephanin stood up, groped among the bedclothes for his robe, and pulled it over his head. Heléri was making gentle excuses, but he was much better than he had been, and if a mindspeaker sought his aid he felt obliged to answer.

He came out of the bedchamber into a larger room that ran the width of the stone hall. Tapestries covered the windows. Turisan and Felisan stood with Heléri near the door, and looked up as he entered.

"Good morrow, Turisan. Felisan. How may I serve you?"

"Forgive us for disturbing your rest." Turisan made a slight bow. "I hope you are feeling better."

"Much better, thank you." Rephanin felt himself smiling, something he had not done much of late.

Felisan stepped toward him. "I have a boon to ask of you, Rephanin. My daughter is in Fireshore, facing many dangers. I would speak with her, if you will aid us."

He glanced at Turisan, and Rephanin understood what he was asking. He wanted Rephanin to use his unique gift, that of speaking with anyone in his presence, to join them in thought. Turisan could then speak to Eliani, and all four of them would be in communication. It was a new use for Rephanin's gift, and that alone made it intriguing.

Turisan met Rephanin's gaze and nodded. He had consented to this.

Rephanin turned to Felisan. "Of course. Does Heléri join us?"

"Yes, if she will. Eliani will be glad to hear her eldermother's voice. You have no objection, Turisan?"

"None."

Heléri indicated a half-circle of chairs before the hearth, where a bed of coals glowed softly. "Shall we sit?"

She brought out pottery cups filled with fragrant, honey-sweetened tea. Rephanin thanked her with a smile as she handed one to him.

A sip brought a swallow fragrant of summer flowers and toasted nuts. He wrapped his fingers around the cup to warm them and leaned back in his chair, settling himself comfortably so that the flesh would not be a distraction. Another swallow, one deep breath to center himself, then he set the cup aside and looked at Turisan.

"Are you ready?"

Turisan nodded. Rephanin closed his eyes, which was not necessary but somehow felt appropriate in this situation, as if it made concession to modesty.

Welcome, then.

In touching the folk in his presence with mindspeech, he became aware of them all, of the differing tones of their khi. Turisan's strength he had felt before, and the deep sincerity and kindness beneath Felisan's outer jollity. Heléri was a pool of calm for which he was glad. A moment later he sensed a new presence: Eliani.

He had never spoken in thought with Felisan's daughter. Like her father, she was a surprise. The gruff face she presented to the world hid a tender heart, one that he instantly knew was both frightened and determined.

He heard Felisan draw a breath, as if to speak aloud. *Eliani?*
Father.

Rephanin withdrew his attention as much as he was able, but the feelings that flowed among these kindred could not be ignored. They communicated faster than words ever could, and with much greater power.

He turned his attention to Heléri, who bade him a small, wordless welcome. This seemed to draw Eliani's notice, for she spoke again.

Eldermother. I am glad you are here.

Heléri opened all the warmth of her heart, and it was as the sun rising. Eliani seemed to tremble in response, as if her fear threatened to break her will.

Something is wrong, eldermother. With Luruthin.

76 ~ Pati Nagle

Luruthin. The name brought his face into Rephanin's mind, a laughing, Stonereach face. He was Eliani's cousin, and also, Rephanin sensed, a former lover.

He was captured because of me. We were able to free him and Othanin, but now ... he is suffering.

Is he wounded? Heléri's question was gentle, full of compassion.

Not physically. He seems weak, and ... afraid.

Give him time.

Rephanin was at a loss to contribute. Perhaps it had been so long since he had felt the draw of kinship that he had forgotten its power. His mother and father had long since crossed into spirit, and he had no other close relatives living. There were those for whom he cared deeply—Heléri, Thorian, and a few others—but none with whom he shared the bond of blood.

Made uncomfortable by the topic, he sought to change it. *Do you return to Southfæld, Lady Eliani?*

Yes, soon. We are ... visiting Othanin's lady, Kivhani. She is the leader of the Lost.

Eliani went on to describe a group of exiles from Clan Sunriding. Rephanin listened in amazement. The Bitter Wars had taught him—had taught all ælvenkind—to hate those who violated the creed by drinking the blood of kobalen. Now Eliani was asking them to sympathize with some who did just that.

They are not like the alben at all. They do all they can to keep the creed, and live in hardship because of their affliction. Father, the Ælven Council should know of them.

Yes, once this war is concluded.

But they could help in the war! And Father—if Fireshore is unhealthy for ælvenkind, perhaps the Lost could return to Ghlanhras. They might harvest darkwood without danger, restore the city.

Perhaps, but that is a consideration for the future. We must reclaim Ghlanhras before we can consider its fate.

I believe the Lost could assist us in that. At the very least, they can help defend Woodrun.

Woodrun?

The alben will go there next.

No one spoke for a moment. Rephanin sensed dismay from both Turisan and Felisan.

Spirits! She is right! Turisan—

I will ride at once to consult Ehranan.

Bring him back with you.

He may want to start for Fireshore immediately.

He can give orders to march, but bring him; we must confer. Rephanin, I understand you have a partner in Glenhallow?

Yes.

Will you ask him to inform Lord Jharan that we wish to meet with him—through your generosity, if you are willing?

Rephanin blinked at this sudden urgency. *Of course, though I may not be able to contact him. Usually he initiates our speech.*

Will you try, when Turisan and Ehranan return? I have the Midwinter ceremony at dusk, and then the feast.

Father?

Yes, Eliani?

I think you should summon the Ælven Council to Highstone.

A pause ensued. They met only a season ago.

Turisan, who had remained silent, now spoke. *I agree with Eliani. Another meeting of the Council is in order. The governors should hear from Eliani herself what she witnessed in Fireshore.*

Felisan's khi was heavy. *Very well. Eliani, if you can alert the Steppes, then the farthest a messenger will have to ride is to Eastfæld. A few days for them to prepare a delegation, then to journey here ... let us say we shall convene on the first of Spring.*

I will send a rider, and inform Othanin and Kivhani of the summons to Council.

Ripples of emotion—surprise, dismay, doubt—went through the group's khi at this announcement. Eliani continued.

We wanted *Othanin at the Council. That is why I came to Fireshore!*

Yes, but....

Kivhani is his partner. She governed Fireshore with him. She should be welcome.

Felisan sighed. *As far as I am concerned she is welcome. Others might not agree.*

She may have to take that risk. Thank you, Father. And thank you, Rephanin, for assisting us.

I am honored to serve you, my lady.

Rephanin withdrew his attention as Eliani and her father made their farewells. A moment later, sensing movement in the room, he opened his eyes.

Turisan was standing, preparing to leave. Felisan rose to accompany him.

"Thank you, Rephanin."

Turisan glanced at Rephanin. "Best make ready to depart."

Rephanin felt a rise of indignation made worse by his awareness that Turisan was right. If Ehranan ordered the army northward at once, he must go with them. He had agreed to continue, though the thought of another battle made him quail.

Felisan and Turisan went out. Left alone with Heléri, Rephanin allowed himself a small sigh. "What do you know of Woodrun, Heléri?"

"Very little. I gather darkwood is harvested there."

Rephanin sat silent, slowly realizing that this town he knew nothing of was about to end his comfort. He leaned forward toward the fire, seeking to banish the chill in his heart. More war.

"What is it?" Heléri laid cool fingertips on his wrist.

"Nothing. Thinking of what lies ahead."

Her fingers closed around his, offering silent comfort. He accepted it, and brushed his thoughts briefly against hers. Warmth and steadiness flowed from her, grounding him, stilling his fears.

For the present.

Riding hard, Turisan reached the army early in the afternoon. They had stopped to rest when they reached the Asurindel, and showed signs of pitching a camp.

Without ceremony, Turisan sought out Ehranan and requested a private word with him. They walked northward along the shore, and when they were out of the army's hearing Turisan quietly told the commander of the conversation with Eliani and Felisan.

Ehranan stopped short when he mentioned Woodrun. "Spirits!"

"Yes."

"We must march at once! Can Felisan provide us with supplies?"

"I am sure he will do all he can. You may ask him yourself. He sent me to bring you to Highstone."

"No, I cannot take the time! We must make all haste..."

Turisan gave him a moment to realize that the army was unlikely to reach Woodrun before the alben. The mounted force could arrive there in thirty days, possibly less. A fast rider from Ghlanhras—no, not a rider; horses feared the alben—but nonetheless a runner from Ghlanhras would be there in ten. A force of warriors might take longer, but not much longer, if they were ready.

"Felisan asks your presence in Highstone. Rephanin can assist us to speak with Jharan. He wants us all to confer before the army marches."

Ehranan nodded. "Very well, let me get my horse."

❈ Fireshore ❈

Tucked beneath a darkwood bough in the small clearing where the party had stopped to rest, Eliani fretted. Her chance mention of Woodrun, and her father and Turisan's reaction to it, had set her thinking.

Of course the alben would seek to control Woodrun. That would secure their hold upon most of Fireshore's darkwood cutting areas, saving only a few smaller places like Bitterfield.

Woodrun must be defended. She should go there herself, not merely send a message, but it must be after her visit with Kivhani was concluded. She would not endanger the tentative friendship they had formed by leaving abruptly. And in any case, she dared not return to the road until she was farther from Ghlanhras.

She gnawed her thumb. How many days to travel to Woodrun? They had come south for two nights, but their progress was slow. It would be at least four days, she thought, and that was probably too hopeful.

The bloom of warmth in her brow was never more welcome. *I am here.*

Ehranan and I are with Rephanin. Your father is on his way to join us.

And Thorian?

Rephanin is seeking to contact him. It is not easy for him.

While they waited, Eliani shared her reflections with Turisan. He agreed that she should not leave Kivhani at present. She suspected he did not wish her to go to Woodrun, but left that discussion for later. He would see that it was important for her to go there, she trusted. She would have to ask Othanin to tell her more about the town.

Felisan is here. Rephanin has reached Thorian.

Very well.

Without further ado, she sensed Rephanin's presence, followed by all the others, a confusion of khi that made her squeeze her eyes shut. Bad enough that she was touching Rephanin in thought, though that was not as distressing as she had expected. The anger he had shown when they first met was gone, burned away by the war, perhaps.

81

Thorian's khi was new to her; she shyly greeted him, then her father took charge of the conference and summarized their concerns for Jharan. After a slight pause, Thorian replied that Jharan understood and agreed. He would come to the Council, and meanwhile he would send another two hundred of the Southfæld Guard north.

Thank you, my friend. Ehranan will no doubt find use for them.

They will be of use. Ehranan's tone was grim. *For now, I will send the mounted forces ahead to Woodrun. There are some three or four hundreds, mostly from Eastfæld and the Steppes. Turisan will command them.*

Eliani sensed her partner's surprise. A moment later Thorian responded.

Your pardon, Lord Ehranan, but Governor Jharan asks if another might as easily command.

No, it must be Turisan. Not only will he inspire the guardians, but he will be able to communicate to us through Eliani, once she returns south. Lady Eliani, if you would consent to join the main army...?

She is to attend the Council in Highstone.

Turisan's response made her smile. Ehranan, in turn, became haughty.

I hope by the time the Council convenes, she will indeed be there. I have need of her first, however. She can inform me of Turisan's progress, and Rephanin can keep Governor Jharan likewise informed.

Eliani swallowed. *It will take me some while to reach the army.*

She did not voice the thought that all might be over at Woodrun well before she could do so. Instead she listened as hasty arrangements were made for the army to march. Riders would be sent ahead immediately to towns along the trade road, warning them of the army's approach and its needs. Her heart sank as she realized the hardships they would suffer, marching as swiftly as they could.

Her father's khi recalled her attention. *I must go—it is nearly time for the Midwinter ceremony.*

Midwinter! She had forgotten!

She made her farewells, including a tender one to Turisan, who promised to contact her later in the evening. As Rephanin released them, she opened her eyes and gazed up at the forest canopy overhead.

Yes, the daylight was waning. She stood, and went around to each of the party, rousing them.

"It is Midwinter. We should honor the ældar." She turned to Othanin. "Will you lead the ceremony, my lord governor?"

He nodded, then held out a hand to Kivhani. "If my lady will assist."

She hesitated, then gave a curt nod. Othanin led her to the center of the clearing, and Eliani and the others gathered around them.

Othanin moved to the east, raised his arms and looked skyward. "Ældar guardians, we greet and honor you on this longest night of all the year. From now until Midsummer, the days will lengthen. We welcome the return of light and all its blessings."

Together he and Kivhani paced the boundary of the circle, pausing to honor the guardians of each direction. Eliani followed with her party. In their faces she saw peace along with solemnity, and was glad that she had asked for this ceremony.

Returning to the center of the circle, Othanin raised his hands again.

"May the blessings of the coming light be with us all in this dark time. Ældar guardians, please watch over us and help us find our best path."

All were still. Eliani glanced down at the ground, thinking of her father conducting his own ceremony in the public circle at Highstone.

At home, and in every ælven town, the Midwinter ceremony would be followed by dancing and feasting. Her little company had no means for such—indeed, their provisions were running low—and she could not summon a merry mood.

Kivhani surprised her by beginning to sing. The song was simple, one that every child learned. It praised the spirits and thanked them for watching over those in the realm of flesh. Kivhani's voice was low and resonant, and Eliani found herself breathing more deeply, feeling uplifted, as she sang along in thought.

The song's end signaled the end of solemnity. The company began to talk, quietly but with enthusiasm.

Eliani went to Kivhani. "Thank you! That was beautiful, and perfect."

Kivhani smiled. "You are kind."

"Many a year she sang that in Ghlanhras's circle." Othanin's voice was filled with sadness.

Eliani drew a breath. "My lord and lady governors, I have a message for you from my father."

Othanin and Kivhani exchanged a glance. Kivhani's eyes hardened, and with a nod of her head she indicated they should seek privacy. They walked a short distance into the woods, then Kivhani turned.

"Your message came through mindspeech."

"Yes, from my lord, Turisan. He has just left Highstone."

"Highstone. That is many leagues away."

Too many, Eliani thought. She pushed aside her desire to see Turisan and concentrated on her message, seeking the right tone of formality in which to phrase it. Diplomacy was not among her strengths. She cleared her throat.

"Governor Othanin, Governor Kivhani, my father Governor Felisan has summoned the Ælven Council to meet at Highstone on the first day of spring. He bids you both attend if you are willing."

"Both of us?" Othanin sounded surprised.

"As governors of Fireshore."

"I am not a governor."

Othanin glanced at his lady. "You were."

Eliani looked from one to the other of them, watching the doubt in their faces. Governors of Fireshore, though they stood in the midst of a forest, fleeing their own seat of government. Othanin might accept her father's invitation with little fear, though he would face uncomfortable questions about the loss of Ghlanhras.

Kivhani turned to Eliani. "I should travel to Highstone, to meet with a Council who may regard me as no different than the alben?"

"Felisan will give you the protection of his hospitality."

Othanin coughed. "If the Council's mood turns hostile, even Felisan may face reprisal."

Kivhani nodded, then fixed Eliani with her dark gaze. "What think you? How will I be received if I go to the Council?"

Eliani thought back to Jharan's Council in Glenhallow, remembering those who attended and which of them had been most hostile and afraid of the alben. She feared Kivhani would have a difficult task to convince them that her people were not the same as alben.

"Governor Pashari will oppose your acceptance, I am almost certain."

Kivhani nodded. "I expect that. Pashari never was fond of me. Will others support her?"

"Some may. That is all the more reason for you to attend. You can argue for your own people more strongly than any of us could, even I, and I most certainly will speak for you. But let them see you...." She hesitated, fearing she had offended, but Kivhani gave no sign of it. "Let them meet you, hear your petition from your own lips. That would be the best way to make them consider you seriously. The courage you show merely in coming to Council will not fail to make an impression."

Kivhani pressed her lips together. "And if I am rejected?"

"Then you would be formally exiled, I suppose. Little loss." Eliani shrugged, glancing around at the forest. This was already Kivhani's way of life.

"Except that we would lose our chance to be accepted as ælven."

"We are approaching war. The longer you wait, the higher feelings of bitterness against the alben will rise, and the less rational folk will be."

Othanin, who had hitherto been silent, spoke up. "What if the Lost could assist in this war?"

Eliani looked at him, pleased that he had made the suggestion. His face, though drawn with sadness and care, held more determination than it had when they had supped together in Darkwood Hall. Truly, Kivhani was his strength. Despite his sufferings, he seemed more like a governor now than when Eliani had first met him.

Kivhani nodded. "We cannot field great numbers, but we know Fireshore well. We could provide guides, and observe the alben's movements."

"You would fight the alben?"

Kivhani bent a stern gaze on Eliani. "With our last breath. The alben are opposed to all that we value."

Eliani smiled. "Then I think the Council will have no choice but to welcome your aid. In fact, you may wish to petition them for recognition of the Lost as a new clan."

Kivhani's eyes widened. "An ælven clan?"

"It would assure you a rightful place among the ælven."

Kivhani blinked, then looked at Othanin. "We shall have to consider this."

"We shall have to consider many things." Othanin turned to Eliani. "I am honored by Governor Felisan's invitation, and of course I will attend the Council, but first I must go to Woodrun."

Eliani's heart sank. "You would be in danger there."

"Yes, but my people are there. Those who escaped Ghlanhras should be there. It is my task to lead them, if they will still permit me the honor."

She was tempted to go with him, and almost offered to. Kivhani spoke before she could do so.

"Lord Felisan honors us." Kivhani's voice was low. "I hope he will pardon me for not answering at once. I think I should discuss this with my people. It is a decision that will affect them all."

"I cannot get a message to him now in any case. When you have decided, I will pass your response to Turisan and he will send it to Highstone at the first opportunity."

They returned to the others and made ready to start forward again. The ceremony seemed to have refreshed them all; even Luruthin seemed reflective rather than distressed. Glad of this, Eliani walked beside him in silence, keeping her doubts and turmoil to herself.

❀ The Trade Road ❀

Returning to the army's camp with Turisan and Ehranan, Rephanin was struck by the changes there. A bustle of activity was taking place around the supply wagons. Rephanin's tent stood alone; no others had been pitched.

Turisan rode away to seek out the mounted companies. Ehranan turned in his saddle to meet Rephanin's gaze.

"We will press harder now. It will likely make you uncomfortable, for which I apologize."

Rephanin swallowed and nodded his understanding.

Ehranan's eyes showed concern. "Rest well. If you have all you need, I will go."

"Go."

Rephanin watched the commander ride away. A guardian came forward to take his horse; he dismounted and yielded it. Really he should learn to care for the animal himself, little though he cared for horses. How useless he was!

He went into his tent, though he doubted he would rest much with all the army busy. To fight the despair he felt rising, he sought activity.

If any of you can hear me, answer now.

Folly, perhaps. He had tried before with much of this army, though new forces had joined them at Midrange. He had little hope of finding another Thorian, but for want of anything better to do, he persisted.

He kept his voice small, a whisper. Over and over he repeated the call. It was soothing in a way, like a cradle song. He was not musical, but he began to play with the rhythm of the words.

Answer now, answer now. If you can hear me, answer now.

What are you doing?

The voice was strong, female, unfamiliar. Rephanin's eyes flew open and he looked around himself. Tent walls, glowing with the fading sunset. He rose and went outside.

Where are you?

With my company. Why do you torment us with this nonsense, magelord?

Do they hear me as well?

A pause followed. Rephanin peered at every face nearby, but the guardians were all occupied, none watching him.

What is your name, please?

He waited, terrified she would not answer. At last she did, sounding less certain.

Filari.

Rephanin drew a deep breath. *Filari, your hearing me among this … chaos, is significant. You may have aptitude for mindspeech. Will you join me?*

I must stay with my company. We are preparing to ride.

You are riding? Then you are with Turisan. Go to him, please, and tell him I have asked for your presence.

He will think me mad!

No, I promise you he will not. Tell him that Heléri is wearing a violet gown today.

What?!

Please, Filari, do this and all will be well.

He swept his gaze across the field, searching for Ehranan, but did not see him. Excitement was building in his gut. Had he truly found another mindspeaker? With all that was happening he was not certain of its significance, except that more mindspeakers meant more points of contact. It could not but be a blessing.

Unable to keep still, he ran. Seeking Ehranan, he came instead upon the mounted force gathered on the river bank west of the main camp.

Turisan would be here. Rephanin hurried along the ranks.

Turisan says I may join you.

Rephanin flinched at the sudden contact. Her voice in thought was strong, laced with doubt and confusion. He would have to teach her the signals he used with Thorian.

Excellent. Please give him my thanks. I am near the mounted force now. Do you see a large oak by the river?

Yes.

Let us meet there.

A pause. *Very well.*

Rephanin walked to the tree. In a moment he saw two riders approaching, Turisan and a Greenglen female. He recognized her from Turisan's escort; he had come to think of her as the one who always scowled.

They dismounted, and Turisan gave him a nod. "Lord Rephanin, this is Filari. I understand she heard your call?"

"Yes." Rephanin bowed to her. "I believe she is a mindspeaker."

Filari's response to this was to frown more deeply.

"Then you wish her to remain with you? The rest of us are riding north shortly."

"If you do not mind, yes. We should get acquainted, explore her gift."

Turisan gave Rephanin an intent look and lifted his chin slightly, which Rephanin guessed was a request for private speech. He took a moment to shield his thought from any outsider, especially Filari.

Yes?

Look after her. She has...had difficulty in the guard.

A vague memory of some scandal in Glenhallow drifted through Rephanin's mind. He would have to get the particulars, but not now.

I will.

And Rephanin—you must leave her alone.

What?

Make no advances. She has been hurt.

Rephanin's heart clenched. That Turisan felt it needful to warn him...but he had only himself, and his past actions, to blame for that.

I will be careful.

Turisan turned to Filari. "I congratulate you. Henceforward, if your mindspeech proves true, you will be honored among all ælven."

Filari blushed crimson and stared at the ground. Her lips moved but formed no words.

"You will travel with the main force. You may keep your mount. Remain with Rephanin, and learn from him."

She looked up at Turisan then, her face filled with unhappiness. No pride in her accomplishment, no gratitude that she was to be spared a grueling ride.

Turisan offered his arm. Filari hesitated before clasping it briefly, causing Rephanin to wonder just how badly she had been hurt. She watched Turisan ride back to the mounted force with hopeless eyes.

"Come, we should find Ehranan. He will be delighted at this news."

She gave him a glance that was almost resentful, then walked beside him toward the main army, leading her horse.

What would come of this? The joy of discovery had changed to doubt, for his new mindspeech partner was, incredibly to him, reluctant.

Turisan rode at the head of his new command. They had greeted him as their commander, though he suspected this brought little joy to them, especially the Steppegards. There were two hundred of these, another hundred Eastfæld riders, and something less than a hundred from Southfæld and Alpinon.

They rode along the Asurindel, eastward toward the plains. Freed from canyon confines, the river sprawled lazily here. Cold stars flickered overhead, and the horses' breath came out as fog. Judging it time to rest them, Turisan raised his hand and called a halt.

The captains led their companies to the water in good order. Turisan led his own horse to drink, then took out a map that Felisan had given him, reading it by starlight. He would strike north, he decided, away from the river toward Greenfield, a small village situated on the river Clerendil where the trade road to Hollirued met the trade road running north toward the Steppe Wilds.

Putting away the map, he sighed. He had a few moments now, and might find no better opportunity this night. He sent the query signal to Eliani.

Yes, love? We are walking.

And we are riding. We shall reach Greenfield tonight.

Fill all your water skins there. You will leave the river afterward, and the next few streams to the north are small in winter.

Thank you.

I told Othanin and Kivhani about the Council. Othanin says he will come. Kivhani has not decided. She wants to consult her people, so we are hastening to their camp.

I wish I were with you.

So do I.

Turisan resisted the urge to elaborate on this theme. It would serve neither of them, and what ease it might give his heart would be fleeting.

Rephanin has found another mindspeaker.

A mindspeaker? Wonderful!

Well, perhaps. We shall see.

Why do you doubt?

It is Filari, one of my escort. She is...troubled.

He had never explained Filari's difficulty to Eliani, not wishing to remind her of Kelevon. He wondered now if he should do so, but thought it would help nothing and possibly distress Eliani.

I hope she finds her path, then.

As do I.

A silence followed. Turisan could still feel Eliani's khi. He closed his eyes, treasuring the contact. It was not enough, but it was better than nothing.

Happy Midwinter, Turisan.

Midwinter. They had hoped to be reunited by now. Spirits knew when it would be, but Turisan was determined to find Eliani as their paths crossed. He ached to hold her again, if only for a little while.

Happy Midwinter, my love.

❈ Ghlanhras ❈

Shalár fretted as she paced the outer chamber of her suite. She wanted to act, to move. She wanted Woodrun, but she had too few hunters to take it and still hold Ghlanhras.

Two nights had passed since she had reclaimed Ghlanhras. Yaras could not possibly have reached Nightsand yet, not even if he ran without rest; it would be many days before she could expect more of her folk to arrive. She was tempted to send a messenger after Yaras to urge his haste, but that would be folly. She needed every hunter here, for she expected the ælven to retaliate.

If she could take Woodrun before they came, she would be at an advantage. Perhaps...

No. The only way she could take Woodrun before her people came from Nightsand was to abandon Ghlanhras, and that she dared not do.

"Bright Lady?"

Naral stood in the doorway, a large rolled parchment in his hands. She summoned him with a gesture.

"These are the plans for a covered passage."

He unrolled them on her work table, and she examined them. "Have we enough darkwood?"

"Plenty, Bright Lady. The wood yard is well-stocked."

"How quickly can this be built?"

"If we may use ælven laborers, it will speed the work."

"Yes, yes. Talk to Banath. How soon?"

"Forty days, Bright Lady."

Shalár scowled. "You must do better than that."

"I will strive to do better, but until the work is underway—"

"Have it done in twenty days."

Even as she said it, the back of her neck prickled. Did the ælven have enough people in Woodrun to mount an attack on Ghlanhras? If so, twenty days was too long. If not...the next closest ælven cities, discounting Bitterfield which was too small to be a threat, were in the Steppes. She might be safe from them yet a while.

She handed the plans back to Naral, daring him with her gaze to protest. He bowed instead, and went away. Vaguely disappointed, she went out to the audience chamber, where her steward stood talking with two of her hunters. They fell silent at her approach.

"I need information. Vamar, find me two good scouts, fast runners."

The hunter bowed and turned to go. In the distance, the sound of repairs to Darkwood Hall disturbed the night. Shalár had ordered all the high window screens to be covered with boards of darkwood, so that the ælven could not again breach them and let daylight into the hall.

She was still restless. She glanced at her steward.

"When the scouts arrive, tell them I want them to make all speed to Woodrun. I need to know how many ælven are there and what weapons they have. Also, they must learn whether the two who escaped are there."

"Yes, Bright Lady."

"I will be inspecting the wall." She strode from the audience chamber and out through the hall to the public circle.

Stars and a cold moon peered down at her. The moon made her frown; even its weaker light stung a little against her cheek. She looked away and started toward the city gates, hoping to distract herself with a review of her defenses.

Luruthin had lost track of how many nights the party had spent walking through the forest. Two? Three? Perhaps more. A handful of Kivhani's people had joined them—white-haired and black-eyed; he disliked looking at them—so for their comfort the party traveled mostly by night. They wore heavy leather hoods and clothing, but during the day they still preferred to hide from the sun.

Luruthin had settled into a state of numbness, which at least was not painful. Whenever they paused to rest he lay on the ground with his head spinning from weariness.

He knew that Eliani worried. He could offer her no reassurance, and did not have the strength to try. Just walking, just moving when it was required of him, took all the strength he had, and it was getting more difficult.

The little food they found, nuts and berries and a few edible leaves and roots, was scarcely enough to keep him going. Eliani was giving most of what she gathered to him.

The ground rose steadily, which slowed their progress even more. They were climbing into the Ebons. The forest had changed enough that he noticed the difference despite his focused weariness.

Darkwoods were fewer and smaller, interspersed with more oaks, and the undergrowth was less tangled. Vines had given way to brush and even small clearings now and then. The understory was much more open, a relief after the confined feeling of the darkwood forest. The air, too, was cooler and less damp.

Luruthin knew the party was setting their pace to what he and Othanin could manage, and so in grim determination he walked on, placing one foot before the other, thinking of little else. When a Greenglen female who was walking ahead of him suddenly stopped, he had to keep himself from stumbling into her.

He leaned against the nearest tree, breathing hard. The khi of the party sharpened and they all fell silent in a way that reminded him of his seasons patrolling with Alpinon's Guard. A quarry had been scented, and all attention turned to its pursuit.

What quarry here? A deer, perhaps? The thought made his empty stomach clench.

He glanced at Eliani, behind him. She was standing still and listening, a slightly puzzled look on her face. After a moment she came over to join Luruthin. He managed to smile for her, assuring her that he was all right.

The Lost hunter who had been at the rear of the party now hastened forward, a sharp look in her eye. Eliani's escort gathered around Luruthin, exchanging curious glances. Vanorin came back down the trail to join them, accompanied by Othanin, who drew them all near with a gesture.

"Kobalen." His voice was a scarcely audible whisper. "My lady and her friends need to hunt. We will wait a while here."

The party exchanged glances again, this time uncomfortably, as they began to look around them for places to rest. Luruthin was surprised he had not sensed the kobalen.

The reminder of the Lost's need for blood was disquieting. The question had not arisen before, but Luruthin now had a fleeting thought that by simply waiting here, by not opposing this hunt, they were complicit.

Felahran sat beneath a scrubby oak. "Would that *we* had something to hunt."

Luruthin sat as well and leaned his back against his tree. Looking up through the forest canopy, he saw a star glinting high above, the first he had seen since leaving Ghlanhras. It gave him great comfort.

Eliani crouched beside him and held up her hands, face questioning, offering healing. He shook his head, smiling his thanks.

She had not given healing to Vanorin, despite his having been wounded at Ghlanhras. Luruthin had suggested it to her early in the journey, but she had shaken her head. Perhaps she had offered, and Vanorin had refused.

Luruthin hugged himself, knowing he must overcome his discomfort. If he was not able to resolve these feelings, he would not be able to tell the others what had happened. How could he tell Jhinani? How could he even face her? More than any other, she would be hurt by it.

He had broken his cup bond to her. However unwilling, he had still broken it, with the worst possible result.

His two children would be born within a season.

Grimacing, he rejected the thought. He would not claim Shalár's daughter. That child was lost to him, and he to her. He must go on as if she did not exist.

A sound distracted him. Footfalls, faint but certain. The Lost were returning.

Around him the other guardians stirred and murmured. Luruthin kept his eyes closed, wishing to avoid conversation. He sensed the khi of the Lost joining the party, sharper and more vital than it had been before. It had an underlying tang to it, which after a moment he identified as kobalen.

He heard Eliani's voice, talking with Othanin's lady. A moment later Eliani summoned her party back to the trail.

They walked, and Luruthin's steps dragged though he tried to lift his feet. He made more noise moving along the trail than all the rest of them together.

The Greenglen ahead of him disappeared into the woods, yet Luruthin could move no faster. Eliani was behind him, not pressing him, but by her concern urging him on. To please her he continued, though he wanted only to collapse beside the trail.

At last they reached a large glen, thickets of thorn twining high overhead, with pockets like small caves around its edges. The trail crossed it and ran on into the woods, but to Luruthin's relief the Lost dispersed when they reached the glen, most seeking places to rest although two stood talking with Kivhani.

He moved to the nearest side of the thicket and dropped to his knees, then stretched out on his back, his breath coming hoarse in his dry throat. Hands touched his; Eliani's hands, wrapping his fingers around a water flask. He lay holding it for a moment, then rolled onto one side and fumbled at the cap with numb fingers.

So weak. He really would not be able to continue much farther. It was not yet close to dawn, so the party must have stopped for him to rest. He felt badly for this, but just now he could not continue.

He drank a little water and leaned on an elbow, starting to regain his breath. Eliani sat nearby, gazing at him in mute concern. He sipped the water again, then capped the flask and let it slip from his fingers onto the leaf-strewn floor of the glen as he lay back. His eyes closed, stinging. Small twitches ran along the muscles of his legs.

He listened to the many and varied complaints of his flesh, trying to identify some part of him that did not ache. His ears rang with weariness. His mouth felt parched despite what he had just drunk.

"Luruthin." Eliani's voice was a whisper.

He opened his eyes and saw her sitting over him, her hands poised near his brow. She gazed at him, silently asking permission to touch him, to bring her healing gift to bear. He nodded.

Warmth filled his head as she laid her hands on either side of it. He inhaled as if to drink in the khi coming through her hands. A slow fire seemed to burn through his head and down into his chest. His eyes fell closed again.

Because he was too weary to control his thoughts, he became immersed in Eliani's presence. The khi that flowed into him was not hers, but it tasted of her, and he could not help the memories awakened by this.

They had served in Alpinon's Guard together for nearly two decades, until his assumption of a theyn's duties had kept him more at home. Even then he had ridden with the Guard from time to time, hunting or patrolling the mountains, a handful of guardians seeing no other company for as much as half a season at a time. Trading stories and singing songs beneath the stars. And lovemaking.

Memory shifted and he saw Shalár's face above him, her face ablaze with triumphant ecstasy. With a start he opened his eyes. Eliani took her hands away and looked at him, questioning.

He pushed himself up and sat rubbing his face with his hands, trying to rid himself of the memory. Eliani watched him with worried eyes.

"Was it too much?"

"No—it was nothing ... nothing to do with you."

He drew a shuddering breath. He did feel somewhat better, though dizzy. He looked around the glen and saw the others of Eliani's party scattered at its edges, resting. Only three of the Lost were present, Kivhani not among them. Othanin sat alone beneath a thorn.

"Where have they gone?"

"Hunting." Vanorin's voice came from nearby.

Luruthin turned his head to look at the captain, who was sitting a little way away. The Greenglen's face looked lean and strained.

"But they just hunted."

Vanorin nodded. "This time they hunt for us. There are deer and small game in this part of the forest, they say."

Eliani glanced at him. "We could have done our own hunting."

"They are stronger than we at the moment, and better armed."

Eliani made no answer. It was true that they had but two bows among them, the others having been lost in Ghlanhras. Luruthin was somewhat uncomfortable at the thought of the Lost hunting on his behalf. He could not hunt for himself, however, even had he had his bow, so he must accept their generosity.

A sound of footfalls made him look up. Three Lost were returning to the glen, their arms full of deadwood. They moved to the center of the space and began preparing to build a fire.

A fire to cook the meat. Luruthin had a mad, momentary wish that they would not bother. He was so hungry he could imagine eating raw game, though he knew it would likely make him unwell.

Eliani stood, her hand brushing near enough to Luruthin's shoulder to raise a tingle in his khi. He glanced up and saw her smile before she walked away, back down the trail. Vanorin's gaze followed her until she was out of sight. Luruthin wondered at it, then realized Vanorin was probably assuring himself she was not going into danger. Jharan had charged him with her safety, and he took the responsibility seriously.

"You should let her heal your arm."

Vanorin glanced at him in surprise. His hand, which lay over the place where he had been cut, moved away and then back.

"It feels good, you know."

A corner of Vanorin's mouth twitched, but did not reach a smile. "I am sure it does."

Flame leapt up, small and golden in the center of the glen, casting shadows of the party against the thorny walls. Luruthin stirred himself to get up and move closer to the fire, taking Eliani's flask with him. Vanorin followed.

Soon Luruthin could feel the warmth on his face. The smell of the campfire was a comfort. They had not dared to build a fire before this, nor needed one in the lower lands. Here it was chill, though. While they were walking it had not mattered, but now he felt it, and was grateful for the fire's growing warmth.

The others drew near. He heard Othanin's voice, speaking in low tones to one of the Lost, asking about water. Luruthin could not make out all the answer, but he heard mention of a spring.

Did they have hot springs in this part of the Ebons? Now that would be a luxury indeed. The thought of soaking his tired body in warm water was almost enough to banish his hunger.

He smelled the meat before the hunting party reached the glen. Raw meat, deer and hare, smelling of fresh blood. His stomach growled and he hugged himself, knowing he had still to wait some while.

Four Lost entered the glen including Kivhani, who had two brace of rabbits already spitted. Two others carried the carcass of a deer slung on a pole.

"I would not have thought the Lost would be so practiced at hunting game."

His comment had been addressed to Vanorin, but one of the Lost at the fire turned to look at him. He could not help flinching from her gaze.

"We hunt for leather and fur." She indicated her clothing. "Usually we give the meat to the kobalen."

Vanorin looked surprised. "They do not fear to take it?"

"At the very first they did, but it has been many years since they hesitated. We leave it hanging near their camps, always in the same manner. They never let it go to waste."

Luruthin nodded. "Generous of you to take such trouble for kobalen."

"It is part of our atonement."

He was silenced. She gazed gravely at him for a moment, then returned her attention to the fire, setting up forked sticks to hold the spits.

Eliani returned with a small cache of nuts she had gathered. She offered them to Luruthin, who took a share and then nodded toward Vanorin. Both hesitated, then Vanorin held out his hand and Eliani dropped a few nuts into it.

Luruthin chewed the nuts one at a time, slowly, making each last as long as he could while he stared at the roasting meat. Soon the first rabbit's fat began to drip on the flames and sizzle. When it was done Kivhani took it from the fire and offered it to him whole. He looked up at her in surprise, saw pity in her stern gaze. Sudden anger made him push the meat away.

"Let it be divided."

"There are four, and there is also the deer. This is not more than your share."

Unable to argue and ashamed of his reaction, Luruthin took the meat and mumbled thanks before biting into it. The hot juices ran into his mouth and he forgot all else as he tore the meat from the bone, not pausing until his jaws began to ache and he became aware that his stomach was full.

Eliani and Vanorin, the three other guardians and also Othanin were all eating rabbit. The deer was now roasting over the fire, the spit being turned by the Lost female who had spoken of giving meat to the kobalen.

Luruthin looked down at the rabbit in his hands. Still plenty of meat on it, but he could eat no more. He offered it to Vanorin, who was nearest him. Vanorin gave him a questioning look, then thanked him and took it.

"Better?"

Luruthin nodded. "Thank you for the food."

"You are welcome."

She offered him a flask of water. He drank two small sips and could take no more. He handed it back.

"You have been very patient with me. If we can rest a little more, I think I can go on."

"We will rest here for the day. It is safe enough. Our hunting parties often camp here."

Luruthin glanced upward. Yes, the canopy's gloom was lightening a little. Dawn was coming.

"Are we close to your main camp?"

"Another night's walking should bring us there."

"Oh."

The journey's end was near, then. This part of the journey, rather. It was only the beginning of the long, tiresome way back to Alpinon.

Trade Road

Filari rode beside Rephanin, silent and sullen, appearing unwearied. Rephanin, whose aching limbs protested his horse's every step, was at a loss for how to approach his new candidate.

Reluctance showed in every line of her face and bristled in her khi. When he spoke to Filari she answered, but with few words and no enthusiasm. She would not initiate a conversation in mindspeech, despite his encouragement. She was withdrawn, and Rephanin did not understand why.

He thought of Ehranan's delight when he had reported Filari's response, of the commander's eagerness to send her at once to Hollirued. He had laughed as he told Ehranan they must first establish the extent of Filari's gift. Now it seemed possible that he must disappoint Ehranan altogether, and that was hard to bear. The commander's approval meant a great deal to him. Perhaps too much.

Rephanin turned his head to look at Filari. The spark of attraction he often felt for one with whom he shared intimate mindspeech was absent. Perhaps it was because of her trouble in Glenhallow; Ehranan had reminded him that she had been entangled with the traitor Kelevon. Her manner had been withdrawn, he assumed on that account, long before this morning. Her behavior toward Rephanin was reserved and formal.

Well, formality would not do, not if they were to become distance speakers together. As she was reluctant, he must exert himself.

Filari, do you hail from Glenhallow, or some other part of Southfæld?

She glanced sidelong at him. *Glenhallow.*

He caught an echo of unhappiness in her thoughts. Keeping his own voice gentle and warm, he tried again.

Your family are there? You must miss them.

She grimaced. *My father gave me to understand he would be grateful if I did not return home.*

Rephanin was astonished. *He cast you out?*

Not in so many words, but he made it clear he thought the Guard was the best place for me.

The Guard, who viewed her with mistrust and barely tolerated her presence. Rephanin frowned, thinking her father must not have known how the Guard treated her. No father who loved his child could wish such a fate upon her.

I am glad we are going to Fireshore.

It was the first voluntary expression she had made. Rephanin glanced at her.

Why?

Folk there do not know me.

Rephanin closed his eyes briefly, sorry for her pain. For a moment he wished to escape it, to abandon the attempt to work with her, but she did not deserve that he should desert her as others had done. What she needed, he thought, was healing, but that was not his gift.

You and Lord Turisan are the only ones who have been kind to me.

He smiled slightly. *We know there is worth in you, Filari.*

She did not answer. When next he looked her way he saw tears upon her cheeks. Dismayed, his instinct was to embrace her and try to comfort her. That could not be done now, while they were riding. Instead he reached a gentle thought toward her, a wordless touch, a tentative intimacy.

She gasped, and in the same instant he felt as if she had struck him a blow, as if the door to her thoughts had slammed in his face. It cost him his balance and he clutched at his mount's neck.

Recovering, he sought to regain his composure. Never in his life had he encountered such a response; Filari's reaction had been violent, something he had not even imagined possible in mindspeech.

Filari coughed. "Your pardon. I was startled."

"My apologies."

"I w-will not do it again."

Rephanin nodded. Despite this assurance, he was hesitant to open himself once more. He rode in silence for a while, thinking of the healers who traveled with the army, wondering if he might approach one of them to work with Filari.

"Please, my lord..."

He met her gaze, saw anxiousness in her dark eyes. Though they were not in speech he could sense desperation in her khi. She feared he would turn away from her as well.

"When you are ready, speak to me."

Her eyes lit with terror for a moment. What had she to fear from him? What had she suffered to make her so afraid?

His gaze drifted to the reins in his hands. All at once he had a strong wish to be back in Glenhallow, in the quiet darkness of the magehall, in the comfort of his circle, who knew him and trusted him.

My lord?

Ah. She could indeed initiate speech with him. Her gift was true. Relief and a tingle of anticipation poured through him.

Yes?

D-do not be angry with me, please.

I am not angry.

I reacted without thinking ... I ...

Filari.

She ceased her restless stammering. He could hear her take in a long breath.

I will never knowingly hurt you. You have my pledge upon that.

T-thank you.

They rode on in silence for a few moments, though the contact remained open between them. Rephanin put nothing forward, leaving it to her to speak first. He sensed her struggling, flashes of emotion reaching him whisper-light, too swift to be understood. At last they faded and she grew somewhat calmer.

It felt like—when Kelevon touched me.

Her fear flared again, so sharply that Rephanin flinched and almost withdrew. Spirits, what had Kelevon done to the child?

I will not hurt you.

I know. I know.

She let out a shuddering sigh, and seemed to be gathering herself. Rephanin remained watchful, as nervous of her as of a horse that might suddenly kick.

Lord Turisan said this would be a way for me to atone, to perform a service that would ... I do not know what he meant by it.

Rephanin paused to choose his words carefully. He had not yet raised the subject of distance speech. He sought now to tell her his hopes in a way that would cause her no alarm.

You said you were glad to be going to Fireshore.

Yes.

What would you think of traveling to Hollirued instead?

Hollirued?

On your own, with none of the Guard to look down upon you.

She seemed to muse on this. *As a child I wished to go to Hollirued. My father journeyed there once, long ago. He said it was the most magnificent city in ælvendom, that it cast Glenhallow into shade.*

If you and I can speak at distance, Lord Ehranan will ask you to travel to Hollirued, to be our voice before the governor of Eastfæld.

She was silent for so long he feared he had frightened her again. Turning his head to look at her, he saw her eyes alight with a fire he had not seen there before.

When? When may I go?

❀ Ebon Mountains ❀

Eliani held her arms across her chest as she walked behind Luruthin on the narrow game track through the woods. Exercise was not enough to keep her warm here. They were high in the Ebons, near the crest of the range. Oaks had given way entirely to tall pines and firs and occasional small stands of bare, white-trunked firespear. The air was thin and sharp with the smell of evergreens. These were comforts, much like the woodlands of her home.

They were far from Ghlanhras now, having crossed the faded track that led to the pass of Westgard. Eliani felt safer here in the mountain heights. Luruthin, before her on the path, walked slowly and steadily, weary but willing and strong enough after rest and food to keep up with the Lost who led the way.

As they topped a rise, the path they were following opened onto a flat, rocky ledge and the party paused there, gathering to look down the east slopes of the Ebons. Shadows traced the tops of the evergreens, and cold stars glinted overhead. Far below, a small scatter of warm, glimmering lights could be seen.

"Bitterfield." Kivhani stepped up beside Eliani. "They have begun to keep a night watch."

Eliani nodded. When her party had stopped there on their way northward, Bitterfield had not kept such a watch, but its people had been wary nevertheless. News of the fall of Ghlanhras, a city they already distrusted, must have prompted the change. If alben fell upon Bitterfield or any ælven town, it would happen at night.

The lights—distant windows, torches in the public circle perhaps— made Eliani yearn for a warm bed and a roof overhead. Instead, the party turned away and ascended another rise, leaving the glimmer of Bitterfield behind.

The path they followed was little more than a game trail, but soon it broadened and met a stream, and turned to follow the watercourse up another steady rise. Kivhani paused at the turning to let the party drink.

Eliani kept an anxious eye not only on Luruthin, but on Vanorin as well. He looked weary and grim, and was drinking one-handed.

"Your arm is troubling you?"

He glanced at her and shrugged. Eliani felt badly for not having offered him healing days ago, but in truth her courage had failed her. She did not wish to cause him grief, and had thought that a healing might do so, being of necessity an intimate contact of khi.

Now she regretted that choice. Vanorin needed healing, plainly, though he would not admit it. Perhaps the same reasons that had made her hesitate to offer had kept him from asking.

Well, no more. She drank another mouthful of water and rubbed her hands on her cloak, then stood and turned to Vanorin.

"Come."

He looked up at her, questioning. She summoned him with a jerk of her head, and moved to a large pine a few paces from the stream. Kivhani caught her eye as she passed, and leaned toward Othanin to murmur something into his ear. Eliani noted that the governor looked weary, but well enough.

At the pine she turned and waited. Vanorin had stood but remained by the stream. She beckoned him with a gesture, then sat down with her back against the trunk. Slowly Vanorin approached.

"We have only a few moments, but it should help." Eliani patted the ground beside her.

"My lady—"

"Hush. Sit down."

She moved aside and made him sit with his back resting against the tree trunk. He stared straight ahead, not meeting her gaze, his face so stern it reminded her of Jharan, which of course reminded her of Turisan.

Eliani hid a wry smile. Peering at the scrap of cloth tied around Vanorin's arm, she frowned.

"This needs washing. It will have to wait until we reach the camp. May I touch you?"

He glanced at her and nodded, then looked forward again, blinking. Eliani first held her hands in the air just over the wound. Khi leapt in her palms, heat drawn toward the injury. Vanorin made a restless movement, then closed his eyes.

Drawing a deep breath, Eliani let herself sink into the absorption of healing. Slowly she brought her hands to rest lightly against the bandaged arm. A small tingle flooded up the backs of her hands as her khi and Vanorin's mingled. His was pleasant, its gentle tone surprising even though she had felt it before. He sat motionless, as if afraid even to breathe.

The cut on his arm was small but fairly deep, and suffered from neglect. Eliani sensed the beginning of a festering and frowned. If she had dealt with this at once the wound would now be well on the way to being healed.

She focused the warmth flowing through her hands on the point where the damage was worst. Healings began on a tiny level, Jhinani had told her, spreading and flowing outward from there. If she could find the source of the pain and festering, she could shift the flow of khi there to set the wound to healing. She let her thoughts follow the thread of dark dullness in Vanorin's khi, pursuing its origin.

Voices disturbed her. Withdrawing until she could comfortably open her eyes, she saw that the party were all standing again, waiting beside the stream.

"We will have to finish later."

She took her hands away from Vanorin's arm, then sat back and watched him open his eyes, blinking in confusion. He glanced at her and color flooded into his cheeks.

"Thank you."

Eliani nodded, then stood and offered him a hand. He hesitated, but then clasped her arm and let her help him to his feet. Yes, she could tell from his khi that the sickness in the wound was beginning to affect his strength. How foolish they had both been, avoiding this.

She let go his arm and smiled briefly, then turned away. What she wished to do was stay close to him, offering comfort, but that probably would aggrieve him. Vanorin was right; formality was their protection. It reminded them of how they stood to one another, which differed from how they felt.

She liked him, she thought as she fell into step behind Luruthin. At first she had thought him somewhat cold, interested only in his responsibilities as captain of her escort. As their acquaintance had grown she had found her admiration for him increasing. Perhaps missing Turisan had some part in it.

The ache of missing her partner intensified. They had not discussed it, but she knew they were both calculating how many days it would be until they might be reunited. Twenty at least. Likely more.

A shift in the khi of those ahead of her made Eliani glance up. They had topped a small rise and were descending its gentle slope toward an open meadow ahead. She could see the lights of campfires between the trunks of the pines. As one, the party quickened their steps, and a moment later she heard the hail of a watcher greeting Kivhani.

There were others in the woods, many others, all with the same white hair and deep dark eyes. Eliani had to shake off the nervousness roused by their appearance, and remind herself that these folk kept the Ælven creed.

The party reached the meadow, which was wide and mostly level. A lone pine stood a little way into the clearing with a large fire circle nearby. Several smaller fires were scattered around the meadow's edges. The main fire was surrounded by huge logs that served as benches, and the Lost who had been sitting there all stood to greet the newcomers. Others gathered, coming from the other fires or out of the woods.

"Othanin!" A white-haired male hurried forward.

Eliani watched the two of them clasp arms. The Lost quickly surrounded the governor, asking anxious questions about friends and loved ones in Ghlanhras. Eliani looked away, knowing the answers would not be happy.

Kivhani's voice rose above the chatter, demanding attention. The Lost fell quiet, all looking to her.

"We have guests." Her voice was not overloud but would reach the edges of the meadow. "Distinguished visitors. Lady Eliani of Felisanin, from Alpinon, and her companions. Please make them welcome."

Faces now turned toward Eliani, who quailed under the gaze of so many black eyes. Think of them as Greenglens, she told herself, and summoned a smile.

"Thank you, Lady Kivhani. We are grateful for your hospitality."

A murmur rumbled through the meadow. The Lost were no more comfortable with her presence here than she, Eliani realized. Perhaps she and her escort were the first ælven to visit the Lost in their camp. Kivhani had not said so, but plainly their arrival was a surprise to many.

A tall male approached and paused a few paces away from Eliani. He was dressed in undyed leather, as were all the Lost. He gazed at her intently, then made a formal bow

"Lady Eliani, I am Inóran. Dare I hope that you remember me?"

"Inóran!"

She had not remembered his face, but then she had been a child the one time that she had seen him, and his appearance was much changed. The hair that was now white had been golden, then, on the day he had handfasted with her father's sister.

She took two quick steps toward him, extending her arm without thinking. He hesitated an instant, glancing at her handfasting ribbons, then smiled shyly and clasped arms. Eliani felt again the strange prickle that she had noticed in Kivhani's khi.

"I saw Davhri some days since. She is sorely concerned for you."

Pain crossed Inóran's face. "I have wanted to send a message to her, but have not known how to tell her...."

"Tell her you are alive, at least. She grieves."

His brow tightened in a frown and his mouth curved downward in bitterness. "My news would not cheer her."

"Of course it would cheer her to know that you live!"

Eliani thought of Davhri, living a barren existence in Bitterfield, a shadow of her former self. During her brief stay there, Eliani had sought to cheer her, but Davhri's despair at the loss of her partner could not be lifted.

"We have no communication with Bitterfield. We dare not approach it, or any ælven town."

She could not bear the thought of Davhri's continuing to suffer, not when she might at least be comforted. Inóran's news might not be happy, but it was better than knowing nothing of his fate.

"I could go to Bitterfield. One of my party is ill." She glanced behind her at the escort. Luruthin and Vanorin had both sat on the ground. The other guardians, Onami, Birani, and Felahran, stood close by, looking nervous. "Two, actually. They could rest here while I go to the village."

Kivhani frowned. "You do not know what welcome you may find there."

"I was just lately there. I am certain Dejhonan will welcome me. I have kindred in the village." She glanced at Inóran.

Othanin, coming to stand beside Kivhani. "Your offer is generous, Lady Eliani, but we need not impose on you so. I will go to Bitterfield. I must consult with Theyn Dejhonan, and tell him what passed at Ghlanhras."

Eliani shrugged. "He will know by now."

"He will not know all."

She met his stern gaze, then nodded. He was still governor, in name if nothing else, and she was encouraged by his willingness to see his duties through.

Kivhani turned to Eliani with a small, kindly smile. "Thus you may rest here a day or two as well. You are welcome for as long as you care to stay."

Eliani accepted this with a nod. She would have liked to see Davhri again, but there were others here who needed her attention as much if not more. Turning away, she went to Luruthin and Vanorin.

"Come closer to the fire."

She led them into the main fire circle, where the Lost hastily moved away, leaving room for them on one of the log benches. Eliani was beginning to feel annoyed at their avoidance, as if she and her party were the ones who were afflicted.

The fire's warmth felt good against her face, and as it began to penetrate her borrowed leathers, she felt a sense of relief. The fire was large, as big as a feast-day fire. The Lost must have no fear of discovery here in this sheltered meadow.

She wondered where they spent their days, for the sun must flood the meadow itself. Looking into the woods around it, she saw the shapes of rough shelters covered in evergreen boughs and had her answer.

Inóran approached, carrying a battered metal urn and three mismatched cups, one of rough pottery, one of metal and one carved of wood. He set down the urn and handed the cups to Eliani and two of her party.

"Tea." He picked up the urn and offered to pour. "It is mint and tealeaf."

Eliani eagerly held out the pottery cup. "Tealeaf grows here?"

Inóran nodded as he poured. "It grows in sheltered places on the eastern slopes. We cultivate a patch near each of our regular camps."

Eliani inhaled the fragrant steam, then sipped at the hot tea. A small luxury and a great comfort.

"Ah, thank you!" She sighed with pleasure. "How many camps have you?"

The sudden silence in the space around her, the stilling of the Lost's voices, told her this question had been a mistake. She had meant it conversationally, but even Inóran's eyes shifted aside with discomfort.

"Perhaps I should not say."

"Of course. Forgive me."

"We have learned to be distrustful, I fear." He gave a small, rueful smile.

"Have the alben troubled you?"

"Not the alben, no. Not until now." He glanced around the meadow. "This is usually a summer camp, but our winter camps are close to Ghlanhras. When we became aware that the alben had crossed the mountains, we decided to move."

Eliani gazed at him, wondering if it had been in the Lost's power to warn Ghlanhras. She decided that if it had been possible to send warning to Othanin, Kivhani would certainly have done so. Most likely, there had not been opportunity.

She sipped her tea, and finding it cool enough, took a larger swallow. Remembering that there were only three cups, she drank as quickly as she could, then let Inóran fill the cup again and offered it to Vanorin, who was sitting beside her with shoulders bowed, staring into the fire. He started when she held the cup before him, as if his thoughts had been far away.

Their khi brushed together as he took the cup. Eliani sensed his weariness and was quietly alarmed at how much his wound was affecting him. She must finish the healing she had begun. She felt an urge to do it at once, but she did not wish to engage in a healing in the midst of all the Lost. Best to stay by the fire until the party were all comfortably warm, then seek a quieter place.

She watched Vanorin drink the tea in small, slow sips. Luruthin had another cup, and the two Stonereaches were sharing the third.

A restless movement drew her attention to the approach of Kivhani and Othanin. Many of the Lost stood gathered outside the fire circle.

Kivhani bowed, with unaccustomed formality. "Lady Eliani, I must beg your indulgence. I wish to consult with my people about the invitation you offered. May we make you comfortable at one of the smaller fires while we use this circle?"

"Of course." Eliani stood at once.

Inóran rose, the urn in his hand. "I will take them to our fire."

Kivhani nodded. "Thank you."

Inóran led Eliani and her friends across the meadow, past two smaller fires to a third just at the edge of the wood. Here the log seats were much smaller, and Eliani and her companions nearly filled them as they sat and huddled toward the flames.

Two Lost, male and female, came out of a shelter nearby, saw Eliani's party and cast alarmed glances at Inóran. He told them of Kivhani's counsel gathering, and they hastened away to the larger fire. Inóran poured the last of the tea into the three cups held eagerly out by Eliani's party, and set about making more.

"Do you not wish to join the discussion? We will be all right if you go."

Inóran glanced up at Eliani as he poured fresh water into the urn from a pitcher. "I think my opinion will be suspect, as I am kin to you. If I may call myself so."

"Of course you are my kindred! Inóran, *who you are* has not changed."

He paused and sat back on his heels, the urn in both hands. "I am glad to hear you say so. Not all would agree with you."

He gazed at her for a moment, then returned to his work, scraping some coals between two flat-topped stones and balancing the urn across them. He then stood up and added wood to the fire.

"What happened, Inóran? If you care to tell of it."

He bent to check the water in the urn, then sat on the ground beside the fire, folding his legs beneath him. His face grew still. At last he spoke.

"I was returning home from Ghlanhras. I did not find the glass I sought there—those who once made it had abandoned their forges on Firethroat. I came back on the trade road through Woodrun, hoping instead to find a small gift there for Davhri."

He paused as his voice went taut with grief. Eliani waited. She knew that the others were also listening.

"By the time I reached Woodrun I was unwell. I took a room at a public lodge and lay sick for three days, wracked with fever. By the end of them I knew something was very wrong.

"I could not eat. My last meal lay heavy in my stomach, and eventually I brought it up. I felt a little better after that and thought I should try to go home, but when I went to the door of the house the sunlight blinded me. It burned my eyes, it was so bright. I could not step into it."

He turned to glance at the urn again, and adjusted its position. "The host, who had been all kindness, became suddenly cold. She told me to leave her house."

Eliani heard a sharp intake of breath from one of the guardians. Such inhospitality was not in keeping with the creed. If someone was troubled, he should be given help. That was the way they all lived, the way harmony was preserved among the ælven.

"I begged to be allowed to stay until nightfall. She agreed, after some discussion and the gift of one of my best trade stones. When darkness came I left the house, but I knew I could not go home. Others would react the same way that my host had done."

Inóran paused to poke at the fire, frowning. "In fact, word of my affliction had spread through Woodrun and a small crowd had gathered in the public circle to see me go. They followed me to the edge of the town, all the way to the trade road. By the time I reached it I had made my choice. I turned north, back to Ghlanhras.

"I knew that Othanin had helped others who had been stricken with the curse. I made my way back to the city, sheltering in the darkwood forest during the day. It was—an unpleasant journey."

He glanced up, meeting Eliani's gaze for a moment. Her heart went out to him. How terrible it must have been, to realize he had suddenly lost all his former life, that he must walk away from everything he loved.

"I sought a private audience with Othanin, and he heard me. He understood at once, and was all kindness. He gave me a few necessities and told me how to find the Lost. I owe him much gratitude. If I had been alone—"

Inóran stopped abruptly and shook his head, then turned away and began fussing with the fire, adding more wood. Eliani thought she knew what he had been about to say. If he had been alone, he might have sought to end his life.

All were silent. Inóran took the steaming urn off of the coals and added tea leaves from a small pouch. The fragrance of mint rose afresh. He set the urn aside to steep and looked at Eliani.

"Tell me of Davhri. Is she well?"

Eliani pursed her lips, composing her answer carefully. "She lives. She is not ill, but I would not say she is well."

He frowned. "How do you mean?"

"There is no joy in her life, no gladness. She appears to have abandoned her work. Dejhonan is looking after her; he sends his daughter to help her about the house."

Inóran's frown had deepened as Eliani spoke. She leaned toward him.

"Davhri lives in despair but cannot give up hope. Inóran, you must end her misery. Send her word of your situation."

He sighed. "It would be better if she forgot me."

"That is foolish. Have you forgotten? Will you ever forget her?"

He looked sharply up at Eliani, then shook his head. He looked almost as miserable as Davhri, she thought. She picked up the pottery cup and turned it in her hand, trying for a lighter tone.

"Besides, you need some new cups. These are wretched. You should ask her to make you a set."

Inóran laughed in surprise, then dropped his face into his hands with a gasping sob. Eliani put down the cup and reached out to touch his shoulder.

"You are partners." She remembered the handfasting in Highstone, the ribbons hanging above Davhri's door. "That has not changed, nor will it."

"But we cannot live as partners." He looked up at Eliani, his face grave. "Some of us have been discussing this. I am not the only one here who is handfasted. We have thought that perhaps, in our case, the bond should be dissolved."

Eliani frowned. "A handfasting is for life."

"One might say this is a different life. What would you wish, if you were in my place? Would you wish your partner to be free?"

Eliani glanced at the ribbons on her arm. "My situation is somewhat different."

"But surely you can imagine it. If you became afflicted, and could not return to your partner—"

"Their situation is different." Vanorin's voice was gruff. "They are mindspeakers."

Inóran turned a startled face to Eliani. "Mindspeakers?"

She swallowed. "Yes."

Inóran's gaze became sharp and intent. "Have you told your partner you were coming here?"

"I told him Kivhani had offered us shelter, yes."

"And he knows where you are?"

"Not precisely. He knows we are near Bitterfield."

"And where is he?"

Eliani misliked the cold suspicion in his voice. Beside her, Vanorin shifted slightly and she sensed his concern.

"He is on his way here, to Fireshore."

With an army of ælven. Inóran would not have reacted well to that news, she thought. He was gazing at her, doubt writ over his face.

"He would never wish you harm. He supports the idea of the Lost being recognized as a clan."

"An ælven clan?" Inóran's eyes widened.

"Yes. That is what Kivhani is discussing now. My father has summoned the Ælven Council to meet at Highstone, and he has invited Kivhani and Othanin to attend."

Inóran gazed raptly at her, his chest moving deeply with his breath. The idea of possible acceptance was new to him, it seemed. His eyes were sharp with sudden, painful hope.

Eliani leaned toward him. "You live by the creed, yes?"

He nodded. "With all our hearts, as far as we are able."

"Then you are still ælven. That is my view, at least. We need only convince the Council of it."

His face fell. "There are too many who despise us."

"That cannot be so."

"It is so. Here in Fireshore, we have been hunted by ælven."

"Hunted!"

Inóran nodded. "In summer a group of us were gathering berries near Darkhollow. We strayed too near the town, and were seen. The townspeople assembled, armed with bows, and fell upon us. Two were slain."

Eliani caught her breath, aghast. "Did they give no warning?"

"None." Inóran shook his head sadly. "They thought we were alben."

Eliani sat up straighter. "That must not happen again. The ælven must be made to understand that you are not alben."

"It may not be easy to convince them. How are they to know an alben from one of us?"

"Clan colors." Vanorin shifted on his log. "If you became a clan, and always wore your colors—"

"The alben would adopt them as well."

Eliani looked at Luruthin, who had hitherto been silent. She had not thought he was following the conversation. The bitterness in his voice troubled her.

"The alben would learn of your clan, and wear your colors to deceive. They care nothing for the creed, only for their own advantage."

Stark silence followed his words. All knew they were true.

Inóran picked up the urn and filled the pottery cup at Eliani's feet, then moved on to pour tea for the others. Eliani sipped, feeling dejected. She could not think of a solution to the problem of differentiating the

Lost from the alben. Luruthin was right, any sort of marking would quickly be adopted by the alben.

Certain words of greeting, perhaps? Not as useful as something visual, and it was possible the alben would discover them as well. They could be changed from time to time, but getting word of the change out to all the ælven settlements would be problematic.

Eliani sighed and drank her tea in silence, still puzzling at the problem. The Lost needed something that the alben could not, or would not, imitate. She could think of nothing.

She filled the cup again and offered it to Vanorin, who shook his head. Handing the tea to Onami, she moved to the ground and leaned her back against the log, inviting Vanorin with a gesture to join her. He did so, and Eliani shifted her position so that she could reach his wound and place her hands over it once more.

Vanorin's eyes dropped shut and he sighed deeply as the warmth spread through her hands. She closed her eyes also and concentrated on finding the source of the pain and illness in the wound.

"Inóran, can you bring some strips of clean cloth? I need to wash and bandage this wound."

"Yes. Hot water as well?"

"If you have it. Otherwise the tea will serve."

She returned her attention to the healing and was lost for a time, delving into the depth of the wound, feeling a shadow of the pain it caused Vanorin, of the ache of sickness in the flesh. She brought light to it, heat and healing to banish the dark dull soreness. She remained so until a sharp crack from the fire startled her into drawing back.

Blinking, disoriented, she saw Inóran sitting nearby, watching. Three small strips of cloth lay across his lap, and he had poured some of the tea into a small bowl. Eliani reached for the bowl, and held out her hand for the cloth.

"You are a healer as well."

"A poor one. My gift is not trained."

She put a strip of cloth into the bowl and set it down while she carefully removed Vanorin's leather arm piece and untied the old bandage from the wound on the underside of his arm. He winced as she pulled it away. He had tied it on just after leaving Ghlanhras, and ignored it thereafter. An unwholesome smell arose from the bandage. Eliani threw it into the fire.

As gently as she could, she bathed the wound. Vanorin held still, but she knew from his khi that she was hurting him. She knew also that she must clean the wound as thoroughly as possible, so she gritted her teeth, poured more tea over the cloth, and pressed it deep into the cut. Vanorin inhaled sharply.

"Forgive me. My clumsy fingers."

He made no answer, nor any further sound as he stood her ministrations. At last she was satisfied that the wound was clean. She laid her hand over it, seeking the darkness that had festered there. The dull ache had turned to a brighter pain, but the darkness was gone.

She bound the wound with another strip of cloth. Inóran carefully folded the third strip and took it away. Cloth must be precious to the Lost, Eliani thought as she watched him go into a shelter. They would have no means of making it themselves. As often as they moved, they could keep nothing so large as a loom.

She placed her hands on Vanorin's arm again and sent healing into the wound. He sighed deeply. A flicker of something went through his khi—regret? Longing? It was gone at once, and Eliani chose to ignore it. She stayed as she was until the heat faded from her palms, then sat back and collected the bowl and the soiled cloth she had used to clean the wound. She was about to throw that on the fire also, then glanced at Inóran. He held out his hand.

"I will wash it."

She handed it and the bowl to him, then took back the empty cup from Onami and poured fresh tea into it, offering it to Vanorin. He took it with a small smile.

"Thank you, my lady."

"You are welcome."

His gaze held hers over the cup, and Eliani felt a different kind of warmth in it, a warmth that brought heat into her cheeks. Vanorin looked away, down at the cup, and then sipped. Eliani gazed into the fire, reflecting that some wounds could never be healed.

❋ Ghlanhras ❋

Shalár sat at a long darkwood table in the chamber she had made her workroom. It had served the same function for Othanin, and she had spent some of the time since her arrival in reading through all of his correspondence. This had mostly to do with the governing of Fireshore, but she had found a cache of personal letters that raised most interesting questions, and they were scattered now before her.

They were cryptic, many of them, and unsigned, but all were in the same hand and all implied affection in their tone, even though the content might be as mundane as the numbers and location of kobalen roaming on the eastern slopes of the Ebons. Othanin's correspondent was a close friend, if not a lover.

Why, Shalár wondered, did this close companion never come to Ghlanhras? None of the letters made any mention of such a possibility.

A knock fell upon the door. Shalár glanced up.

"Come."

Ranad entered. Shalár had made him her attendant for the nonce, until Galir should arrive from Nightsand. Ranad was a poor substitute, young and eager, impatient of such tedious tasks as guard duty, but at least he was untroubled by being sent on the most trivial of errands.

"Scouts to report to you, Bright Lady. Torith and Gavál."

"Very well. Bring Torith first."

He left and returned a moment later with Torith, whose faded black leathers were coated with dust. He had come to her straight from the road, then. She gestured to a chair.

"Be at ease. Ranad, bring water and wine."

Ranad bowed briskly and left, quietly shutting the door behind him. Torith took the chair Shalár had offered, slouching into it with a sigh. He brushed loose wisps of hair back from his face.

"What news?"

"I reached Woodrun, but could not enter it. They have set a watch at the road and another to patrol the edges of the town night and day."

Shalár frowned and swept the letters she had been reading into a rough stack. "So they know we are here."

"Undoubtedly they know. Three of the party that attacked our gates escaped thither—I heard the watchers talking of it."

"What of Othanin? Is he there?"

"I heard no mention of him."

Shalár bit her lip. Woodrun was alert, and so would not be easy to capture. She must rethink her plans.

"How many would you say are dwelling there?"

"Four or five hundreds, at least."

"That many? Woodrun was the merest village...."

The merest village when she had dwelt here before, but that was centuries ago. Being here again, in her childhood home, sometimes made her forget how long it had been.

Torith leaned against her work table. "Woodrun is Fireshore's main city now. All the darkwood trade has moved there, as have many of Ghlanhras's people."

Shalár nodded. After capturing Ghlanhras she had found that many of the houses here were long abandoned. She planned to fill them with her own people, when they arrived. Then she would have the strength to capture Woodrun. For now, she must hold off.

Ranad returned with goblets and two ewers. Torith declined the wine, but drank two cupfuls of water in quick succession. Shalár watched his face, thinking she saw a slight pinched look about it.

"Have you other news?"

He finished his second cup of water and set the goblet on the table. "No, Bright Lady. I spent a night listening to the watchers, but they talked mostly of the darkwood harvest. A new milling site has been made, close to Woodrun."

A tremor shook the room. Shalár clutched at the edge of the table, then made herself relax.

There had been a number of tremors since their arrival; not unusual in Fireshore, though new to most of her people. She herself was unused to them, but she remembered them from early childhood.

The water ewer teetered slightly with a small, metallic sound, then was still. She gazed at Torith, who stared back, wide-eyed.

"Take your rest, then. You may share a kobalen with Gavál after I have seen him."

"Thank you, Bright Lady."

Torith stood up, bowed briefly, and left. Shalár reached for the wine and poured herself a cup.

The door opened again and Gavál came in. He had made the effort of grooming his hair before coming to her; it lay loose about his shoulders. He bowed deeply and scarcely met Shalár's eye, looking apprehensive. Disappointing news, then.

"Be seated. Have some wine or some water."

"Thank you, Bright Lady." He sat, but did not reach for drink.

"What news?"

"Bright Lady, we could not catch the ælven attackers."

"Why not?"

"They appear to have split up. Some left the road at a stream crossing. They must have followed it into the forest, but we could find no sign of their passing. We searched both east and west, as well as on the road."

Shalár's eyes narrowed. She took hold of his khi, swiftly so that he had no chance to hide his thoughts. He gave a small gasp.

She searched his mind and found no deceit. Going so far as to explore his recent memory, she saw that he had earnestly sought the ælven in the darkwood forest. She released him.

"Take your hunters and search eastward. If you find no sign of them in two nights, return."

"Yes, Bright Lady." His voice was a whisper.

Shalár reached for a scrap of parchment and dipped a pen in ink. "Go with Torith to the kobalen pens. He will choose a feeder. When he is finished with it you may share what remains with your hunters."

She handed Gavál the written order. He stood as he took it, swallowing.

"Thank you, Bright Lady."

"You had better hurry. The sun will soon rise."

Fear crossed his face, and he hastily bowed and left the room. Shalár stared at the closed door, drumming her fingertips against the table.

So the ælven were most likely lost to her. Othanin, who would have been useful as a trade offering, now gone. This irked her, but not so much as the loss of the other, the Stonereach.

She had hoped to breed him again. One success offered hope of others.

She put a hand to her belly and opened her khi, hoping for a word or a sign from the spirit of her child. She sensed its presence, but distantly.

A year from now the child would be born. Born of winter, born of strife. Appropriate for a future leader of her people. Shalár smiled slightly, then reached for Othanin's letters again.

Othanin's correspondent was in the Ebons, west of Ghlanhras, not east. She frowned. Perhaps her guess was mistaken, and the ælven would not be fleeing to the Steppe Wilds. She almost called Ranad to summon back Gavál, but decided to wait. Gavál would not leave the city until nightfall.

She searched through the letters again, seeking reference to a place of shelter, but it seemed that the writer moved often, mentioning Firethroat in one message, the Great Sleeper in another. Unlikely, then, that Othanin would seek refuge with this friend, for he might not be able to find her.

Her, or him. No—her, Shalár decided, looking at the pages in her hands, seeking information in the whispers of khi that clung to them. It was mostly Othanin's khi, but there was that hint of another, of the writer.

Her. Othanin's lover. Shalár was certain of it.

"Ranad."

He came in at once, face inquiring. Shalár gathered up the letters again, slipping them into the silver ribbon that had bound them.

"How many ælven were captured in the Hall?"

"Seventeen, Bright Lady, including the governor and—"

"Yes, yes. So fifteen remain?"

"Three of them have crossed, my lady."

She frowned. "Go to the house where they are kept, and bring back whichever of them attended most closely on Othanin. Hurry, I want you back before daylight."

"Yes, Bright Lady." He bowed and swiftly left.

Three crossed. Yielding their flesh in their despair. They gave up too easily, these ælven. Shalár wondered how she might prevent their seeking death, but apart from giving them more comforts, she could think of nothing.

She stood and left the chamber, passing down the hallway to her private rooms. A memory was tickling at her, something she had glimpsed among Othanin's belongings. She could not recall it exactly. She went into the bedchamber and threw open the darkwood wardrobe that had held Othanin's clothing and now contained hers.

Her new leathers hung here, with her cloak and three of the robes that had been Othanin's, dyed with the superior dyes available here in Fireshore. The leathers and the grey garments had been dyed to black, the orange to blood red. The cloak had resisted dying and was now a dullish green-gray, its falcon-head clasp replaced with one of iron in the shape of flames. Shalár stared at the clothes, frowning.

Not these, but something close. She pulled open the three inner drawers of the wardrobe one by one. The first two held silken tunics and legs, also recently dyed to Darkshore's colors. The third held a clutter of small items she had not yet sorted: a jumble of pouches, sashes, and ornaments, mostly grey and orange. A flash of dark green showed among them, though, and Shalár caught at it.

A ribbon. She pulled it free of the tangle. It was three ells long, a thumb's width, and beautifully woven. Orange and gray entwined with the russet and dark yellowy green of the Steppegard clan, interspersed with images of darkwood trees and scrub pines, running horses and Firethroat.

A handfasting ribbon.

Shalár repressed a sneer. Othanin was handfasted, to a Steppegard it appeared. She searched in the drawer but found no second ribbon. His partner had taken it with her, then.

Shalár frowned. She had found no sign of a second occupant in Othanin's chambers, nor any room that appeared to house a partner. The guest chambers were plainly that alone, and the household attendants had their own separate dwelling behind Darkwood Hall.

Othanin's partner had not resided here, then, or at least not recently. Shalár held the ribbon in both hands and sought through it with khi. The exploration was unpleasant, for the blessings that had been laid into the ribbon by its maker rang against her own khi.

Ælven held great store by pledges, and the handfasting pledge was the most binding of all. Shalár, who made no promises, detested those who revered them. A pledge was a limitation, and she accepted none such.

Deep within the weave, an echo of the handfasting ceremony whispered. Shalár sensed a female, sensed Othanin's delight in her, a hint of her scent, the brush against skin of a long swath of waving bronze hair. Deep, abiding love.

Angered, Shalár threw the ribbon from her. She opened her eyes and stood staring at it. It lay crumpled on the floor, a snake, a tether, but only a symbol of the pledge that was the greater object of repugnance.

Fools, to bind themselves so! Where were they now? Not together, she knew.

Othanin's correspondent was his partner. She was sure of it now. Handfasted, but dwelling apart. What did it mean?

She picked up the ribbon again and searched its length. Sometimes the couple's names were woven into their handfasting ribbons, along with the images and blessings. Shalár found no names here, but the initials "O" and "K" adorned each end of the ribbon, entwined with firevine.

Slowly she coiled the ribbon, then chose a plain grey pouch from the drawer in which to store it. Pulling the strings tight, she cast the pouch behind her boots and closed the wardrobe.

She returned to her workroom and found Ranad there, standing over a black-haired ælven male who was on his knees, head bowed, hands bound behind him. She gazed at the ælven for a long moment, then gestured to Ranad to loose his bonds. Ranad gave her a doubtful look, but knelt to obey.

The ælven came out of his stupor as his hands were untied. He glanced up at Shalár, blue eyes startled, then quickly looked away. His face was strained and somewhat gaunt.

Shalár gazed at him. "Are you not given enough to eat?"

He rubbed at his wrists but did not meet her gaze. "We are given enough."

Starving themselves, perhaps. That might be how they were dying. She would inquire about it later, of those who guarded the houses where the ælven were held. One housed those captured in Darkwood Hall, three others the rest of the ælven taken in Ghlanhras.

Ranad stepped back, the ropes dangling from his hand. Shalár gestured to him to leave the room. He opened his mouth to protest, but shut it again and obeyed.

"Come, sit here." Shalár waved at the chair before her table. "There is wine if you wish it."

The ælven cast a wary glance at her, then got to his feet and sat in the chair. He stared at the tabletop and made no move to take wine.

Shalár returned to her own chair and gazed at him. "You were Othanin's attendant?"

"Steward of the hall."

"For how long?"

"Two decades and more."

"Othanin must have been pleased with your service."

He made no answer. Shalár watched him, wondering how best to approach him. She could wrest what she wanted to know from his mind, but that was taxing and sometimes inspired greater resistance. Ælven were not easy to control, and she wished to conserve her strength for the building of her child's body. She would try first to coax what she wanted from him.

"You must know Othanin's lady, then."

His startled expression told her she had guessed aright. After the first glance he returned his gaze to the table, frowning.

"Tell me about her. What is her name?"

He was silent. She could taste fear in his khi, see it in his breathing. Knowing her power, she smiled and leaned toward him.

"I can find it out easily enough. Spare me the trouble of fetching others." She wrapped her khi around his, let him feel it. "Her name."

His eyes widened, breath shortened. "Kivhani."

"A Steppegard."

He blinked. "Yes."

"Why did she leave Ghlanhras?"

For a moment he did not answer. "Many have left. They fear the hunger."

"Why did *she* leave?"

She saw him swallow, knew he was debating what to say. He glanced up at her.

"Why should I tell you? What will it gain me?"

She twisted his khi and he cringed, making a small, strangled sound. When she released him he fell forward, catching himself against the table. Slowly he pushed himself upright.

"Spare yourself. Tell me why Kivhani left her lord."

"The hunger."

Shalár frowned in impatience. "She did not leave him for fear of the hunger." She tightened her hold on the ælven's khi.

"No! She left when she was struck with the hunger."

Surprised, Shalár gazed at him. "But she did not seek death."

"I do not know."

"She wrote to Othanin."

"I do not know."

Shalár took up the bundled letters and held them before his face. "As steward of the house all messages passed through your hands. Have you not seen these before?"

He stared at them, then glanced at her fearfully and shook his head. "No."

She shoved the bundle toward him. "Is it her hand?"

He turned his head to look at the writing. "Yes."

Shalár set the letters aside. "What did Othanin say of her?"

"He did not speak of her after she left. He mourned her absence."

The ælven fell silent and stared at nothing, as if lost in memory. Shalár doubted he knew much more that would be of use. She sat back in her chair.

"Ranad!"

The ælven looked up. "Wait."

The door opened and Ranad looked in. Shalár held up a hand to stay him. "In a moment."

Ranad glanced at the ælven, then withdrew. Shalár looked expectantly at the male before her. His dark hair hung lank about his face, and a look of hunger had come into his eyes.

"If I tell you something you will be glad to know, will you reward me?"

"I do not bargain with captives."

"You will be glad to know this. It could save you from a danger."

Shalár peered at him. Extracting information whose nature was unknown would be difficult. When she entered another's mind it was best to know what she was seeking. She tilted her head.

"What reward do you desire?"

He met her gaze. "Free my daughter."

"No."

To set any of her ælven captives free would be to send information about her people and her position in Ghlanhras to her enemies. There was no question of it, and the ælven looked as if he knew it.

"Then ... spare her from being used to breed."

His face went hard with the words. Shalár felt a ripple of anger in his khi.

Her custom always had been to encourage her hunters to breed with ælven captives. She would reward any of her people who bred successfully, as they well knew. Here in Ghlanhras there were far more ælven available than she had ever had at a time in Nightsand, so she doubted any one of the captives was overused. Still, she understood their hatred of such treatment. Interesting that this ælven did not ask to be spared himself, but made the request only on behalf of his child.

"What is your daughter's name?"

He looked up at her, fearful and hopeful at once. "Teshali."

"Very well. If I find your information useful, Teshali will be spared."

"Your word on it?"

Fool. He expected her to behave as an ælven.

"You have my word."

Shalár smiled. Perhaps she actually would spare the daughter—once. Just to torment the father with the fact that she had quite literally kept her so-valued word.

Or perhaps such strong concern for his daughter might be used to make him do Shalár's bidding. A cooperative ælven might well be of use. He could be sent into Woodrun to gather information. He would not be suspected, and he would certainly return, knowing that to fail would be to doom his daughter to unimagined torments.

He was watching her, searching her face. Shalár raised an eyebrow. Her patience was not infinite.

He licked his lips. "Kivhani is not alone."

"What do you mean?"

"There are others—many have been cursed with the hunger. Not all seek death."

Shalár leaned forward. "What do they seek?"

"They go into voluntary exile."

"Where?"

"West. At first they were sent away. Governor Minálan would not allow them to remain in Fireshore. He sent them across the Ebons."

Shalár knew of ælven who had occasionally wandered into her lands. Once in a great while such a one was taken captive, and if they showed sign of the hunger, was offered a place among her people, which was usually refused. More often they were found dead of sun poisoning or starvation, pathetic bodies discovered by her hunters, shriveled in lonely death on the rugged western slopes of the Ebons. It had been some decades since any such had been found.

"Governor Othanin was more lenient. He gave them help, tools and supplies to make some kind of life, when he sent them west."

Shalár's eyes narrowed. "How generous."

"He never spoke of them afterward, but everyone knew...."

Shalár coiled her khi a little tighter around the ælven's. He closed his eyes.

"Knew what?"

"That they were together. They had made a life, together."

She knew nothing of this. A community of ælven who suffered the hunger, yet did not seek refuge with Clan Darkshore?

"How many are they?"

"I do not know."

"*Where* are they?"

"I do not know."

Shalár brought pressure to bear on his khi. He winced, and his breath came short, but he shook his head.

"I do not know! West, only west. I know no more."

She relented. "Is Kivhani with them?"

He squeezed his eyes shut, as if anticipating pain. "I do not know. Othanin never spoke of her again."

She watched him for a moment, seeking any sign that he was withholding information. At last she released him. He gave a small, choked gasp.

"Ranad!"

Her attendant opened the door and looked in. Shalár gestured toward the ælven.

"Take him away."

"The sun has risen, Bright Lady."

"Hold him here until nightfall, then. And give him something to eat."

Ranad moved to take hold of the captive's arms. The ælven looked up at Shalár. "My daughter?"

"Ah, yes." Shalár looked at Ranad. "When you return him to holding, bring back a female named Teshali."

The ælven jerked against Ranad's hold. "But you said—"

"You want her spared from being bred. My people have access to any of the ælven in the holding houses. I have given them my word." Shalár watched his face, enjoying the dismay that crossed it. "She may dwell here, if she does as she is bid. I need someone to look after my chambers."

The ælven stared at her, his expression desperate. "She will not be troubled?"

"I expect not."

Shalár smiled, and with a gesture told Ranad to take him away. She was well pleased with what she had learned, and with what looked to be a useful arrangement. If the daughter cared as much for her father as he for her, they could each be made to do Shalár's bidding for the other's sake.

And the information he had given was of value. Shalár took up Othanin's letters. She did not recall any mention of others in them, but she would look through them again with an eye to finding hints about these voluntary exiles. A band of ælven outcasts, wandering together in the west. The steward had been right that such might be a danger to her. She would have to learn more of them.

❈ Ebon Mountains ❈

Eliani felt confined when she entered Kivhani's shelter, but she kept the thought to herself. No more than a framework thickly covered with evergreen boughs, the shelter was a single small room that smelled of pine sap and dust.

The ground on which Kivhani invited her to sit was cold. No fire, for to make a smoke hole would be to admit sunlight. The opening left as a doorway in the side facing the meadow was covered by a curtain of deer hide.

Kivhani sat across from Eliani, gazing at floor between them. Her hair was braided tightly back as always, but a wisp had escaped near her neck and it curled in a pale white spiral across her shoulder. Othanin sat beside her, but it was she who spoke.

"My people have decided. The discussion was long, and not all agree with our choice, but the majority wish to petition for recognition as an ælven clan." Kivhani raised her head to meet Eliani's gaze. Her own black eyes were troubled. "So I will attend the Council at Highstone."

Eliani nodded. "Good. You have my support, and my father's. Lord Turisan asked me to give you his as well."

"My thanks to him. It will be needed, I believe."

"Have you considered a clan name?"

"Yes." Kivhani smiled wryly. "The debate over that was almost as heated as over whether we should seek clan status. We have chosen Ebonwatch for a clan name. Our colors will be white, for atonement and to honor our ælven heritage, and night blue."

"That is fitting. Ebonwatch."

"We mean it to express our willingness to do our part against the alben. That is one thing upon which we are all agreed, that the alben are enemies to the creed and so our enemies as well."

"This will stand you well with the Council."

"If they will hear it, and believe it."

Othanin shifted and raised his eyes. "I will testify that it is so. If the Council has any respect left for me."

Eliani looked at him. "The Council will hear you. They need to hear you, to understand how it has been in Fireshore."

He nodded and gave a rueful smile. "I have been remiss in communicating the state of our affairs. I confess I was afraid...."

"Never mind. Your coming to the Council will mend that."

Eliani hoped she spoke the truth. She herself had been suspicious of Othanin not long ago, but having heard his account of the devastation caused by the return of the hunger to Fireshore, she was convinced of his integrity. Convinced, also, that the hunger was a sickness and of the need for all ælven to recognize this.

"Do you still plan to visit Bitterfield?"

"Yes. Then I will continue to Woodrun."

"Woodrun is too dangerous!"

"I am yet governor of Fireshore, and my people have gathered at Woodrun. I will seek to resume governing there." He smiled wryly. "Theyn Doriavi and I have had disagreements of late. It is possible she will seek to claim the governance of Fireshore."

Dismayed by this, Eliani sought words of reassurance, but could not form them. The governance of Fireshore was in disarray, most certainly. By leaving, as he soon must, to attend the Council, Othanin might be jeopardizing his position. Yet his presence was needed at the Council, both to reassure them he had not abandoned his duties and to support Kivhani's petition.

Othanin glanced at her with a crooked smile. "Bitterfield first, though."

"May I give you a message for Davhri?"

Kivhani reached for her pack. "I have paper and ink you may use."

"Thank you."

Paper and ink must be hard for the Lost to come by. Othanin must have provided them, while he dwelt in Ghlanhras. Eliani glanced at him and caught him exchanging a loving look with Kivhani. She looked away, suddenly missing Turisan.

Kivhani handed her a small piece of parchment, a corked bottle of ink, and a quill cut from a raven's feather. Eliani smiled her thanks.

"I will leave you, if I may. I wish to look in on Luruthin, he has not been well."

Kivhani nodded. "We will talk more this evening."

"Thank you."

Eliani stood and carried the writing tools out of the shelter, slipping through the curtain with care to keep from letting daylight in. She did wish to visit Luruthin, but she also wished to give Kivhani and Othanin privacy together, since Othanin meant to leave on the morrow.

The meadow, a few paces away, was flooded with sunlight. Eliani walked out into it, breathing a grateful sigh to be outside again. A bird startled up at her approach and flew away, chittering.

Looking across the meadow Eliani saw the fire circles all abandoned, the fires sunk to ash and coal. Vanorin sat on the grassy hillside across from her. He did not seem to notice her. No others were in sight.

She sought the shelter that Inóran shared with three others. "Inóran? It is Eliani. May I come in?"

"Yes."

She entered and stood for a moment by the curtain, letting her eyes adjust to the darkness. Luruthin lay resting beside one wall, his eyes closed, brow slightly creased. Inóran and another male sat by the opposite wall, both working a piece of deerskin with polishing stones. Two females lay facing one another at the back of the shelter, talking quietly.

Eliani knelt beside Luruthin and put down her writing things. Reaching her hands toward his head, she made the lightest contact with his khi, only to sense how he fared. He was calm, though she sensed a general discomfort. Possibly it was weariness from their journey hither. Eliani left him be and moved closer to Inóran.

"I am about to write to Davhri. Would you like to add a message?"

Inóran swallowed, then nodded. Eliani picked up her parchment and spread it across her knee, then carefully opened the ink and dipped the quill.

Dearest Davhri,

She paused, thinking, and had to freshen the quill before continuing. She barely touched the quill to the page for fear of piercing the parchment against the soft support of her flesh.

I regret that I must leave Fireshore without seeing you again. I am in haste, and will not be passing through Bitterfield, so I must send you my warmest affection on

this bit of paper. I hope and trust that you will be happy
at the news that follows. With fond love, Eliani.

She had used a little more than half the page. She blew on the ink to
dry it, then offered the letter and the quill to Inóran. He put aside his
stone and took them, read the letter, then sat musing for a while.

Eliani looked away, at Luruthin again. He seemed peaceful enough,
though she did not like the strain she saw in his face. It had been there
ever since Ghlanhras, and showed no sign of abating.

She heard the scratch of the quill and looked up. Inóran was writing,
frowning at the page. Not wishing to disturb him, she closed her eyes
and called to Turisan. He answered immediately with a rush of warmth
that set her loins tingling.

*And I miss you as well, my love. Can you stop to write? This message
should be sealed, I think.*

A pause preceded his answer. Eliani noticed that Inóran's quill had
gone silent.

Yes, it is time we rested the horses. Give me a few moments.

Eliani opened her eyes and saw Inóran staring at the letter, looking
distressed. He glanced up at her and held the page out toward her.

"I cannot say any more. Will you finish it?"

"Of course."

She read the two lines he had written:

Davhri, my love, I ask your forgiveness for my absence. I
was struck with the alben's curse in Ghlanhras, and have
gone into exile.

Eliani's heart was wrenched by this simple declaration, for she saw
all the pain behind it in Inóran's eyes. He offered her the quill and ink
with unsteady hands. She took them and added to the bottom of the
page.

He is well, and with friends. He is safe, Davhri. He hopes
you will understand why he cannot return to you, and
that you will be at peace.

"I have left room for you to sign." Eliani held out the letter and the
pen.

Inóran took them again, read what she had written, and nodded. He added a few words and signed his name.

"Thank you." He laid down the letter and gazed at it, his face full of sadness. "I should have done that long ago."

"She will be glad to receive this."

He smiled, though tears were brimming in his eyes. He turned his head away.

I am ready.

Eliani made herself comfortable and closed her eyes. She deepened her contact with Turisan until she could taste a hint of dust on the wind, feel the cool breeze across the plains.

Tell my father that Kivhani and Othanin will attend the Council. Tell him also that I have found Inóran. And ask him to procure cloth for a clan pennant, white and night blue.

For the Lost?

Yes. Heléri can help—I am sure she would be willing to make the pennant.

Is that not somewhat premature?

If the clan—Ebonwatch, they have chosen—is approved, then to see their colors carried forward will secure their status in the minds of the Council.

Turisan was silent for a moment. *I think it might anger some.*

Well, the pennant need not be displayed until the Council has made its decision.

But they will know that it was prepared in advance.

Eliani bit back impatience. *It shall be my gift to the new clan. If anyone is angered they may take it up with me.*

All right, love. I shall include your instructions.

He paused to write. Eliani savored the whispers of sensation she felt from him. A cold, sharp day on the plains. She thought she smelled a hint of storm.

What else would you say?

My love, of course, and regards to Heléri.

Are you certain that is all? I cannot send many more riders back to Highstone.

I am certain.

She smelled the wax he was heating to seal the letter. Opening her eyes, she reached for her own letter to Davhri. She had no wax, and doubted Kivhani would have any, but it was not needed. Othanin would place the letter in Davhri's hands. Finding it dry, Eliani folded it and wrote Davhri's name on the outside.

Done.

Thank you, Turisan.

She sent him warm, wordless love, then allowed the contact to fade. Feeling lonely in the absence of his touch, she shivered and stood up.

"I saw Vanorin outside. Do you know where the others of my party are?"

"Havaran and Gelasan offered them shelter." Inóran gestured. "The next lodge."

"Thank you. I think I will see how they are faring."

She went out into the sunlight again. Vanorin was no longer sitting where she had seen him. The meadow was empty, quiet. Dry grass and blooms of seed on the stalks of wildflowers told of the coming winter. The seed looked like a new set of flowers, all white where before there had been violet, yellow, red.

Gone white. Eliani closed her eyes, thinking of the Lost, hoping for the success and acceptance of their new clan. It still chilled her at times to be near them, when she remembered how they fed. Yet she was convinced of their complete devotion to the creed, and it was the creed, more than anything, that made the ælven who they were.

She went to the lodge Inóran had indicated, seeking her guardians. The two Lost within told her they had gone to a warm spring nearby, and directed Eliani how to reach it. As she had not bathed in many days, she turned eager steps toward it, finding the landmarks easily and locating the small path that climbed a rocky bluff beside the course of a trickling stream.

Green grass clung to its banks, still thriving in the warmth of the water despite the lateness of the season. The path left the stream partway up the bluff, angling off to the side to climb the steep rise. Eliani reached the top slightly out of breath and paused.

A few stunted pines grew in the shallow soil atop the bluff. The footpath ran plainly between them, and as she turned to follow it, she heard a burst of laughter ahead. Grinning, she began to loosen the lacings of her leathers as she walked.

"Reveling in my absence, are you?" She spoke as she came in sight of the spring, and stopped abruptly.

Vanorin was in the water with the others, his body pale against the dark sandy floor of the pool. Their gazes met and Eliani felt heat rush to her face. She looked away and continued to unlace her leathers. To retreat now would be worse than to carry on.

Birani answered with a merry laugh. "You were taking counsel with Kivhani. We did not wish to disturb you."

"Well considered, but I have finished now, so you must make room for me."

Eliani pulled off her leathers and the tunic and legs beneath them, and slid into the water between Birani and Onami. It was warm, not hot, but still an immense pleasure.

She glanced around at the others. Felahran and Vanorin had both bathed with her before; all of them had, in Highstone. There should be not the slightest cause for uneasiness. Still, she felt it, and hoped that it was not obvious to her companions. She was thankful for the water's disrupting effect upon khi.

She pulled at the thong that held her braid, untangling it and tossing the leather aside. Shaking out her hair, she sighed and lay back, feeling the tresses float atop the water before slowly sinking. She rubbed her scalp with her fingers, and scooped handfuls of sand to scrub lazily along her limbs, wishing for a pot of Heléri's soap.

"Not quite the Guardian's Reward, but close."

Felahran grunted agreement. "Reward enough."

Eliani gazed up at the crisp, deep blue of the mountain sky. "They must come here only at night."

Onami sighed. "How sad never to see the sun. To spend every day in those small lodges, or in a cave somewhere."

"Perhaps there will come a time when they can dwell in houses."

Eliani glanced at the others for their reaction. Birani looked surprised, Felahran thoughtful, Onami doubtful. Vanorin showed no sign of having heard. He closed his eyes as she glanced at him, and sank beneath the water.

Eliani sat up, her wet hair going cold at once in the chill air. She found a comfortable rock to lean against and slid down again until only her head was above the water.

"I am surprised the water does not harm your ribbons."

Eliani glanced at Onami, then raised her right forearm to inspect the handfasting ribbons. Their colors were as bright, the weave as tight as on her handfasting day.

"Heléri promised me it would not."

Birani joined the discussion. "Heléri's work is beyond compare. She made my eldermother's handfasting ribbon."

"Did she?"

"It stayed brilliant all her life, and her partner's. The day they both crossed, their ribbons fell to dust."

An image Eliani did not wish to think on. She lowered her arm again and touched her ribbon possessively beneath the water.

The conversation strayed from handfastings to cup bonds to the Midwinter celebrations they had missed. Eliani listened, adding a comment when she could think of one, half-distracted by consciousness of Vanorin's every movement. He, too, mostly listened to the conversation, answering only when directly addressed by one of the others.

Birani was the first to leave the pool, declaring that it was past midday and the day would get no warmer. Eliani wrung out her hair as well as she could, then stood and quickly climbed out of the water, hastening to put on her tunic and legs, grateful for the heavy protection of her leathers. The pool was not hot enough to have warmed her against the winter air. She wished once again for her lost cloak.

She felt much better for being clean, however, and was able to banter jokes with the others as they dressed and returned to the Lost's meadow. Vanorin hung back, remaining silent as he brought up the rear of the party. While the rest sat around a cold fire circle, he crossed the hillside to where he had sat earlier.

Eliani turned back to the circle. "Shall we build up the fire?"

"Yes!" Onami smiled. "My hair is cold."

Felahran went to a small stack of firewood nearby. "We could build them all up, come dusk. Have them burning when the Lost come out."

Eliani smiled. "A good thought. Let us build this one and finish drying out, then gather more wood."

They busied themselves with the fire, stirring the ashes and finding a few coals from which to kindle new flames. Eliani brought two logs forward to add to the fire, then sat and stretched her feet toward it.

"Do we journey back to Alpinon now, my lady?"

Eliani nodded to Felahran. "Yes, in a day or two. We have fulfilled our task."

Birani sighed. "I confess I will be glad to see Highstone again."

Eliani thought privately that she would be glad to see Althill, where she hoped to find some of her guardians who had fallen out of the party along the way. Others had returned to Clerestone. She would be glad to find them again as well, for too many had been lost.

Costly, her errand to Fireshore. She had learned much of value, but it was hard to think that the information, however important, had been gained at the expense of ælven lives.

Birani began braiding Onami's hair for her, attempting a Greenglen braid with the aid of Onami's advice. Eliani watched, smiling as they laughed together. Looking westward, she saw that the sun was already approaching the mountain peaks, glinting in the tops of the tall evergreens. Evening was not far away.

Felahran went foraging up the hillside for downed wood. Eliani watched him for a few moments, then allowed her gaze to wander to where Vanorin sat gazing up at the sky, much as he had been that morning. Gathering her courage, she stood.

"I will find some more kindling."

She walked away toward the woods, and soon found a pile of cut brush that looked to have been collected as kindling. Filling her arms, she started back toward the meadow, but did not go straight to the fire circle. Instead she walked to where Vanorin was half-lying, leaned back on his elbows, his face turned to the declining sun.

"Vanorin."

He started and looked at her, then sat up. "My lady?"

Eliani knelt and set down her load of kindling, brushing dust from her leathers. "I wanted to say—"

"Please do not."

Surprised, she gazed at him. He smiled, a little uncomfortably.

"Do not apologize for showing me your beauty. It was a pleasure, not a hardship."

"Oh. Vanorin—"

"You need not fear me."

"I *do* not fear you." She met his gaze. "I fear to hurt you."

He smiled again, this time seeming more at ease. "Well, I shall never be hurt by the chance to admire you."

Eliani closed her eyes briefly, then opened them and searched his face. She saw no pain there, only a gentle sadness. If he felt pain he hid it well.

She swallowed. "I owe you much more than gratitude, Vanorin. More than respect. I care for you, as much as I may."

A slight flush of color rose into his cheeks. He blinked, glancing downward. "Thank you."

She watched him for a moment, then sighed. "Your hair is still damp, and we should bind your arm afresh."

"It does not trouble me."

"It will if you leave that wet bandage on it. Come and join us at the fire."

"Yes, my lady."

The wry note in his voice made her glance up sharply. She saw him smiling, laughter dancing in his eyes. She grimaced at him, but was silently pleased as she turned to collect her kindling.

Vanorin's wounds, whatever they might be, were not dangerous. He would be all right.

Luruthin sat by Inóran's fire near the edge of the meadow, watching the others prepare to depart. It was not yet dawn, though morning was not far off and the Lost had begun to move into their shelters for the day.

Some brought meat and fruit to Eliani and the other guardians, helping them stow the supplies into deerskin packs. Luruthin had no possessions to manage, and Eliani had sternly bidden him to rest and not concern himself with the preparations.

Resting was all he had done in the three nights they had spent here with the Lost, but he was not inclined to argue. He felt better, but his heart was yet numb.

He had begun to think more of home, of Clerestone and Highstone, and of Jhinani. It now seemed possible that he might reach them. He yearned to feel safe again, to feel at peace. Perhaps that would come, in time. He could dare at least to hope for it now.

Memories of Ghlanhras still intruded, but less often and with less intensity. He had a little more strength against them. He was not ready yet to talk of it, but the grip of terror and pain had eased somewhat.

He shifted his seat on the log, moving a little closer to the fire. Inóran had lent him a blanket, which he pulled more closely about himself.

Inóran had befriended him, remembering that Luruthin had been at his handfasting. Luruthin's memories of that distant day were vague—he had been preoccupied with pursuing a comely Stonereach maiden at the time—but he did recall chasing his young cousin Eliani, then a child and in a particularly mischievous mood on the occasion of Davhri's handfasting, into a creek and returning with her to Felisanin Hall quite thoroughly muddied. Inóran quietly teased him for it, and Luruthin had no choice but to smile.

Two nights since, Inóran had taken him to the warm spring that

Eliani had praised. There beneath the blanket of a clouded sky Inóran had talked a little more of Davhri, of their life together in Bitterfield, of his love for her and her work. He expressed worry that she had abandoned her pottery, and Luruthin listened with sympathy, oddly relieved to think about another's troubles instead of his own. He offered what encouragement he could, and supported Inóran's hope that Davhri would send him an answer through Othanin.

Kivhani had now gone to meet Othanin, leaving just after sunset to journey to a meeting place she and her lord had agreed upon near Bitterfield. She had not yet returned, and Eliani had begun to cast anxious glances toward the way to Bitterfield.

"Luruthin." Inóran's voice, beside him.

Luruthin opened his eyes. The Lost was standing before him, offering a steaming cup.

"Have some tea. 'Tis a chill morning."

"Thank you."

Luruthin took the cup, wrapping his cold fingers around it and sipping cautiously. Inóran sat beside him.

"I shall miss your company. It has been pleasant to remember Highstone."

"You were there for all of a day." Luruthin grinned.

"And two nights. The happiest of my life."

Luruthin watched the wistful smile fade from Inóran's lips. A voice raised in greeting drew his attention.

Kivhani was coming down the hillside, accompanied by two of her folk, each burdened with a large pack. They approached Eliani, and Luruthin stood up, drawn by curiosity away from the fire.

"Othanin sends his greetings." Kivhani smiled as she took off her pack and threw it open. "He and Dejhonan send you best wishes and a few small gifts for your journey."

"Blankets!" Eliani pounced on them. "Oh, thank you!"

"There is wine as well, and bread and cheese. Also soap and other small comforts."

"Oh!" Eliani dug through the pack as eagerly as a child opening a name-day gift. She looked up, smiling, at Kivhani. "Give them our heartfelt thanks, when next you see Othanin."

"I shall."

Kivhani reached into her tunic and brought out a handful of letters. Most of them she handed to Eliani.

"From Davhri, Dejhonan, and Othanin, and this is for Felisan from Othanin. I have a letter for him as well, I will fetch it anon."

Kivhani turned toward where Luruthin and Inóran were standing. With a quiet smile she offered a last letter to Inóran.

"This is for you."

Inóran's eyes lit with joy and painful hope. He took the letter, said a strangled word of thanks, and with a glance at Luruthin hastened away to sit by the fire, bending over the letter and devouring it with hungry eyes. Luruthin smiled, glad for him, and looked back at Eliani. She had one of her own letters open and was perusing it.

"Ah! Our wounded sent a message to Dejhonan from Woodrun."

Luruthin nodded. "Good news."

"Yes." She glanced up. "Kivhani? May I impose upon you for another piece of paper?"

"Of course."

They went away together to Kivhani's lodge. Vanorin and the others were distributing the additional supplies among their packs. Luruthin watched for a little while, drinking his tea. When it was gone he returned to the fire and set the cup down beside the log where he sat.

Inóran was still absorbed in his letter. It was several pages long, and he went through them twice while Luruthin watched. At last he looked up.

"She wants to see me."

Luruthin smiled. "Did I not tell you she would?"

Inóran laughed with sheer happiness. "She scolds me for failing to bring her the glass I promised! She demands compensation!"

"Ah. So she loves you still."

Inóran laughed again, and wiped at his eye. "A lapse in judgment. At least, her father always thought so."

"Did he? Yet he sanctioned your handfasting."

"Davhri gave him no choice. You are right about her strength of will." His face went grim. "Her father did not want her to come to Fireshore."

Luruthin had no answer. Fireshore had certainly brought misfortune to them. It had brought misfortune to many, himself included.

Turning away from that grief, Luruthin sought to encourage Inóran. "Othanin and Kivhani have found a balance. You and Davhri will do the same."

Inóran nodded. "Yes. Even if we must remain apart." He held the letter to his bosom, closed his eyes and whispered. "I am so grateful."

Grateful despite the curse under which he lived. Luruthin was moved. He, too, had cause for gratitude. He had a son coming. He allowed himself to dwell on that for the first time since Ghlanhras, thinking how it would be to hold his child in his arms. How it would be to teach him, watch him grow. Show him how to make a bow, and take him hunting. Teach him the benisons and tokens of respect to offer in thanks for the prosperous hunt. Teach him the creed.

These pleasant thoughts occupied him until Eliani emerged again from Kivhani's lodge. Vanorin and the others were finished with the packs. With a start, Luruthin realized their departure was near. The sky above the treetops at the meadow's east side glowed with the first blue hint of dawn.

Eliani held a scrap of paper in her hand, and she showed it to Vanorin and the others. Luruthin got up to join them. The page was a map.

Eliani displayed it for them. "There are no trails, but this is the easiest way to the headwaters of the Basarindel. They have marked hazards and springs for us. We can stay off the road."

"Springs!" Jhathali's face lit with delight. "Thank the Spirits!"

"Thank the Lost." Felahran looked amused as he peered at the map. "This should take us no more than twenty days, if the weather holds."

"Less than twenty, I hope." Eliani glanced up at Luruthin and smiled. "But we shall see. Are you all ready?"

"In a moment."

Luruthin turned to go back to the fire. Inóran was reading Davhri's letter yet again, but he glanced up at Luruthin's approach.

"Your blanket." Luruthin took it off and folded it. "Thank you."

Inóran stood up, folding the letter and tucking it into his tunic. "Ah, yes! Stay a moment."

He accepted the blanket and hurried into his lodge. Luruthin edged nearer the fire, already feeling chilled. He had only the tunic and legs he had been wearing when he was captured—clean, now, at least, but beginning to be tattered at the edges.

Inóran returned holding the deerskin he had been working over the past days. Luruthin had seen him stitching it, though he had paid little attention. Inóran now held it up, and Luruthin saw that it was made into a simple tunic. It had no sleeves, but the shoulders were wide and would drape downward a little.

"Not a cloak, but it will guard you a little from the cold."

Touched, Luruthin accepted the gift. The skin was soft and supple. His throat tightened with gratitude.

"Th-thank you. I did not expect this."

Inóran smiled. "Put it on. You are shivering."

Luruthin slipped the tunic over his head and settled it on his shoulders. It was not a cloak, true, but it made him feel warmer at once.

"Thank you, Inóran. It is a fine gift."

Inóran smiled and offered an arm. "Spirits guard your path."

"And yours."

Luruthin clasped arms. The warmth of friendship shone through Inóran's khi.

"You are welcome here, for my part."

"Thank you." Luruthin smiled as they let go, thinking privately that despite the generosity of the welcome, he hoped never to avail himself of it. He would be glad if he could be assured he need never return to Fireshore.

Rejoining the others, he saw Eliani raise an eyebrow at his tunic. Luruthin smiled.

"A gift from Inóran."

"Kind of him."

She glanced toward Inóran and waved a hand in farewell. Luruthin did the same, and Inóran waved back before returning to his lodge. At the same moment, Kivhani came out of the woods with another of the Lost, each carrying bows and quivers full of arrows fletched in white. Kivhani stopped before Eliani.

"Please accept these, Lady Eliani, with our wishes for your safety as you journey homeward."

Eliani looked astonished as she took one of the bows and ran her hands along the arched wood. "Thank you! These are fine work. You honor us."

"As you have honored us, with your understanding and friendship."

Kivhani came to Luruthin with a bow and quiver, smiling as she offered them. Accepting them, he felt a wash of gratitude. He had not had a weapon since his capture, and the sense of safety it gave him was surprising in its power. He bowed.

"Thank you, Lady Kivhani."

"You are most welcome."

She offered an arm and Luruthin clasped it. Her grip was firm, her khi stronger than he expected. She smiled again briefly.

"If ever we may be of service to you, call upon us."

"You and Othanin are welcome to break your journey in Clerestone, if you wish. It is a day's travel from Highstone."

Kivhani gazed at him. "If that will not trouble the people of Clerestone."

Luruthin lifted his chin slightly. "My house is open to you. My people will welcome my honored guests."

"Thank you, Theyn Luruthin." She held his gaze for a long moment, then glanced eastward. "I must retire. Fare you well, and may spirits watch over you."

Vanorin distributed the deerskin packs of supplies. The one he handed to Luruthin looked less full than the others. Luruthin glanced inside it, found a blanket, two pouches of dried food, and a water skin. He looked at Vanorin, wanting to protest that he could carry more, but he suspected that even this light burden would become a trial before long.

He settled the bow and pack at his back and started off after Eliani, who was already walking up the hillside toward the trail that had led them hither. As the trees closed in around them and the path became a narrow track, Vanorin took the lead, followed by Birani, Eliani, Luruthin, and the other two guardians.

Luruthin glanced back, but the meadow was already hidden by trees. Wishing the best to Inóran and the others, he turned his thoughts toward home.

❀ Ghlanhras ❀

Shalár stood with Torith on a high platform beside the city gates, gazing over Ghlanhras. Work on the enclosures was progressing. The way from the gates to Darkwood Hall was now completely covered, and passages to the platforms overlooking the north road and the other guarded points along the walls were roofed and partially enclosed.

The darkwood used on these passages was salvaged from vacant houses on the west side of the city. Shalár had ordered their destruction to make way for a holding pen for kobalen. She could see the pen from where she stood, some hundred or more kobalen huddled within it. Another hunt would be needed before long.

Shalár's blood stirred at the thought, though she knew she could not lead the hunt. She must consider the safety of her child, and too many matters required her attention for her to leave Ghlanhras just now. Nor would she care to be absent when her people arrived from Nightsand.

Her gaze rose to the peak of Firethroat visible above the darkwood forest, steaming sullenly in the night. A flash of orange light told of some small disturbance within the volcano's maw.

Shalár frowned. She would have to observe Firethroat more closely. The night was young enough yet for a walk to the shore.

"Thank you, Torith. Carry on."

He bowed. "Bright Lady."

Shalár climbed down from the platform and started back to the hall, but a hail from outside the gate made her pause. She listened to Torith exchange words with the newcomers, and recognized Gavál's voice. Interested, she turned to await the opening of the gates.

The massive darkwood gates swung inward, passing beneath the roof of the enclosure, which had been built high at the gates to accommodate them. Gavál and three other hunters came in, pushing before them two bound ælven, a Stonereach and a Greenglen, both male. The Greenglen limped. All came to a halt before Shalár.

A moment's hope was extinguished—the Stonereach was not the one she had conceived with. Still, she examined both captives with interest, walking all around them. The ælven did not look at her. She turned to Gavál, who appeared pleased with himself as he bowed deeply before her.

"Bright Lady, we found these by the Lanarindel. They were fashioning a raft."

"Were there others with them?"

He shook his head. "No sign of any others."

Disappointing, but she could not blame Gavál for their absence. He had at least caught two of the ælven who had attacked the city.

She stepped toward the gate and addressed the Stonereach. "Come here."

When he did not respond she took hold of his khi and compelled him. He gave a strangled cry, then shuffled after her.

Shalár glanced at the Greenglen, who hastened to follow. She led them just outside the gates, to where the head of an ælven attacker killed in the fighting, another Stonereach, was impaled on a spear set at the side of the road.

"Is this a friend of yours?"

She made the Stonereach look at it. He said nothing, but his eyes widened in dread. The Greenglen glanced at the head, then quickly looked down again.

Feeling she had made her point, Shalár led them back into the city and signaled for the gates to be closed. She turned to Gavál.

"Well done. Bring them to the audience hall."

"Yes, Bright Lady."

She released the Stonereach, who drew a gasping breath. Ignoring him, Shalár strode along the passage to Darkwood Hall.

She would visit Firethroat another night. She wanted to question these captives. They would not be kept with the other ælven, she decided. These were warriors, and might incite the more docile city folk to unrest. No, she would keep them where she had kept her Stonereach and Othanin, though she would make certain first that the rooms were secure.

Passing through the hall to her private chambers, she glanced around for her ælven chamber attendant. The female sat on the floor by the door between Shalár's workroom and bedchamber, as Shalár had commanded. She was rather gaunt and wore an air of dejection. Her black hair was braided back severely, without ornament.

Shalár went into the bedchamber. "Help me out of these leathers."

The female rose and silently obeyed, her fingers fumbling a little at the buckles. Shalár stood still, observing the attendant's khi, watchful for any flare of resistance, but the female was submissive, as she had been since the first night of her service. Shalár had subdued her quickly then, with judicious application of khi and the threat of killing the female's father should she disobey. She had not had to repeat the lesson.

"Boots."

The attendant knelt and pulled off Shalár's boots. The second came off with difficulty, and the female's tugging nearly pulled Shalár off balance. Shalár thrust a heel against her chest in rebuke, pushing her backward. The ælven sprawled and lay still for a moment, then slowly sat up.

"Bring me the broidered robe, then put those away."

The female obeyed, keeping her gaze averted as she got to her feet and went to the wardrobe. She returned with the robe and held it for Shalár. It was silk, scarlet with firevines finely wrought in silver thread, one of the finest of Shalár's new garments. She donned it, then went out without another glance at the ælven.

Ranad was hovering idly at the door to the audience hall, and brightened at her approach. Shalár paused.

"Bring me that steward again, and bring a set of fresh clothes that will fit him."

Ranad looked curious. "Yes, Bright Lady."

She brushed past him into the hall, mounting the dais where her governor's chair stood. Its cushion had been covered in red at her orders, and flames carved into the curling smoke of its darkwood back. Darkshore ruled in Ghlanhras again, and all who sought audience with her would remember it.

Gavál was waiting at the back of the hall with his hunters and the ælven captives. Shalár beckoned one of the hall guards to her and gave him orders for the preparation of the holding rooms. He hastened away and she summoned Gavál with a gesture. He brought his prizes forward and made them kneel before her.

Shalár gazed at them for a moment, debating what information to seek of them. She already knew who they were, as far as she cared to know. She knew why they had come to Ghlanhras—to rescue Othanin and the Stonereach.

She knew from questioning the ælven attendants of Darkwood Hall that the female Stonereach who had escaped during her capture of the city was the daughter of Alpinon's governor, and she had found among Othanin's letters the messages that female had brought from the Ælven Council and the governor of Southfæld. It had amused Shalár to learn that Kelevon had escaped from them; she had assumed they would kill him. Fatally softhearted, the ælven.

She leaned forward, brushing her khi against that of the Stonereach. He flinched as if she had slapped him.

"Whither is your governor's daughter bound?"

He stared at the floor, blinking rapidly, silent. Shalár wrenched his khi and he cried out, but still did not answer. She twisted harder, until he fell into a faint. Releasing him, she turned her attention to the Greenglen, who hastily looked away from her gaze.

"Where is she bound?"

"I do not know."

She felt her way into his khi, found the dull pain of an arrow wound in his thigh, and sent fire into it. The ælven gasped and collapsed forward, then rolled onto his side clasping his leg. She waited for a moment until she was sure he would hear her, then spoke again.

"Where did you leave her?"

He gasped. "Outside the city. Oh, please stop!"

"She came here to deliver letters. Does she return to Southfæld?"

"I do not know. I do not know!"

"How many are with her?"

"T-ten? There were—twelve of us."

"Including your friends at the gates, I presume."

He made a gulping sound, but did not answer. Shalár let him go and he curled into himself, weeping and shivering.

She was annoyed at his lack of knowledge, but unsurprised. She did not share her plans with her own warriors. No doubt the Stonereach leader kept hers to herself.

Eight warriors with her, and they had all slipped through Shalár's grasp. Disappointing. Most likely they were in Woodrun by now. In the Stonereach's place, Shalár would be inciting the people of that town to fight, to arm and come against Ghlanhras. She needed to know if that was indeed coming to pass.

"Take them away, Gavál. Check the holding rooms yourself. If they make trouble, you will answer."

"Yes, Bright Lady."

Gavál bowed, then signaled his hunters to take the ælven out. Two of them carried the Stonereach, while the third prodded the Greenglen to his feet and made him limp from the hall. Shalár watched his slow progress, musing.

How quickly would an attack from Woodrun be organized? Several days had passed since the news must have reached the town. Shalár would need more kobalen before long, but if an attack was coming she could not spare the hunters from Ghlanhras.

Voices from the far end of the hall roused her. Ranad had returned with the steward, and was answering the hall guard's challenge. The steward's hands were bound behind him and a sack was slung across his shoulders, dangling at his back. Ranad shoved him to his knees at Shalár's feet before sweeping a bow.

"Bright Lady, here is the ælven you wanted."

"Thank you. Where are the clothes?"

"In that sack."

"Unbind him and bring the sack."

Shalár rose from her chair and waited for Ranad to obey her. He loosed the ælven's bonds and glanced at her, then picked up the sack.

The ælven was staring at the hem of her robe, where the firevines twined in silver on the silk that had once been orange and was now red. His troubled frown told her he recognized the garment. She smiled in amusement, then led the way to her private chambers, with Ranad hastening the steward behind her. In the workroom she turned to Ranad.

"Put it by the door."

The ælven steward's face lit with relief as he caught sight of the chamber attendant.

"Teshali!" He took a step toward her, then caught Shalár's eye and stopped, averting his gaze.

Shalár glanced at the attendant, whose face was alive with unaccustomed emotion. She, too, looked away.

Shalár watched them, trying to decide if their excitement would carry them to violence against her. She doubted it, but for the sake of her child's safety, she decided to keep Ranad in the room. She looked at him.

"Close the door."

Ranad obeyed, taking up a stance beside it. Shalár stepped up to the steward, who stood unmoving.

"You see? I have kept my pledge to you. Your daughter spends her days here, now, safe and doubtless bored out of her wits."

The steward made no answer. His daughter raised her eyes and a glance passed between them. Shalár sensed the intensity of their love in their khi. Useful, no doubt.

"I have a task for you."

Both ælven looked at her. She glanced at the female, then turned her attention to the male.

"If you cherish your daughter's safety, you will obey me exactly."

His brow creased with worry. He gave a single nod.

"You will go to Woodrun. Take one of the horses in the stables. You should be able to go there, spend a night, and return in seven nights, if you hasten. If you do not return by the seventh night hence, she dies."

The steward closed his eyes and nodded again. She saw a swallow move in his throat.

"I want information. You will spend one night and one day in Woodrun, visiting the market and every public lodge and tavern. You will listen, and ask questions only if you can do so without raising suspicion. You will say nothing of Ghlanhras, of me or my people. Do you know why I can trust you to say nothing?"

He glanced at her, surprise and confusion in his face. Shalár smiled.

"Because the longer it takes your ælven to learn about us, the longer it will be before they come against us. The next time ælven attack this city, your daughter dies."

The steward gasped, dread coming into his eyes. He looked at his daughter, but said nothing.

"Find out how many of the ælven who attacked Ghlanhras are in Woodrun. Find out if their leader is there—she is a Stonereach, daughter of Alpinon's governor—or any of her people, or Othanin. Find out if there is any movement to organize a force against us, and if so how many are raised. Do you understand?"

He nodded. Shalár gestured to Ranad to bring her the sack. He picked it up and strolled forward with it, lazily watching the ælven. Shalár took the sack and tossed it to the female.

"Help him bathe and dress."

Turning away, she left the room, taking Ranad with her. Outside she told him to stay near her chambers and inform her when the steward had departed.

"Your pardon, Bright Lady, but is it wise to leave them alone together? They may scheme—"

"Let them have their touching moment. It will make him the more eager to return. They can make no scheme that will mar my plans."

"Yes, Bright Lady."

"Were there any others seeking audience tonight?"

"No, Bright Lady."

"I will be in the gardens."

Ranad bowed as she strolled away, down the corridor that led to the elaborate private gardens behind Darkwood Hall. Moonlight smote her face as she stepped outside, bright enough to tingle against her skin. She frowned up at the orb that blazed out amid drifting clouds, then stepped into the shade of a laceleaf tree.

These gardens had been her favorite haunt as a child. She had played here, hidden here, buried her treasures beneath the trees and bushes and vented her youthful woes to the silent statues. She wandered the paths of crushed black stone now as she had then, seeking respite from her cares.

A large house to one side of the garden had accommodated the attendants, cooks, and others who served in Darkwood Hall. Now it housed Shalár's hunters. She glanced at it, then continued along the black path into the depths of the garden, where trees hid the buildings of Ghlanhras from view and one could pretend one was in a peaceful forest.

Water trickled in a stream alongside the path, chuckling now and again over small falls where the stones were carefully placed to create the most musical sounds. It masked the noises drifting to the gardens of the destruction of another vacant house and the work on the covered passages.

The moon did not show itself again to trouble Shalár, but remained cloaked in the gathering cloud. Shalár wandered the garden paths, discovering them anew, for this was the first night she had ventured here since her return. She frowned when she encountered some small change the ælven had made, and smiled with delight at finding others of her favorite places unaltered. At last she found herself in a glade she remembered all too well, standing before the statue of the fire maiden.

Carved from a single piece of ebonglass, the maiden stood atop a boulder of black rock taken from the mouth of Firethroat. She was fair and terrible, gazing sternly down at Shalár, evoking even now a whisper of the awe Shalár had felt as a child. The ælven who had long ago carved the statue had laid in subtle enchantments of khi, so that flickers of firelight seemed to dance in the maiden's hair of flame. Shalár had wanted to be like her.

She scarcely remembered the legend. Some nonsense about the maiden giving herself to the flames to appease Firethroat's wrath, as if the mountain were a living thing that cared in the least what its disgorgements destroyed, or could sense and appreciate the maiden's sacrifice. Instead of dying in the volcano's maw, the maiden was supposedly transformed and lived on as a spirit of flame, watching over the safety of Ghlanhras. Foolish as all ælven tales.

Not foolish.

The words were a whisper in her mind, and not her own. With a tingling in her flesh Shalár realized it was her daughter speaking to her. She held still, straining to hear more. She felt the child's presence as she often did, and had a sense that the spirit was trying to tell her something of importance.

You are like her.

Shalár glanced up at the fire maiden's face, smooth glass curving, cheeks gleaming as if wet with tears. She had given her life to the survival of her people, if that was what the spirit meant. It was the only way Shalár could think of in which she was at all like the fire maiden.

The tingling faded as her sense of the child diminished. No more would be said tonight. It must take a great effort to say even so much, Shalár concluded. She felt frustrated, and wondered if the child felt so as well.

These moments were gifts, however fleeting. She closed her eyes, treasuring it up as a memory.

Like the fire maiden, am I? Well, the ælven shall soon see that it is so. While I breathe, I will fight to keep Fireshore for my people.

A whisper troubled the leaves of the trees, and a moment later she felt the gentle brush of raindrops on her face. She opened her eyes and gazed upward into the gray sky. A distant rumble, felt underfoot as much as heard, told of Firethroat's restlessness.

"Even you. I will fight even you."

She stayed a moment, as if waiting for an answer from the uncaring mountain. None came, of course. She looked at the fire maiden again, real drops sliding down the statue's face now. The flickers in her hair had gone dark.

Turning her back, Shalár walked away, back to the hall where she oversaw her people's well-being.

❀ Ebon Mountains ❀

By the time the sun rose, Luruthin was starting to be weary. The track they followed was little more than a game trail, and at times it disappeared altogether as they crossed rocky outcrops and ridges. They were traveling nearly straight south, with the winter sun behind their shoulders.

Ahead, rising into the cold blue sky, was the towering shape of the Great Sleeper, its upper shoulders dusted in snow, its peak shrouded in cloud. They would skirt its eastern flanks and continue along the mountains as they passed into the Steppes. Though it was harder going than the trade roads, Luruthin was in complete agreement with Eliani's wish to avoid the roads until they were well out of Fireshore.

Shalár's face came unbidden to mind and he shuddered, shaking his head to rid himself of the memory. He had no breath to spare, but he could think through a song in his mind, and he did so to keep other thoughts away.

He chose a humorous tune, long and repetitive, of the sort he and Eliani and other guardians had often sung around campfires at night while on patrol. Setting his steps to its rhythm, he was able to keep pace with Eliani, and the foolish story staved off unwelcome memories.

At midday they crossed a small stream and Vanorin called a halt to let the party rest and eat a little. They filled their skins with the frigid water and sat in spots of sunshine that broke through the evergreens here and there.

Luruthin found the sun too bright and moved into the shade of a cluster of fir trees. He took a strip of dried venison from his pack and chewed at it without enthusiasm. Eliani came to sit nearby, glancing at him with concern.

"Are you tired?"

"Yes, but I can continue."

"You will tell us if you need to stop."

"Well, I hope you will notice if I fall on my face."

Eliani smiled, but the concern yet creased her brow. He found the pitying looks she turned toward him upsetting, so he closed his eyes until Vanorin called them back to the march.

The captain gave him a hard look as he got to his feet. "Are you fit?"

Luruthin slung his pack, which indeed seemed heavy now, over his shoulder. "Fit enough."

Vanorin gazed sharply at him, then gave a nod and started forward, leading them upward. Soon the trail disappeared and they had to push through the forest, slowed by heavy undergrowth and uncertain footing.

The sky clouded over with a thin veil of gray, and the sun when they glimpsed it was a pale, shrouded light. The air was still, cold but not sharp. Luruthin was glad to be moving, for the walking kept him warm.

Late in the afternoon Vanorin called another halt, and left the party waiting while he climbed a tree to get a view of their progress. Luruthin sat down at once, wincing as dry needles pricked him through the thin cloth of his legs. He could wish for a pair of deerskin legs to go with his tunic. Ungrateful, he knew.

He shrugged out of his pack and lay down with it pillowing his head. Above, the clouds seemed to be thickening. The forest was quiet, its creatures watching, waiting for the onset of a storm.

Luruthin realized that he had withdrawn his khi from any awareness of the living woodlands. He was holding himself closed, a state he had assumed as defense in Ghlanhras. There was no need for it now, and he sought to alter it, reaching out experimentally toward the nearest tree, an ancient fir. He felt its life, slow, silent and powerful in roots that spread deep into the earth. It gave him heart with an intensity that surprised him.

Live in the world, a tenet of the creed. One he had ceased to uphold for a while. It would be best if he resumed it, but slowly, slowly. He could not open himself all at once.

He was glad to be with his people, his kindred and companions. Glad to be walking free beneath the sky. These were the gifts he should hold in his thoughts, as a light against dark memories.

And Jhinani. It almost hurt to think of her, but she, too, was a gift. He should compose a message to send to her. Some cheerful news, some word of hope. When he tried, he could only remember the dark truth that he must someday share with her, and his heart recoiled. Not yet, not yet.

Footsteps hastening toward them made him sit up. Vanorin was returning, slightly winded.

"There is a ridge ahead that we can reach by nightfall, if we hasten. It will be a good place to camp." Vanorin drank from his water skin, then looked at Luruthin. "Can you bear a push until evening?"

Luruthin rubbed his thighs. "I think so."

"Eat some fruit, it will give you strength."

Luruthin was not hungry, but he knew the sense in Vanorin's words and reached for his pack. He ate a dried stonefruit and kept out the pouch, tying it to his waist with a leather thong that he found in the bottom of the pack. There was a comb there, too. A simple thing, to be able to comb one's hair when one wished, but also an enormous comfort.

Another gift. Luruthin's lips twitched in a smile. Giving thanks was also part of the creed. He was trying, with all his heart, to be grateful.

Vanorin hastened them onward, crossing a valley and pointing out the ridge on its far side. It seemed rather distant to Luruthin, and the climb would be steep on the opposite side of the valley, but he resolved to keep up.

For a while the way was clear of brush, allowing them to make good speed as they followed Vanorin back and forth across the steep slope. As they approached the valley bottom the rushing sound of water reached them. The stream was small but swift, and Vanorin secured a rope to a tree before crossing, tying it to another at the far side. This was for his sake, Luruthin knew, feeling slightly ashamed and annoyed.

He held the rope as he crossed, cold water stabbing into his lower legs and the rocks slippery underfoot. The others all used the rope as well though he suspected they did not need it. Onami came last, untying the far end of the rope and gathering it as she came. Just before reaching the bank she slipped and caught herself with the rope, splashing out of the stream to take Vanorin's reaching hand.

They paused to fill their water skins. Luruthin drank as much of the icy water as he could stand, and ate another stonefruit while he stamped his numb feet and tried to shake off the cold. He was too sensitive to it, he thought. Usually he was stronger than this. He was holding better than he had on the journey to the Lost's camp, though.

Vanorin pushed them onward, crossing back and forth on the south slope as they climbed, now. Before long Luruthin's breath rasped in his throat, and his lower legs began to burn with the effort. Twice Vanorin halted to let him catch his breath. The second time Luruthin noticed tiny snowflakes beginning to drift down. Looking up, he saw a thick sky above the treetops, and many more flakes falling.

It would snow well into the night, he realized. There was no wind to push the storm away. This was why Vanorin wished to reach the ridge by nightfall. He must be hoping to find a good shelter against the snow. If need be they could cut boughs of fir and pine to protect them, and such a shelter would be easier to make against a rock wall.

Luruthin drank, forced himself to eat one more fruit, and nodded to Vanorin. His stomach complained at the cold water. He ignored it and trudged after Eliani, too tired even to think of a song.

Dark had fallen by the time they reached the ridge. A thumb's width of snow lay on the ground, and the flakes continued to fall, larger and thicker now.

Vanorin found a small, clear place that was fairly level and sheltered by a crop of rock that looked ready to tumble at the first tremor. Luruthin leaned against the rock while the others set about cutting branches, brushing away the snow, gathering firewood. He was too weary to help, to his dismay.

Eliani dumped an armload of dry sticks beside him. "Can you kindle us a fire?"

Luruthin nodded and pushed away from the rock. Leaving his pack, bow, and quiver beside it, he took up two handfuls of the kindling and moved to the center of the tiny camp. Piling the sticks together, he held his hand over them and focused his khi upon the dry heart of one twig, building warmth within it, growing it into heat, into a spark.

He found it difficult to concentrate on the task, one so easy every ælven child learned it before learning to write. His lungs burned with cold as he drew in deep breaths. He was angry with himself, and he used that to feed the feeble spark he had made.

At last a yellow tongue of flame flickered. He fed it with more twigs and with scraps of shreddy bark handed to him by Birani. He became aware that the others were in the camp, moving about. Glancing behind him he saw them building a low roof against the rock outcrop, covering cross poles with boughs of evergreen.

Returning his attention to the fire, he fed it carefully, building it up with heavier sticks and the first of a pile of small logs that Felahran had brought. The guardian must have acquired a woodcutter's knife somewhere, among the gifts from Bitterfield, perhaps.

Snowflakes hissed as they vanished in the flames. Luruthin began to feel the fire's warmth against his knees, and sighed gratefully.

"Ah, excellent!" Vanorin crouched beside him and held out his hands toward the fire.

Luruthin glanced up and saw that the roof now extended over him, with a notch left for the fire's smoke. The others gathered beneath it, close quarters, but that was an advantage in the cold. They dug in their packs for food. Eliani produced a loaf of soft bread and tore it into six portions. She smiled as she handed one to Luruthin.

"You are getting stronger. You would not have made that climb a few days ago."

Luruthin pulled off a bit of the bread and ate it. Its flavor was good, but he was not especially hungry.

He glanced at Vanorin. "I wonder if we will be able to move at all, tomorrow."

"A good question."

If the snow fell all night and fell deeply, they would not be able to continue southward. They would have to return down the valley and seek lower ground for their journey. They were well south of Bitterfield, now, but not out of Fireshore. That would take another day or two, at least.

Eliani offered Luruthin a slice of cheese from her knife. He took it and ate it, but the taste was sour in his mouth and he refused a second piece. He nibbled at the bread until he could not manage more, and handed what was left back to Eliani.

"Too many stonefruits?"

The teasing in her voice reminded him of childhood. He smiled, then poked at the fire with a stick of kindling.

Vanorin hung two of the blankets across the front of the shelter, trapping more of the fire's warmth inside and keeping out the drifting snow. Gradually the party settled down to rest, their feet toward the fire, sharing the remaining blankets.

Luruthin lay with Eliani on one side and Felahran on the other. He tried to clear his thoughts, empty his mind for rest, though lately doing so had opened the way for dark memories to rise up. To counter that he thought of pleasant memories, old times with the Guard. He could imagine himself on patrol now, in the high reaches of Alpinon, guarding the roads below from kobalen.

He became aware that his thoughts were drifting, aware of deep silence around him. The night seemed to press down on him. No stars, no friendly light. Darkness enwrapped him, a darkness so heavy he felt trapped by it, so intense it seemed the sun would never breach it.

With a gasp he sat up and threw off the blanket covering him. He stumbled to his feet and out of the shelter, nearly pulling down one of the blankets in his haste.

Outside he stood gasping in the cold, blinking as snowflakes settled on his face. The snow lay nearly a handspan deep, and the cold swiftly penetrated his legs, but he stood shuddering, drinking deep gulps of the night air.

He heard someone emerge from the shelter and turned his head swiftly. Vanorin stood there, concern writ on his face.

"Luruthin?"

"I h-had to get out. Get some air. I felt confined."

His throat tightened on the words. He glanced away again, into the swirling snow. The panic he had felt was fading.

"I see. Stay a moment."

Vanorin went into the shelter and returned with a blanket. He wrapped it around Luruthin's shoulders.

"Th-thank you."

"Will you be all right?"

"Yes. Thank you."

Vanorin gazed at him, worry in the dark eyes. "Do not go far."

Luruthin stared back, realizing the captain feared he would leave, wander off into the frozen night. He drew the blanket closer.

"I will return."

Vanorin nodded, then went back into the shelter. Luruthin turned away again, gazing at the falling snow. He felt calmer though he was not yet ready to go back inside.

He was annoyed with himself for panicking so, for disturbing the rest of his fellows. Perhaps he *should* walk away into the snow and cease to be a burden on them.

But to do that would be to waste the effort they had spent to free him. The *lives* that had been spent.

He closed his eyes, swallowing. He could not do that, render their sacrifice meaningless. The worst was over. It was his obligation to make the best of the gift of freedom the guardians had given him.

Glancing toward the shelter, he saw the snow piled on the boughs of its makeshift roof. That was what had made him feel confined—the muffling layer of snow. Now that he knew what it was, he thought he could return inside.

He took a last deep breath and gazed upward at the fat flakes drifting out of the darkness. The air was no longer quite so still, and the snow danced and swirled over his head.

Father—

Luruthin gasped and for a moment lost his balance. He shifted his feet and blinked as a snowflake struck one eye. He shook his head vigorously, then listened.

It had been his daughter's voice, he was certain. He stood still, straining to hear more.

No sound came, but through the drifting snow he saw a pair of golden eyes in the darkness, blazing with the rage and hunger of a catamount. He took a step back instinctively. The eyes faded, leaving him staring into the snowfall.

For a long time he stood straining to hear or see more. No more came, though, and at last the cold drove him back into the shelter.

Faint heat rose from the coals of the fire. Luruthin stirred them and added wood, pushing the coals close on either side so that it would burn slowly. Vanorin lay uncovered between the others, so Luruthin settled beside him and threw the blanket over them both.

Lying back, he tried to relax. The stillness caused by the snow layer overhead closed around him again.

To keep himself calm he reached out to the woods, touching the khi of the many trees outside the shelter, feeling their strength and their deep, silent patience. In their roots they knew the snow would not last forever. It would stop falling eventually. It would melt, not at once, perhaps, but in time. The sun would return again.

The sun would return, and he would find his way out of darkness. The memory of the glowing eyes troubled him, but not knowing their meaning, he could make no response. He sensed no catamount near, nor any other creature moving in the forest. He would have to wait out the storm, and see what the morrow might bring.

"Eyes?" Eliani frowned as she watched Luruthin toy with the fire, which he had built up again after sunrise. The snow had ceased, but it had fallen fairly deep, and Vanorin had decided to let the sun work at it a while before they moved on.

Luruthin nodded, frowning himself as he mused. "I thought they might belong to a catamount. They were angry, and hungry."

Her stomach growled. She dug a piece of bread from her pack. "You think it was a vision, not a real animal?"

"I know it was not really there. It may have been a warning."

"Spirit-sent."

Luruthin gazed toward the front of the shelter, seeming not to see the blankets that blocked his view. After a moment, he nodded.

Eliani tore the chunk of bread in half and offered a share to him. He shook his head. He had not broken fast, save for a few sips of water, and this worried her.

His vision worried her as well. She had never heard of eyes appearing as a warning. She wished she could ask Heléri about it, for Heléri knew more about the spirit world than anyone else of her acquaintance.

Glancing aside, she saw that Vanorin was watching them. She offered him the bread Luruthin had refused, and he took it with a nod of thanks. She held his gaze for a moment, silently questioning. He glanced at Luruthin and gave a small shrug.

Well, they would go carefully today. They would have to take care in any case, for the snow would make crossing the heights treacherous. She glanced toward the smoke vent in the roof, where the sky showed bright, sharp blue. At least they had sun.

By the time the snow covering their shelter began to drip with melting, Vanorin had everyone ready to march. They took down the last two blankets and stowed them away in packs, scattered the coals and doused them with snow, and pulled apart the roof, taking the stripped support poles for walking sticks.

Vanorin took up the lead again, prodding at the snow ahead with his stick. It was not deep, but in places it drifted as high as his knee. They went slowly, carefully.

Eliani was glad for the occasional splashes of sunlight across her shoulders, though the brightness of the snow blinded her whenever they crossed open spaces. They climbed higher, making for a hot spring marked on Kivhani's map. If they reached it they would spend the night there.

Vanorin called fewer halts, possibly because their careful pace seemed to tire Luruthin less. Whenever Eliani glanced back at him he was walking with his head bowed, frowning, squinting against the bright snow. Her thoughts kept returning to his vision, and she was watchful, keeping open to any change in the khi of the forests around them.

Glancing westward she searched for signs of another storm, and was glad to see that the sky was clear. The Great Sleeper was powdered white down to its shoulders. She felt safer here in the heights, despite the cold and the hazardous snow, than she would down on the trade road.

In the afternoon the wind picked up sharply, and she and Luruthin took out their blankets to use as cloaks. Their progress continued slow, although Eliani could see that they were steadily gaining ground. By dusk they had come near a jutting finger of rock that was a landmark on the map. The spring was some distance beyond it, and Eliani resigned herself to not reaching it until the next day.

Vanorin found a curved hollow in the rocky mountainside that would accommodate them all. Using their sticks as poles again, he and Felahran set up a frame over which to hang blankets across the front of the space.

There was no room to make a fire. They would have had to dig beneath the snow to find firewood anyway, and it was enough to be out of the wind, sharing the warmth of their bodies in the close space.

Eliani joined Luruthin as the party settled in together for the night. "Will you be all right?"

"Yes. It was the snow overhead that troubled me before. I felt trapped in darkness ..."

Dismay crossed his face as words failed him. He shook his head as if to clear it. "This will be all right."

She smiled to encourage him, then lay back between him and Birani. Outside the wind moaned among the rocks and whispered in the evergreens, a sad sound.

Eliani felt her brow grow warm and smiled as she closed her eyes. *Yes, my love?*

We are making camp. Where are you?

On the shoulders of the Sleeper, crouched behind our blankets. Come and warm us.

I wish I could. More snow?

No, it is clear tonight, but bitter cold.

They shared what little news they had, then settled into comfortable silence, holding each other's thought as they might have held hands were they together in flesh. Eliani tried to lie still, but found it difficult not to fidget. The close quarters, everyone touching his neighbor, helped to keep them warm but made it difficult to relax. She was aware of everyone's khi, and knew that the others, too, were waiting out the uncomfortable night.

At length Vanorin sat up and remained so. Eliani watched him as he listened, frowning, to the low moaning of the wind. It had fallen off somewhat, she thought. She felt cold on one side, and turning her head saw that Birani was gone, then remembered that the guardian had stepped out some while ago.

With a cold sinking in her heart, Eliani realized that Vanorin was listening for Birani's return. He turned his head to meet her gaze, then stood.

Eliani got up as well, folding her edge of the blanket around Luruthin. She followed Vanorin outside.

The wind had indeed fallen, though the air was bitter and the stars glittered overhead like sparks of white fire. Birani must have gone to the place they had agreed on for use as a privy, for no other footprints were visible in the snow than the trail worn down by the party. Eliani felt the need to make use of the privy herself, now that she was out in the cold.

She followed Vanorin until he suddenly halted. Eliani looked past him to where a dark shape lay in the snow.

"No!" She clapped a hand over her mouth at Vanorin's sharp glance.

Her heart hammered. She followed Vanorin's cautious advance and stopped when he held up a hand. He crouched and pushed the figure over. It was Birani, blood clotted at a wound upon her throat, just beneath one ear.

Eliani moaned softly. Vanorin gently touched Birani, seeking a pulse. Eliani knew that he would find none. There was no spark of khi in the air around the guardian. She was dead.

Luruthin held his blanket close as he hurried after Eliani. He had known something was wrong when he heard her startled cry. Now she turned and gestured to him to stay away, but he had already seen what lay beyond.

A female, dead. Birani, their clan-sister.

Shock and horror swept through him, then his gaze fixed on her throat, where dark, frozen blood had scarcely closed a sharp cut. He could smell the blood despite the cold, and it sparked a strange twist in his gut. Turning away, he stumbled a few steps and then fell on his knees in the snow, retching.

Hands gripped his shoulders as his stomach heaved. When the spasms ceased, he felt shaken and weak.

"Come away." Eliani's voice was gentle.

She helped him stand, retrieved the blanket he had dropped and shook it free of snow, and supported him as they walked back to the hollow. Felahran and Onami came toward them, faces anxious.

"Birani has been attacked and killed. Please help Vanorin."

Looking alarmed, they hastened past. Luruthin wished that he could help as well. He felt angry at his weakness.

When they reached the hollow he sat down, huddling in the blanket. "Go and help them, I will be all right."

"I will not leave you alone."

A shudder passed through him. Eliani knelt beside him and wrapped her arms around him. Warmth spread through him from her touch. He sighed and bowed his head, closing his eyes. He had not realized how cold he was.

"So your vision *was* a warning."

He remembered the savage eyes he had seen, then the image of dead guardian returned to him even more vividly. Frozen blood black against her flesh, black spatters in the snow.

"But this was the work of no beast. Her throat was cut, not bitten."

"Kobalen, perhaps."

"Up here, in the snow? I doubt it."

Eliani made no answer. If it had not been kobalen, it must have been alben. Yes, alben.

Horror shook him, making him shiver again. Eliani's arms tightened around him. How had the alben found them? Had they hunted him even into the heights of the Ebons? The eyes in his vision had been golden, not black.

Fear froze his thinking, but he was able to find a flaw in the reasoning that alben had attacked Birani. If the alben had followed them, why had they waited so long, and why had they not attacked the entire party?

Sounds reached him from outside, voices and shuffling footsteps. They had brought Birani back with them, he realized as he heard them laying her down. Vanorin was talking of finding wood for a pyre.

Eliani raised her head, listening. Luruthin drew away.

"Go ahead. I am all right."

She got up and went out. Alone behind the blankets, Luruthin shivered as he listened to their plans.

In the morning they would build a pyre for Birani, cut wood for it if they had to. They would take her sword and a few of her belongings back to Alpinon to give to her family. They had no leisure to make a conce, but they could set a plain stone to mark the place where she had fallen, and later it could be replaced with a conce, if anyone wished to make the journey.

Luruthin closed his eyes. Honoring everyone they had lost on this mission would require setting conces from Alpinon to Ghlanhras. He had never expected that so many would fall, that the hazards would be so numerous and so deadly. Most of the misfortune could be attributed to the alben, some directly to Shalár. A twist of anger tightened in his chest.

Someone pulled the blankets aside, letting in a gust of cold air. Luruthin looked up and saw Eliani, burdened with Birani's leather armor. He could smell the blood on it, and his empty stomach tightened into a knot.

"Put this on."

He stared at her, aghast. He shook his head.

"It will keep you warm. Put it on."

Her voice was stern and commanding. She dropped the armor beside him and went back outside.

He gazed at the crumpled heap of leather, tears welling in his eyes. He did not feel right benefiting by Birani's death, but Eliani was correct. He must avail himself of every advantage.

Poor Birani. He remembered her dancing a few steps around the campfire in the Lost's meadow, just two nights since, laughing and tossing her freshly braided hair. She was slighter of build than he. With trembling fingers he reached out to loosen the straps of the leathers.

"Vanorin, do not go alone." Eliani could not keep the dread from her voice.

"Onami may come with me. Stay here."

Onami glanced at her, then followed Vanorin down the trail back toward where they had found Birani. Eliani watched, feeling helpless, foolish, frightened. She wanted to command their return.

She was about to go back to the camp when she heard Vanorin's startled cry. She ran, heart pounding.

At a turning she saw Vanorin on his knees, Onami sprawled, sword fallen from her hand. Blotches of blood, dark on the snow, and a face snarling at her.

"Kelevon!"

He let his snarl become a grin. "Hello, my sweet."

Even as she reached for her sword, she heard footsteps behind her. Kelevon threw his knife, and Eliani heard the thud of it striking home.

Half turning, she glimpsed Felahran, the knife lodged in his throat. She let out a cry of dismay as she turned toward Kelevon, drawing her sword.

Pain swept over her; khi that was fire, angry fire. Stunned, she stumbled, then it was gone and Kelevon was at Vanorin's side.

"No!"

Eliani lunged forward, sword swinging. Kelevon sprang away, laughing.

"Farewell, sweet Eliani!"

He turned and fled. She would have pursued but for fear that Vanorin needed her help.

"Coward! *Traitor!*"

It felt good to scream that at him. An arrow hissed past her as she turned; Luruthin stood over Felahran, bow in hand. She met his gaze, then knelt beside Vanorin.

"Are you wounded?"

He shook his head, breathing unsteadily. "Help the others."

She put a hand on his shoulder briefly, and was reassured. His khi was far from calm, but he was unhurt.

She stood, swallowed, and went to Felahran.

Luruthin lowered his bow. Kelevon was out of sight, now, lost among the trees. Becoming aware of the sound of anguished weeping, he looked down and saw Eliani on her knees beside Felahran. She turned him on his side, and blood oozed from around the knife in his throat.

The smell of blood smote Luruthin again, so powerfully he gave a small gasp. Looking around, he saw Onami lying crumpled, her blood melting the snow around her. Vanorin had struggled to his feet and was coming toward Eliani.

A powerful cramp gripped Luruthin's stomach. He was empty, and suddenly desperately hungry, and for a wild moment the blood smelled like food. Swallowing, he shook his head and took a step toward Eliani and Vanorin.

Vanorin was speaking. "You cannot help him. He is gone."

Eliani raised a tear-streaked face. "Onami?"

Vanorin shook his head, then glanced up at Luruthin. "We need to move them. Can you help?"

Luruthin nodded, though he felt faint with hunger. He slung his bow at his back, and the three of them moved Felahran and Jhathali up to the side of the cliff where they had camped, laying them beside Birani.

Vanorin took a small woodcutter's knife from his pack and they went out to gather wood, staying together, watching and listening, keeping close to the camp. They worked in silence.

Luruthin's thoughts went from grief to anger to fear that Kelevon would attack again, or had gone to fetch others. Vanorin seemed to fear that as well, for he pushed for speed. He cut down dead saplings whole and Eliani and Luruthin dragged them up to the camp, stacking them to make a pyre. When Vanorin judged they had enough, he and Eliani prepared the three bodies for burning, taking their swords and pouches to carry away.

Luruthin sat against the rock wall, arms across his anguished stomach as he watched. The blood smell pervaded his awareness, making it hard to think of anything else. He considered trying to eat, but though he was hungry his stomach rebelled at the thought of food. He took a few sips of water instead, which eased him a little.

Vanorin summoned him to help lay the dead across the pyre. Luruthin's arms trembled as together they lifted the three fallen guardians one by one. He, Vanorin, and Eliani stood gazing at them for a moment, then Vanorin looked at Eliani, who coughed and spoke.

"Spirits, welcome those who have left this flesh to cross into your realm. Birani, Onami, and Felahran. Their service shall be remembered. May they walk in light henceforward."

The last words came out sounding strangled. Fresh tears streaked her cold-reddened cheeks. Vanorin wept silently as well, and Luruthin felt his own tears falling, drawing lines of cold down his face.

Eliani raised her hands toward the pyre. Vanorin and Luruthin did likewise. Luruthin felt khi stinging in the air as the three of them summoned fire within the dry wood.

The pyre burst into flame. Luruthin stumbled back from the sudden heat. Feeling weak, he backed against the cliff wall and sank to the ground once more.

Eliani glanced over her shoulder at him, then returned her gaze to the fire. Vanorin went into the hollow. Luruthin could hear him moving behind the blankets, going through the packs, consolidating supplies.

They must leave here. They could not stay, nor did Luruthin wish to stay and watch the flesh of their companions burn to ash. He looked southward, though he could not see very far toward their goal. His gaze drifted upward, to the sky filled with shining stars. Did their friends walk up there, now, among the stars?

No, the spirit realm was not among the stars, though the custom was to look skyward when speaking of spirits. He thought again of his daughter's voice, and remembered the eyes that he believed she had shown him.

With a start he sat up. Golden eyes! Steppegard eyes, Kelevon's! She *had* been trying to warn him.

Kelevon's eyes were still golden, Luruthin thought, frowning as he tried to remember. The traitor's hair had gone half-white, though. He was becoming alben.

Sickened, Luruthin leaned back against the rock again. That one who had been ælven could attack his own kind so brutally horrified him. With bitterness he remembered Kelevon's past unkindness to Eliani— trivial compared with what he had done this night, but indicative that cruelty was part of his nature. In that sense he had been like the alben all along.

Vanorin emerged. Luruthin was surprised to see him empty-handed. Vanorin glanced at him and summoned him with a gesture. Luruthin got to his feet, pausing as a cramp seized his gut.

"Let us place a stone where Birani fell."

Slowly Eliani turned her head to look at Vanorin, then nodded. "No need for one here. This place we will remember."

The three of them walked back to the spot where Birani had been killed. Compared with where the others had fallen near the cliff, there was less blood here.

Kelevon had drunk it, Luruthin realized with a fierce pang of anger. Immediately another cramp bent him nearly double. Vanorin looked at him sharply, but Luruthin shook his head as the cramp passed. He straightened, and helped Vanorin and Eliani roll a small boulder to the place where Birani had died.

The effort left him dizzy and winded. Eliani placed a hand on his shoulder, her face concerned. Khi blazed through him at her touch. He closed his eyes, letting it flow through him, wanting more. It did ease him somewhat.

"We must go." Vanorin's voice.

Luruthin opened his eyes, feeling a stab of anger though he knew Vanorin was right. In silence he followed the others back to the hollow.

The pyre was melting snow from all the trees nearby. The space before the hollow was wet, and the water had begun to soak into the bottom edges of the hanging blankets. Vanorin pushed one aside and fetched out three packs, two of them heavily loaded. He handed the lightest to Luruthin, along with a sword in its scabbard on a belt.

"Felahran's. You might as well have the use of it."

Luruthin nodded and strapped on the belt while Vanorin strapped Jhathali's sword to his own back. Eliani used Birani's scabbard to hold her own sword, tossing her makeshift sling of tangled net onto the pyre, and wrapped Birani's blade in a blanket before tying it to her back. She shouldered her pack over it, and her bow and quiver over them.

Luruthin lifted his own pack, bow, and quiver. He knew Vanorin had made his burden as light as possible, but with the added weight of the leathers he wore, he felt weary before they had even begun to march.

Vanorin left the blankets hanging and the spare supplies behind them. He handed a walking stick to Luruthin and one to Eliani, keeping a third for himself.

They paused to gaze at the pyre once more, now so hot they could not come within an armspan of it. At last Vanorin turned away, starting southward.

"Come."

Eliani gestured to Luruthin to go second, but Luruthin shook his head. Kelevon was roaming these woods, and Eliani's back should be protected. He managed a smile.

"I will shout if I cannot keep up, or perhaps you will hear me tumble down the slope."

"You look pale. Are you well?"

"Not very, but I will manage."

He took three long swallows from his water flask and left it slung at his hip. The water churned in his stomach as he walked, but eased the hunger pangs somewhat.

As before, Vanorin tested the ground ahead with his stick. The snow was not too deep, but their progress was slow. Even so, Luruthin soon found himself lagging behind. He glanced eastward and saw the dawn beginning to lighten the horizon's edge. He pushed himself forward, straining to catch up to the others.

Vanorin and Eliani paused at the top of a ridge. Luruthin saw Vanorin pointing southward, and as he reached them the captain turned to glance at him. Breathing hard, Luruthin saw a river glinting cold in the valley below. Not the Basarindel, he knew. Some lesser watercourse.

Vanorin looked at him. "The spring is on the far side. Can you continue?"

"Yes, if you will give me a moment to catch my breath."

Realizing that his legs were trembling, Luruthin sat down. He pulled off his pack, knowing he would not be able to stand again with it on his back.

Eliani sat beside him and opened her own pack, taking out a pouch of dried fruit. She offered one to Luruthin. He took it and raised it to his mouth, but the smell repelled him and his stomach clenched in protest. Shaking his head, he gave it back.

"You must eat. Some meat?"

"No. Not now."

He closed his eyes, breathing deeply, trying to calm the pounding of his heart. They could not stay in this high place. Too cold, too exposed. He thought about reaching the river. That much he could manage, and then he would think about the next goal.

Vanorin's footsteps roused him. Opening his eyes, he saw the captain returning toward them from the east.

"I find no sign of Kelevon behind us, or below. I think he has gone."

Eliani's face hardened. "I should have killed him. He used khi as a *weapon!* I was so surprised...."

"He will not surprise us again."

"No." Eliani looked up at the captain. "What did he do to you?"

Vanorin's face went grim. "As you said, he used khi."

Remembering how Shalár had done the same to him, Luruthin shuddered. It was an outrageous invasion, painful and terrifying. A horrible distortion of what should be a respectful intimacy.

"It is plain that he cares nothing for the creed." Vanorin glanced at Luruthin. "None of us goes anywhere alone."

Luruthin nodded. Even if Kelevon was not following them, they were vulnerable to other dangers. A catamount might attack a solitary ælven. Kobalen in any numbers would not hesitate to strike.

"Perhaps we should turn east and make for the road."

Eliani sighed wearily. "We must cross this river in any case. Let us cross it high, where it will be smaller. Let us find the spring, then we can decide."

"Very well."

Vanorin glanced toward Luruthin. Suppressing a groan, Luruthin stood up, pausing for a moment to get his balance. He looked down at the river. The descent was steep, but not too far. He thought he could manage it. He hoped so.

He drank a little more water, then lifted his burdens. His calves complained as the party started downward. The snow was deeper here, under the shade of the thick evergreen forest. Vanorin broke a trail for them, turning across and across the steep slope. He paused at every turn to let Luruthin catch up.

Each step seemed to jolt Luruthin's aching knees. He felt numbness beginning to claim his mind, the same sort of weariness he had felt as they fled through the darkwood forest.

By the time they neared the river the sky was growing light, the glow of dawn visible between tall treetops. A roaring sound was growing in the back of Luruthin's awareness. He thought at first that it was caused by weariness, but when Vanorin paused to await him, he saw that the others heard the sound as well.

They were pointing eastward, nodding in agreement. As Luruthin reached them Vanorin looked at him.

"A waterfall. We are near its head. Eliani would like to view it, if you agree."

Luruthin shrugged slightly, then shifted his pack to ease an ache in one shoulder. He was too weary to be charmed by the thought of admiring a waterfall, but would be glad of any chance to rest.

Vanorin started eastward, no longer turning but making steady progress downward toward the river. The roaring grew louder, much louder, then suddenly Luruthin could see the water ahead through the trees, looking black in the shadow of the valley. The river was perhaps three rods across, flowing level and silent toward its fall.

They turned to walk along its course. Ice dripped into the river from the snowy bank. A cool breeze blew across the water, and the glow of the coming sun increased above the mountain ridge on the far side. Luruthin found himself blinking at its brightness.

They reached the top of the cascade and paused to look down. The water poured over a shelf of rock that stretched over openness for perhaps a rod, the space behind it broken back, as if some softer rock beneath the shelf was crumbling away. Eventually the shelf would break and fall. Looking down, Luruthin saw huge blades of rock from earlier collapses in the pool below, vanishing and reappearing out of the drifting mist.

The sight made him dizzy and he took a step backward. The cascade was not the highest he had even seen, nor the most powerful, but it was troubling enough. Water always disrupted khi, and so much water churning with such force made him feel out of balance.

Eliani looked at him. "It is higher than the Three Shades, I think."

Though her voice was casual her words sent a shock ringing through Luruthin's soul as he remembered the last time he had been at the Shades. Vanorin met his gaze and Luruthin saw that he remembered as well.

They had been together, on that twilit evening when they had seen one of the shades that gave the falls its name. A vivid memory returned to Luruthin of watching the maiden in white leap into the falls, then drift with impossible peacefulness in the churning waters of the pool before fading into its dark, cold depths.

The vision had terrified them, and even now fear and bewilderment returned to shake Luruthin. Heléri had said that it was the shade of Josæli, who had leapt to her death in the falls many centuries before. She had also told them that the appearance of a shade was often a response to some great disturbance of khi, and that a shade had appeared in the falls before the first Midrange War.

Well, now there had been another battle at Midrange. Luruthin wondered if that had been what summoned the shade, or if she had appeared in response to something more immediate, in response to the fate that awaited him and Vanorin in Fireshore.

Shuddering, he turned away from the falls, walking upstream a few paces to where the roar was somewhat less overpowering. Here the water was silent as it glided toward its violent descent. Silent and black. He glanced across the valley and winced at the brightness of the coming sunrise.

"Luruthin?"

He turned to see Eliani and Vanorin approaching. Eliani looked concerned.

"Are you all right?"

"I was dizzy for a moment. I am better now."

Eliani glanced at Vanorin, then at the river. "We cannot cross here."

Vanorin nodded. "Upstream, perhaps."

They set off along the river bank, climbing over ice-slick rocks, sometimes moving into the woods for better footing. Slow going, and weary work.

Luruthin felt himself beginning to flag. His mouth hung open as his breath rasped cold in his throat. A throbbing ache filled his head, and his feet dragged as he walked.

They reached a pool at the foot of a much smaller fall, perhaps two rods high, barely more than a ripple in the river's long journey down the narrow valley. Gray rock, capped with patches of snow and carved into hollows by the water, surrounded the small pool where the river seemed to pause for rest before continuing on its path. The sun had risen above the far ridge at last, and Eliani stepped into a splash of sunlight at the water's edge.

Luruthin did not think he could walk much farther without rest. He felt ill at ease, had felt so ever since looking over the falls and remembering the shade. He found a tree whose lower trunk was bare of branches and leaned against it, trying to catch his breath.

Vanorin came to him, dark eyes appraising. "We can rest here a while. Come into the sun, it will warm you."

Luruthin was disinclined to move, but he obediently pushed away from the tree trunk and followed Vanorin toward the river. As he stepped into the sunshine a hot prickling poured over him and he gasped, stumbling back. He caught himself against evergreen branches and stood wheezing in the shadow of the forest.

Vanorin turned to look at him. "What is it?"

Luruthin stared at the pool of sunshine, terrible in its brightness, painful to look at. "It stings!"

"Luruthin?" Eliani hurried toward him, her face taut with concern. She stopped before him, her voice dropping to a whisper. "Luruthin?"

Dread filled Luruthin's heart as he returned her gaze. "I cannot go into the sun."

❀ Falls ❀

The look on Luruthin's face tore at Eliani's heart. She gazed at him, her cousin and her friend, watching the dread grow in his eyes.

"The curse." His voice was choked. "It has taken me."

Vanorin's footsteps came toward them. Eliani glanced at him, saw that he was holding two blankets.

"There is a cave beside the fall. We can shelter there."

"I cannot go there." Luruthin stared past him toward the sunlit pool.

"We will shield you." Vanorin handed corners of both blankets to Eliani. "Two steps and you will be out of the sun."

Vanorin spread the blankets double and draped them over Luruthin, he and Eliani holding up the front corners just enough that Luruthin could see where he walked. They moved to the edge of the woods.

"There, to the right. That crevice."

Luruthin paused as if gathering himself, then nodded. Together they stepped swiftly out of the woods and across to the crevice, which opened into a cave that went surprisingly deep into the rock.

Ice made its uneven floor treacherous in the lowest places. Luruthin stumbled and Vanorin caught his arm, preventing him from falling.

Backing against the cave wall in the deepest shadows, Luruthin sank to the floor and sat hugging his knees, shivering. Eliani and Vanorin tucked both blankets around him, then Eliani took off her pack and knelt beside him.

"Let me give you healing."

"No, leave me." Luruthin was shaking badly. He raised his head and whispered. "Please leave me be."

Biting her lip to keep back tears, Eliani rose and stepped backward, leaving her pack beside the wall. She watched Luruthin lay his head upon his knees.

"My lady."

She looked up at the captain, saw him nod toward the pool. They went outside together, leaving packs and weapons behind, leaving Luruthin to find what peace he could.

The warmth of the sunshine soothed Eliani, though this comfort was marred by the knowledge that Luruthin could not share it. She followed Vanorin toward a broad, flat rock at the pool's edge. The sun had not yet warmed the stone, but she sat there, hugging her own knees and turning her face to the light.

"What will we do?"

Vanorin was filling his water flask from the pool. He glanced up at her, his brow creased in thought.

"Travel by night. We had better take him back to the Lost."

Eliani drew a sharp breath. It was the best solution, but she could not bear to suggest it to Luruthin.

Vanorin offered the water flask to her. "Hand me yours and I will fill it."

She did so, then took a deep drink. The water was icy, sending cold through her chest and lying heavy in her stomach. She opened the pouch of dried fruit that she had tied to Birani's sword belt and ate a piece, then remembered that Luruthin had refused it.

"He has not eaten in days."

Vanorin met her gaze, his own eyes troubled. He glanced toward the cave, but made no answer though his frown deepened.

Eliani's brow grew suddenly warm, almost hot. She lay back upon the rock and closed her eyes.

Turisan.

What is wrong? Is it Kelevon again?

No.

His anxious concern was palpable in his khi. No doubt he had sensed her distress. She struggled to find a way to explain to him. She did not want to tell him, did not want to charge him with conveying yet more bad news to her father.

During their weary march to the river she had told him of Kelevon's attack. His response was to offer to send more guardians to her, but his company was several days away yet and would travel fastest by remaining on the road. She had asked him to send a message to Felisan, so that he in turn could inform the fallen guardians' families of their fate and send word to Jharan, who could go in person to Onami's kin. Such news should not be told in a letter.

Eliani? My love, what is it?

Luruthin is ill. Very ill.

She felt tears slide down either side of her face, into her matted hair. She had not combed it out since they had left the Lost, she thought inconsequentially.

Is it the hunger?

Eliani gave a sob. She sat up, trying to master her grief, struggling to quell the gasping sobs that continued to rise. Wiping at her face, she saw Vanorin watching her with concern.

I fear so. He has not been able to eat, and now he cannot bear the sun.

Oh, my heart. I am so sorry.

Eliani moved to the edge of the rock and scooped up handfuls of water from the pool to splash on her face. The cold stung, distracting her, helping her conquer the tears. She sat back.

I do not know what to do.

I wish I could advise you. I wish I could hold you, love.

So do I.

Silence fell between them, though Turisan stayed with her. Greatly comforted by his closeness, Eliani tried to turn her thoughts toward helping Luruthin.

His choices were few now. To continue to Alpinon would be difficult, though Luruthin might wish to say farewell to his folk and to gather his belongings. Some time would pass—she did not know how much— before his appearance changed. He would be safest with the Lost, and it might be best for him to go to them at once. They could succor him, teach him.

Teach him their way of hunting. Eliani swallowed dismay. She did not want to think of what he must now to do survive.

She wiped away a stray tear and sighed. Feeling disheveled as well as miserable, she pulled her hair out of its tangled braid. Her comb was in her pack, inside the cave. She stood up and went to fetch it.

Luruthin lay on his side where she had left him, curled up in the tangle of blankets. His eyes were closed and he was shivering. She knelt and reached toward his face, feeling the heat of fever before she touched him. Alarmed, she hurried to the mouth of the cave.

"Vanorin!"

The captain had been standing by the pool, gazing skyward. At her call he hastened toward her. Eliani glanced back at Luruthin.

"He is in a fever. We should build a fire, it is too cold in here."

With a nod, Vanorin came inside and fetched the woodcutter's knife from his pack. Eliani told Turisan what was passing, then bade him farewell and went out with Vanorin to gather dead wood.

Returning to the cave, Vanorin chose a place that was high enough to be free of ice, fairly level, and lay beneath a water-carved crack that was open to the sky. He and Eliani made the fire, fed it until it was burning steadily, then went to where Luruthin lay. He was still shivering, still throwing off far too much heat.

"Luruthin."

He stirred and frowned, but did not open his eyes. Eliani laid a hand gently on his shoulder.

"Luruthin. We have made a fire. Come."

At this he opened his eyes and blinked at her, seeming not to recognize her. His lips were cracked, she saw. A thin, dark line of blood divided the lower.

"Come to the fire. Can you stand?"

He pushed himself up and sat for a moment, swallowed, then slowly got to his feet. Eliani let him lean on her as they walked the few steps to the fire.

He glanced fearfully toward the open sky above, but though the sun was high by now it was also well to the north, and did not come into the cave. Sinking down again beside the fire, Luruthin looked at Eliani and this time seemed to know her.

"Thank you." His voice was a croak. He coughed.

Eliani went outside to fetch the flask she had left beside the pool. It was warm from lying in the sun. She took it in and handed it to Luruthin, who drank greedily, emptying it.

Eliani took it back. "More?"

He shook his head slightly, then winced as if the motion had pained him. He pulled his blankets closer and lay down upon the rock, facing the fire.

Eliani fetched his pack and lifted his head onto it. His flesh was burning. Alarmed, she stayed beside him, gently smoothing his hair. She could feel the khi of healing flowing through her hand, though now it felt cool rather than warm, especially in comparison to Luruthin's burning flesh.

"That feels good. I ache so."

Eliani bit her lip until she could answer in a steady voice. "It is just a fever. It will pass."

"Inóran said he was fevered, did he not?"

"For a while, yes."

"But I think this is from the sun. My face feels burned."

Eliani closed her eyes, struggling to keep back the tears that threatened again. "You will be better presently."

He did not answer. She stayed by him, touching him gently, offering him what comfort she could. It was not enough, she knew. It could never be enough.

Why? Why did this happen? Why is this his path?

No answer came from the spirits to whom she had called. Tears won the struggle and slid down her cheeks again. She sniffed defiantly and wiped at them with her free hand.

Vanorin returned with more wood. He stacked it against the cave wall, then added one branch to the fire. He glanced at the smoke rising out of the cave and Eliani knew he was thinking that it betrayed their presence.

They would be watchful. If Kelevon came after them again, she thought with a grimace, she would make him deeply sorry.

Vanorin pulled a small metal ewer from his pack and went outside, returning with it filled with water. He arranged two stones to support it over a corner of the fire, then sat back to wait for the water to boil. He took some dried meat from his pack and offered a piece to Eliani. She accepted it, knowing she should eat though she had no desire for food.

Luruthin was resting calmly now. He no longer shivered, and some of the strain had left his face.

When Vanorin's water was hot, Eliani roused Luruthin to make him drink some of the tea Vanorin made. There was but one cup, and they gave it first to Luruthin. Vanorin watched him drink, then rinsed the cup with a little of the tea and poured it out before filling it again and offering it to Eliani.

She sipped the tea and sighed. There was no way to know if they were risking contracting the hunger by staying with Luruthin, by sharing a cup or a flask with him. They knew too little about this ailment and how it behaved.

Within her heart she felt secure, and did not fear the curse. She had been exposed much more directly when Kelevon had drunk from her wounded hand, yet that was so long ago now that she was beginning to feel confident she was not in danger, at least from that contact.

She stayed beside Luruthin as the shadows deepened within the cave, kept back only by the flickering firelight. Looking out of the cave's mouth, she watched the sunlight grow golden-hued, then climb the far side of the valley as a line of shadow crept upward behind it, turning the evergreens to dusky blue.

Luruthin was gazing at the fire now, lying on his side. Eliani touched his brow and was relieved to find it cooler, though still unnaturally warm. The fever was breaking.

He was better, but she doubted he could travel far tonight. It would be best if he rested longer. A night and another day here? She glanced at Vanorin, saw him watching Luruthin with a worried frown. He met her gaze, and she knew he had concluded as she had. They would not try to move Luruthin tonight.

Vanorin went to where the packs sat against the wall and took out a blanket. He glanced at Eliani, offering with a gesture to bring another for her.

"Yes, thank you. Bring my pack, will you please?"

He brought it over to her, then settled himself on the opposite side of the fire, lying on his back with his sword unsheathed beside him. Eliani found her comb and went to work untangling her hair. She signaled Turisan, who answered at once.

Is all well?

As well as can be. Luruthin is somewhat better, but we will let him rest tonight and tomorrow.

I did not seal my letter to your father. Shall I tell him about Luruthin?

Eliani closed her eyes. She did not want to face this. To tell her father was to admit that it was real.

Yes, but please ask him to tell no one else as yet.

She felt as if she had betrayed Luruthin, passed judgment on him. Once Felisan knew of his affliction, he must as Alpinon's governor seek to find a new theyn for Clerestone. It would be Mathran, most like—Luruthin's steward. A faithful friend, loyal in service.

She set aside her comb and braided her hair again, tying it with the worn bit of leather thong she had used all through this journey, then arranged herself to rest. Pillowing her head on her pack and lying so that she could see the cave's entrance, she pulled her blankets close, seeking comfort against the bitterness in her heart.

Luruthin lay still, watching the fire that had gone to glowing coals, listening to the others and waiting until he knew they were at rest. His head had cleared at last. While he had lain in fever his thoughts had been confused, but he now had ample leisure to consider his situation, as little as he wished to think of it.

He could not return home. He would not see Jhinani, nor ever hold their son. All that he had known and treasured in life was lost to him now.

He closed his eyes wearily. He had no more tears in him, and his heart was once again numb. The hopes that had begun to flicker there were quenched. He had nothing left.

Slowly, with all the stealth he could command, he got up and left the cave. The falls whispered restlessly. The small pool at their foot lay dark, shadows crossing it as fitful clouds hid the sky. Luruthin stood gazing at the water, then followed the stream as it left the pool and continued down the valley.

The air was sharp but he ignored the cold. This was no more chill than a walk to the Three Shades.

He thought again of the last time he had been there, of the vision he and Vanorin had seen. Perhaps Josæli had not been drawn by the trouble at Midrange after all. Perhaps she had been drawn to him.

Walking warmed him a little. The way was easier now than it had been in the morning. He was going downhill, and he was rested. Nor was the sun shining to trouble him. Thinking back, he realized he had been avoiding the sun of late.

He reached the high fall and stood looking over it, down into the mist that drifted about the sharp rocks in the pool. They frightened him, but he could not let that stay him. He stepped down onto a dry space, a slightly higher ledge of rock just beside the cascade. Looking over its edge, he breathed the mist that rose up to him, listened to the roar below.

It would be quick, he hoped. No more than a moment's pain. A swift end to all his troubles.

How strange to be standing here, contemplating ending his life. He had never really understood, until now, why an ælven would make such a choice.

Ælven lives were long; it was thought that they could be endless, yet eventually each chose to abandon the flesh. The eldest ælven whom he knew had seen the Bitter Wars. None remained who had seen the first attacks of kobalen on ælven villages, or the founding of Clan Ælvanen and the setting of the creed.

By comparison to those eldest he was extremely young, not even a full century behind him. Sad to have come to this so soon, but he could not bear to think of spending centuries in fear of the sun, in fear of both ælven and alben, living by the suffering of others. He would rather walk in spirit, and hope someday to try again to make a life in the world of flesh. This life was broken beyond mending, he feared.

"Luruthin!"

Eliani's voice, so close that it startled him. Alarm tingled through his limbs. He should jump before she reached him, but he could not help turning his head.

"Luruthin, no!"

She was running along the river bank, slipping and scrambling in her haste. He knew a stab of fear for her. Vanorin was behind her, though. He would take care of her.

Luruthin looked down at the water again. The chill was beginning to reach him now. He shivered briefly.

"Cousin! I *will not lose you!*"

"Eliani, no!"

Vanorin's cry and a scuffle made Luruthin look back again. Vanorin had caught Eliani's arm, keeping her from jumping down to where Luruthin stood. A wise act, for the ledge might have crumbled beneath both of them had she succeeded.

"I am sorry." Luruthin looked up at her, knowing it was useless to try to explain. He shook his head helplessly. "I am so tired."

Suddenly the pain returned. Unexpected tears slipped from his eyes. Eliani stared back at him, her face anguished.

"Tell Jhinani I love her."

Eliani scowled. "How can I tell her that if you abandon her? She bears your child!"

Luruthin closed his eyes briefly. "He is lost to me now."

"No! Not if the Lost become a clan! Luruthin, you can help them! You can speak for them at the Council."

"Kivhani will speak for them."

"But she is not known to the Council. You are!" A passionate fire lit Eliani's eyes now, a look he knew of old. "They have named you a hero! If you join your voice to hers they *must* listen!"

A call to service. He frowned, not wanting to answer it, not wanting to let his heart reawaken, let the pain in again.

"They need you, Luruthin. The Lost need you, and *I* need you! Do not leave me, Cousin, I beg of you!" She gave a gasping sob.

Luruthin turned away, gasping himself as he gazed down at the rocky death below. Was it selfish of him to seek escape?

"Luruthin." Vanorin's voice, steady and controlled as ever. "Three of us are safer together than two. Stay for her sake."

It broke his will. How vexing of Vanorin to remind him of his pledge. While there was breath in him, his sword was hers.

Luruthin turned away from the falls, stepped toward the river bank, and slipped on unseen ice. He fell, landing hard on one knee, and felt the rock crack beneath him.

"Luruthin!"

He flung up a hand. "Stay back! The rock is crumbling."

His heart was pounding. He shifted his weight and felt the ledge shift as well.

Looking up, he saw Vanorin push Eliani unceremoniously back and kneel at the edge of the bank, reaching down to him. Luruthin stretched his arm, not daring to move his legs. He had to lean forward to reach Vanorin's hand. As they clasped each other's wrists, the rock beneath him broke away.

Eliani gave a sharp cry as he fell, rock bruising his knees and his arm jerked so hard he let out a grunt of pain. Vanorin's grip held. The captain leaned back, straining to pull him up.

Luruthin's arm felt like fire, like it would pull free of his shoulder. He scrabbled with his other hand for a hold on the bank, but could find no purchase. He saw Vanorin's feet slipping as the captain strove to push backward.

His flailing hand was seized and pulled upward. Both shoulders protested with pain as Eliani and Vanorin hauled him onto the bank.

The three of them tumbled together into the snow, gasping for breath. Snow was in Luruthin's face, in his eyes. He pushed himself up to his knees, wincing as the one he had fallen on protested his weight.

"Forgive me."

Eliani threw her arms around him. In that moment he was glad to be alive. He would have to hope for more such moments, to ease the darkness of his path.

He stood, with Eliani's help, and found he could hobble well enough. They returned to the cave, and Vanorin built up the fire again. Luruthin sat beside it, shaking now, unable to stop the chattering of his teeth. Eliani wrapped blankets around him and stayed holding him until the shivering subsided.

After a while, Vanorin stood and left the cave, carrying the little cup with him. Eliani frowned, then got up to follow.

Luruthin watched her go, then returned his gaze to the fire. Spirits, he was more tired than he remembered ever being. He stared at the flames, content to think of nothing.

Eliani found Vanorin kneeling on the flat rock, the knife he had held in the fire and the cup he had taken with him sitting before him as he unlaced one leather bracer from a forearm. She stepped onto the rock and stood in front of him.

"What are you doing?"

Vanorin glanced up at her. "He is too weak to travel," he said in a voice so low it barely reached her.

He set his bracer aside and pushed up the sleeve of his tunic, then held his arm over the cup and picked up the knife. Aghast, Eliani crouched before him.

"No!"

"There is no choice. There are no kobalen this high in this season. He cannot continue without food."

"Vanorin—"

He had set the blade to his flesh, though, making a neat cut from which blood quickly welled. Eliani watched as the blood dripped into the cup.

"You will weaken yourself."

"A little will not harm me."

"You cannot do this every day!"

"No."

His face was calm, a little stern. He glanced up and met Eliani's gaze. Suddenly decided, she began to unlace her own bracer.

"I will contribute."

"There is no need—"

"This will be from both of us. It is better so." She held his gaze. "It will not be easy for him."

Vanorin's eyes showed his understanding. He made no further protest as Eliani picked up the knife and pressed it to her own flesh, hissing a little as she cut herself. She held her arm over the cup, nearly touching Vanorin's, so close she could feel his khi. It would have made sense to wait, let him give his share first before giving hers, but she was ever impatient.

They sat silent as they bled together. Eliani felt a great warmth toward Vanorin, who had convinced Luruthin to live, who had pulled him to safety, who now gave of his very flesh for Luruthin's sake. Always giving, never expecting thanks. Her heart swelled with fondness for him.

When the cup was close to full they withdrew their arms. Vanorin handed Eliani a kerchief with which to stanch her cut. She pressed it to her arm, staring at the blood which now steamed gently in the cold night.

A snowflake drifted into the cup, melting as it touched the warm, dark liquid. Eliani glanced up. She had not noticed the sky clouding over.

Snow again. She looked at Vanorin, saw him frowning. The snow would slow them, possibly even trap them. She regretted having been so insistent upon avoiding the roads.

Her arm had stopped bleeding. She handed the kerchief to Vanorin and pulled down her sleeve, then put on her bracer again and pulled the laces tight. Picking up the cup, she sighed.

"This will be the proof of it. Not that proof is needed."

She waited for Vanorin to put on his bracer and they returned to the cave together. Luruthin was sitting exactly as she had left him, staring into the fire. She cleared her throat, feeling awkward about making this offer.

"Luruthin..."

She could not continue. Instead she came toward him, knelt beside him, and held out the cup.

He stared at it, his nostrils flaring, eyes widening as he realized what it was. His gaze flew up to meet hers.

"No!"

"It is done. You need sustenance. We have a hard journey ahead."

"Eliani—"

"This is our gift to you. Vanorin's and mine."

An anguished frown wrought his brow as his gaze shifted back to the blood. His mouth fell open and his eyes sharpened with need. His breathing was shallow. He shook his head, even as he reached for the cup.

Eliani wrapped her fingers around his, steadying his hand. He brought the cup to his lips, gave her a horrified glance, then closed his eyes and drank.

188 ~ Pati Nagle

After the first cautious sip he lunged forward, gulping at the rest, nearly spilling it. Fear tingled through Eliani as she helped him drink. This was not her beloved cousin, this being with such animal need. He tipped the cup upward to drain it, then let go and sat back, gasping.

Eliani set the empty cup down beside the fire and watched Luruthin catch his breath, amazed at how swiftly color came into his cheeks. His pallor of the last few days vanished. He gazed at her from eyes more clear than they had been in days, clear and filled with wonder.

"Oh."

Eliani glanced at Vanorin. Very rarely did the captain betray surprise, but it was on his face now as he gazed at Luruthin.

The frown that Luruthin had worn so constantly of late was gone. He sat up straighter and rolled his shoulders as if to ease some stiffness, showing none of his recent weakness as he looked from her to Vanorin.

"Thank you." Luruthin's voice was notably stronger. "And please do not do that again."

He stood up, stretching, then went to the cave's mouth. Eliani got to her feet.

"Luruthin..."

"Do not worry, Cousin. I will not waste your gift."

Eliani hastened to the entrance and stood watching as Luruthin walked to the edge of the pool. Snow caught in his hair and on the leathers he wore. He looked up at the falling flakes, laughed softly, then began to take off the leathers.

Vanorin joined Eliani in the entrance. They watched Luruthin strip, then gather the leathers and his clothing and carry them back to the cave. He grinned as he heaped them in the entrance.

"Out of the snow." He turned and went back to the pool, walking straight into it up to his waist.

Eliani caught her breath just thinking of bathing in that icy water. Luruthin shook out his hair, then dove beneath the surface.

They watched him swim around in the pool for a short while, then come dripping back to the cave, his cheeks reddened with cold, his eyes bright. He stood by the fire, shaking out his wet hair over the rising heat.

"Perhaps we should start before the snow becomes deep. We have half the night, we can make good progress."

Eliani traded a glance with Vanorin. "Which way do you mean to go?"

Luruthin looked at her in surprise as he pulled on a boot. "To

Alpinon, of course."

Eliani drew a breath. "We thought perhaps it would be best to return to the Lost's camp."

Luruthin looked confused, then dismayed as he took her meaning. "Oh. I see. I was thinking of the Council."

He looked so hurt, Eliani was smitten with remorse. "You might travel with Othanin and Kivhani to the Council. They do not know the roads."

He nodded, then turned away, reaching for his pack. He took his water skin and Eliani's flask out to the pool.

Eliani gazed after him. "I am such a clumsy wretch."

Vanorin picked up a blanket and began folding it. "There was no gentle way to say it."

Eliani gathered her own belongings. Hiking through a snowfall was not her preferred way to spend the night, but as Luruthin could not travel by day, there was no other choice. She was glad he felt well enough to move, instead of needing more rest. One less day lost.

❀ The Trade Road ❀

Rephanin sat a short distance apart from the army. Ehranan had called a brief halt where a stream crossed the road. Westward, the mountain peaks were shrouded in cloud. Here on the plains the sky was clear, stars glittering coldly and a chill wind cutting through Rephanin's cloak. He drew it closer.

His body ached in unaccustomed places, even after several days of riding. He bore it silently, knowing his own softness was the cause. Had he been told a year ago that he would make a march like this, he would have laughed aloud.

Filari sat beside him, still sullen but less wary. She surprised him by raising a new topic. "You are from Eastfæld, are you not?"

"In mindspeech, Filari."

Your pardon. Are you from Eastfæld, my lord?

Long ago, yes.

Why did you come to Southfæld?

I suffered a disappointment, and wished to escape painful memories.

Her eyes narrowed. *A disappointment in love?*

You might say so.

And you never went back.

I grew accustomed to Glenhallow. It is a fair place to live.

It is that. Though I have heard Hollirued is fairer.

Hollirued. Rephanin sighed, searching far back in memory. *It is very fair, and very old, and its ways have changed little over the centuries. Folk are more open minded in Southfæld.*

Is that why you stayed?

Perhaps it is.

You used to host gatherings of pleasure.

He met her gaze, the sting of recollection haunting him. *I did.*

Now they were approaching his own pain, but he could reflect on it with less distress since Heléri had come back into his life. Filari was

191

probably old enough to have attended one of his gatherings. He wondered if she had done so.

I was curious about them. Her eyes narrowed again and the whisper of a sly smile touched her lips. *I suppose I shall not have a chance, now.*

She knew it all, then. Of course. Everyone in Southfæld had heard of the tragedy.

I fear not.

A pity. It sounded enjoyable.

It was enjoyable. He almost said so aloud, then left it. Filari had heard much about his entertainments, no doubt. He had made no secret of them, and indeed folk had come from far away to attend them, which was why it had been such a shock to find that Soshari had been unaware of their nature.

Leave that. He wished to avoid the trap of remorse over past events. No good could come of further self-blame.

I regret that I had to discontinue them, but it was needful. They could never have been the same.

Filari nodded. *One must go on.*

Yes.

She met his gaze and silent understanding passed between them. One must go on, live down the past and atone for it as best one might. It was sometimes unpleasant, but regret was a part of atonement.

A movement nearby distracted him. Ehranan, watching them with curiosity.

Will you excuse me?

Of course.

Rising slowly, his stiff limbs complaining, Rephanin faced the commander. They had not had mindspeech for some days now, not since Rephanin had left the battleground. He had needed the respite, needed to find his balance again.

Ehranan regarded him steadily for a moment, then gestured toward the stream. They walked along it together, away from Filari and the rest of the army. At length, Ehranan pulled his cloak about himself and sat on the ground. Rephanin did likewise.

"You are still sore?"

"I will manage."

"I dare not slow our pace—"

"We have discussed this. I will manage."

Ehranan ran a hand over his face. "I am hurting you again."

Rephanin hesitated. "May I speak to you?"

A faint smile crossed Ehranan's lips. He nodded gravely.

Rephanin reached toward him in thought. Suddenly Ehranan was present in his mind, the familiar tone of his khi like a favorite melody remembered. A homecoming, it seemed, which surprised Rephanin. They had not shared mindspeech for very long—no more than a season —but the intensity of their work together had brought them close.

He drew a careful breath. *I am here voluntarily, like all the rest. I need no coddling.*

Ehranan gave a huff of laughter that expressed his disagreement. *Are you well enough to search for more mindspeakers?*

Rephanin blinked. *I am still getting acquainted with Filari. We have not tested her gift at distance. She is eager to serve, though—when I mentioned she might go to Hollirued—*

We need more. I want a mindspeaker in every realm, at least one. Keep searching, Rephanin.

Yes, my lord.

Now I have angered you.

No. But it is not so simple. I will try—I am not saying I will not try—but I cannot promise you I will find more.

He looked over the army, most of whom were from the Southfæld Guard. He had already tried them in the search that had led him to Thorian. The Steppegards and Ælvanen who had joined the army at Midrange he had not tried, so there was some potential there, perhaps.

Potential was necessary—that could not be created—but potential could be trained. It had not previously occurred to him that a distance speaker could be made, rather than found, but that in essence was what he had done with Thorian, and was doing with Filari.

To make a mindspeaker. That would certainly earn him a place in the ballads of history. He had far rather be remembered so than as a somewhat talented mage whose self-indulgence was legendary.

Ehranan looked eastward, then stood. Dawn was not yet near, but the horizon was beginning to glow with blue.

"We had better prepare to continue."

Rephanin hid a grimace, and accepted the arm Ehranan offered to help him to stand.

❀ Ebon Mountains ❀

Eliani waited with Luruthin while Vanorin went a short distance ahead, studying the crag they were climbing. They had strayed from their earlier course, hampered by the snowfall which had thickened as the night wore on. It must not be long before dawn now, but the storm was so heavy around them that there was no way to tell whether the sun had risen.

She looked at Luruthin, worried that the sun might somehow affect him through the cloud. He met her gaze.

"I have been thinking, Eliani. If I remain with the Lost, you will only be two."

"Sunahran and the others meant to return to Bitterfield. We will join them there, or catch up with them on the road."

"Ah." He nodded, though she thought he looked a bit disappointed.

Her brow grew warm. She glanced at Vanorin, his blanket-cloaked form almost hidden by the swirling snow, then closed her eyes and answered.

Hello, love.

It is snowing? Where are you?

Somewhere on the shoulder of the Sleeper. Yes, the storm is growing stronger, I think.

I thought Luruthin was too weak to travel.

Eliani swallowed. *He is better now. We—I must confess something to you, love. We fed him.*

She sensed Turisan's confusion. *You found a kobalen?*

No. Vanorin and I bled into a cup for him.

Turisan was silent. She feared he was angry. Nervous, she spoke the first thought that came to her.

The change it brought over him was quite striking. He is much stronger now.

Yes, it is remarkable how quickly they change.

You have seen this?

A faint ripple of amusement went through Turisan's khi. *Yes, I have seen it. I must confess to you in turn that I fed Kelevon when he was being held in Glenhallow.*

Kelevon!

Fury woke in her heart at the thought of Kelevon drinking her partner's blood. She tried to keep her anger from Turisan, but was so distraught she knew she had likely failed.

Turisan's khi filled with warmth and gentleness. *I did not tell you at the time because I feared to distress you. If I have erred I ask your forgiveness.*

I....

She could not form a reply. Shaking with anger, she opened her eyes. She could no longer see Vanorin through the snow.

I had two reasons for feeding him. One was that he was suffering. As we held him against his will, we were responsible for his welfare. The other reason was that in exchange for being fed he gave us information about the alben.

Eliani drew a deep breath, cold in her throat. *I am not angry with you, love. But Kelevon....*

Yes. We did not know then how destructive he was.

If I meet him again I will kill him.

I pray you will never meet him again.

Eliani let out an exasperated sigh. *So do I.*

She peered through the snow, seeking a glimpse of Vanorin. The flakes were swirling thicker now, agitated by an increasing breeze. Luruthin shifted beside her and she met his glance. She sensed movement from Turisan and focused her attention on him.

You are riding?

Yes.

Has the sun risen?

Not yet, but it will not be long.

All is darkness here. Love, I will speak to you later. I think we must find shelter.

Very well. Spirits guard you.

Thank you, my heart. May they walk with you also.

A last wave of warmth from him faded slowly. She gazed after Vanorin, but saw only swirling snow.

"Vanorin?"

Silence answered. Perhaps the snow had muffled her call. She tried again, more loudly. Luruthin added his voice to hers. They listened, then

Eliani heard Vanorin's voice, indistinct with distance.

She looked at Luruthin. "I could not tell what he said."

"Nor I."

She paused, thinking she had heard Vanorin's voice again. After a moment she called his name. There was no answer. She tried to find his khi, but the snowfall confused her perception.

Eliani stamped her feet in the snow, both to warm them and to curb her impatience. She pulled her blanket closer and shook snow from her hair, wishing for her lost cloak and the comfort of its hood. It had been Turisan's cloak, his first gift to her after their handfasting. She was sorry to have lost it, for many reasons.

A sound caught her ear; the fall of a loose rock, muffled by snow. She stared but did not see it, though she heard it continue down the mountainside below.

"Vanorin?"

"Here."

His voice was stronger than it had been, and came from above. Eliani tilted back her head and peered into the falling snow.

"Where are you?"

"On a ledge. There is another ridge beyond this, and the other has caves."

"Good! We need shelter."

"Can you follow my tracks?"

Eliani peered at the footprints he had left. They were mere dimples already, nearly filled with snow.

"If we hurry. The snow falls heavy."

"Let me come down to you."

Eliani waited, listening to his descent. She glanced at Luruthin, who was gazing eastward, frowning slightly. He sensed her gaze and turned to meet it.

"I think the sun is rising."

"You can feel it?"

"I feel uncomfortable. Not burning, but ... if this storm clears suddenly...."

"We will find shelter before then."

Eliani heard Vanorin's tread off to the right and peered through the snow toward the sound. A moment later she saw his huddled shape coming toward them. Snow lay thick on his hair and shoulders. As he reached them Eliani saw that his cheeks were flushed with exertion.

"A short climb, perhaps five rods. I sought a way around but there is no other. Can you manage it?" He looked at Luruthin, who nodded.

"I can manage. There are caves?"

Vanorin paused in drinking from his water skin. "Several. I only looked into the first, which was small though it would shelter us. I think we will have no trouble finding better."

Eliani took a sip of her own water, then slung it behind her. Vanorin started off again, following his own trail. Eliani fell into step behind him.

The path climbed as the mountain slope steepened. Eliani trod on a stone hidden beneath the snow and lost her balance, flailing. Luruthin caught hold of her from behind, keeping her from tumbling down the slope. Together they fell heavily against the rock wall uphill from them.

Vanorin had turned, and now returned to them. "Have a care, my lady."

Setting forth again, Vanorin walked more slowly. After a short while he turned back across the slope and began to climb the craggy rock. Now and then his foot dislodged a loose rock, and Eliani watched it tumble down and away to disappear in the snow.

They reached a narrow ledge, Eliani assumed the one on which Vanorin had stood to call down to them. There they paused, clinging to the rock wall, crowded together in the small space.

"Another rod or two to climb. Are you fit for it?"

"Yes."

Vanorin started upward again. The rock had plenty of cracks for handholds, but some broke away under Vanorin's hands. Eliani watched where he found steady footing and followed his path up the steep cliff. She could hear Luruthin behind her, his breathing beginning to labor with exertion, as did her own.

A broader ledge came in view above. Vanorin had almost reached it.

His foot slipped as he was pulling himself up to the ledge. With a startled cry he slid back, clung with both hands to the rock, then dropped.

"Vanorin!"

Eliani heard him scrabbling down the cliff, ending in a heavy thump. Clinging to the rock, she craned her head to see beneath her.

He lay face down on the narrow ledge, his head and one arm hanging over its edge.

"Vanorin!"

The captain stirred, pushing himself back from the edge, rolling onto his back. Even through the falling snow Eliani saw his grimace of pain.

Luruthin looked up at her. "Stay where you are, Eliani. I will go to him."

Eliani held still, her heart pounding. She tried to slow her breathing, tried to think what was best to do.

Looking down again, she saw Vanorin sitting up, both arms wrapped around his right leg. Luruthin knelt beside him on the ledge, searching inside his pack.

"Are you hurt?"

Luruthin looked up. "He has twisted an ankle. He cannot climb. We can raise him with rope, if we can find a place to tie it."

"Shall I come down?"

"No, climb up if you are able. I will throw you the end of the rope."

Eliani swallowed, looking at the short distance she had left to climb. It was nothing, a mere leap, yet she feared it. She tried to remember exactly where Vanorin's foot had slipped, but that was useless. Drawing a deep breath, she started upward.

In three breaths she was pulling herself onto the ledge. She got to her knees, then looked down at her companions.

"I am up. Throw the rope."

She watched Luruthin twist the rope twice about his wrist, then fling the rest of the coil up toward her. It passed her hands as a gust of breeze pulled it beyond her reach. Hoping to catch it as it fell onto the ledge, she lunged after it, but the rope did not fall.

Hands had caught it. Gloved hands, reaching from beneath a furred cloak. Eliani scrambled backward, looking up at a male, white hair whipping around his face and his black eyes boring into her.

✖ The Great Sleeper ✖

Scrambling to her feet, Eliani drew her sword. The alben male took a startled step backward and raised a hand.

"Stay your sword! I mean you no harm."

"Give me that rope!"

He tossed it to her. She caught it, then stood staring at him, breathing hard, wondering what to do. Snow swirled around her, making her blink. She could not hold the stranger at swordpoint and manage the rope as well.

"Eliani!" Luruthin's voice from below.

The alben's glance flicked toward the cliff. "May I be of assistance?"

"Who are you?"

"My name will mean nothing to you, but I give it you. I am Ulithan."

"That is an ælven name!"

A smile twitched at a corner of his mouth. "Yes."

Eliani frowned. "Are you one of the Lost?"

His brows rose in surprise. "One could call me that."

"Eliani!"

She took a step sideways toward the cliff's edge and glanced down at Luruthin. He had tied a loop in the rope and settled it under Vanorin's arms.

"Is your friend hurt?"

Eliani's eyes narrowed as she looked back at Ulithan. "We seek shelter from the storm."

Ulithan nodded. "There are several caves along this ridge. You are welcome to shelter there. Shall I help you?"

He gestured toward the rope. Eliani hesitated. She tried to get a sense of the stranger's khi, but in the gusting snow it was difficult.

No malice showed in his face. He seemed unusually calm, in fact—untroubled by her sword, unhurried for an answer.

After a moment he unbuckled the belt at his hips, which held a long knife in its sheath and a battered water skin, and set it down by the cliff wall. He took off his cloak and laid it over the belt. He was dressed in deerskin, with furs strapped about his lower legs.

"There. I am unarmed. Shall I help you or no?"

Reluctantly, Eliani gave him the rope. He pulled up the slack, then set himself to haul and glanced at her.

Eliani looked over the edge. "Are you ready?"

Luruthin looked up at her. "Yes. Shall I come up?"

"Not yet."

She stepped back and nodded to Ulithan, who began to haul at the rope. When she heard Vanorin coming near the top she sheathed her sword and went to help him over the edge.

The captain winced in pain as he crawled onto the ledge; Eliani felt sharp flashes of it in his khi. Her hands went at once to his ankle, which she could feel had swollen inside the boot.

After a moment she sighed. "Not broken."

She glanced at Ulithan, who still stood holding the rope. Carefully, she took the loop from around Vanorin's shoulders and tossed it down to Luruthin.

"Send up his pack and bow."

A sound of shifting made her glance up. Ulithan was stepping toward his belongings, still holding the rope. Eliani rose to her feet, hand to her sword hilt, but relaxed when she saw him pick up his furred cloak and shake off the snow. He carried it toward her, offering it at arm's length.

She laid the cloak over Vanorin and knelt beside him. His eyes were closed, his face twisted in pain.

Luruthin called his readiness. Eliani nodded to Ulithan, who began hauling at the rope again. She watched him bring up Vanorin's gear and stack it away from the edge. She could hear Luruthin climbing now.

Ulithan coiled the rope, laid it beside Vanorin's gear, then moved to where his belt lay. Eliani kept an eye on him, not yet ready to trust him. He put on his belt and stayed by the cliff wall, watching her with his black eyes.

Luruthin reached the ledge, caught sight of Ulithan and paused halfway over the edge, staring in alarm. "Who is that?"

"A friend, I think. He helped bring Vanorin up."

Ulithan came toward them. "May I help you as well?"

Luruthin heaved himself over the edge, wincing as he set his weight on his knees. He got to his feet and stepped between Eliani and Ulithan, glaring at the alben.

"This is Ulithan." Eliani met Ulithan's gaze. "I am Eliani, and this is Luruthin, my cousin. That is Vanorin."

Ulithan nodded. "You are welcome to shelter in any of the caves, but I think you should come into mine for now. I have a fire there. Shall I carry him?"

He stepped toward Vanorin, looking to Eliani for approval. She nodded.

"Yes. Thank you."

He knelt and gently picked up the injured captain. Luruthin caught Eliani's eye, frowning. She gave a shrug and reached for Vanorin's bow and quiver, while Luruthin took up his pack.

They followed Ulithan along the ledge through the gusting snow, passing the dark mouths of several caves before Ulithan stopped at one. He glanced back at Eliani and Luruthin, then stepped into what looked like a mere hollow in the cliff wall, higher and narrower than the one where Eliani and her party had sheltered the night of Kelevon's attack.

Eliani closed her eyes as she pushed away that memory. When she opened them again she saw Ulithan step around a protrusion of rock and disappear. She hurried after him, and found herself in a narrow corridor that ran deep into the cliff.

Vanorin gave a startled gasp as his injured foot brushed the wall. Ulithan murmured an apology and continued forward.

There was almost no light in the passage, though Eliani could see Ulithan's form moving before her. Despite the closeness of the walls she was relieved to be out of the snow and wind. She caught a whiff of wood smoke, and a faint, pungent smell of dried leaves, then saw light ahead as the passage opened into a larger cave.

It was roughly circular, perhaps three rods across, and was lit by a small bed of glowing coals at one side. A circle of rocks contained the fire, and the smoke rose into a small crack in the cave's ceiling.

The walls were dotted with rows of pegs from which hung deerskin clothing, untrimmed skins, furs, bunches of dried herbs, a bow and two quivers. Small shelves mounted high on the walls held wooden bowls and cups, rough pottery jars, gourds, feathers, and animal skins. One longer shelf held a large number of what looked like more skins, these small and rolled, neatly stacked.

Ulithan went to the fire and gently laid Vanorin on a heap of furs beside it. Luruthin entered the cave, set Vanorin's pack against the wall, and took off his own.

Eliani unshouldered hers as well, sighing with relief. She left it with Vanorin's quiver and bow and her own, though she kept both her sword and Birani's with her.

She went forward to the fire and knelt beside Vanorin. Ulithan moved back to give her room.

She glanced at him. "Thank you for your kindness."

He smiled slightly and nodded, then stood up. "Please make yourselves at home. It is long since I had any visitors."

Luruthin came to sit beside Eliani. He, too, had kept on the sword he wore, and his hand rested on its hilt as he watched Ulithan go to a shelf and take down a gourd and a pottery jug. Trusting Luruthin's suspicion, Eliani turned her own attention to Vanorin's injury.

Gently she drew the fur cloak—rabbit furs, she now noticed, meticulously stitched together and wonderfully soft—away from Vanorin's foot. He lay with eyes closed, breathing shallowly. Eliani held her hands above his ankle, careful not to touch it as healing began to flow from her palms.

Vanorin gave a soft moan, and his breathing slowed somewhat. Eliani closed her eyes and let go of all thoughts beyond the khi flowing through her. She guided it into the swollen flesh, felt it ease pain and begin to mend the damage. She stayed still, unaware of time passing until at last she noticed her hands growing cool.

When she opened her eyes she saw Luruthin still seated nearby, watching Ulithan. Their host was stirring something in the pottery jug, which sat over the coals at one side of the fire. Minted steam rose from the jug, a comforting smell. Ulithan sensed her gaze and glanced up, smiling shyly.

"A healer." His voice was soft and low. "Welcome indeed. Will you have some tea?"

"Thank you, yes."

He took the jug from the fire and poured from it into a wooden cup, which he then offered to Eliani. He had taken off his gloves, and she saw that his fingers were long and dexterous. All his movements were unhurried and fluid.

She watched him as she sipped the tea, its warmth spreading through her chest. Ulithan offered tea to Luruthin, then poured a third cup and glanced inquiringly from Vanorin to Eliani.

She shook her head. "Let him rest."

Ulithan nodded and returned the jug to the fire, settling back and sipping from the cup himself. Eliani gazed at him, wondering what to make of him. Though his coloring proclaimed him a victim of the alben's curse, something in the lines of his face reminded her of Greenglens.

She glanced from him to Vanorin. Yes, the angle of the brows, and the high cheekbones, were similar.

Now that they were out of the wind and snow she could better observe Ulithan's khi, and what she sensed reassured her. As far as she could tell he was sincere in his wish to be of service. She could detect no ill will. He seemed entirely content to host three strangers in what was plainly his home.

He asked no questions. He seemed at peace, and that reminded her more of Heléri than anyone else. It was the strongest sense she had from him, that he was one who had found peace.

She took another sip of tea. "Do you live here alone?"

Ulithan smiled softly. "Yes."

"What of your kindred? Your clan?"

The smile faded. "I have no clan."

He took a log from a small stack nearby and laid it over the coals. Wisps of smoke began to rise from beneath it, drifting toward the crack in the roof.

"Everyone has a clan."

Ulithan glanced at Luruthin, black eyes gone hard. "Darkshore cast me out, and no other would have me."

"Darkshore!" Eliani stared at him in surprise. "How long have you lived here?"

Ulithan's lips curved again, this time in amusement. "Twenty-seven centuries, and a few years."

Eliani was stunned. "You saw the Bitter Wars!"

"I saw the first, and heard about the second. By then I had already left Ghlanhras."

Eliani gazed at him in awe. He was one of the oldest souls she had ever met, and though countless questions leapt to her mind, she was shy of posing them. Ulithan had chosen to live alone, in voluntary exile perhaps, for centuries. She had no wish to intrude upon his privacy.

Luruthin was not so reticent. "Why did Darkshore cast you out?"

Ulithan gazed at him for a long moment. "Because my ways did not agree with theirs."

"How so?"

Eliani directed a warning frown at Luruthin, who showed no sign of noticing. He was watching Ulithan, his expression suspicious. Eliani wished he would show more courtesy to one who was so much their elder.

Ulithan in turn was watching Luruthin, his air of amusement increasing, though it was tempered with a slight frown. "I favored upholding the creed, for one thing."

Luruthin seemed to relax somewhat. "Oh."

Eliani gave a slight cough. "Perhaps you have not heard of the Lost."

Ulithan turned an interested gaze on her. She finished her tea and set the cup down before her.

"A group of folk who suffer the alben's curse, but who live by the creed. They have dwelt in the woodlands of Fireshore for a century or so."

Ulithan shook his head. "I had not heard of them, no. I am glad to hear they live by the creed. I tried to convince Darkshore they should live so, but they were too bitter, and would not hear me."

"I am sure the Lost would welcome you."

He glanced at her, laughter glinting in his dark eyes. "Think you so?"

"Yes. Their leader is Kivhani, who governed Fireshore with her lord until she was stricken with the hunger. She is a gracious lady, deeply devoted to the creed. I know she would make you welcome."

He gazed at her, the smile playing about his lips. "I think I am best here. I have dwelt alone too long now to wish for constant company."

Eliani felt her cheeks reddening. "It is most kind of you to welcome us."

His smile widened. "Oh, I am glad to have visitors. It has been a long while since anyone came this high onto the Sleeper. What brought you here?"

"We were trying to retrace our path northward, but missed our way in the storm."

Ulithan's face went serious. "Was it you who lit the pyre two nights since?"

"Yes. You saw it?"

"I smelled it."

Eliani lowered her gaze to the fire, where small tongues of yellow flame were now licking at the new wood. "We were attacked. Three of our party were slain."

"Half your party?" Ulithan's brows rose. "By what? Not a catamount."

Eliani shook her head. "An alben."

"Kelevon." Luruthin's voice was bitter.

Ulithan glanced at him, then looked back to Eliani. "An alben who is known to you?"

"Sadly, yes."

All were silent for a long moment, then Ulithan said softly, "So not all the alben are west of the Ebons."

Luruthin put down his cup. "No."

Eliani glanced at him and saw the familiar haunted look in his eyes. He was thinking of Ghlanhras, she knew. She changed the subject.

"Kelevon is—unusual. He suffers the alben's curse, but he does not claim kinship with them. He only recently acquired the hunger."

Luruthin shook his head. "He is traveling north. That implies he is going to them."

"He could be returning to the Steppes."

"There are alben in the north?"

Luruthin made no answer. Eliani glanced at Ulithan. He had a right to know about the upheavals in Fireshore, for they might affect him.

"The alben have taken Ghlanhras. Two hundred warriors or more, led by their ruler, Shalár. We were there when the city fell."

Ulithan's brows rose. "Shalár? Would she once have been called Shalári?"

Luruthin's head came up sharply. "You knew her?"

Ulithan gazed thoughtfully at him for a moment. "Shalári was a child when the wars began. Her father was head of Clan Darkshore and governor of Fireshore, until he was killed in the war. So she survived?"

Eliani looked at Luruthin. He had drawn up his knees and was resting his chin on them, plainly unwilling to discuss Shalár.

"Apparently."

Ulithan picked up the pottery jug and offered to pour more tea for Eliani "I saw a group of alben traveling northward not long ago, though on the west side of the mountains. It must have been Shalári and her warriors."

Eliani sipped the tea and sighed. She tried to think of something else to talk of, if only to spare Luruthin's feelings. His face had gone grim, and he sat frowning at the fire though she doubted he saw the flames.

Her brow grew warm. She closed her eyes.

Yes, love? I cannot take long, I am in company.

I wanted to ask if all was well. I thought you were troubled, earlier.

I was, but all is well now. I will explain later.

Opening her eyes again, she saw Ulithan watching her. His expression was unreadable, though she thought it was partly curious. He glanced away toward Vanorin, who had risen to his elbows and was blinking at the rabbit fur cloak that lay over him.

Eliani set down her cup and moved to Vanorin's side. "How do you feel?"

He looked up at her with a chagrined smile. "My foot feels somewhat better, and I feel rather a fool."

"Anyone might have slipped there, in this snow."

"Hm."

Vanorin looked around the cave. When his glance fell upon Ulithan his eyes widened and he sat up sharply, wincing a little at the movement. Eliani's hands twitched toward his injured foot, but she kept them back.

"This is Ulithan. He has been kind enough to make us welcome in his home."

Ulithan nodded in greeting. "I have balmroot, if you would like some for your pain."

Vanorin stared at him, then glanced at Eliani and seemed to conclude from her manner that Ulithan was no danger. "Thank you, I am well enough for now. You are very good to shelter us."

Ulithan smiled and offered tea to Vanorin. A gust from the roof crack raised a cloud of sparks from the fire, and Eliani glanced upward. If the storm continued, they might be trapped here for a while.

"Is that a handfasting ribbon?"

She glanced at her arm, where the glints of gold and silver showed at the edges of her bracer. "Yes."

"Your partner does not travel with you."

Eliani met Ulithan's gaze. "He is with the army."

"Ah."

Ulithan smiled, a little wistfully, she thought, and a tingling of realization passed through her. He had been alone here for centuries. He must not have had a lover in a very long while. Pity moved in her heart, though his isolation had been by choice. Had she not been bound....

Foolish to think that way. She *was* bound, for life.

And he suffered the curse. Strange how quickly she had almost forgotten that. He reminded her of the Lost in a way, though he was also different. The Lost were always watchful, always cautious. Ulithan must be no less alert, or he would not have survived so long alone, yet he seemed more at ease.

She wondered how often he had to hunt. He must have to descend the mountain to find kobalen, possibly on the western side. Perhaps he would take Luruthin with him, if they stayed a few days, and advise him. Eliani swallowed and reached for her teacup, not wanting to think about that.

"Is there more?"

"I can make more." Ulithan reached for the jug.

Vanorin drained his own cup. "We have some tealeaf."

Ulithan's face brightened. "I have not had leaf tea in ages!"

"It is in my pack."

Eliani stood up. "I will get it."

She went to their packs at the side of the cave and rummaged in Vanorin's for the tea. She took out the metal urn and cup they shared, thinking as she set them down that Ulithan might consider them rare treasures.

Such simple things, and she took them for granted, but he would not have the means for making or acquiring their like. She glanced at him, wanting to offer them to him, but her party needed them and perhaps he would be offended by what might seem like charity.

She found the tea, and from her own pack brought out a pouch of dried stonefruit and the last of the bread. Returning to the fire, she handed the pouch of tealeaf to Ulithan.

"Bread?"

"Yes. Would you like some?"

She tore off a quarter of the loaf and offered it to him, remembering that the Lost ate small amounts of regular food after hunting. He accepted it with a quaintly formal bow.

"Many thanks! This is a rare treat indeed."

He set the bread aside, then opened the tea pouch, inhaling its scent with a smile of delight. The jug was filled with fresh water and sat upon the fire, but was not yet boiling. Ulithan set the pouch down carefully before him, then tore off a bit of the bread and ate it.

Eliani watched him close his eyes, savoring the food. She had spent enough patrols living on trail fare to know how one might relish a bit of fresh bread, but she could not imagine what it must be like to live for centuries without such comforts.

She glanced around the cave, looking for any object that could not have been made by Ulithan. She saw none, save for the long knife he had worn, which now hung from one of the pegs. No other metal was in view, nor any crafted thing save for the wooden bowls and the pottery, which he must have made himself.

The furs and skins must be his handiwork as well. She was impressed at the variety of skills he must have developed, but then, he had had plenty of time to hone them.

Her gaze fell upon the quiver of arrows hanging from a peg beside the knife. She glanced at Ulithan.

"May I look at your arrows?"

"Certainly, if I may look at yours."

Smiling, she got up and fetched Ulithan's quiver and her own, bringing them back to the fire. She handed her quiver to Ulithan and drew an arrow from his, admiring the straightness of the shaft, the fletching of striped feathers perfectly aligned, and the wicked point of sharpened ebonglass.

"Glass points, like the kobalen use on their darts."

Ulithan glanced at her, one of the Lost's arrows in his hands. "Yes. I have not the means to work metal. I make knives of glass as well, for everyday use."

She held the arrow tip up and peered through the point at the firelight. It set up a smoky glow in the glass.

"How do you keep the points from breaking in the quiver?"

"A handful of fleececod in the bottom."

Eliani handed the arrow to Vanorin, who was watching with interest. "Fleececod? That does not grow in the mountains."

"No, I found it when I was traveling in the west. If it grew close by I would try my hand at weaving cloth, but it is too distant for that to be practical. Skins and furs are much easier to come by."

She gazed at Ulithan. "You must know the Sleeper very well."

He smiled. "Yes."

The jug was now steaming, and Ulithan turned his attention to it, shifting it over the coals. When it boiled a moment later he took it off the fire and added tealeaf to it, carefully pouring a small amount of leaf into his hand first, then stirring it into the hot water, brushing the last bits from his palm.

"Ah." He smiled as the fragrant steam arose. "How delightful. You brought this from Alpinon?"

"No, it was a gift from the Lost. They cultivate it near their camps."

"In Fireshore? I would have thought it too warm."

"Inóran said they find sheltered places to grow it."

"Perhaps I could grow some on the lower slopes."

"I am sure they would give you cuttings."

Ulithan stirred the tea. He was silent for a moment, then looked up at her.

"You see, I am not certain I wish my presence to be known."

She saw the depths of years in his dark eyes, and was reminded again of Heléri. Part of her wanted to protest, to point out the many advantages he would gain by associating with the Lost, not the least of which would be companionship. Yet, he could have sought companionship if he truly desired it.

Or perhaps he could not. It was unlikely that any ælven would welcome intimacy with one who suffered the alben's curse. Then, too, Ulithan seemed to hold no love for the alben. If he had been open to them, he would have sought their company west of the mountains.

"We will respect your wishes, of course, but we would be happy to carry a message to the Lost for you."

"Thank you. I will think on that."

The tea being ready, he filled all their cups, then held his own in both hands, savoring the steam before taking a sip. Eliani watched him, touched by the pleasure he took in a simple cup of tea, and resolved to be more grateful for her own blessings.

Vanorin reached for the bread, tore off a share for himself, and offered it to Luruthin, who gazed at it for a moment, then shook his head. Eliani wondered if he was beginning to be hungry again. He looked well enough, but the amount of blood they had given him was small. She had no idea how often he would need to hunt. The Lost had not hunted every day, though that might have been only because there were no kobalen nearby.

She opened her pouch of stonefruits and offered them first to Ulithan, who took three, then to the others. Luruthin accepted one and nibbled at it, though he seemed to take no pleasure in it.

Vanorin took three of the fruits. "All we need is a song to make this a regular feast."

Ulithan glanced up, smiling. "Yes, a song! You must know many that I have not heard." He turned to look at Eliani. "Will you sing?"

She laughed. "Not I! My voice is as sweet as a jay's."

"Truth." Luruthin glanced sidelong at her with a grin, his first contribution to the conversation in some while.

Relieved, Eliani grinned back, then looked at the captain. "Vanorin has a pleasant voice. Will you sing for us?"

Vanorin nodded, finished chewing a mouthful of bread, then drank some tea. He sat thinking for a moment, then set down his cup and drew breath.

> *The shepherd's fair daughter to market did carry her fleece,*
> *All on the fairest of midsummer mornings,*
> *And there she did meet with the woodworker's comely young*
> *son,*
> *Dally, heigh dally till midsummer moon.*

Eliani sat back, enjoying the tune, which she had heard often around the Guard's campfires, and had even sung herself when the wine was flowing and the company was uncritical. Ulithan listened with evident delight to the frivolous tale, laughing at the clever parts, and applauding when Vanorin had finished.

"That is wonderful! May I note it down? I would like to remember it."

Vanorin nodded, and Ulithan got up and went to a shelf, returning with one of the small, rolled skins, a quill-cut feather, a small bowl and a tiny gourd. He poured some dark powder from the gourd into the bowl and added water, stirring it to make ink, then unrolled the skin.

"A parchment skin." Eliani admired the beautiful, thin and supple skin. "I never learned how to make them."

"All it takes is patience." Ulithan smiled as he dipped his quill.

Eliani looked up at the shelf that held many of the skins. She had not realized at first what they were.

"Have you written on all of those?"

Ulithan followed her gaze. "Yes. Most are about the events leading up to the wars. I thought I should record them. It was a way of occupying myself, and I wished not to forget the causes of those troubled times."

Eliani gazed in wonder at the shelf laden with history, history so ancient that it was little more than legend now. Events leading up to the Bitter Wars, as seen through the eyes of a member of Clan Darkshore.

What a treasure to find in the cave of a recluse high in the mountains! Nothing like it had been known among the ælven. She glanced at Luruthin, who seemed as awed as she.

"Ulithan, may I read them?"

He glanced up at her, looking slightly surprised, then at the shelf. "If you wish. They are numbered. The first ones are at the left." He turned his attention to Vanorin. "It begins, 'The shepherd's fair daughter'?"

As he and Vanorin murmured together, Eliani stood and went to the shelf full of scrolls. She hesitated to touch them, wondering how old they must be.

Ulithan must have recopied them from time to time as the parchments began to crumble, for as she looked at them more closely the scrolls seemed relatively new. She reached for the topmost scroll at the left end of the shelf, taking it down carefully. The number "1" was written on an outside corner. Smiling with quiet pleasure, she carried it back to the fire and settled down to lose herself in reading.

❀ Ghlanhras ❀

When she felt night descend, Shalár arose from her rest. She poured water into her basin and splashed it onto her face, then donned the tunic and legs and the robe laid out for her. Silken slippers, once orange, now red, sat near her bed. Stepping into them, she sighed with deep appreciation. She had not forgotten the lean times in Nightsand, when such luxuries as these were unknown even to her.

"Come and comb my hair."

The ælven female who waited on her came into the chamber and took up brush and comb from her dressing table. Shalár sat in a cushioned chair by the table and closed her eyes. The brush felt good against her scalp.

"Your father has not returned."

The female said nothing. Shalár had expected no answer, but she smiled.

"He may be on his way. For your sake I hope so. I will give him until the morning."

No answer still, though the brushing slowed. Shalár observed the ælven's khi, watchful for any sign of rebellious intent. There was none. The ælven was not stupid. If she intended anything, it was escape.

Shalár knew how unlikely the female was to succeed at that venture. She need not trouble herself to discourage it, for if the ælven tried to escape she would be stopped by Shalár's hunters, either within the palace or at the city gates, or if the female was more adventurous than Shalár thought, at the wall.

Dismissing the matter, Shalár turned her thoughts to the night ahead. No word yet from the west. Too soon still. Woodrun must wait.

Tonight she would venture to the foot of Firethroat. The volcano had fallen silent, which troubled her far more than the frequent tremors had done. No tremor had been felt in Ghlanhras for the past three nights.

The ælven put down her brush and began to separate strands of

Shalár's hair with the comb, preparing to braid it. Shalár brushed her hands away.

"No, leave it. I will have it braided later."

Standing up, Shalár went out to her workroom. She picked up a handful of notes—her own, and messages from her subordinates. All writ on beautiful paper that was made here in Ghlanhras. Another luxury, and one she intended never to forgo again. Some of the ælven captives had already been put to work making more, using tools left behind by their fellows.

Paper. Cloth. All manner of wooden things, crafted of darkwood. These products were already in train. When her people arrived from the west, they would take up these crafts, which their forebears had abandoned in the struggle to survive.

Other crafts had yet to be revived. The working of glass, done in hot caves on Firethroat's restless slopes, would be next, Shalár thought. She wished also that she might rediscover the working of steel, though that required not only fire but skill with khi, and such gifts were rare among Clan Darkshore.

Frowning, she pondered whether any of her ælven captives might have skill with metal. She had not thought to inquire. She glanced through the open doorway into her bedchamber, where the ælven female was straightening her bed.

"Come here."

The ælven silently obeyed, coming to stand before her with downcast eyes. Shalár gazed at her, musing.

"Who among your people knows the working of metal?"

The ælven looked startled, then her brows drew together. "Gelithan. He works copper and tin."

"Who works in sword metal?"

"No one now. Thelani once did, but she left Ghlanhras years ago."

"No others?"

The ælven shook her head. Frustrated, Shalár caught her by the jaw and forced the ælven to meet her gaze.

"Are you certain?"

Fear glinted in the female's blue eyes, and also a hint of disdain. "Yes, I am certain."

"Where did this Thelani go?"

"To Woodrun."

"Sword metal is not worked in Woodrun. Where did she go from there?"

"I do not know. S-she spoke of traveling south."

Shalár pushed her away. South meant Southfæld, most like. She knew of no place between Firethroat and Midrange where the mountains' bellies were hot enough for the making of swords.

Lost to her, then, that one. Mayhap she would find another, or mayhap the coppersmith's skill could be turned to harder metals. She wanted swords for her hunters, for the coming fight with the ælven.

Bows, in the meantime, and darts as the kobalen used. She had a few captured throwing sticks, and could put the ælven to work making more.

She carried her notes out to the audience hall, where the hunters she had placed in charge of the various alterations to Ghlanhras waited to give her their nightly reports. Having heard them and heard from the keepers of the ælven and the kobalen, she gave instructions for ælven to be set to work making weapons, then accompanied the kobalen's keeper back to the holding pen.

The sky was overcast, heavy with the threat of rain. She glanced to the northwest, looking for the angry orange glow of Firethroat against the clouds, but the mountain's maw was dark. Frowning, she hastened to the house where the kobalen's keeper dwelt, and where she kept the cup and knife she had selected from the governor's trove to use here.

She was hungry. She had not fed for two nights, and while in Nightsand far fewer feedings had kept her, here she was more lavish. She wanted strength for her child, and that meant feeding whenever she felt the slightest desire.

In the house she took her cup and knife from the shelf, and sat beside the hearth where embers lay dying. Wahral, the hunter she had set to watch over the kobalen, reached for wood to add to the fire. Shalár waved her away.

"Choose a strong one and bring it to me. Hurry."

"Yes, Bright Lady."

Wahral left the house, and Shalár drew her chair closer to the fire. She put a small log on the coals and poked at them, urging them to new life. There was not enough heat in them to light the wood, so she added a handful of tinder from a box nearby. The scraps of wood began to smoke.

She heard Wahral returning, accompanied by the heavy tread of a kobalen. Standing, she followed the keeper to a wall where shackles had been mounted, and waited while Wahral bound the kobalen in place.

218 ~ Pati Nagle

It was a male, deep chested and angry looking. Shalár took hold of its khi and its eyes showed the shock of her more thorough control. Wahral's skill was adequate to her tasks, but Shalár had greater strength.

She held the kobalen motionless while she opened a vein in its arm and let blood run into her cup. Wahral stood ready with another cup, and when Shalár's was full Wahral held hers beneath the wound while Shalár drank.

Strength flooded through her. She took a second cup, then gestured to the keeper to stanch the cut.

"The rest will go to the builders making the passage to the east outpost. I will send them."

Wahral bowed and pressed dryleaf to the cut on the kobalen's arm. Shalár waited until Wahral had hold of the kobalen's khi before relinquishing her own grasp of it. The creature stirred, straining against its bonds, then was still.

Shalár returned her cup and knife to their shelf, then turned back to Wahral. She nodded toward the cup the keeper held.

"Enjoy your share."

"Thank you, Bright Lady."

Shalár left, the lazy sensation that accompanied a large feeding descending on her. She would rest a while before walking to Firethroat. Returning to Darkwood Hall, she sent Ranad to fetch the chosen workers to their feeding, then retired to her work chamber to make new notes on the night's progress.

The ælven female was there. No attempt yet to escape, then, or perhaps she had explored the palace and discovered how closely she was watched. She gave no sign of noticing Shalár's entrance, but remained sitting on the floor beside the bedchamber doorway, silent and still, eyes downcast.

Perhaps she was meditating, as the ælven were wont to do. Dwelling upon her fate, seeking to explain it, to justify it as some form of atonement, no doubt. Far be it from the ælven to accept the simple dominance of strength, Shalár thought with a wry smile.

She proceeded to make her notes, then wrote a message to the watchers at the gates and summoned Ranad to carry it. As she handed him the folded page she noticed him cast a speculative look at the ælven.

"Leave her alone. If her father does not arrive by dawn, you may have her before she dies."

Ranad met Shalár's gaze, then grinned. He looked again at the ælven, whose cheeks had paled. Ranad made a swift bow toward Shalár, then left.

Shalár stood and looked at the ælven, who remained motionless. As silent as the fire maiden's statue, and as devoid of thought, no doubt. Shalár brushed past her into the bedchamber.

"Bring out my leathers and boots."

The ælven obeyed, fetching the leathers while Shalár pulled off her robe and tossed it upon the bed. The female helped Shalár into the leathers, then handed her the boots. Shalár noted a smear of mud on one heel.

"You did not clean them properly."

"Perhaps your next attendant will do better."

The words were softly spoken, but Shalár did not miss the bitterness beneath them. She smiled.

"Your father has until the morning. You may yet be redeemed."

"Someone must have hurt you very badly, to make you take such pleasure in tormenting others."

Staggered by this insolence, Shalár glared at the ælven. The female seemed as modest as ever, gaze downcast, quietly kneeling, hands folded as she waited for the next command. Shalár's eyes narrowed as her anger swelled. How dare this timid female presume to judge her!

Shalár spread her khi into the ælven's, then clenched it into a knot. The female gave a soft cry and flinched, her hands fluttering slightly as if groping for a support they would never find.

"You would do well to remember that I am bound by no pledges. I will kill you now if it pleases me."

As it happened, that prospect did not please Shalár. She was far more interested in the female's possible usefulness, assuming her father did indeed return. The ælven needed a lesson, however, so Shalár drew upon her khi, drinking it into herself, enjoying it as she would a fine wine. Her flesh was already sated, but she had never known a satiation of khi. She suspected it was not possible. It might be interesting to find out if an ælven could be killed in this way, but not now.

Releasing the female, Shalár finished pulling on her boots. The ælven collapsed upon the floor, still conscious, but barely so. Stepping over her, Shalár went to the wall and took down her sword, strapped it on, and strode out of her chambers, much refreshed.

The night was half gone, and the threatening rain had not yet fallen. The sky was dark and sullen as Shalár strode to the city gates, choosing to walk in the open rather than through the sheltered passage.

She selected two hunters to accompany her, then left Ghlanhras and turned northward, toward Firethroat and the shore. She ran for the pleasure of stretching her legs, and the hunters kept up with her, though they flagged a little as they started up the trail that climbed Fireshore's southern slope.

The path was disused, beginning to be overgrown. That would not do.

Shalár dropped to a walk and brushed aside a dangling firevine. She would have this way cleared, then have the coppersmith fetched out of the holding houses under guard and brought here to work. If he could be made to work sword metal, the effort would be worthwhile.

Her hand went to the hilt of her sword. It had been her father's, her most precious possession, perhaps, though not as fine as the sword she had taken from her Stonereach, with its crystal-studded hilt and guards. That sword she would save for her daughter.

Shalár smiled, thinking of her child. She could feel her near, though the child rarely spoke. The small body inside Shalár's womb was as yet too unformed to accommodate her, but there was not long to wait. A year was nothing.

The path leveled and widened as it reached the entrance of a passage that struck deep into Firethroat. Shalár remembered coming here with her father to watch the smiths and glass makers work, before the hunger and the wars.

She had come once since then, with her mother after they had fled Ghlanhras. Shalár's heart clenched as she remembered the fearful days spent here, the suffering of those who sheltered within, and her mother's decline. When Shalár had left this place, she had been alone, carrying only a few necessities and her father's sword.

Drawing a deep breath, she strode into the mountain, her two hunters following. A faint taste of sulfur was on the air. Firethroat was silent, but not sleeping. Shalár felt a tension in the air that she misliked.

The tunnel had begun as a natural cave and had been widened centuries ago by the first ælven to work metal here. Openings on either side led to storage rooms, now empty. Shalár hurried past them, picking up a run again as she drove deeper into the mountain.

The air became warm, then hot and stifling. She reached the main chamber of the works, a wide, high-ceilinged cavern, empty save for years of dust and a few scattered tools whose purpose was unknown to her.

Fire pits, where lesser metals and glass could be worked over ordinary heat, were filled with cold ash. A large anvil remained, too heavy to be moved without great effort. Several boulders had been used to shape metal, their tops worn with beating.

Shalár walked to the far recess of the cavern, to the place where the swordsmiths had summoned fire from the mountain's belly to work their craft. That took fine control of a powerful force of khi. Shalár knew that it was beyond her to grapple with the mountain. She laid a hand against the glass-smooth wall which the smith's art would open, awed anew by what she remembered from her childhood visit.

One of her hunters coughed. Shalár turned to look at him, and he met her gaze with a rueful expression. Well, she had seen enough, and the air was indeed close in this place.

She led the way back out of the abandoned works, striding swiftly. One of the hunters gave a small gasp of relief as they came out of the passage into the cool, damp night air.

Firethroat loomed high and steep, the forest climbing up its feet but giving up before reaching its shoulders. The mountain's jagged maw was ominously dark. Shalár frowned as she gazed at it. She needed to know what was happening within.

A rumble sounded, but it was thunder from the clouds overhead, not the mountain. Shalár walked a few steps southward and turned to gaze up at Firethroat, then explored the forest nearby with khi.

No night birds here. She reached instead toward the shore, where nighthawks hunted to the muted growling of the waves. Catching hold of one, she made it fly inland, up Firethroat's side. She squatted on the path and closed her eyes so that she could give more attention to what the bird saw.

Firethroat's mouth was lower to the north, where it often belched fire into the sea. There was no sign of a recent flow, and the air was clear of fumes. Shalár's brows twitched together and the bird responded with an angry cry.

Soaring over the jagged rim, she saw only darkness below. At first it seemed that the mountain had fallen dead, but as she gradually saw more clearly through the bird's night-blown eyes, she realized with dread that it was far from so.

Within the mountain was no hollow bowl. A swell of rock had grown inside it, like bread rising in a kitchen's warmth. Shalár knew what the bloated dome portended. She had seen it before. She had seen Ghlanhras shrouded in a fine, gray dust that choked and smothered everything it touched.

Releasing the bird, she stood. "Come."

Without waiting she turned southward again. When she heard the hunters following she hastened her stride. By the time they left the mountain path they were running again, and the storm broke over them. Rain drenched them as they sped toward Ghlanhras.

Dawn was near as they entered the gates, though the sky showed no light through the storm. Shalár sent her two hunters to the holding pens for their reward, and returned to the hall and to her chambers.

The ælven female had recovered enough to put away Shalár's robe and sit in her accustomed place, though she leaned against the doorway with her eyes closed. She started and looked up as Shalár came in, and there was fear in her glance.

"I want to bathe. Go to the kitchens and tell them to send hot water and my tub. Then go pick me some greens from the garden, wash them and bring them to me."

The ælven got slowly to her feet. For a moment she seemed about to fall, then she steadied herself with a hand against the wall. Her eyes were vague and her face weary, her hair disordered. She left the chamber without saying a word, without meeting Shalár's gaze.

Shalár went into her bedchamber and took off her boots and leathers, leaving them heaped on the floor. By the time she was out of them, down to silken tunic and legs, her bath had arrived. While three attendants placed the tub and began to fill it she rummaged for a pot of soap she had found among Othanin's things, spicewood scented and rich with oil. She found it and brought it to the tub along with a comb.

"This is all the hot water that was ready, Bright Lady. More is being heated."

She dismissed the attendants with a nod and glanced into the tub, no more than two handspans deep in water. Steam curled from its surface. Shalár set down her soap and comb on a low table that one of the attendants moved beside the tub, then sent them all away and pulled off her tunic and legs.

She stepped into the water and sighed with pleasure as its heat soaked into her feet. Sitting down in the tub, she cupped handfuls of water over herself, then began to spread the soap along her limbs and rub it into her flesh. Attendants returned with steaming pitchers, enough to fill the tub and enable her to wash her hair. By the time she had finished bathing and stepped out of the tub to dry herself with soft cloths, she had begun to wonder what had become of the ælven female.

She donned fresh clothing and looked out into the hallway. Ranad loitered there, and glanced up at her.

"Where is the ælven?"

Ranad shrugged. "I saw her going to the kitchens. I have not seen her since."

"I sent her to the gardens. Go and find her."

"It is nearly dawn."

Shalár raised an eyebrow at him. "You had best hurry, then."

He looked mildly alarmed, then turned and left, his stride quickening to a run. Shalár returned to her bedchamber and combed out her hair. She did not feel tired, so she returned to her workroom and made notes about the metal works on Firethroat, and about her observations of the mountain.

She pondered whether to wait before sending the coppersmith to the works. If the mountain erupted, he might be killed, and she was loathe to lose a skilled craftsman. Best to wait, she decided.

A knock on her door made her glance up. "Come."

The door opened to admit one of the gate's watchers, accompanied by the ælven Shalár had sent to Woodrun. The watcher pushed the ælven forward, then left at a nod from Shalár.

The ælven coughed. He looked winded, soaked and travel-weary. His hair hung damp and lank, and his legs and shoes were spattered with mud. Shalár leaned back in her chair, eyebrows raised.

"Well. I had all but given up hope of seeing you again."

The ælven's eyes searched the chamber. "My daughter?"

"Give me your news and you have time to save her."

A look of horror crossed his face, then he began to speak rapidly. "There are two Greenglens and two Stonereaches in Woodrun. The governor's daughter is not with them. Another Greenglen rode for the Steppes. They have told the theyn to gather warriors, and she is doing so. I heard no mention of a plan to attack Ghlanhras."

"How many warriors has she raised?"

"Some seventy as yet, I believe."

"Does she expect to raise more?"

"That I do not know. They expect to be joined by a force from the south. A large force, from the way they speak of it."

Shalár frowned. These were ill tidings, save only in that it seemed an immediate attack was not planned. The ælven would wait for their larger force to join them before moving against Ghlanhras.

"Please. My daughter?"

Shalár glanced toward the doorway. Ranad had been too long in fetching the ælven. She stood up, wondering if something had gone wrong, if the female had summoned more courage than Shalár expected, courage enough to attack Ranad.

A rumble of thunder sounded overhead. Shalár narrowed her eyes.

"Come with me."

She led him down the corridor toward the back of the hall, to the garden's entrance. She paused, knowing the sun had risen. Storm was some protection, but not complete protection, and she did not wish any risk to her child.

The door into the gardens faced north, so she could look out of it without risk of being touched by the sun. Shalár was just about to open it when a thump fell against it and the door swung inward.

Stepping back, she watched Ranad enter carrying the ælven female lewdly against his hips, her legs hanging limp to either side of him. She looked unconscious, and they were both drenched, the female's gown clinging wetly to Ranad's leathers. He leaned his back against the door to push it closed, and looked at Shalár.

"The sun is up." He grinned.

The ælven stepped toward them. "Teshali!"

Shalár pushed him back, then glared at Ranad. "What are you doing, fool? Put her down."

"Alas, Bright Lady, I cannot obey you." Ranad's grin widened and he cupped a hand beneath the female's chin, raising her face to his. "We are bred even now, are we not, my sweet?"

"Teshali!"

The ælven male lunged toward them in greater earnest. Shalár stopped him with a backhanded blow that sent him sprawling. Rage was in his face as he looked at his daughter in Ranad's embrace. He got up and rushed at them again.

Shalár threw him down, and when he made to rise she kicked him until he was still. He lay gasping for breath, then raised his head to glare at her.

"You promised she would not be harmed!"

"Well, she is sure to be untroubled now. Her honored state protects her." She looked at the hunter. "Are you certain, Ranad?"

"Oh, yes. The child will be a male, he tells me." He laughed drunkenly, and slid down against the door until he was sitting on the floor.

Torn between exasperation and admiration of his ability to get himself indoors while in such a condition, Shalár stared at Ranad, debating what to do. He and the female would be coupled for some while, yet. She did not wish to leave them where they were, but the only chambers nearby were her own.

"Walk a little farther, Ranad, and you may rest in my chambers."

"You honor me, Bright Lady, yet I fear I cannot get up."

"Help him." Shalár prodded the ælven male, and bent to lend her own assistance.

Between them they hauled Ranad to his feet once more. The ælven touched his daughter's face with tender concern, but she did not rouse. He hovered beside them, his expression shifting from grief to anger and back again, as Ranad staggered his way to Shalár's chambers with the weight of the female on his chest.

They passed the kitchens and workrooms where curious attendants stood watching in the doorways. Shalár ignored them, and none dared to raise a question.

Shalár led Ranad to her bedchamber, where he collapsed backward onto the bed and heaved a great sigh. The ælven male made a small, anxious sound and darted forward to move one of his daughter's legs from an awkward position. Shalár dragged him away, back out to her workroom, and made him sit across the table from her.

"You may not think it, but this is good fortune for your daughter."

He glanced angrily at Shalár, but said nothing. She smiled.

"She is now certain to live for at least a year. I shall probably allow her to nurse the child. You should be glad, for Ghlanhras is sure to be attacked before then, and I would have kept my pledge to slay her."

A swallow moved the ælven's throat. His face was set in grief, but he made no protest. Wise of him, she thought.

"Of course, I will not hesitate to kill both her and the child if you disobey me."

He raised his head, but did not meet her gaze. Instead he stared at the wall beyond her with dread-filled eyes.

Shalár straightened the papers on her table, setting aside the notes she had made earlier. She was well pleased with what she had learned this night, though some of the tidings were ill news.

She was pleased that the ælven spy had shown the wisdom to return from Woodrun, and pleased also with Ranad for siring a child. Shalár would not slay the mother and child, despite what she had told the female's father. She gazed at him, wondering if he had the wit to surmise as much. Even if he did, she doubted he would risk her wrath.

"Now, then. I understand there is a coppersmith among the ælven in the city. Tell me all you know about him."

❀ The Trade Road ❀

Turisan's gaze rose to the Ebons, where a few drifts of cloud played yet around the highest peaks. Fresh snow lay well down upon the mountains' shoulders. He looked to the north, toward the Great Sleeper, where Eliani lay somewhere curled in the warmth of a stranger's home. A cave, she had said. The most comfortable cave she had ever seen.

Impatience smote him. She should not lie anywhere without him. He knew it was senseless, but that was his feeling. He knew also that if they were to be useful as mindspeakers, they must often be apart.

Not like this, though. Not now. They had been parted long enough for now.

Though he had held off from speaking to Eliani, he was weary of waiting for her to explain. He sent her the signal requesting her attention, and after a moment she answered.

Yes? Is it morning?

It is, and we are marching. Are you still reading?

I finished a short while ago. I have been thinking.

Turisan waited, but she said no more. All manner of foolish feeling assailed him: jealousy, worry that he had lost her love, anger at the nameless friend who had so distracted her. All nonsense, he knew. He closed his eyes, trying to release it all.

Turisan?

Yes.

Our host does not know that I am a mindspeaker, and so I cannot ask his permission to tell you about him. May I ask you to keep what I am about to say private for the nonce?

Turisan wanted to ask why, but he knew he must trust her. *All right.*

He has been living here a very long time, since the Bitter Wars, and he has not decided whether he wishes to be known. I have given him my pledge to respect his privacy. I ask you as my partner to honor this pledge as well.

Very well.

My love, I think he can influence the Council.

Turisan blinked in surprise. He had not expected the Council to figure in the conversation.

How so?

The scrolls I have been reading are a history. They are his work, his reminiscences of the Bitter Wars and how they began.

Turisan waited, certain there must be more. He had himself read several histories of the wars, some from citizens of Southfæld who had long since crossed, some copies that his father had commissioned of documents that rested in Hollirued.

Love, he was a member of Clan Darkshore.

Darkshore?

Yes. His history is of how they saw the crisis.

Clan Darkshore were traitors to the creed!

But he was not. He urged them to keep the creed, and was cast out of his clan for it. He lives by the creed now, I am certain of it.

Turisan was silent for a moment, absorbing the import of her words. If this unnamed elder had truly seen the wars, and could tell the tale as Darkshore saw it, he might well influence the Council, but to what purpose?

The most important part of it is the description of how the hunger swept through Darkshore. I consider it proof that it is an illness. The Councils at that time all assumed it was a choice, but truly those who were stricken had no choice. Ulithan's history makes that painfully clear.

Ulithan. The name was unfamiliar, but Turisan would not forget it.

The only choice that was made, and it was a fateful one, was that of the Governor and head of Clan Darkshore to stand by those of his people who were stricken, to help them and try to live in harmony with them. That choice led to Clan Darkshore's being cast out of the ælven. After all their struggles, to be chastised so made Darkshore deeply bitter. I wish you could read the history yourself, love. I am not expressing its depth.

Turisan gazed toward the Sleeper, wishing most intently that he could be there with her. He would read all the scrolls she wished if only he were beside her.

So, what will you? Take the scrolls to the Council?

I mean to ask him if I may take copies of the first five. I do not think he would send his only copies with me, nor should he. His history has been preserved so long, it should not be placed at risk of any accident.

Turisan had to smile. She meant that it should not be entrusted to her care. Anything Eliani possessed was immediately in danger. He laughed softly, remembering her contrition as she had told him of the loss of her cloak, as if such a thing mattered. Only she mattered to him. As long as she was safe, he cared for naught else.

The others are stirring, love. I must go. I will speak to you again today.

Please do. I have missed you.

She sent a wave of love that made him ache for her, then withdrew. Turisan gave his attention to the road ahead, the long weary leagues that lay between him and Eliani. He wanted to urge his horse to a gallop, to speed across the distance to her side, but his duty lay in Fireshore.

❁ The Great Sleeper ❁

Ulithan came in from the passage. "The storm has lifted."

Eliani nodded, then sat back on her heels and looked at Vanorin, whose ankle she had been examining. "All the swelling is gone. You should be able to walk on it, if you take care."

"I shall take care not to fall down another cliff." He smiled wryly as he reached for his boots.

Eliani smiled back and stood. Stretching her arms toward the cave's ceiling, she could just brush it with her fingertips.

She decided to look outside and try to judge how much snow had fallen. If it was very deep they might have to wait another day or two to travel onward, though she hoped to avoid that. Though she enjoyed Ulithan's company, she was sure he must be wishing to have his home to himself once more.

She pulled on her leathers for warmth, and walked out through the passage to the ledge outside the cave. Bright sunlight gleamed from a snow-laden landscape, setting her eyes to watering. Drifts of snow lay along the ledge and within the hollow that marked the entrance to Ulithan's cave. Eliani stepped forward and shaded her eyes with a hand as she gazed northward, her breath fogging on the chill air.

She could not find the place where they had lit the pyre. Overcoming hesitance, she searched with khi for any sign of Kelevon in the wooded slopes below, and found none. Snow lay heavy for several leagues, at least a day's travel in deep snow, if they left today.

Tonight, she amended. Luruthin could not travel in daylight. Well, perhaps the snow would melt a bit by nightfall.

She heard someone coming out of the cave. Vanorin, she thought, coming to see for himself the result of the storm. She waited, gazing across the snowy mountains.

"I am going to fetch water. Would you care to walk with me?"

Eliani turned, astonished. Ulithan stood smiling at her, a large water skin over his shoulder, his hair gleaming white against the snowy cliff behind. Fear seized her.

"Ulithan! The sun!"

His gaze flicked toward the sky, then back to her as he smiled in amusement. "It does not trouble me."

"How can that be?"

His smile turned wistful. "When the alben's curse, as you call it, came over my family, the only mark it made upon me is what you see."

Eliani stared at him in disbelief. Without doubt he looked alben; the white hair and black eyes still gave her alarm at odd moments. Out here, in daylight, his skin seemed so pale as to be nearly white as well.

Yet he stood smiling at her in the sunshine, untroubled as he claimed. She remembered Luruthin's distress after only an instant's exposure to the sun.

"Then you—you do not have to hunt ...?"

Ulithan shook his head. "When I hunt it is for game, even as you do."

"I misunderstood."

As she gazed at him in amazement, she realized that his khi had no trace of the prickling she had come to associate with those who suffered the curse. She had not noted its absence before.

"Forgive me. I have never heard of such a...."

"Nor I of another such." Ulithan smiled again, sadly. "I am alone in this, as far as I know."

"And this is why Darkshore cast you out."

He nodded. "Partly why."

"And no other clan would have you."

"None believed me. The war was underway. Everywhere I went I was met with fear and suspicion. My attempts at explanation were not heard. Some folk even drove me away with threats of violence. At last I gave up trying to find a place among my people."

"Oh, Ulithan! How terrible."

He shrugged. "It was a long time ago. I am content." He shifted the water skin over his shoulder. "Will you walk with me to the spring?"

"Yes."

He led the way northward along the ledge, his boots making deep tracks in the drifted snow. Eliani followed, stepping in his footprints, musing on his strange fate. How could it be that the curse had afflicted him, yet left him untouched save for his appearance?

She felt this was important, that if she could understand it, she might find a way of fighting the curse itself. She knew so little of such matters, though. She wished yet again that she could consult with Jhinani.

Ulithan stopped at a frozen pool no more than an armspan across. Water trickled over a cascade of ice that issued from a crack in the cliff wall a little above the pool. Ulithan knelt beside it and broke the tiny frozen waterfall with his fingers, setting the spring free to sparkle in the sun as it poured from the rock. He held the water skin beneath the flow.

Eliani squatted across the pool from him and tapped its surface with a finger to test how hard it had frozen. The sunshine would melt it by midday, she thought.

"Ulithan?"

He turned his head to look at her, black eyes inquiring. Eliani cleared her throat.

"My father is the head of my clan. He would welcome you to join us, I know."

Ulithan's eyes widened and color came into his cheeks. A look of astonishment crossed his face. In the few days she had known him, she had not seen him so moved.

"That is most kind of you. You honor me. Please do not be offended if I decline." He glanced back at the spring and shifted the water skin, then laughed softly. "I have grown accustomed to my solitary ways. I no longer wish to live otherwise."

Eliani nodded, unsurprised. After so long alone, he would likely find Clan Stonereach an unbearably boisterous company.

"The invitation stands. I know I can speak for my father in this."

Ulithan gazed at her thoughtfully. "Your father is head of Stonereach?"

"And governor of Alpinon. I will make you another invitation on his behalf, which I know he will support. He has summoned the Ælven Council to meet at Highstone on the first day of spring. We would be greatly honored if you would attend."

"The Ælven Council?" Ulithan looked bemused. "I am so far removed from ælven affairs, I cannot see how I could serve the Council."

"Your presence would be of service. Your very existence proves we do not fully understand the alben's curse. Ulithan, the Lost plan to seek clan status at this Council. I think your presence would be of great help to them."

"The Lost." He nodded as if recalling her words. "Those who live with the curse, but live by the creed. Their path must be hard."

"It is."

"And you think I can help them." He gazed at her, frowning slightly. "I do not know."

He looked away, back at the spring. The water skin was beginning to bulge and he shifted it again to let it fill more easily.

Eliani thought he would refuse to attend the Council. The idea of going into an ælven city was likely a frightening one to him, after so long.

"Whether or not you decide to attend, I would like to ask a boon of you. I would like to take copies of your history to the Council."

He met her gaze. "Those events are known. I have told nothing new."

Eliani shifted her footing, laying clasped hands across her knees. This was important, she felt. Deeply important.

"You have told how Darkshore came to fall. This is not understood among the ælven. If I can take the first five scrolls of your history to the Council, it will change how they understand the curse. Please, Ulithan. I will make the copies myself, if you will allow."

He blinked as he gazed at her. For a long moment he said nothing, and Eliani began to fear he would refuse this as well.

"I will make copies for you, if you think it so important."

"I do." Eliani breathed relief. "I do think it important. We are facing the same dilemma that caused the Bitter Wars. The curse has arisen in Fireshore again. Ghlanhras was dying before the alben attacked it."

Sadness deepened in Ulithan's eyes. "I am sorry to hear it." He shook his head. "Ghlanhras was ever cursed, I fear."

"All our troubles have come from a failure to understand that curse. I am certain of it. And I am certain your history will be of help."

He gazed at her long and steadily. "If you think it will help, then I am honored to contribute."

"Thank you, Ulithan!"

"I would ask a favor in return."

"Of course."

"Tell no one where I dwell, or how to find me."

Eliani drew a breath, disappointed but unsurprised. "You would find friends among the ælven, I believe. Among the Lost, certainly."

He smiled softly. "But their ways and mine differ."

She nodded. "Yes."

"And though I believe your assurance that your father would welcome me, there would be others in your clan who would not understand, who would fear me." He shook his head. "I put aside that struggle long ago. I have no wish to take it up again."

"I understand. I will honor your wishes."

"Thank you."

They sat in silence while the water skin filled. Eliani watched him, gazing at the lines of his face, trying to commit them to memory. She was sorry he had chosen to remain alone.

"How long do you think it might take to copy the scrolls?"

"Some few days. I will have to make more parchments. I fear I have filled all the ones I had ready with Vanorin's songs."

His eyes glinted with mischief as he grinned. Eliani smiled back. Ulithan had made Vanorin sing him every song he knew, while they waited out the storm. Some they had sung together, Ulithan's voice clear and rich, the harmonies Vanorin taught him filling the cave.

Eliani traced a swirling knotwork on the surface of the frozen pool with a fingertip. "My father loves music. He always has several bards at his court."

"You are trying to tempt me."

She chuckled. "Yes."

"I thought when I first saw you that you would grieve me."

She looked up and saw him smiling softly at her. A rush of tenderness filled her heart. She cared for him, truly, this strange and solitary soul. He had such patience, such gentleness.

"I have no wish to grieve you."

His smile broadened, then he looked away, jiggling the water skin. "Perhaps I will visit your father someday. I have never been to Highstone."

"You would be welcome."

Ulithan lifted the water skin away from the spring and carefully closed it. The spring water splashed onto its frozen pool and began to spread across it, flowing over Eliani's design. When it reached the edges it swelled for a moment, a liquid mirror, then spilled across a low place to trickle down the mountainside.

"You had best not wait while I copy the scrolls."

Eliani agreed, though she would have enjoyed staying longer. Luruthin needed to hunt. He was showing strain, now, and she thought he was beginning to suffer.

"We mean to go to the Lost's camp. They are near Bitterfield at present."

"You will start tonight?"

Eliani met his gaze, realization tingling through her. Ulithan knew they must travel by night. He knew, though none of them had mentioned Luruthin's affliction.

"Forgive me." Ulithan spoke with gentle sadness. "I have seen it many times."

Eliani sighed, nodding. Her throat tightened and fresh grief washed through her.

"He will join the Lost." Her eyes were blurring with tears, and she rubbed at them impatiently.

"It is fortunate he has such friends to go to."

Eliani nodded. "Yes."

Suddenly the grief overwhelmed her and she gave a gasping sob. Angry with herself, she stood and turned away, leaning a hand against the cold rock of the cliff as she struggled to control her emotion. A moment later a hand touched her shoulder, and warmth spread through her.

Startled, she held still. At first she thought it was healing, but then she knew it was merely the strength of Ulithan's khi, warm and gentle, filled with subtle power. She was awed by its depth. She turned, tears forgotten, and gazed into Ulithan's eyes, then laid her head upon his shoulder as if that were the most natural thing to do.

The water skin sloshed as he dropped it. His arms folded around her and Eliani closed her eyes. She felt a deep satisfaction ripple through his khi, and realized that he had longed for this, only a simple embrace, for centuries.

They stood still for a long while, breathing together, sharing khi. Eliani's brow grew warm and she returned the signal for delay. She would explain this to Turisan later. This did not breach her vow, and she needed it as much as did Ulithan.

At last the sound of approaching footsteps made them part. Eliani stood blinking at the bright snow while Ulithan bent to retrieve his water skin.

"Eliani?"

She looked back toward the cave and saw Vanorin hurrying toward them, following their tracks in the snow, concern in his face. Her own face was burning. She hoped Vanorin would not notice, or would think it caused by the cold.

"I was beginning to worry."

"We were talking."

Vanorin looked at Ulithan and started in surprise. He glanced at Eliani, who nodded.

"Ulithan does not suffer the effects of the curse. Only his appearance was changed by it."

Ulithan stepped forward with the water skin slung over his shoulder. "I have been so discourteous as to suggest that you should leave here tonight, not because I tire of your company, but because your friend hungers."

Vanorin looked at him sharply. "I suspected you knew."

"You will find no kobalen above the snowfall. You must travel down to the foothills, and even there you may not find them. Follow the Varindel down to the edge of the steppes, then cut north to the Bitterfield road." Ulithan looked at Eliani. "It is not the most direct path to Bitterfield, but in this season the road is your best choice."

Eliani nodded, resigned to it. This far south, pursuit from the alben was unlikely, and at least near the road they would have a better chance of finding kobalen.

"You have been very kind to shelter us. You must be wishing us gone."

"No."

It was said softly, with a tenderness that rang in Eliani's heart. She looked at Ulithan and saw him smiling at her with an expression so fond it made her cheeks burn afresh. She smiled briefly in return, then turned away and started back to the cave. Vanorin fell into step behind her.

The warmth of the cave was a comfort. Luruthin looked up as they entered, and managed a wan smile. Eliani smiled back as she joined him by the fire. She put another stick of wood on the coals and rubbed her hands together over them.

"Cold outside?"

"Yes, but clear. The sun is out."

He gazed at the fire. Eliani saw a swallow move his throat.

"We will start tonight."

Luruthin glanced at her, then nodded. "I have delayed you."

"The storm delayed us. No matter. We would not have met Ulithan otherwise, and that would have been a great loss."

She felt Luruthin's gaze upon her. She reached out to shift the wood,

238 ~ Pati Nagle

pushing it to a better position. A small flame appeared beneath it.

"Ulithan has agreed to let me show his history to the Council."

"He will give you his scrolls?"

"No, no. He will make copies."

"Ah."

Eliani had encouraged Luruthin to read the history as well, but he had not cared to, and she dared not press him. He was grieving his own fate, and to read of other sufferers would be no comfort. She feared his sorrow might yet drive him to abandon his flesh.

Vanorin sat down between them. Ulithan moved about the cave, humming as he hung up the water skin and fussed among his shelves. Eliani watched sidelong as he took a large skin from one of the pegs and began to stretch it over a frame of lashed branches.

"We can reach the edge of the Steppes tonight, if we go swiftly."

Eliani looked at Vanorin. "Will your ankle bear it?"

He nodded, then briefly smiled. "Thanks to your ministrations, my lady."

Eliani sighed, wishing her ministrations could help Luruthin as well. She leaned her back against the cave wall and closed her eyes. Turisan was waiting. With some trepidation, she sent him the signal asking his attention.

Eliani!

He said no more, but she could feel his unhappiness and confusion. She reached out gently, very gently, with a warm thought.

Forgive me, love. I have been talking with Ulithan.

Talking!

Yes. And he held me for a moment, when I was overcome with sadness for Luruthin.

Turisan's dismay rolled through her in waves. She felt his fear that she would betray her oath to him, and knew that she had caused it. The flash of anger that rose in her at this mistrust she set aside. Her atonement would be to reassure him.

Here is how it was, my love.

She opened her memory to him, showing him Ulithan for the first time, laying all she had learned of this strange new friend bare to Turisan's exploration. It was frightening; she had not opened herself so completely since the night of their handfasting. Had Turisan held any ill will toward her, she was entirely vulnerable.

There was no ill will, though; only the fear which was fading now, the ripples smaller and smaller until they grew still. Turisan traced her memory of the conversation by the spring. She gave all to him, trusting that he would honor the promises she had made to Ulithan.

At last there was no more to remember. They were silent together for a long while. Eliani waited, hoping Turisan would understand and be reassured that he was yet, and always, her only love.

You comforted him as much as he you.

Yes.

Why is he so stubborn in keeping alone? He would benefit by visiting an ælven town now and again.

Eliani smiled at hearing him express her own opinion. Only picture his reception, love. *They would not understand.*

I suppose not.

Roguish mirth swept through his thoughts. *Perhaps we can find a volunteer to offer him consolation.*

Eliani chuckled aloud. *Will you send out the call, or shall I?*

Hm.

No, we cannot. I have promised to tell no one where he dwells.

A stirring nearby made her open her eyes. Luruthin had put another stick on the fire. Beyond him, Eliani saw Ulithan seated before his stretched skin, but he was not working it. His hands lay still at his sides as he gazed intently at her. A tingle went through her shoulders.

He knows, love. He knows we are mindspeakers.

How can he know? You have said nothing, nor would the others.

He can feel it.

Ulithan looked away, picked up a sharpened stone, and began scraping at the skin with long, gentle strokes. Eliani felt her cheeks flood with color, and wondered, though she thought it impossible, if Ulithan was aware they had been talking of him.

❀ Ghlanhras ❀

The Steppegard bowed low before the edge of the dais where Shalár sat, not meeting her gaze. "Bright Lady."

She gazed at him a moment, taking in the changes since she had last seen him. His curling hair was now streaked with white, and his clothing showed the wear of many nights outdoors. The hunters who had escorted him forward stood watching him with suspicion.

Shalár smiled. "I did not expect to see you again, Kelev."

He tilted his head upward just enough to look up at her. "You once offered me refuge, Bright Lady. I have come to see the wisdom of accepting, if I may yet claim it."

"Come to see wisdom?"

She saw him tense, and knew that he feared she would seize his khi. That fear was enough.

She stood and walked toward him. To keep his gaze on her he must either kneel or stand. He chose the latter, which she expected. He had always been a prideful creature. Her hunters bristled.

She stopped at the edge of the dais. "Yes, I remember offering you refuge. What can have possessed me, I wonder? I ceased long ago to make such offers to ælven who acquired the hunger. They were never able to adjust."

"Perhaps you saw a greater potential in me, Bright Lady."

She raised an eyebrow. "Perhaps I did."

He lowered his voice. "Perhaps you felt there were ways in which I might serve you."

Shalár's lip curved in amusement. "I am certain there are ways in which you might serve me."

She turned away, summoning one of the hunters with a gesture as she strolled to one side of the dais. "Go to my chambers and take up watch at the door. I want to speak to this one in greater privacy."

The hunter nodded and went away down the corridor. Shalár looked

241

back at Kelev.

"Come."

She beckoned him with a jerk of her head and went after the hunter without looking back to see if Kelev obeyed. After only the slightest hesitation, she heard him following.

The hunter took up a place outside her door. Leaving it open, she led Kelev into the work room, seated herself at the table, and waved him to a chair. He sat and waited, gazing about the room while Shalár dipped a black quill in ink and pulled a page toward her.

"A pity about your hair."

"Is it?"

"Yes. It means you cannot go among the ælven to gather information for me."

Kelev gave a cough of laughter. "Lady, I could not go among them in any case. I have become rather notorious, I fear."

"Oh? How so?"

"The Ælven Council saw through my deception."

Shalár's eyes narrowed. "Unfortunate. How come you here, then?"

"I escaped."

He offered nothing more. She leaned forward, arms crossed on the table top. "Escaped from Glenhallow, when they knew you to be a deceiver? How did you manage it?"

"I found a willing friend."

He let his voice drop on the words, and his gaze lingered on Shalár's throat. She sensed his desires—all of them—and ignored them.

"Your friend did not journey hither with you."

"She would have slowed me."

"Ah."

"Particularly as I had to feed from her."

Shalár frowned. "Does she live?"

"I assume so. I did not kill her."

"How generous."

"Well, she had been of help to me."

Shalár made no further comment, but picked up a sheaf of papers and leafed through them. It angered her that Kelev had violated the one rule she had set for herself—never to feed upon the ælven—but she had first led him to do it, so she could hardly be surprised.

With that thought came the memory of their last coupling. It had been frenzied, the unexpected aftermath of a glut of feeding on ælven blood. The first ælven blood she had tasted, and the last she hoped to taste. There were few things she would not do for her people, but that was one of them. It was wrong.

She glanced up at him and saw him smiling at her with open appreciation. His smile widened to a grin as their gazes met.

He glanced toward the hunter and lowered his voice. "I was thinking of when we were last together. I did enjoy that."

"It was not for your pleasure. I wanted a child."

"I will gladly try again to give you one whenever you wish it, my lady."

His gaze shifted to the curtained doorway behind her. She almost laughed aloud at his presumption, but instead she merely smiled.

"I will let you know when I wish it."

She withdrew a page from her sheaf, studied it, then laid all down and looked at him. "What were you, when you dwelt among the ælven?"

"I trained horses."

She scoffed. "Well, that is useless now. Have you any other skills?"

"I was a guide. I led trade caravans throughout the ælven realms."

"How well do you know Fireshore?"

"I know the trade roads. They are few enough. I traveled less often here."

"Do you know the darkwood camps?"

"I have seen some of them."

Shalár nodded slightly and wrote another line, then put up her quill. She pushed aside her papers and gazed thoughtfully at Kelev. He returned her gaze, waiting.

"You have no other skills? Carpentry, perhaps?"

He laughed. "I am a poor hand at that. I can plan something pretty, but my hands will make a mess if I try to build it."

"What if others did the building?"

He blinked. "You have a particular project in mind?"

She stood and retrieved a large roll of paper from a shelf, then spread it on the table before him. "I want covered passages to give access to key places in Ghlanhras. This plan is underway, but it is going too slowly."

The Steppegard leaned forward, peering at the plan. "Perhaps I can help. Your folk are doing the work?"

"No. It is being done by captives."

"Ah. I may indeed be able to help, in that case. I can be persuasive."

His voice rose on the last word, making it almost a question as he looked up at her.

"Hm." She rolled the plan up again. "Take this and study it, go and observe the progress, then return and give me your opinion."

He accepted the page with lowered gaze. She sensed a flash of something in his khi—anger? Impatience? It was gone at once.

"As you wish, Bright Lady."

"But first, you are no doubt wishing for a meal and a rest." She drew a half-page of paper toward her and scrawled on it, then stood and handed it to the guard.

"Take Kelev to the pens and give that to Wahral. You may have what remains of his feeder. Show him to a house near the circle."

The guard bowed. "Yes, Bright Lady."

The Steppegard stood, and she regarded him. "The houses are in disarray, but you will not mind that. Choose one you like and set it in order."

Kelev bowed. "Thank you, Bright Lady."

She watched him go, wondering how he had managed to escape. She should have questioned him about the ælven in Glenhallow, but there would be time for that. He was unlikely to leave after asking for refuge. There was nowhere else he could go.

❀ Fairhollow ❀

Rephanin gazed out of the window over the town of Fairhollow, infinitely grateful to be indoors. Ehranan had bespoken rooms for him and Filari at one of the public lodges. A bed and a roof seemed extravagant luxuries, and he felt a slight pang for the army who were camped outside the town, but at least they, too, would have comforts they had not known in some days. The town was already preparing a feast for them.

Fairhollow was fairly large, a trading center for local farmers and hunters. Houses built of the blond stone common to the plains climbed up both sides of a shallow valley. A small river ran down its center, the road crossing it on a wide bridge built of darkwood, and smaller footbridges connected the two halves of the town on either side of the road.

Folk here were dark-haired, for the most part; Ælvanen in appearance, which roused Rephanin's memories of his first home. Here and there he saw a head of dark brown hair, sometimes curling, instead of black.

"Your pardon, my lord."

He turned to find the host of the lodge standing in the open doorway, holding a tray with an ewer and cups. She was one of the brown-haired folk, and her eyes were dark green; a hint of Stonereach blood in her.

"I brought some wine for you and the lady." She glanced over her shoulder toward Filari's room. "Should I have brought separate trays?"

"No, no. We can share. Thank you kindly."

She blushed at his smile, and hastened to set the tray on a table near the fire. Rephanin crossed the hall and knocked on Filari's door.

"Filari? Would you care for some wine?"

The door opened and Filari looked out, suspicion in her face. Rephanin gestured toward his room, where the host was building up the fire. Filari gazed at her for a long moment.

"All right."

The host seemed even more in awe of Filari than of himself. He doubted Ehranan had told her, but she had plainly learned that they were mindspeakers.

Filari carried a chair in from her room and put it before the hearth. Rephanin reached for the ewer but the host was before him; she poured wine for them both, offered to bring food, and finally withdrew after Rephanin told her rather firmly that they had all they needed.

Settling into his chair, he stretched his feet toward the fire and sipped his wine. "This is pleasant."

Filari said nothing. She was in her most common mood: grim endurance. Poor company; he sought to change it.

Filari, what is it?

She was distant, withheld. For a moment he thought she would not answer, then she spoke so abruptly it startled him.

Do you expect me to spend the night with you?

Defensiveness bristled in her khi. Rephanin took another swallow of wine.

I expect nothing, though you are welcome if you wish to stay.

Filari appeared to relax somewhat. *It is what they are all saying. That you have chosen me as a lover.*

Camp gossip. Shall I deny it?

They would only believe it the more.

Rephanin chuckled. *I fear you are right.*

She took a deep swallow of wine. Rephanin wondered if he should not have accepted the host's offer of food.

Filari.

What?

I think you must have been hurt. Do you care to tell me of it?

She stared long at him, breathing sharply, then lowered her gaze. *I do not see what that would serve.*

It might help me avoid causing you further pain.

She pressed her lips together, then drank more wine. After a moment she put down the cup and closed her eyes.

It was the alben. Kelevon.

Rephanin nodded, though she could not see. He waited, not wishing to press her. She drew a ragged breath and sighed, rubbing at her eyes.

He—took control of me. In mind and in flesh.

Rephanin blinked. What she seemed to be saying was inconceivable.
He used khi to do this?

Yes.

Horror spread through Rephanin's awareness. This was a violation of the creed at its most basic level. One did not interfere uninvited with another's khi. To do so was to dishonor that other, and so to dishonor oneself.

Have you told anyone of this?

The healer who tended my hurts, but I think she did not believe me. She blamed me for his escape.

Filari stopped speaking abruptly and buried her face in her hands. Rephanin watched, his horror turning to anger against Kelevon.

You are not to blame.

I am. I knew in the back of my mind that he might deceive me, yet I persisted.

Blame is useless. Let it go.

She sat still, saying nothing. Listening, he thought. Waiting to hear exculpation.

Filari, remember when we talked of going on? That is what you must do now. Let go of the traitor, and know that any blame was his, not yours.

She did not answer. He could see her breathing deeply, steadily, and wondered if she was weeping. His instinct was to offer comfort, but he knew now that he must be very cautious in approaching her in any way. No wonder she bristled so.

If we are to succeed together as partners in mindspeech, we must learn to trust one another. I have sworn never to hurt you, and I stand by that, Filari. Yet if it hurts you to be touched at all, then I do not know how we shall manage.

She raised her head, blinking. Her eyes were dry, though her countenance was strained. She looked at him, and he could see the depth of her fear in her soft, dark eyes.

Poor child. To have been wounded so, and then blamed for it by her people. Pushed away by her family, and shunned by the Guard.

Rephanin reached his hand toward her, laying it on the table between them, palm up. She gazed at his hand for a long while, then slowly moved her own above it, holding it a handspan away, not touching but close enough that the khi from their palms began to blend. It tingled softly in Rephanin's flesh. He held still, leaving it to her to decide when and how far to go further.

You are very patient.

Rephanin smiled. *Sometimes. Not always. I make no promises there.*

Her lips curved slightly and her frown eased. She moved her hand a little closer and the tingling in his palm grew stronger.

Your khi is not like his.

She sounded surprised. Turning her head to meet his gaze, she looked thoughtful.

His was ... sharp. No, that does not describe it.

She seemed to be struggling for words. Rephanin watched her frustration.

You could show me.

She looked at him sharply, questioning. Fear leapt in her khi, then subsided.

With mindspeech we can show memories to each other, or even present sights, though that can be confusing. May I offer an example? May I share a memory with you? It means deepening our contact.

Filari blinked a few times, then gave a sharp nod. She was breathing rapidly, and he knew this frightened her.

Close your eyes.

She did so, and after a moment seemed to relax a little. She drew a deeper breath and let it out slowly.

Rephanin closed his own eyes and summoned a memory of Hollirued, of the coast near the city where he had often gone to gaze across the endless waters. He filled his mind with it, then opened the sight to Filari.

He heard her draw breath sharply. His own heart leapt with fear lest she react with violence again, for he had opened himself now and was unprotected. She did not, though. She slowly moved into his awareness, taking in the full sensation of the memory.

The sea. I have never seen it.

Rephanin offered her the smell of the water, the calls of the gulls. She embraced them, and he could feel her wonder. She had forgotten to be afraid, and in so doing had moved into a deeper bond. He remained still, open to her exploration, ready to withdraw if she became uncomfortable.

How beautiful. Thank you.

Rephanin smiled, knowing she would feel it. Instead of using words, he sent the thought of welcomeness to her, in all its shades of meaning.

"Oh!"

Suddenly she was gone. Not with the violence of her earlier reaction, but with a swiftness and finality that left Rephanin breathless. He opened his eyes and saw her hugging herself, rocking slightly.

"Too close? Forgive me."

She looked at him and ceased rocking. She swallowed, sniffed.

"I ought to get used to it. You are right, we have to trust...."

"We have time. No need to hurry."

"Th-thank you."

She looked down to where his hand still lay, then laid her own over it. The physical contact brought their khi together. Rephanin returned the clasp lightly, and was unsurprised when she immediately withdrew. She reached for her cup and tossed back the remaining wine.

"More?" He picked up the ewer.

"No." She glanced sharply at him, then frowned at the cup. "Well, yes."

"I pledge I will not attempt to seduce you." Rephanin kept his voice light as he poured.

"It would take more wine than this."

A jest. The first she had made all day. Rephanin put down the ewer and smiled as he watched her sip the wine. There was hope for their partnership, he thought, though he would have to treat her carefully.

"Would you like to try showing me a memory?"

She gazed at him, blinking. *Not of him.*

Very well. Make your own choice.

She thought for a moment, sipping her wine, then put down the cup. Rephanin watched her close her eyes, and closed his own when her vision began to intrude on him.

She showed him a river, the Silverwash, he thought, but broader than it was near Glenhallow, flowing lazily through a plain of grass. A stream joined it, and bushes grew along the stream's bank. These were the focus of the memory. They were heavy with goldenberries, and the smell of the juice came to him, sharp in his nostrils. Berry-picking, he realized, smiling.

Thunder came into the memory, not the thunder of a storm, but the rumbling of many hoof beats. A herd of horses was approaching. Rephanin was surprised to see no riders; they were wild on the plains, golden-coated, white-maned horses like those the Southfæld Guard preferred to ride.

They leaped across the stream, then splashed into the river with riotous noise, crossing it in a few bounds and galloping onward until they disappeared into the plain. The sound of their hooves faded until all that was left was the breeze stirring the grasses.

Rephanin smiled. *Lovely.*

Filari said nothing, though he sensed that she was pleased. The memory faded, leaving them alone together in silence. Sensing that she needed to be restful in this state, to feel at peace while sharing khi, he remained still, open, calm.

Thank you for the wine.

It was our host's doing, not mine, but of course you are welcome.

And thank you for your patience.

Rephanin smiled softly. *Thank you for yours. We shall find a balance.*

She nodded, managing a smile. She withdrew with the odd twist of khi that was becoming her signature—a mental bow, a quaint formality. Rephanin thought it might be that she did this to complete the severance of contact, to declare for her own comfort that her solitude was absolute.

She stood and went to the door, carrying her cup with her. To his surprise, she paused and looked back at him.

"I will see you at supper."

He nodded, smiling, and watched her go into her room. For the first time, he felt they had made true progress.

Dark had fallen and Eliani could no longer delay. She was loathe to leave Ulithan's cave, and fussed with her saddle packs, lashing and relashing them together so that they rested comfortably on her back. It mattered less than she affected, and at last she shouldered them and stood to take her leave.

Ulithan accompanied them out to the ledge and along it to where they had climbed up. The snow had retreated under a day's sunshine so that only the deepest drifts remained. The sky was clear and cold, glittering with starlight.

In that light Ulithan reminded her very much of the Lost, with his clothes of skin and fur, his white hair and black eyes. She turned to him and smiled.

"Thank you for your help, and for all you have shared with us."

He smiled in return. "Thank you for your company. Your music." He nodded to Vanorin. "I have enjoyed your visit."

"Keep this knife, with our gratitude."

She held out a sheathed belt knife, one of several that Dejhonan had sent from Bitterfield for the party's use just before their departure. It was a commonplace knife, a small tool and useful. Eliani knew that to Ulithan it would be a rare treasure, and she saw his deep appreciation in his eyes as he accepted it with a bow.

"Many thanks."

"May we come again?"

"You must, for the scrolls. Come to the cave by the little falls on the Varindel. You saw them as you came up, yes?"

Eliani nodded, remembering the cave where they had sheltered Luruthin. She glanced at her cousin, but his face showed only patience and the strain of his hunger. He was silent of late, which she thought an ill sign.

"I will leave the scrolls in that cave, so that you need not climb all this way."

"Then I shall not see you again?"

Ulithan smiled softly. "Not this season."

Eliani nodded, accepting his wish to be left alone. Disappointing, but it was his path to choose and she must respect it. She shifted the packs on her shoulders.

"Well, I hope I may visit you again one day."

"Perhaps you will bring your lord to meet me."

"Yes. I know he would be honored."

Ulithan's smile widened, and she had the feeling that he understood how very true were her words. She *did* know, for she had discussed it with Turisan, and Ulithan seemed to perceive this.

Eliani stepped toward the cliff and made to climb down, but was stayed by a touch on her arm. Vanorin stood beside her.

"Let me go first, my lady."

"Is your ankle steady enough to find footing?"

"If it is not, I would not wish to fall upon you."

He started down the cliff, and looked secure enough. Luruthin moved past Eliani to follow him. Left alone with Ulithan, she offered him her arm. After a slight hesitation he clasped it, his khi strong and deep as she remembered.

"Farewell."

She could not help smiling with fondness, and Ulithan returned the smile as he released her and stepped backward. Eliani began to climb down, knowing that he stayed to watch her, that he would stay watching until they had passed out of his sight.

The climb seemed much shorter in calm weather than it had in the storm's fury, and in moments the three of them were standing together on the ledge where Vanorin had fallen. Ulithan had told them of a trail that led down to the river Varindel, which they easily found. Following this path they made much better progress than they had coming up through the woods, and before the night was half gone they had reached the little falls and the cave.

The snow was less deep here, only a handspan at most. They paused to drink from the pool, the icy water biting Eliani's hands and chilling her insides.

Vanorin stood upon the broad stone gazing up at the sky, no doubt calculating how much longer they could travel that night before seeking shelter. He sensed Eliani's gaze and met it, and she saw that he shared her concern. Luruthin must hunt, and soon.

Eliani glanced at her cousin, who had taken water from the pool and was now pacing its edge rather restlessly. She remembered bleeding into a cup for his sake, along with Vanorin, on this very rock.

"Luruthin...if we cannot find kobalen tonight—"

"No."

Eliani pressed her lips together, then took a breath. "Only enough to get you through—"

"No!"

Anger flared in his eyes, making him look savage for a moment. He squeezed them shut and appeared to struggle briefly. When he looked at her again it was with her own kindred's affection.

"Thank you for your generosity, but no. I have no wish to...."

"We understand." Vanorin glanced at Eliani, warning in his eyes. "We shall have to find kobalen, that is all. Are you ready?"

They started downriver once more, following the bank as they had done before. Soon the roar of the larger cascade reached them, first whispering at the border of hearing, then growing to a constant rumble.

Ice hung in long spikes from the snowy shore into the water, which must be piercing cold. Drifts of chill mist reached them from below. Luruthin's face was hard as he gazed down at the broken rocks in the pool.

"A bitter drop."

Eliani took a step nearer to him and he turned his head to look at her. She slid her hand into his and gripped it. The prickling in his khi was much sharper now, unpleasant against her palm, but she kept her grasp and gently pulled Luruthin away from the falls.

"Watersmeet? The Steppes?"

Filari's brow furrowed with worry. Rephanin realized she must be thinking of Kelevon, who hailed from the Steppe Wilds.

Kelevon will not dare go near Watersmeet. Pashari would have his head.

Ehranan took a slice of meat from the platter between them. "The Steppes are closest to Fireshore. Communicating with them is more important than with Eastfæld at present. Governor Pashari will welcome you, be assured. I will give you a letter for her."

Rephanin watched Filari, who had stopped eating and sat staring at her plate. None of these assurances seemed to comfort her, even his private one. He gave a slight cough.

"We have not yet tested Filari's ability to speak at distance."

Ehranan raised an eyebrow. "You spoke from opposite ends of the column."

"Less than a league apart."

"Well, she must speak to you several times a day, then, to be sure that she still can."

Rephanin stifled a sigh, and looked at the feast laid for them by the host. It had overflowed the table in the private room Ehranan had taken; several dishes waited atop the dresser, fated to be ignored. Rephanin selected a piece of apple and chewed it thoughtfully.

"She might reach Watersmeet faster if she rode."

A horse would also gain her the attention and respect of the Steppegards. He knew Ehranan was aware of this.

"If there is a mount to be had at Waymeet, by all means."

Rephanin looked at Filari, unsurprised to see that this did not cheer her. *It will not be so bad. At least you will be away from the army.*

But you made me want to see the sea.

I ask your pardon.

The corners of her lips curved slightly at this. She sipped her cider.

Ehranan put down his knife and turned to her. "You will be doing a great service for all ælvenkind. Your sacrifice will not be forgotten."

Filari colored deeply and looked down again. "Thank you, my lord."

And you will not be in the Steppe Wilds forever.

A flicker of sadness went through her khi and was gone even before Rephanin recognized it. She raised her cup to sip again.

It will be better than home, no doubt.

A tragic thought. He could think of no answer. Centuries ago, he had felt the same way.

It was well past midnight when Luruthin and his friends left the snow behind. The hunger was painful now, and Luruthin fought the desire to break into a run. Waves of cramp gripped his gut, making it difficult to think of anything save for putting an end to the torment.

The trail they followed stayed near the river. They passed numerous cascades, all lesser than the high waterfall above.

His fall. His folly. Would it have been simpler for all of them if he had succeeded there?

Vanorin began to search for shelter among the steep crags of the valley wall. It need only accommodate Luruthin, of course. Eliani and Vanorin could rest outside, in the sunlight. Or continue without him. Perhaps that would be best.

Vanorin paused to peer upward at a high, narrow cliff of black rock that divided the valley they traveled from another running down from the north. He pointed toward a dark hollow on the side of the cliff.

"There is a cave there, but we would have to climb to it."

Luruthin scowled. "We have had enough climbing."

He started forward again, along the base of the cliff and toward the convergence of the valleys. Vanorin and Eliani caught up with him at the edge of a stream that ran briskly there.

The water was swift and too wide to leap across, swollen with snowmelt from the mild day just past. They could not cross here.

Luruthin caught his breath. Smoke!

Eliani smelled it too—he saw her nostrils widen. They all stood silent, watching and listening, questing up the valley with khi for a sign of the fire's makers. Luruthin found it and swallowed.

Kobalen. A small group, camped on the south side of the valley near the stream, perhaps half a league away. The running water made confusion of their khi but he was certain there were several kobalen together.

He crouched as he gazed up the valley toward the unseen camp. How to capture a kobalen? Separate one from the group and take it alive? He had hunted them often but only to kill them.

He remembered Kivhani saying something about the hunter's benison, and wished now that he had asked to know more of how the Lost hunted. It was strange to think of kobalen as game.

By the creed, game were given a quick and merciful kill if possible, but he suspected it would be easier to take blood from a living kobalen. The creature need not die; he would not need that much blood. When he recalled the strength that a single cup had given him...

A shiver went through him at the memory. That would not happen again.

He glanced at Eliani, then started forward up the valley, moving with a hunter's silence through the scrubby oaks and greenleaf trees that grew along the stream. With Eliani and Vanorin following, he strode onward until he reached the kobalen's camp.

Six adults, two young, sleeping around the remains of their fire. One family, or perhaps two. He closed his eyes, hating that he must destroy their peace.

To attack the whole party was needless, and also dangerous. Eliani's safety must be considered. Had that not been the case, had they merely been on patrol to keep the Ebons near ælven towns clear of kobalen, he would not have hesitated to slay the whole group.

Eliani and Vanorin came to stand beside him. He glanced toward his cousin and saw her take something from her belt, a dark bundle. The glint of starlight on metal told him what it was.

An alben throwing net. Yes, she had kept one. He had forgotten. He shivered.

She offered it to him. With a shudder he shook his head.

He would not use one of their nets. He preferred not to touch it or even to look at it. Fighting the evil memories it aroused, he looked away, back at the kobalen.

One of them stirred. Luruthin held his breath, watching as the young male sat up, then stood and stretched. It walked to the stream bank and stood relieving itself into the water.

Instinct and need together drove Luruthin forward. He stepped out of the woods, moving silently until he stood behind the kobalen. In one swift movement he put his arm around its throat. At the same time, and purely by instinct, he took hold of its khi, silencing it more effectively so than mere physical dominance would ensure.

The kobalen struggled feebly for a moment, then sagged, its weight dragging Luruthin forward. He held on, knowing the creature was not dead, was perhaps feigning helplessness.

He turned his head and saw Vanorin beside him. The captain picked up the kobalen's legs and helped carry it into the woods. They took it some few rods downstream, stopping in a small clearing between stands of oak.

They laid the kobalen down on the dry leaves. Luruthin made certain it was truly unconscious, then looked up.

Eliani stood at the edge of the clearing, gazing toward the kobalen's camp. She glanced at him and shook her head, then returned to watching.

The kobalen had not missed their companion. Not yet.

Luruthin knelt beside the creature, anxious to be done with it. The strong, musky smell of the kobalen was not appealing, but he was in no case to be fastidious. He drew his belt knife, wondering how to proceed.

Vanorin had unshouldered his pack and now held out the cup they had shared. The same cup from which Luruthin had drunk their gift. He met Vanorin's gaze, swallowed, and accepted it. Better to drink from a cup than to lay his lips to the creature's hide.

Vanorin lifted the kobalen by its shoulders and held its head, exposing the neck to Luruthin's blade. Chagrined at this assistance, he hesitated no longer and made a cut beneath the kobalen's ear, where the heavy veins lay.

The smell of blood rose bright and hot into the night air, making him gasp with need. Luruthin held the cup beneath the cut with a trembling hand, gathering what flowed from the wound. It took far too long, with his anguished stomach demanding what he smelled.

When the cup was half full he could wait no longer. He gulped down its contents, then returned it for more.

The blood struck his gut like a ball of fire. Kobalen's blood, and kobalen's khi especially, was much heavier than that of ælven, and he tasted and felt the differences. Still, the rush of returning strength was like what he had felt before, the ebb of anguish a familiar relief.

He looked down at the kobalen. Vanorin held its head between his hands, ready to control it should it rouse. How humbling that he should need help in this, that Vanorin should debase himself so far, stepping outside the creed to do harm to this creature for his sake.

His fingers were slick with blood, he realized, warm and sticky where they pressed against the kobalen's throat. He shifted the cup to a better position and watched the blood flow until it was nearly full, then drank again, more slowly this time, pausing to breathe between swallows.

Much better. His senses sharpened, free of the blinding hunger. He heard the stream's rush and the cry of a night bird hunting down the valley, smelled the kobalen and their fire a short distance away, saw a mouse scurry away beneath the oaks.

One more, he decided, returning the cup to the kobalen's throat again. That would sate him, and he hoped he would need no more for a while.

A sound reached him, a voice raised in query, sending a tremor of fear through him. He glanced up at Eliani, who came toward him to whisper.

"They have missed him."

Vanorin pushed the kobalen off of his knees and let it fall on the ground, reaching for his pack as he stood. Luruthin gulped what was in the cup and followed Vanorin and Eliani down the valley, moving swiftly and silently.

Vanorin paused and pointed to the stream. It spread wide in a shallows, curling around boulders before plunging through a narrow cleft in a small cascade. Eliani nodded and Vanorin scrambled down the bank into the water, which came to his waist. Holding his bow overhead, he began to cross the stream.

Luruthin licked blood from his fingers and from the cup as he watched Eliani follow Vanorin into the water. When he saw that she was steady and in no danger of being swept away, he followed, still clutching the cup, holding his own bow high with one hand.

He gasped at the icy water. The blood in his gut churned as he slogged across. Uncomfortable, but far better than the pain of being empty.

Shouting reached him from upstream. The kobalen had found their friend. Luruthin hoped they would concern themselves with tending the injured one's hurts, and not with pursuing his attacker.

Vanorin reached the far bank and climbed it, then turned to help Eliani. Luruthin slipped on a loose stone as he followed, and nearly plunged face first into the stream. He managed to keep his bow out of the water but his other hand went into it and he lost the cup as instinct made him grab for support. Finding his feet again, he peered down into the water but saw no glint of metal.

"Never mind." Vanorin beckoned to him from the shore.

Luruthin scrambled out of the water and stood dripping, shivering. His stomach grumbled and he wished to lie down and rest, but knew he could not risk staying this close to the kobalen's camp. Vanorin led them downward again, following the stream once more and setting an easy pace.

Dawn was beginning to lighten the eastern sky by the time Vanorin called a halt. Luruthin eyed the strip of glowing blue as one might watch a dangerous beast. He knew the sun would not rise yet for a while, but already he sensed a whisper of its burning power tingling in the air.

The valley was less steep here, dense with trees and brush in its bottom where the river flowed swift and cold. No cliffs; instead wooded slopes thick with evergreens reaching skyward.

Luruthin doubted they would find caves here. His heart began to race with fear.

A shelter, then. There was time to fashion one, and it would suffice. He remembered the Lost's shelters at their camp. Simple frames draped with skins and covered with boughs of evergreen. He and his friends had no skins, but they had blankets that would serve.

Vanorin and Eliani were filling their water skins from the river. Luruthin's gut rumbled. He wanted greens, but they did not grow in the mountains in winter.

Remembering the food in his pack, he took it out and ate two dried stonefruits, which eased him a little. He ate one more, then put the pouch away and looked at the trees between the river and the slope.

Vanorin came toward him. "I will look for a cave. Stay here with Eliani."

Luruthin nodded. "I will cut branches for a shelter, in case you find no cave."

"Yes. Take my woodcutting blade." Vanorin unslung the blade in its sheath and handed it to Luruthin, then started toward the woods.

"Vanorin."

The captain paused, eyes questioning. Luruthin took a step closer. "Thank you for your help."

Vanorin smiled slightly, then nodded and left. Luruthin watched him walk into the woods, thinking that his words of thanks had been inadequate. Vanorin helped him for Eliani's sake, yet help for any reason was crucial to him now. Alone, he would surely have perished.

Eliani came to him, offering water. He shook his head, hefting his own skin, which was more than half full. He had drunk no water since taking blood, and as yet wanted none. The fruit had helped.

He would have to pay close attention to his body's changing demands. Feeling a return of grief at the thought, he pushed it away and walked to the nearest evergreen, selecting a long, straight limb to cut.

By the time Vanorin returned, Luruthin had cut ten poles and Eliani had stripped them of lesser branches. The band of blue on the eastern horizon had widened and grown paler at its edge. Warmed by the work of cutting, Luruthin paused and wiped his brow as Vanorin joined them.

"No caves, but there is a wash down the slope where the trees are thick. A good place to make a shelter."

"Very well."

Luruthin sheathed the blade and picked up the poles he had cut, balancing them on his shoulder. Eliani and Vanorin carried his weapons and pack as Vanorin led them into the forest.

The wash was narrow and less than a rod deep, filled with rocks and damp in its sandy bottom. Luruthin glanced westward, wary of a storm that would bring down a flood, but the sky was yet clear.

With Vanorin's help he built his shelter, stacking evergreen branches thickly across the south-facing front, nervous lest a single ray of sunlight find its way in. The sky was growing brighter moment by moment, and his skin had begun to prickle by the time he crawled inside with his pack and nodded to the others to lay branches across the last gap.

Eliani peered in at him, looking worried. "Shall I come in with you?"

Luruthin shook his head. "There is not much room. You will be more comfortable outside."

Out in the sunshine, where he could never again go. His throat tightened suddenly and he looked away, fussing with his pack. The light dimmed as Vanorin covered the entrance with tree branches.

Luruthin watched the slivers of light that speckled the rocks around him disappear as his friends piled more boughs over the entrance. For a moment the panic of being held captive returned to him, and he had to force himself to be still and not fly from the enclosure.

He took deep breaths and looked at the blanket and poles overhead, reminding himself that he had made this place, that he was here by choice. Pressing his lips together so that he would make no sound, he leaned his back against the rocky wall of the wash and wrapped his arms around his knees.

It was chill inside the shelter, but he did not mind. Better that than the sun.

He listened to the sounds of his friends settling themselves for the day, to the few words they exchanged, to the song of birds greeting the dawn. He felt as if he had disappeared. Another wave of panic came over him, and to fight it he spoke.

"Has the sun risen?"

Vanorin replied. "It is rising now. Are you all right?"

Luruthin's breath came short as he stared at his roof, wondering if it was enough to protect him. He moved to the far side of the wash, which was deeper in shadow.

"Y-yes. So far I am well."

Fear gripped him. Between the sun and the dread of confinement, he felt he might lose his wits and flee.

"Sing that s-song, will you, Vanorin? The one about the shepherd's child?"

Vanorin began to sing softly. The tune calmed Luruthin, who had heard it often enough in Ulithan's cave that he could follow it and join in on some of the verses.

It was long and rambling, and very foolish, and it comforted him. By the time the song had ended, the sun was fully up. He could feel it in his bones. Staring apprehensively at the roof of his little shelter, he was able at last to convince himself that it was enough.

"Thank you, Vanorin."

"Do want another?"

"Not now."

As the morning progressed, Luruthin tried to rest, as he knew the others were doing. He had not the concentration required to meditate. He had not done that for a long time, spending his thoughts instead on dread of the new life he must lead, on regrets for all he must leave behind.

The air around him grew warmer as the day went on, and his thoughts moved away from the immediacy of his situation. For a long while, since Ghlanhras, he had thought only of surviving the present day. Now he was beginning to be able to think of a future, of a day when he would feel no suffering, or much less suffering at least.

A day when he could feel safe among others who shared his fate. Bitter a fate as it was, he was beginning to believe that he could bear it.

These musings carried him until the light began to fade and he knew the sun was westering. He sat listening as evening came on, as the birds and woodland creatures made ready for night.

He knew the moment the sun was down. Standing, he pushed against the boughs that covered his shelter and they slid in a jumble to the ground. He stepped over the heap of branches into the twilit evening.

Eliani and Vanorin were sitting nearby, their backs leaned against tree trunks. Eliani looked at Luruthin, then suddenly jumped up and threw her arms around him. He returned the embrace lightly before drawing back. A tear glinted on Eliani's cheek and she brushed it away.

"Are you all right?"

Luruthin nodded, smiling a little to reassure her, then turned to break his camp. Vanorin helped him, and soon they were ready to walk on. They followed the Varindel down its valley, which widened and became filled with the grey, leafless wraiths of greenleaf trees.

"This is the way we came from Twisted Pine Pass."

Luruthin nodded. Eliani's comment had echoed his thoughts.

He thought of the shade he had seen in the falls near Highstone, and of his fear that she portended a dark fate for him. He did not think so now, or at least, not a death like to hers. He had passed through that trial, and though unsure of exactly where his path would lead him, he now saw it and had the strength to follow.

❁ Ghlanhras ❁

Shalár emerged from Darkwood Hall immediately after sunset, eager to inspect progress on the city's defenses. Kelev had assumed the task of overseeing construction of the network of sheltered paths that now gave access to all levels of the city.

The paths stretched from Darkwood Hall to the outer walls at the four watch platforms and the gates, and ran all along the inside of the city wall. Since Kelev had taken a hand, the work had gone more efficiently. Shalár could now walk to any part of Ghlanhras in daylight, if need be.

She found Kelev at the northwestern watch platform, revising its structure so that the access ladder could be withdrawn up into the platform at need. He had a small crew of ælven laborers at work, and seemed to have no trouble compelling them to work quickly and well.

He nodded in greeting at her approach. The white in his hair had spread, so that now it was the few remaining brown strands that seemed an intrusion. Curling white hair around a golden face, quite striking, though the golden skin was beginning to pale somewhat.

"An improvement." She nodded toward the ladder. "Will you do this at each platform?"

"This is the last. The others are done."

Shalár nodded again, impressed anew. She would have to think of something more for Kelev to do.

"I have a suggestion, Bright Lady."

"Oh?"

"Let me make an inner yard at the front gates, a defensible enclosure. If the gates fall, the enemy will still have to fight to get into the city."

"Interesting. I would want to see plans."

"I have made some sketches. Shall I bring them to you?"

She gave him a guarded look. She did not wish to encourage him to think he might demand her attention whenever he wished it. He was one of her people now, but had no more consequence than any other. He seemed not to understand this. Natural arrogance, perhaps.

"You may bring them to the Hall later this evening, when I hold audience."

Kelev made a slight bow. "Thank you, Bright Lady."

She turned away and walked the covered path to the next watch platform, then visited the others in turn. Kelev's work was excellent.

Hungry now, she went to the kobalen pen, where some twenty newly-caught kobalen roamed restlessly. Ranad's hunting had kept the city well supplied, and Shalár had no hesitation in feeding whenever she wished. Such a change from the hardship of Nightsand. She smiled with pleasure at the thought of becoming soft, though she would never let herself lapse so far that she lost strength.

A rumbling underfoot made her glance northward. The sky was smudged with grey cloud hanging heavily about Firethroat's peak. Steam had been seeping from the volcano for several nights now. A relief, for it meant that some of the pressure beneath the mountain had eased.

She chose her feeder and drank her fill, leaving the rest for the keeper. She toyed with the thought of sending it to Kelev as a reward for his excellent service, but decided his self-importance needed no encouragement. Let him ask, if he hungered.

Returning to the Hall, she went to her chambers to don a robe for her audience. Her ælven attendant silently brought out a robe of black silk with gray edges, silently took it back when Shalár demanded another. The female had been listless, entirely passive, since her conception with Ranad. She never spoke unless Shalár demanded an answer.

Shalár watched her closely as she moved about the chamber. Her face looked strained, a little gaunt. Shalár suspected she was not eating enough. That would not do. The child she carried, a Darkshore child, must be nourished.

"Yes, that will serve." Shalár accepted a scarlet robe with swirls of gray smoke dancing along its hem. It was of Eastfæld make, and the smoke curls shifted with each movement. The orange silk had taken the scarlet dye without loss of this art. She could wish the smoke was black instead of gray, but its beauty consoled her for this lack.

"Go to the kitchens and fetch me some greens, and some cakes or bread. Whatever is at hand."

The ælven left the chambers without a word. Shalár hoped the kitchens would tempt her to eat. She had already given orders that the ælven who served there should make whatever foods her attendant desired, and should always have something savory ready to be eaten.

A pity that the girl's father was no longer useful. His anger at her conception made sending him again to Woodrun too great a risk.

Shalár could not be certain he would obey her; his daughter's life was no longer a useful incentive, for he knew Shalár would protect her until the child was born. He might seek vengeance for what he perceived as a wrong done to his child—though in fact it was to her benefit—by passing information about Ghlanhras to the ælven.

Shalár donned the robe and brushed out her hair. She decided to leave it loose and merely catch it back from her face. She needed a scarf or a band for that.

She rummaged in the lowest drawer of the wardrobe, which still contained a jumble of Othanin's things. She found the pouch into which she'd stuffed his handfasting ribbon, and toyed with the thought of wearing it in her hair. That would be amusing, but she decided against it. The latent khi in the ribbon would be a distraction.

Looking further, she found a circlet of plain silver rubbed with a dark polish to make it gray. She held it in her hands, remembering a distant past. Her father had worn a circlet of state, when he was governor. This was rightfully hers.

She carried it to her mirror and put it on, tucking strands of her hair back from her face. She was governor of Fireshore, now. She had achieved her wish of resuming her father's place.

But the circlet was an ælven custom. She took it off and tossed it back into the drawer. Instead she chose a length of smoke-colored gauze heavy with glistening beads, all black and gray. She tied it over her brow, letting the long ends dangle down her shoulder.

A sound in the outer chamber drew her notice. The ælven, returning with a platter of fresh greens dressed with sunfruit oil and spices, and a dish of assorted cakes and sweetmeats. She set them on the table and retreated to her customary place on the floor by the door to the bedchamber.

Shalár ate most of the greens and two of the cakes, then turned to look at her attendant. "Have you tried these? They are quite good."

The female shook her head. Shalár picked up the plate and carried it to her.

"Have one."

Again, a shake of the head. Shalár felt a rising anger.

"Have one, or I shall make you eat them all."

Alarm flashed through the ælven's eyes. She took the nearest cake off the plate and bit into it, then coughed, choking. Shalár put down the plate and hauled her to her feet.

Struggling for breath, the ælven coughed and retched, then drew a gasping breath and dropped to her knees, sobbing. Shalár stood gazing down at the wretched female with mingled annoyance and pity. This weeping was worse than the silence. She knelt and took hold of the ælven's shoulders, compelling her to look up.

"I am not trying to be cruel. I want you to be well."

The female looked away, avoiding her gaze, but began to calm. Shalár fetched her own goblet and filled it with water.

"Drink." She watched until the ælven had swallowed half the cup. The female still looked wretched. Shalár gazed at her with a critical eye.

"You have worn that same gown for many days now. Have you no other?"

"Not here." The female's voice was a rasping whisper.

"Hm. I will send for your clothing. Meanwhile, bathe yourself. You may put on the black robe you took out earlier. That gown you have on is past mending, I think. Send it to be burnt."

The gown was not so terribly worn, but as it was what the ælven had been wearing when Ranad had taken her, Shalár thought disposing of it might improve her mood. The ælven merely nodded, slipping back into silent obedience. Shalár picked up the plate of cakes and put it in her hands.

"Try to eat a little. Please."

The female was still, silent. Shalár left her alone, though if she would not eat, Shalár would have to force her. No Darkshore child would be born a weakling.

❀ Fireshore ❀

Near midnight the forest began to change, oaks giving way to the occasional darkwood. Eliani felt unease at passing near their twisted trunks, at the way they seemed to close in on her. She and the others fell silent as they pushed their way through the thickening undergrowth, their mood further daunted by a drizzle of rain.

At last they reached the road and were able to quicken their pace. Striding westward toward Bitterfield, they made good progress and were soon within sight of the town.

"Halt!"

Eliani obeyed, startled at finding watchers posted on the road. There had been none when they had first come here, but that was before Ghlanhras had fallen.

Vanorin stepped in front of her. The voice came again from the forest ahead.

"Who are you, and what is your business?"

"I am Eliani of Felisanin, and these are my companions. I was here some few days since. Theyn Dejhonan will remember me."

"I remember you. Your pardon, Lady Eliani."

The watcher stepped from the forest, lowered bow in hand, and pushed back his hood. He was one of the villagers Eliani had met on her earlier visit, a tall male with Greenglen coloring, though his eyes were a lighter shade of brown. He bowed.

"We are required to stop everyone, even friends."

"I understand."

"You are here to see the theyn?"

"Yes, and to see Davhri, my kin."

"Walk on, then."

Eliani thanked the watcher, who pulled up his hood again and returned to his post in the forest. She hastened forward, anxious to get into the village and find shelter for Luruthin before the sun rose.

She was struck again at the guarded appearance of the village, by the windowless back walls of the outer row of houses, the hearthroom doors that stood merely ajar where in Highstone they would have stood wide. This deep into night the hearths were mostly down to coals, but now and again she saw one where a fire burned brightly.

"I do not wish to disturb Dejhonan's rest. Let us go to Davhri's house. We can sit in the hearthroom if she is not receiving company."

She led the way along the path between the outer two rows of houses, searching for the withered goldenberry bush that struggled to grow in Davhri's garden. She spied it and wondered for a moment if it was dead, for the stalks were altogether bare of leaves now.

It was winter, though, she reminded herself. Goldenberry dropped its leaves in winter, apparently even in this snowless land. As she stepped into the yard and looked more closely at the bush, she saw that its branches were green and bore the first tiny buds of new growth.

The garden had been cleared, she noticed. The kiln, which on Eliani's previous visit had looked neglected, had been set to order. All the weeds and overgrowth were gone, and a small kitchen garden showed freshly-turned earth. A rosemary bush that had been a wild tangle was now neatly trimmed.

Eliani smiled, her heart lifted by these signs of change. Perhaps it had been done by Mishri, the theyn's daughter, who helped Davhri about the house. Even if so, a more cheerful garden must be good for Davhri.

The door of the house stood ajar, and the hearth was deep in ashes where before it had been bare. Davhri was receiving again, then. Eliani held her hand out toward the hearth and felt the warmth of a fire only recently faded.

The entrance into the house from the hearthroom was curtained, and Eliani saw no light at its edges, so she gestured to the others to sit. It was pleasant to be out of the rain. She added wood to the fire and coaxed it to flame. The three of them crowded around it, stretching chilled hands toward it.

A noise from within the house drew Eliani's attention. Footsteps hastened toward them. The heavy curtain was pulled aside, and Davhri looked out at them.

"I thought I heard voices! Why did you not ring the chime?"

Eliani rose, smiling as she saw how well Davhri looked. Her eyes were clear and bright, her hair and clothing neat, her movements quick and full of the strength Eliani remembered from long ago.

"We thought you might be resting."

"And so I was, but that is no reason for you to sit out here. Come in, come in!"

Davhri beckoned them into the house, and they followed her. Eliani marveled at the change in the place. Where before it had seemed empty and lifeless, now it was full of color and the pleasant clutter of Davhri's craft.

Finished pieces of pottery, and some that were yet to be glazed, stood along the shelves. The large table was covered with jars and pots of glazes and colored earth, and a wheel on which stood something draped with a heavy, dampened cloth.

"You have taken up your craft again! I am glad."

"I was given to understand that my lord is in need of better cups."

Eliani met her gaze and saw a glint of humor there, though it was replaced by earnestness in the next moment. Davhri stepped toward her.

"Thank you for finding him."

Eliani smiled, and on impulse threw her arms around Davhri, who returned the embrace with quick fierceness before stepping back and turning to the others.

"Luruthin. Welcome again."

She held out her arm and Luruthin clasped it. Davhri froze for a moment, gazing at him.

"You must be tired. Will you not rest here, and give me a chance to make up for my inability to host you before? My guest room is ready, and there are beds for two. Eliani may share with me."

She glanced at Vanorin, who stepped forward. "We did not meet when I was here before. I am Vanorin."

Eliani winced. "Forgive me. Davhri, Vanorin is captain of my escort. Vanorin, please meet Davhri, my father's sister."

Davhri smiled and clasped his arm briefly. "Welcome. Come sit by the fire. You must all be chilled, walking in this rain."

Luruthin and Vanorin readily accepted this hospitality. The fire on the main room's hearth had fallen to coals, and Vanorin set about at once to build it up. Eliani followed Davhri to the kitchen, where Davhri put her to work slicing bread. Eliani's stomach rumbled as she set the knife to it, and she was hard put not to gobble a piece right away. Instead she swept up the crumbs and let them melt on her tongue while she watched Davhri come and go with kettle and ewer, cups and plates.

Davhri took down a small, bright yellow pot and uncovered it, releasing the sharp scent of sunfruit. She set it on the plate with the bread and a smooth knife.

"Take that out, now, and share it with your friend. The tea will soon be ready."

Eliani carried the plate out to the main room, wondering why she had said "friend" and not "friends." Vanorin had the fire crackling brightly, and Davhri's kettle was hanging over it, beginning to steam. The captain had unbound his damp hair and was absently combing through it with his fingers.

He looked up at Eliani, his eyes lighting at the sight of the bread. Eliani pulled another chair over to the hearth, set the plate of bread down on it, then spread sunfruit preserve on a slice and handed it to Vanorin.

"Thank you. Mmm."

She offered another slice to Luruthin. He shook his head.

"Some without preserve?"

"No, thank you."

Eliani saw a swallow move his throat. She felt badly, eating when he could not, but she knew he would say that was foolish. She pulled up a chair for herself and took a bite of the bread, the taste of sunfruit bursting sharp and sweet in her mouth, bits of the tangy golden peel threaded through the preserve.

Davhri came and fetched the kettle, set a plate of sliced cheese beside the bread, then hurried back to the kitchen. In a few moments she returned with a tray bearing cups, the grey ewer, and a smaller ewer of dark blue.

Davhri picked up the blue ewer and uncovered it, holding it out for Luruthin to smell. "This is winterbalm and honeyleaf. My lord finds it soothing. Would you like to try some?"

Luruthin looked up at her sharply, then glanced at Eliani. Everyone was still for a moment.

Eliani drew a sharp breath. "You can feel it."

Davhri glanced at her. "Yes. Only because I have lately seen Inóran. I doubt I would have noticed, otherwise."

Luruthin gave Eliani a questioning glance. She had not told him that she could feel his affliction, for she had not wished to distress him. He turned a wary gaze on Davhri, then nodded.

"I will have some. Thank you."

Davhri poured the tea for them all. "Forgive me, I should have offered you dry clothing right away. Let me fetch some."

Eliani looked up from her tea. "Please do not trouble—"

"No trouble. I have plenty to spare. Inóran has little use for robes now." She gave a small, sad smile, then hastened away into the back of the house.

Luruthin drained his cup. "Is there more of this?"

"I think so." Eliani lifted the lid of the blue ewer. Yes."

She poured for him, watching his face. He took a sip and glanced up at her.

"I did not know you could feel my...."

"Your khi is different. Altered." She glanced at Vanorin. "Had you noticed?"

He nodded. "I was not certain why, at first."

"Nor I, or I would have mentioned it. I am sorry, Cousin."

A smile flashed across Luruthin's face and was gone again. He leaned forward with the cup in his hands, elbows on his knees, rocking slightly.

"I suppose it does not matter. It is a small thing, compared to all the rest."

Eliani's heart ached for him. She wanted to rage at the ældar for allowing him to be hurt so, at the spirits for failing to protect him. She tried to reconcile herself to the tortured path he walked.

Not by choice. How could it be by choice? Supposedly each soul chose its path, but why would anyone choose such suffering?

Davhri returned with two robes over her arm and two pairs of soft house shoes in her hands. "These should fit you well enough, I think."

She handed a pair of shoes to Vanorin and set another beside Luruthin's chair, then shook out the robes. Both were grey and heavy, one a little darker than the other, and smelled faintly of whiteflower. She gave them to Luruthin and Vanorin, then turned to Eliani.

"Come, you may have your pick of my robes. Remember when you used to come and play in my wardrobe?"

Eliani grinned. "I remember the time you shut me in."

"Foolish of me. I hoped it would discourage you."

"Instead I thought it a great game, and tried to kick my way out."

"Much to the detriment of my furniture."

Davhri caught Eliani's arm and pulled her away, leaving the males to change their wet leathers and clothes for the warm robes. Eliani glanced

272 ~ Pati Nagle

at the door to the hearthroom as they passed. A single handfasting ribbon hung there, where before she had seen two.

"Only one ribbon at your door."

"Inóran has mine. He took it with him."

"He was here?"

Davhri closed the bedchamber door and went to a darkwood wardrobe, throwing its doors wide. "Very briefly, a few nights ago. He came near midnight and left before dawn. He had asked if he might bring me to visit the camp, but was forbidden."

"Oh, Davhri. I am sorry."

Davhri turned a smiling face toward her. "No matter. I saw him. It was enough. To know that he is alive, that he is ... well, as far as he can be. It is such a relief, after all my fears."

"But to be kept apart from him must be dreadful."

Davhri gazed at her, one brow rising slightly in a way that reminded Eliani very much of her father. "I imagine you know how dreadful it is."

Eliani felt warmth rising to her cheeks. "But we have the hope of being together again."

"So have we, child. We have not given it up." Davhri pulled a robe of palest orange from the wardrobe, its color so light it seemed almost white, like the blossoms of a fruit tree. The sleeves were lined with a brighter flame, and the same color touched the collar.

"I think this might suit you. Let me help you out of those leathers."

"Thank you. Is Othanin still in Bitterfield?"

"Yes. He is staying in a guest house on the public circle. The one with firevines over the door."

"I will visit him in the morning."

Davhri gathered up the robe and held it for Eliani, who raised her arms to the sleeves. The robe slid down over her, clinging warmly to her limbs, wonderfully soft. She sighed.

"Ah, much better. Thank you."

Davhri smiled and handed her a pair of soft shoes. "It looks well on you. I have never been very fond of orange, but it does wear well on a Stonereach. When I first put on Sunriding's colors to please Inóran, I received many compliments."

Eliani paused in putting on the shoes to look up. "You left your clan for him, and now you must dwell apart."

Davhri smiled sadly. "I asked to be allowed to come and live with them, but they refused me. I even offered to swear my allegiance, but no.

I am not one of them, therefore I am forbidden to join them."

"Oh, Davhri!"

Davhri picked up Eliani's tunic and reached for her discarded legs. "It is not so hard. It is true that I could not ply my craft if I dwelt with the Lost. I can ply it for their benefit, now. I am making them some things in their new clan colors."

"Inóran told you of that?"

Davhri nodded. "They are all very hopeful about it."

"It is by no means certain of acceptance." Eliani wriggled her feet into the warm shoes.

"I know. They know it, too, but they have decided to act as a clan whether or not they are accepted by the Council. Ebonwatch sounds better than Lost, does it not? I think it was a good suggestion, Eliani. Your father will be proud of you."

Discomfited by this praise, Eliani began to collect her leathers. Davhri picked up the two bracers and handed them to her.

"These are very handsome, by the way. Fine work."

"Thank you. They are borrowed, actually. Mine were left in Ghlanhras."

"Ah. I thought you had worn blue leathers, not green, when you came before. Though I was not thinking very clearly then." She smiled wistfully.

"I am glad to see you better, Davhri."

"Thanks to you, child. Come, let us set those leathers by the fire, and see about washing these."

Luruthin and Vanorin had put on their robes and were sitting before the hearth, still sipping tea. Davhri collected their clothing and bustled away to the kitchen again. Eliani arranged her leathers on a chair to dry, then sat in another chair and poured herself more tea.

She glanced at Luruthin. "You will come to the Council, will you not?"

He sighed. "Yes, if Othanin and Kivhani will have me."

"Good."

"I want to see Clerestone again. To say goodbye."

Eliani swallowed a mouthful of tea too hard, raising an ache in her throat. She set aside her cup and rummaged in her pack until she found her comb. Untying her hair, she leaned toward the fire as she combed the dampness out of it.

Vanorin followed her example and combed his own hair, braiding it back in a simple plait instead of the hunter's braid he usually wore. Eliani got up and went to stand behind Luruthin, untying his hair.

At her first touch he jumped, then he sat stiffly, but gradually he relaxed and leaned his head back. She combed his hair slowly, gently, until it was smooth and free of tangles, then kept combing it while the fire's warmth dried it.

Vanorin was watching. Perhaps wishing himself in Luruthin's place, she thought, but when she glanced at him his face wore a look of pity as he gazed at Luruthin. Leaning forward a little, she saw that Luruthin's eyes were closed, his cheeks wet with tears.

Eliani blinked away the threat of her own tears. Time enough for grieving after they must say farewell. For now, she would not add to Luruthin's pain by visiting her own upon him.

Davhri returned from the kitchen and came to the fire. Luruthin sat up, wiping at his face, though Davhri was busy hanging the kettle and seemed not to notice. She added a piece of wood to the coals, then turned to Vanorin.

"Let me show you the guest room. You and Luruthin may put your things there, and take your rest whenever you wish."

"Thank you." Vanorin stood up and picked up his pack.

Luruthin followed, his hair spilling loose over his shoulders, gleaming warmly in the firelight. He caught at Eliani's fingers as she handed him the strip of leather that had tied his braid.

She watched them go, then put away her comb and carried her own pack to Davhri's bedchamber. A moment later Davhri came in, stepped out of her slippers and sat on the bed.

"I am sorry for Luruthin. It must have come over him very recently, no?"

"Some few days ago, though I think it had been coming on for a while."

"Has he...?"

"Yes, but not lately."

"I thought so." She smiled sadly. "Inóran fasted before coming to see me. He wanted me to have no illusions."

Eliani watched Davhri put out the lamp at her bedside and slide into the bed, marveling at her calm acceptance of Inóran's fate. Perhaps she had done her grieving and was finished with it.

Eliani crawled beneath the covers with Davhri and closed her eyes, thinking of the Turisan. He and his riders were nearing the Steppe Wilds.

Her spine tingled at the thought of how near he was, only a few days' travel away.

Not long. Too long. A day was too long. She was weary of sacrifices, though she knew that henceforth her life would be filled with them. She had chosen the path willingly. Her gift had demanded no less.

❁ Bitterfield ❁

Luruthin sat on the bed, gazing at nothing. Vanorin moved about the room, preparing to rest. When morning came, Vanorin would leave to find the guardians of his command, while Luruthin would remain here. Trapped. Hiding.

The familiar panic rose in him, but Luruthin fought it down. It was senseless, he knew it, and he was beginning to have better command of it.

If only he were not so hungry.

Vanorin sat down on his own bed, facing him. "Is there aught I can do for you?"

"Thank you. No."

Rather abrupt, he knew. He misliked the concern on Vanorin's face, so he tried again.

"You have been most patient and generous. Thank you, Vanorin, for all your support."

Luruthin held out his arm, and Vanorin clasped it with a small smile. As they touched, the brilliance of Vanorin's khi nearly struck Luruthin breathless. He knew an urge to draw upon it, and pulled his arm away as if he had touched fire.

Vanorin's frown deepened. "What is it?"

Luruthin squeezed his eyes shut. "You recall how the creed forbids one to draw on another's khi?"

"Yes."

"I nearly did so, just now."

Vanorin was silent. Luruthin took a deep breath and looked at him. The Greenglen looked troubled.

"If it would ease you–"

"No! Thank you, but no. I will not f-feed upon my friends."

He pressed his dry lips together, struggling to master his grief and his hunger. It was not as bad yet as the worst he had felt, but it would

278 ~ Pati Nagle

not be long. He feared he would lose self-command in another day or two.

"This is a cruel fate." Vanorin's voice was quiet. "I am deeply sorry for you."

Luruthin managed a smile, but could not bring himself to speak words of thanks. The rage inside him overpowered gratitude. He was angry at his fate, at the alben and their vicious leader, and most of all at himself, for succumbing.

He lay on his back and stared at the heavy beams overhead. Darkwood. No escaping it in Fireshore, where it seemed nearly everything was made of darkwood.

It reminded him strongly of the room where he had been held in Darkwood Hall. It was not that room, he told himself over and again. He was nonetheless trapped here for a day's time, and that raised all his fears again.

When the sun rose he knew it, despite the shelter of the heavy darkwood and the clouds that yet covered the sky. He lay listening to small sounds: rain still falling gently, a footstep out in the house, the crack of a fresh log on the fire.

Vanorin stirred and arose, then began to comb his hair. Luruthin was reminded of Eliani's kindness to him earlier. How good it had felt, to be touched with gentleness and affection. How painful to know he might never feel such again.

He sat up, found his comb, and set his own hair in order, braiding it loosely and tying it off halfway down its length, leaving a long span free below the tie. He peered at it, searching for white threads among the auburn.

Too soon, but it would come. He remembered Kelevon's appearance in the mountains, his hair all streaked with white and blowing in wild curls about his face.

Luruthin wished now that he had followed Kelevon and hunted him down. He had been weak and ill at the time, though now that he knew why, he saw Kelevon's attack somewhat differently.

Vengeance was against the creed. He might not hunt Kelevon for vengeance's sake, but he could hunt him to stop him causing further harm. Luruthin knew, remembering that bloody night, that Kelevon would hunt ælven again.

Vanorin went out. A soft knock at the door made Luruthin look up. Eliani opened it a small way and leaned in.

"I am going to see Othanin now. Shall I...tell him? Or ask him to visit you?"

Luruthin swallowed. "Ask him to visit, if it suits his convenience." Anything to break his sense of confinement.

Eliani gave a nod and a wan smile, then withdrew. Davhri took her place, carrying a small tray with the blue ewer and a cup upon it. She poured tea for him and let the ewer on the bedside table.

"I have some books if you care to read..."

Luruthin shook his head, knowing he would not be able to concentrate on a book. "Thank you, no. I think I should try to meditate, and rest."

"Very well. Call if you need anything. Even just company."

She left the room, closing the door again, shutting him into silence. He sipped his tea slowly, savoring it. It reminded him of Heléri, his eldermother, who was famous for her delightful blends of tea. He was glad he had decided to attend the Council, for it would give him a chance to see Heléri once more, to bid her farewell.

So many friends he must bid farewell. He brushed the thought aside, knowing that to dwell on it would only grieve him. He finished the tea in his cup and filled it again, then piled pillows and cushions against the headstead of his bed, and leaned back against them.

Luxurious, this. He had not enjoyed such comfort in many days. The nearest to it had been Ulithan's cave, but not even Ulithan had been able to offer a true bed. He closed his eyes, determined to enjoy what might be his last night in such a bed.

Sunrise set the sky aglow, casting a gentle warmth on the houses of Bitterfield. Eliani drew a deep breath, enjoying the smell of damp earth overlaid with the scent of morning fires. The rain had ceased, though a clouded sky suggested this was temporary.

As she and Vanorin walked into the public circle they were hailed by Mishri, the theyn's daughter, who ran up to them smiling, a cloth-covered basket in her hands.

"Welcome back! I am so glad you survived your adventures!"

"No more glad than we. I gather our friends are here?"

"Yes, I was just bringing them some food. They will be happy to see you."

Mishri led them to a guest house. As soon as they entered, they were surrounded by members of Eliani's escort, all talking at once. Mihlaran, Cærshari, Sunahran, and Revani all greeted her joyously. She was surprised to see a fifth guardian with them.

"Hathranen! We thought you—were lost at Ghlanhras!"

He clasped the arm she offered, and she noted a tone of distress in his khi. "Not there, but I became lost as I fled. I could not get to the gates, so I ran through the city and climbed over the wall. I intended to cut through the forest to the road, but lost my bearings and ended up wandering for days."

"How dreadful!"

Sunahran smiled in sympathy. "He stumbled into Woodrun three days after we arrived there. You should have seen him then."

"Well, I am glad to see him now. All of you!"

Mishri had laid out the contents of her basket on a long table, and now called the guardians to break their fast. Eliani declined their invitation to join them.

"We have broken fast. I have another errand, so I will bid you farewell for now."

Accompanied by Vanorin and Mishri, she went back out. Folk were stirring in the town, traders beginning to set up their wares in the public circle. A market day. It seemed strange to Eliani, such a normal activity. These folk must be aware of the threat in Ghlanhras, yet here they were, offering gourds and bread and jewelry for trade.

Eliani turned to Mishri. "Has Othanin broken fast?"

"Yes, I took him some food earlier. He spent half the night talking with my father."

"Will you take us to his house?"

Mishri nodded, and led them to the same house where she had stayed on their earlier visit to Fireshore. Othanin welcomed them and invited them to sit by his fire.

"I am glad to see you again, Eliani."

"And I you, Governor. I have a boon to ask of you."

"Oh?"

"Luruthin...." She swallowed, her throat suddenly tight.

Vanorin came to her rescue. "Luruthin asks that you visit him. He is at Davhri's house."

Othanin nodded. "I will be glad to."

Eliani cast Vanorin a grateful glance. "Thank you. Have you planned your trip to Alpinon?"

"First I must go to Woodrun."

"I advise against that. It would place you in needless danger."

"Woodrun is where my people have gone. I must make contact with them, and confer with the theyn."

"The ælven armies are on their way there. Until they arrive, there is too much risk in your going there. You could go after the Council. You must leave soon for that, in any case."

Othanin gazed at her. "You do not think my people will see that as cowardice? I fear many of them think poorly of me as it is."

"You have suffered enough at the hands of the alben." Vanorin's voice was gruff. "Let any who doubt your courage speak to us. We shall enlighten them."

A small smile flickered around Othanin's mouth. "That is kind of you."

Eliani leaned toward him. "Write a letter to Theyn Doriavi. I will carry it to the army, and see that it is delivered to her. Tell her you will come to Woodrun after the Council."

The governor gazed into the fire. After a long moment, he stirred.

"I will think on this. Meanwhile, I will visit your friend."

❈

Luruthin had just poured the last of his tea into his cup when he heard voices out in the house. Davhri had a visitor, a male. Sitting up, he listened more closely and was certain the voice was Othanin's.

He got up, set the cup aside, and straightened his borrowed robe. He felt nervous, which was absurd considering what he and Othanin had been through together. Yet Othanin was governor here, and he only a supplicant.

A gentle knock was followed by Othanin's voice. "Luruthin?"

Luruthin opened the door and saw Othanin in a robe the color of live coals, with his black hair loose across it. His dark eyes were clear and determined, more so than Luruthin had seen them before. He looked strong, and well, and Luruthin knew a pang of envy.

"Come in."

Luruthin closed the door and gestured toward the beds. Othanin sat on that which had been Vanorin's, and Luruthin sat facing him.

"Thank you for coming. I have... I must ask..."

"You wish to join the Lost."

Luruthin looked up sharply. "Eliani told you."

"No, she said nothing."

"Is it so obvious?"

Othanin's eyes softened. "Kivhani and I suspected your condition by the time we reached the camp. I hope your realization was not too painful."

Luruthin sighed. "Why did you not tell me, if you knew?"

"You must forgive us. It seems unkind, I know, but we did not wish to give you news that would likely anger you against us. It might have made you reluctant to return."

"Oh."

Luruthin looked down at his hands, which were tightly clenched. He pulled them apart, and found himself at a loss what to do with them. He laid them on his knees.

"What must I do? Should I write to Kivhani?"

"No, no. She is expecting you. I will take you to the camp tonight."

Relief rained through Luruthin. He had half feared being turned away, he realized.

"You are fortunate that the clan is still nearby. They are planning to move their camp soon."

"Why?"

"Too many outsiders know of their presence here."

Luruthin frowned. "We—Eliani and Vanorin—would never betray them."

"Not intentionally, but a chance word, a stray remark ... it is too great a risk. The Lost's ways are strict, but with good reason. Much thought and much bitter experience have gone into their making." Othanin's lips curved into a slight smile. "Even I do not know to which camp they will go."

Luruthin was surprised. "If they trust anyone it is you."

"They do trust me, but only to a point." Othanin rose and made as if to go. "I will return this evening to take you up."

"Othanin?"

"Yes?"

The governor paused, looking back at him. Luruthin stood and stepped toward him.

"When you and Kivhani depart for the Council in Highstone, I would like to accompany you."

Othanin's brows twitched together. "Why?"

"Eliani suggested that I would be a good advocate for the Lost, since many of the Council know me. She thought also that you might be glad to have a guide. If we wish to avoid other travelers we may have to leave the road. I know where to find water, and good camp sites. And I know where kobalen range."

Othanin's face grew sober. "We can discuss it with Kivhani tonight." He offered to clasp arms. "I am glad you returned, though sorry that it was needful. You will be glad as well, I believe."

Luruthin gazed at Othanin's arm, knowing that to take it would tempt him again as he had been tempted with Vanorin. Knowing as well that Othanin would feel the difference in his khi. He should be grateful, he supposed, that Othanin offered the gesture in spite of it.

He clasped arms briefly, then quickly let go. Othanin seemed to understand. He went to the door and Luruthin followed him.

"Thank you, Othanin."

The governor turned, a gentle expression on his face. "A bitter path is easier when one walks it with friends. I will return after sunset."

Luruthin closed the door behind him and returned to his bed. Jhinani was in his thoughts now, and he could not evade the bitter truth that he must never see her again, that he must let her go.

He knew so little of her, but he had spent long enough looking forward to knowing her better that the loss was as bitter as any he felt. She was his partner, though he had broken the bond. She carried his son. He had tied all his hopes up in her, and now they were never to be realized.

He grieved now as he had not let himself grieve before, for Jhinani, for Clerestone, for all his friends and kindred. He knew he must leave them.

From grief he drifted into a numbness, a kind of peace. All seemed grey to him, no spark of joy to hope for on the path ahead.

He wondered what purpose could be served by his living on under this affliction. To talk to the Council, perhaps. He could not imagine that his words would have much effect, but Eliani wished it and so he would try.

To hunt Kelevon and prevent him causing further harm. Luruthin felt a grim determination take hold inside him. That would be a service he would be glad to perform for his people. And when Kelevon was removed, perhaps he could turn his mind to removing Shalár.

He sat up suddenly, gasping with fear at the thought of going near her again. He was not ready to face that, though in truth there was little more she could do to harm him.

He rubbed his hands over his face, struggling to banish her from his thoughts. He could not get near her even if he wished to, entrenched as she was in Ghlanhras. He would not think of it.

Deciding to meditate, he sat on the bed and breathed deeply, willing away the tension in his flesh, watching from a distance the stray thoughts that entered his mind and dismissing them as they came. When he was calm and no longer troubled by random thoughts, he hesitantly opened his awareness to the khi of his surroundings. He sensed Davhri at work in the room outside his door, the hot storm of the fire on her hearth, and the gentler glow of the sleeping garden beyond the window.

Rain was still falling, a quiet, steady rain, blurring his awareness of all the living things nearby, though he could still feel them. Small creatures lay in their burrows, awaiting the sun's return. Birds nestled patiently in the shelter of their nests in the forest beyond the village, the leaves of tree and bramble protecting them from the wet.

Slowly he became aware that he was not alone. He wondered for a long while whether this should trouble him. He held back from seeking to know who it was who was near, for in not knowing he had no cause to be afraid.

It was someone he knew. That understanding came unbidden, and with it woke curiosity. Before he could form an intention, he found himself opening his awareness further, seeking to identify the other.

He became aware of a brilliant glow of love surrounding him. Surprised, he reached out to the source, and found it the familiar presence he had sensed.

His daughter. Shiláni.

Wonder and gratitude filled him, and also a wish to know why. Had she been drawn by his grief, or by his seeking peace in meditation? Before he could shape an inquiry, he was startled by a knock upon his door.

"Luruthin?"

He opened his eyes, blinking, disoriented. It was Davhri's voice that had called.

He cleared his throat. "Yes?"

"I have finished my work for the day. I thought you might like to come out and sit by the fire."

He took a couple of breaths to steady himself, then got up and went out into the main room. Davhri had draped her windows and the doorway to the hearthroom, though he could see glints of daylight at the edges of the tapestries. He went to the fire and sat gazing at it, thinking of Shiláni.

This was not the first time she had come to him. Why her, and never his son?

That was a selfish thought, he supposed. The answer might be as simple as that she was nearer, though he had heard it said that distance in the world of flesh was not a barrier to those in spirit.

Davhri returned to the room, a folded mass of grey silk in her hands. "Your clothes are clean, but they are rather worn. Will you accept these in their stead?"

Luruthin took the silks she offered, two tunics and two sets of legs in the soft grey so common in Bitterfield. He looked up at her.

"Inóran's?"

"They were, yes. He will only keep two changes with him, though, and he has many more than that here. I know he would be glad to have them go to use."

Luruthin rubbed the silk between his fingers. It was much newer than the tunic and legs he had been wearing ever since Ghlanhras. He would be glad to abandon those. Let them become rags, or paper, and so be given a new life.

"Thank you, Davhri. Thank you for your endless generosity."

"This is but a small thing." She flashed a sad smile. "I am glad to help. It makes up a little for my not having been able to help Inóran."

She stepped to the large table and brought back Luruthin's leather tunic, neatly folded. "This is stained, I fear. I did my best, but could not get it all out."

Luruthin unfolded it and looked at the bloodstains down its front. Glancing at Davhri, he saw her watching warily.

"I put on Birani's leathers after she was killed. We were in a snowstorm, and I had no cloak."

Though it might as well have been the blood of the kobalen he had fed upon. Luruthin laid the tunic aside, and put the silks on top of it. He was feeling unwell, and in the next moment a cramp seized hold of him. He hugged himself, leaning forward in his chair.

"Tea! I will fetch it."

Davhri hastened from the room, leaving him to struggle alone. He grimaced, breathing shallowly. He hoped this would pass, that he would have the strength to travel this night, for he must.

Davhri returned with a steaming cup. "Shall I hold it for you?"

Luruthin shook his head and took the cup in both hands, careful not to touch Davhri for fear he would draw upon her khi. He could feel it even so, bright enough to be almost painful.

He brought the cup to his lips and sipped, burning his tongue on the hot liquid. Another small sip, then another. His hands were shaking. He clutched the cup and drank the tea little by little, and gradually felt the cramp begin to ease.

"Thank you. It does help."

He sat back in the chair. The pain faded, leaving him feeling wrung.

Davhri returned to the kitchen and came back with her own cup of tea and a bulging cloth pouch. The latter she laid atop the grey silks.

"That is more of the tea. I promised it to Inóran, if you do not mind carrying it."

"I would be glad to."

"Would you take him a note from me as well?"

"Of course."

"Thank you. Othanin exchanges messages with them every few days, but I do not like to impose on him."

"I doubt he minds."

"Even so." Davhri sipped her tea. "We are supposed to go each our own way, Inóran and I, but I cannot say goodbye to him. Not yet."

Luruthin understood her feelings only too well. He wondered if she knew that the Lost would soon leave their camp above Bitterfield. Not his place to tell her, he supposed.

He felt adrift, his loyalties and obligations shifting. It would be better once he had formally joined the Lost, he thought. It meant relinquishing his clan, he realized with a stab of sadness.

Glancing toward the window, he saw that the rain-gray daylight was fading. He put aside his cup, took up his clothing, and stood.

"I had better put these on."

He went to the guest room and dressed swiftly, cinching his belt tight over his querulous gut. Putting the spare silks and Davhri's tea into his pack, he carried it out to the main room and set by the hearthroom door with his quiver and bow.

Davhri was sitting at her table, writing. Luruthin put on Felahran's boots, which he hoped the guardian's family would not begrudge him, then gathered up Birani's leathers and laid them against the wall with Felahran's sword, where Vanorin would find them.

Voices out in the hearthroom made him turn his head. Davhri rose and went to greet Eliani and Vanorin, who came in with raindrops glinting in their hair.

"You found Sunahran?"

Eliani smiled. "Yes, and three others. Hathranen made his way alone through the forest to Woodrun. I could not have done it!"

"Good news."

"Yes. I have an escort once more, and Vanorin a command. He was beginning to miss it, were you not?" She cast a sly glance at Vanorin, who returned a quiet smile.

"I was certainly missing the horses. It will be good to ride again."

Davhri brought tea for them. "I will start a stew."

"No, no, we are all asked to sup with Dejhonan and his family." Eliani turned to Luruthin. "I wish you could join us. We shall miss you."

"And I you."

Eliani's smile faded. "Cousin..."

"We shall meet again at the Council."

The hearthroom chime sounded. Davhri went to answer it and brought Othanin back with her. He declined the tea she offered, and came to stand beside Luruthin, wearing a dark grey cloak over grey tunic and legs, and high boots of soft dark leather.

"You are ready. Good, then let us begin. It is a long walk."

Luruthin stood. Eliani and Vanorin rose also, each murmuring words of farewell. Luruthin clasped their arms briefly, and held still when Eliani caught him in a tight hug.

"Oh, Luruthin!"

He stepped back from her, trying to smile. Tears were starting in her eyes, and he felt his own throat tightening.

"Thank you for seeing me safely here." He glanced from Eliani to Vanorin. "May spirits watch over your path."

Vanorin nodded. "And yours."

Eliani said no more, frowning up at him as a tear slid down her cheek. Without thinking he put a finger to her chin, lifting it. Her khi shone bright against his flesh.

"Keep you safe, Kestrel."

He turned away before his own grief could spill out. Othanin followed him to the door, where he picked up his belongings. Davhri joined them, bringing a grey cloak which she put around Luruthin's shoulders.

"It is raining. I wished to send this to Inóran, so you might as well wear it."

"Thank you, Davhri. Thank you for all."

She smiled, pressed a letter into his hands, then held aside the tapestry. A bright fire crackled on the welcoming hearth. Beyond, the rain had darkened the sky to make the evening seem later than it was.

Luruthin tucked the letter into his tunic, then stepped out, pulling the cloak's hood up over his head. Grey, like the silks.

He was all grey now, no color to him. He walked between colors, between lives. He stood in the silent garden, looking up at the rain, feeling it on his face. He needed no tears. The sky wept for him.

❀ Ghlanhras ❀

Kelev was in the audience hall, a roll of paper in his hands. Shalár ignored him, turning to the hall attendant whose duty was to record the business of petitioners as they arrived.

Three others stood waiting, and it happened that two of them preceded Kelev. Shalár heard their reports and requests, and gave orders in response. When Kelev's turn came, the attendant announced him as "Kelevon, supervisor of the walks."

Shalár turned a cold gaze on Kelev. "We do not use ælven names here."

"Your pardon, Bright Lady. I am yet unaccustomed to your ways."

"What is your request?"

Kelev stepped to the hall attendant's small work table and unrolled his papers atop it, causing the attendant to snatch up his inkwell in haste. Shalár disliked being compelled to go where Kelev directed, but it would be foolish to require him to spread his work on the floor at her feet, and inconvenient to view it there. She stood and went to the table.

Kelev pointed to the drawing. "These are the city gates as they are now. I propose converting these houses—which are empty except this one, in use by the watch at the gate—to a walled court that can withstand attack should the enemy achieve the gates."

"The covered paths would allow them to pass around the walled court."

"I will alter the paths at either side of the gates, adding a lesser gate to each which may be barred from without. Here are my plans."

Shalár watched and listened with interest as he showed her several sketches. He had planned well, and thoroughly. Plainly he had given the idea much thought.

Shalár tried to imagine an ælven attack on the city, the benefit that Kelev's inner court might yield. Certainly it would give her more time to prepare and carry out her next plan, whatever that might be. Perhaps it would be worthwhile to make such a court at each of the watch platforms, since they might also be vulnerable to attack. She would have to think on that.

"Very well. You may build this."

"I thank you, Bright Lady. May I make a small request in return?"

She looked at him, watching his eyes. Golden eyes, though they were beginning to darken.

"I would like an ælven to look after my house."

"You desire an attendant?"

"For myself, no. But I have been directing all my energy to the tasks you have given me, and the house you were also so kind as to give me is in a state of neglect. I would ask for an ælven to set it to rights."

"Why an ælven?"

Kelev looked surprised. "I did not suppose you would set one of your own people to such a menial task."

Shalár gazed at him, thinking there was more to his request than he claimed. Perhaps he wanted the use of an ælven for his pleasure. She would not deny him that, any more than she grudged it to any of her folk. She encouraged all attempts at breeding, but a perverse whim made her decide to thwart Kelev at this turn.

"Very well. I shall send an ælven to attend to your neglected house."

She would send her own attendant's father, who was otherwise fairly useless, and no pleasant company. Let Kelev make of that what he would.

Kelev bowed, a smile of satisfaction on his lips. "Thank you, Bright Lady."

He withdrew, rolling up his plans again. Shalár turned her attention to the hall attendant, who called forth the next seeking audience. This was Torith, with a report of what scouts had lately learned of Woodrun. The most significant news he brought was that the Greenglens had all left the town, riding south.

Shalár dared not hope that this portended a complete withdrawal. More likely, they were gone to rouse others to fall upon Ghlanhras and wrest it away from Clan Darkshore. She frowned as she listened, wondering how quickly Kelev could make his inner court.

A commotion at the back of the hall distracted her. Frowning, she glanced up and saw several hunters there, disputing with the guard who refused to let them in. Shalár glanced at the hall attendant, who hastened to the back of the chamber and returned shortly, looking excited.

Shalár raised a hand to stop Torith's report. He fell silent and followed her gaze to the attendant, who bowed deeply, then broke into a grin.

"Bright Lady, by your leave, Gæleth has arrived from Nightsand. He brings two hundred hunters."

Shalár's heart leapt with delight. Now she could hold Ghlanhras. This was but the first wave of Darkshore to return to their homeland. She leaned back in her chair, smiling.

"Show him forward."

✳ Ebon Mountains ✳

The walk was indeed long, and more than once Luruthin was seized with cramp and had to stop until it passed. Othanin stood by him, calmly waiting, offering no help for there was none he could give, and both knew it.

As they ascended the mountains Luruthin's breath began to rasp. He ached all over, as he had done on the first journey hither. His concentration narrowed to the task of walking, of moving one foot and then the other.

At long last a challenge rang out. Luruthin stood swaying while Othanin answered the watcher. Their words passed over him, no meaning lodging in his foggy awareness. Slowly he realized that the rain had stopped.

"Come." Othanin lightly touched his shoulder.

Luruthin moved forward once more, sparing no strength to answer. They walked on and on, far too long, it seemed to him, but at last he saw the light of a fire ahead.

The Lost's meadow. Relief sang through him. He followed Othanin toward the fire, but before they reached it Kivhani appeared before them.

"Welcome." She looked at Luruthin. Her face shifted, the smile replaced by a stern expression. "You need to hunt. Come with me."

Othanin frowned. "Do not go alone."

"No." Kivhani glanced over her shoulder toward the fire. "Inóran may come, and Vethalin."

Two others came toward them. Luruthin was too weary to greet them, too occupied with keeping himself upright. He felt dizzy, he realized. That was not good.

"Leave your bow, you will not need it."

Obediently he unslung the bow and quiver and dropped them at his feet. He took off his pack as well, and though it was not much burden, he was glad of the difference. Raising his head, he saw Inóran beside him.

He tried for a smile.

"Inóran. This is your cloak."

Inóran smiled back slightly. "Keep it on for now."

Kivhani stepped between them, caught and held Luruthin's gaze, then beckoned to him to follow. He obeyed, lengthening his stride to keep up with her as they left the meadow and struck into the forest. He heard Inóran and the other following.

Kivhani walked swiftly, and soon Luruthin was out of breath once more. He tried to be silent, but now and again he stumbled, or stepped upon a twig that cracked.

Clumsy. A poor hunter he made, in this condition.

Kivhani slowed her pace a little, for which he was grateful. She turned her head to glance at him.

"Have you hunted before?"

Luruthin swallowed, feeling his cheeks burn. "Once."

"Did you kill the kobalen?"

"No."

"Good."

They walked on. A sudden cramp sent Luruthin to his knees, retching dryly. Kivhani and the others murmured over him until it passed, then helped him up and onward.

When Kivhani stopped, Luruthin nearly stumbled into her. She caught his gaze and gestured for silence, and that he should stay where he was, then looked past him and jerked her head in summons. The Lost he did not know joined her, and both disappeared into the woods.

Kivhani must have scented kobalen. Luruthin was unaware of them, but then he was not much aware of anything, just now. He tried to feel the khi around him, to extend his senses through the woods, but he was too tired. He could sense Inóran's khi, that was all.

A nighthawk's cry cut the air. Inóran stirred, then touched Luruthin's arm and gestured to him to follow. They had not walked far when they came upon Kivhani and the other, with a female kobalen lying at their feet.

The other Lost squatted at the kobalen's head, his hand upon its brow. Its eyes were closed.

Luruthin felt mixed revulsion and relief. He looked to Kivhani, who spoke in a low, intent voice.

"We will teach you the ways of our hunting, but now is not the time. For now you need only give the benison. Say these words after me."

She beckoned him closer to the kobalen. Luruthin's knees trembled from weakness as he came near. He dropped down beside the kobalen, and Kivhani knelt beside him.

"Ældar guardian of this creature, accept my thanks for the sustenance it gives me."

Luruthin repeated the familiar words, the beginning of the hunter's benison. He had often said them over deer, or boar.

"Forgive me for the harm I cause to her. Accept my pledge of atonement."

Atonement was not normally a part of the benison, though it was understood that the hunter would not waste the bounty of the hunt, and would foster the well-being of the breed he hunted. Luruthin repeated the pledge.

She pressed a cup into his hands. It was metal, cool in the chill night. Kivhani gestured to him to hold it against the kobalen's arm. He obeyed, and with her knife she made a small cut above it.

Blood welled, filling the air with its hot scent, slipping into the cup held by Luruthin's trembling fingers. He shifted his grasp, careful to catch the flow, ignoring the raging urge of his flesh to throw away the cup and drink straight from the wound. He could hear his own pulse throbbing in his ears as he watched the cup slowly fill, a tiny curl of steam rising from it.

Kivhani held another cup close by, and gestured to him to take his away. She moved the fresh cup to the wound as he did so.

Luruthin did not wait for permission to drink, gulping greedily until he had emptied the cup. He sighed and closed his eyes, tilting his head back as renewal washed through him.

The sensation was amazing. First the pain drained away, then strength flowed through his veins, and with it the return of awareness.

He could hear the nervous shifting of a squirrel in a tree, smell the damp, rain-freshened earth beyond the bright and pungent smell of kobalen, feel the deep-sleeping khi of the trees around him. It was as if a veil had clouded all his senses, and was suddenly lifted.

"Here."

Luruthin opened his eyes and Kivhani reaching for the cup he held. He gave it to her, and she switched it with the other, offering the full cup to him. He drained it, not quite so quickly, and felt his strength increase further.

Once more she switched the cups, and now Luruthin sipped more slowly at the blood. He noticed its flavor, and the heaviness of the khi in it. When he had drunk half the cup he was sated, and could swallow no more. He lowered it and looked at Kivhani, who nodded toward Inóran.

Luruthin held out the cup. Inóran took it with a nod, murmured the benison over it, and drank.

Luruthin watched while he drank another cupful, then changed places with the other Lost, who also took a cup. Luruthin realized all at once why they touched the kobalen's brow—they were controlling it with khi, even as he had done by instinct at his first clumsy hunting.

Instinct, or experience? He had never previously used khi so upon a kobalen, or on any living thing. It was Shalár who had shown him that practice, who had practiced it upon him.

He swallowed. It was she who had passed the curse to him. Another cause for his rage against her.

Kivhani was now stanching the kobalen's wound. He had not seen her take a cup. Perhaps she had hunted recently, and felt no need. He looked at the kobalen, saw that it breathed. It lay peacefully, Inóran's hand at its brow.

"What gift can you give her?" Kivhani asked in a whisper.

Confused, Luruthin met her gaze. She nodded toward the kobalen, and he realized she meant he should give a gift to the creature.

"I have nothing with me."

"Nothing at all?"

He frowned, thinking. He had nothing of his own—he had lost everything in Ghlanhras, and now even the clothes he wore belonged to others. The few things he had lately acquired were all in his pack, back at the camp. All he had with him were a water skin and a belt knife. He took these out and showed them to Kivhani.

"The knife."

He met her gaze, wondering at her intention to arm a kobalen with a weapon of ælven make. She was quite serious, he saw. As she was to be his leader from now on, he did not question her decision, but removed the sheath from his belt and slid the knife into it, then placed it in the kobalen's slack hands.

"Good. Now, the mark."

Kivhani took her own knife from her belt and carefully cut a curl of fur from the kobalen's brow. The bare patch left behind looked odd. She handed the cut fur to Luruthin.

"Keep that. Tomorrow you will use it in your meditation."

Luruthin was confused and a little repelled, but he closed his hand around the fur. He watched as Inóran placed a pouch in the kobalen's hands, and the other Lost a string of clay beads.

Kivhani stood and stepped away into the woods along with the other Lost. Luruthin followed, trying to remember his name. He moved behind a tree, watching as Inóran slowly rose, his hand held out toward the kobalen, still holding it with khi. He, too, moved into the woods, and the kobalen stirred.

A stab of remorse struck Luruthin. It had been easy to ignore that the kobalen lived, that it had thought and feeling, when it had lain still before him. Not so easy now as he watched it wake in confusion and stare blankly at the knife in its hands.

Atonement. The knife was a gesture of atonement. He remembered one of the Lost saying they left meat for the kobalen. He was beginning to understand that their relationship with their prey was more complex than he had thought.

A brush of khi against his arm drew his attention. Kivhani summoned him, and he followed, silently now and steadily, joined by the other two as they moved through shadows away from the scene of their hunt.

They did not speak, but moved swiftly through the forest. Luruthin had no trouble keeping pace now, and he gave silent thanks again for the relief of feeling well and strong.

The journey back to the camp seemed much shorter. Soon Luruthin could see firelight through the trees, and hear the murmur of quiet voices. Othanin rose from the large fire circle to greet them. He smiled at Luruthin.

"You look better."

"I feel better." Luruthin turned to Kivhani and made a small bow. "Thank you, Lady."

Kivhani acknowledged this with a nod and a slight smile. "You are welcome. Now that you are fit, we must discuss why you are here."

Othanin turned to her. "I will join you, if I may. There is the Council to discuss as well."

Kivhani quirked a brow at him, then nodded. "Let us go to my camp."

They returned to the meadow and went to the small fire pit outside Kivhani's shelter. Othanin set about making a fire while Kivhani invited Luruthin to sit with her. She put back her hood and gazed at him, her black eyes deep, her pale brow slightly drawn with concern. When she spoke, her voice was soft and low.

"I am sorry for your suffering. You are welcome to come and live with us, if you are willing to abide by our ways."

Luruthin nodded. "I am grateful for the welcome."

"Hear what we require before you decide."

Her tone was serious, and Luruthin felt a qualm of misgiving, but he was willing to listen. He had little choice.

"Have you ever killed a kobalen?"

The question surprised him. "Countless. I was in Alpinon's Guard for decades."

"Well, you will never kill another."

Luruthin stared at her, blinking in astonishment. "But they are a danger to ælven settlements!"

"That is for ælven settlements to address. To us they are a blessing, to be respected and fostered. Without them we would have no hope."

Luruthin was silent, absorbing this. He could understand it, he supposed, yet it seemed very strange. All his life he had thought of kobalen as vermin. Kivhani spoke of them with reverence.

A bright flame leapt up from the fire pit. Luruthin glanced toward it, watching Othanin feed it with bits of shredded bark.

"You must leave your past life behind. You must never return to your former home. To live among us is to yield all other allegiance. You may never tell an outsider where we camp, what our numbers are or our names."

"With some exception." Luruthin glanced at Othanin, who met his gaze.

"This is the first camp I have been to. I shall probably never see another, nor this again after tonight."

Kivhani handed him a larger piece of wood from a pile near her seat, then glanced at Luruthin. "It was my decision to bring Othanin here, along with you and your friends. I felt the circumstances merited an exception. There are some who still disagree, and I respect their views. Othanin is a friend to many among us, but he will not return to our camps."

Luruthin felt a pang of sadness for them both. He glanced again at Othanin, but the governor's face showed nothing, though shadows danced across it with the shifting firelight.

"He is our link to the ælven world, and to all the gifts that world brings us." Kivhani's gaze rested softly on her partner, and Luruthin sensed both great love and great sadness in her eyes. "Therefore we do keep contact with him, but at meeting places of our choosing. Without Othanin, we could not trade for tools and little luxuries. Our life would be much harder."

"Perhaps the Ælven Council will change that. Perhaps you will no longer need such caution."

Kivhani gazed at Luruthin, doubt in her eyes. He recalled Inóran's tale of being hunted by ælven, and suppressed a shiver.

Othanin moved back from the fire, which was now burning briskly. "Lady Eliani suggested that Luruthin might speak on behalf of the Lost at the Council."

Luruthin hastened to explain. "I was at Jharan's Council in the autumn, so many there will know me. I believe Eliani's idea was that seeing and hearing from one they know who is now—afflicted—would make an impression."

Kivhani's brows rose. "Possibly one you would not enjoy."

Luruthin could not help grimacing. "Well, that is inevitable. At least I could try to convince them of your merit. They know nothing of your people, Kivhani—of your dedication to the creed, of the hard choices you have made. The three of us together can show them that the Lost are far different than the alben."

Kivhani held her hands out toward the fire, looking thoughtful. "I suppose it would be of value to have one the Council knows speak as one of us. You are willing to undertake the journey?"

"Yes. Alpinon is my homeland. I can guide you along the mountain road, where we are less likely to meet others."

"Your homeland?" Kivhani's face darkened. "You are not to return to your home."

Luruthin blinked. "Forgive me, Lady Kivhani, but why is this forbidden?"

"Because it only brings grief to all. Your family will cling to you, promise you it does not matter, that you may still live with them and they will care for you." Kivhani's face hardened. "But it does matter. We cannot dwell among the ælven. They fear us, and fear wakens cruelty. The last of us who stayed at home with family was slain by her own kindred."

Luruthin drew a sharp breath. He could not imagine his friends and family turning against him, but nor could he doubt Kivhani's words.

Othanin coughed gently. "Luruthin wishes only to bid his folk farewell. Perhaps he could take his oaths after we return from the Council."

Kivhani turned her head to gaze at him, frowning. "And live among us unsworn until then?"

"It is only for a few days. We must leave soon for Highstone in any case."

Luruthin watched their faces, thinking they engaged in a wordless debate. Not mindspeech, perhaps, but something close to it. Thus the understanding between lifelong partners. He felt a pang at seeing it.

At last Kivhani turned to him. "I will not require oaths of you now, but I will ask that you abide by our ways while you are among us. You must learn our way of hunting."

"Gladly."

"Also we require that one spend a part of every day in meditation on the subject of atonement. You will use that bit of fur to perform a blessing for the kobalen."

"I cannot commit to practices I do not know, but I will pledge to do my best to honor them."

Kivhani nodded, seeming satisfied. "Very well. After the Council, if you choose to dwell among us, you must swear to keep our ways."

"I understand."

A brief silence fell. Thinking that the governors would like to be alone together before Othanin must depart, Luruthin stood and picked up his things.

"I will go and find Inóran, if I may. I have a letter for him."

Kivhani frowned slightly but said nothing. She disapproved, perhaps, of Inóran's communicating with Davhri. Having seen how much joy and relief the contact had given to both of them, Luruthin could not agree. Perhaps he would take issue with that someday, but not now.

Othanin rose and extended an arm. "Thank you for your offer to guide us. I expect the journey will be hard."

Luruthin clasped arms briefly. "Long, certainly. And cold. Bring your warmest garments."

He left them, crossing the meadow toward Inóran's camp. He paused to look up at the stars, which seemed to glimmer with added brilliance after the rain. Standing in this meadow, he felt a calmness enfold him. With a small smile he acknowledged what it was: a tentative feeling of being at home.

❀ Bitterfield ❀

"Do you await Othanin's return?"

Eliani glanced up at Dejhonan as she chewed a mouthful of braised fowl, part of the excellent dinner the theyn and his lady had provided for her and her friends. Their last such meal for some while, she expected.

She had debated the very question Harangue had asked all day. It would be wise to confirm that Othanin would travel south and not try to reach Woodrun. Her heart, though, wished to be riding for the trade road.

Turisan was coming; he was in the Steppe Wilds now. If she missed him, reached the road after he had passed....

No, she could not even bear to think of it. She would ride as soon as she might.

She turned to the theyn. "No, but I will ask you to give him a message for me, and to talk to him yourself. Try to persuade him not to go to Woodrun."

Harangue filled Eliani's cup with more of the sharp local wine. "I will try. I cannot promise success."

"Has he named a nextkin since Ghlanhras fell?"

Saharan's brows rose. "I do not know. That is an excellent question, and one I will put to him."

"Thank you. I trust he will listen to you."

"He may say that his nextkin is in Woodrun."

"If that is the case, he should stay away, so that they are not both at risk."

"Mm."

"If all goes well, Turisan will be at Woodrun in a few days. Best he wait here for the news, if he does not leave at once for Highstone."

Dejhonan smiled. "I will do my best, my lady. Our governor may seem soft, but he has much determination."

"So I have discovered."

Eliani sipped her wine and looked at her plate, but her appetite had fled, replaced by a knot in her gut. She wished she could leave now, which would be rude, or immediately after the meal, which would be unkind to her friends and to the horses.

She took a forkful of tender greens, knowing she might have no more for some days. They gave her no pleasure but she ate them, clearing her plate of them while she listened to her escort chatter.

They were a family now. The bonds they had made would go with them back to Alpinon and Southfæld, and perhaps assure that Clan Greenglen and Clan Stonereach were more than allies.

The thought increased her loneliness. Even as she sat resisting the urge to speak to Turisan—impolite, when she was in company—she felt the warming of her brow.

She took a swallow of wine. *I am in company, love.*

I will not distract you. We are halting for the night at Riversease.

A tingle went through her. Riversease was the last town in the Steppe Wilds before the trade road entered Fireshore.

It will be our last chance to resupply.

Eliani could summon no simple response. She should say something polite, but all she could think of was how soon she might be in Turisan's arms.

She closed her eyes, trying to control her thoughts. A leader did not let personal wishes interfere with the good of her people.

I miss you as well, my heart.

She gave a cough of laughter and opened her eyes. Vanorin was watching her; the others were listening to Sunahran describe Woodrun's condition. Eliani had already heard his report and shared it with Turisan. The city was sending its children and weaker folk to Bitterfield—some had already arrived—and preparing to defend itself with some two hundred armed citizens.

And she should be thinking of how to help them, not indulging in selfish thoughts of reunion with Turisan. She took another mouthful of wine.

This will be a long night.

She knew her tone was bitter and regretted it, but Turisan seemed not to notice.

For me as well. It may indeed be selfish, but I intend to find you on the road, my lady. So dismiss any noble thoughts you may be having.

Her heart leapt with delight. Lowering her gaze, she allowed herself a small smile.

Yes, my lord.

❈ Waymeet ❈

A sharp wind tossed Rephanin's hair as he stood with Ehranan and Filari in the public circle at the village of Waymeet. They were in the Steppes at last, a land less soft and bountiful than the western plains of Eastfæld they had left behind. Harsh bluffs of reddish rock had replaced the rolling hills deep in grass. Small pines, gnarled and twisted, clung to the bluffs in defiance of the wind.

The trade road continued north from this place, while a second road struck northeastward into the Steppes, leading eventually to Watersmeet. Filari would take that road henceforth. An escort of eight guardians waited a short distance away, ready to accompany her.

Rephanin was relieved in part that she was leaving, for the need for constant vigilance in her presence was tiring. Yet he was pleased with her, and proud of her courage. He doubted that most understood how much courage she had. Turisan, perhaps, but no other, not even Ehranan.

She stood gazing at the Watersmeet road, squinting a little against the rising sun. Rephanin stepped toward her.

"I have a small gift for you, Filari. May I give it to you now?"

She frowned. "A gift? Why?"

"Merely a remembrance. We may not see each other again for some time."

"Oh. I have nothing—"

"Please do not feel obligated to make a gift in return. It is I who wish to be remembered."

He smiled, then withdrew a cord from his inner sleeve: white and gold, Eastfæld colors. The small coil glinted softly in the morning light. Filari held out her hand, and Rephanin pressed the cord into it

"There is khi in it." She unwound the cord to look at it.

"Yes. Blessings for your safety."

She glanced at him, uncertain but no longer frightened, he thought. "Thank you. This is kind of you."

307

308 ~ Pati Nagle

Rephanin spoke softly. "Whenever doubt assails you—and it will, that is certain—remember that you are not alone. Spirits are watching over you, and you have friends who wish you well. You are safe."

She gave a cough of laughter. "I will try to believe it."

Believe it.

With the contact he was suddenly aware of the dread that gripped her. She was eager to be away from the army, but she feared going to the Steppes, a fear so deep and irrational that Rephanin knew its source.

Kelevon is far away. He cannot touch you, nor would he dare approach Watersmeet.

I know that.

She was breathing rather sharply, and had twined the cord around her wrists. Rephanin placed his hands over it.

Filari.

Slowly he coaxed her to ease her grip. He unwound the cord and coiled it again, pressing it into her palm. She did not resist, and seemed to take comfort in his touch, so he prolonged it, gently holding her hand between his.

He wished he could banish her fears, but he did not know how. She needed healing that he could not give her.

Suddenly tears welled in her eyes and spilled down her cheeks. Rephanin's hands instinctively tightened on hers.

"Oh, Filari. Child."

I am not a child.

To me you are.

She pulled her hand from between his, stood swaying for a moment, then with a gasping sob threw her arms about his neck. Surprised, Rephanin held still at first, then gently embraced her. He smiled softly, sadly as he held her, allowing her to weep the tears she had denied for so long.

He heard Ehranan stepping away, giving them privacy. He felt a stab of heartache, but suppressed it. Ehranan understood, he hoped. Was it not obvious that his relationship with Filari was not intimate?

Gradually she calmed, then abruptly pulled away and wiped at her face. "Well, I should waste no more time. Thank you again for your kindness."

She met his gaze with eyes that belied the gruffness of her voice. Rephanin smiled.

"Thank *you*, Filari."

She glanced toward Ehranan, who was watching from a little distance. He strolled to her and held out a sealed letter.

"Give this to Governor Pashari, and tell her you come to serve the Steppe Wilds in this time of war."

Rephanin raised an eyebrow. "Does not your letter explain that?"

"Yes, but Pashari is fond of ceremony."

Filari slid the letter into her satchel. "I hope she will not refuse to see me."

"You come from me. She will see you. Your escort will confirm this."

Filari scowled. "I wish you would not make me take them."

"No mindspeaker rides unescorted."

Filari looked up sharply at that, as if still surprised to be called a mindspeaker. Rephanin smiled, then offered his arm. She clasped it, looking once more into his eyes, and he was glad to see that she was steadier. She exchanged a brief arm-clasp with Ehranan, then walked away to join her escort.

"Have you sought another mindspeaker?"

He turned to Ehranan, irritated by the question. "Every day. Every time we halt."

Ehranan raised his hands, a gesture of yielding. "I thought you might have forgotten."

"No. Shall I try again now?"

"I meant no offense."

The weariness in his voice dispelled Rephanin's annoyance. His instinct was to offer unspoken reassurance, and he reached out without thought, opening his heart to Ehranan.

A moment's stillness, a sense of a chasm before him, the sudden awareness of the expanse of Ehranan's soul opened and waiting, familiar and unfamiliar. Not the simple openness to communication that was usual when Rephanin spoke to another, but the complete baring of a heart who knew what it was to unite in spirit.

Rephanin hesitated, thinking a bird about to take wing must feel thus. He knew Ehranan's soul—had shared it in the battle by necessity— but this was no battle. This was the lonely, frightened heart of one who bore a great burden.

The soul beyond Ehranan's care-worn eyes was vast and rich. Rephanin embraced it, offering his own khi, feeling it mingle with Ehranan's, flowing together as they had not done since Midrange.

Then, there had been distractions, obligations, the emergency of war.

Now there was nothing to keep them from sharing all that was in their hearts. Ehranan's anxiety over the many details he must manage, over the welfare of those who accepted his command, over what they would face in Fireshore, all the worries he felt he should keep from the army were revealed. Rephanin was overwhelmed, and could only offer sympathy, wordless comfort, understanding.

He heard Ehranan give a small gasp. The commander stepped toward him, and suddenly their embrace became physical as well. A new level of tension filled Rephanin's awareness.

It is all right. It is all right.

It was his own voice he heard, repeating the assurance over and again.

Gradually the agitation in Ehranan's khi subsided, leaving them drifting together, sharing comfort, reaching a balance of peace.

They were together. Neither was alone. There was much solace each could give the other, much support, much affection.

Another possibility lay open to their exploration, one that Rephanin had tried to keep from his thoughts. This close, he could hide no thought from Ehranan, nor could he hide the rousing of his own flesh. He sensed Ehranan's dawning understanding, the long moment of stillness while Ehranan paused to consider the possibilities.

Rephanin made no advance, no offer, no invitation. He was still, so still he scarcely breathed. He could not deny or hide the feelings building within him, the urgency in his flesh. He waited, and at last he sensed a flicker of response, a tiny stirring of curiosity.

Ehranan wrenched himself away, mind and body, stumbling. Rephanin nearly fell, disoriented by the sudden shift. He strove to catch his breath, to calm the thunder of his heart, to still all the frightened thoughts within him.

Ehranan stopped a few steps away, both hands bunched into fists. He stayed thus for several breaths. Rephanin could see the tension in his shoulders.

"Forgive me." Ehranan's voice was rough.

"It is all right." The assurance rose to Rephanin's lips without volition.

"No. No, it is not. I apologize."

Ehranan turned, unhappiness writ in his face. It made Rephanin angry with himself, for the carelessness that had turned comfort to something unwelcome.

He swallowed. "I should not—"

I am cup-bonded.

Taken aback, Rephanin blinked. Ehranan slowly came back and stood before him, an arm's length between them.

I am cup-bonded until Midsummer.

His gaze was sharp, demanding, filled with need. He had resumed contact only on the lightest level, only enough to speak. Rephanin sought no more.

I see. A...a long-standing connection?

Ehranan let out an exasperated breath. *We have been occasional lovers for some time. At last Midsummer's feast we were carried away and made our pledge. I did not know then that I would be going to war in the next season. Mirlani was less than pleased when I departed.*

Oh.

I have had but two letters from her since I left Hollirued. I doubt we shall renew our bond. However....

However. It was a solemn pledge, not as lasting as handfasting but every bit as serious. Rephanin closed his eyes, frightened anew at how near he had come to compromising that pledge.

I ask your pardon—

Do not. You need not. The fault was mine.

Ehranan's tension echoed through the words. Rephanin wished he could offer comfort, but that was not possible now. He met the commander's gaze, saw the hunger there and felt a shadow of the same revive in his own flesh.

Ehranan's mouth twisted in a wry smile. *I did not think to mention it to you. Forgive me.*

Rephanin sighed and rubbed at his brow. *I would like to say there was no reason you should think you need warn me you were pledged, but that is sadly untrue.*

Ehranan chuckled. *Oh, Rephanin. Have you not let that go?*

Ehranan met his gaze and held it for a long moment. A whisper of the chasm's breeze teased Rephanin. Finally Ehranan looked away and shook his head.

I ... it is useless to speculate. We do not know where either of us will be at Midsummer.

Roasting in a darkwood forest, perhaps.

Perhaps. A smile tugged at the corner of Ehranan's mouth. *Until then we had better forget we had this conversation.*

I doubt I can manage that, but I will try not to remind you of it.

Ehranan gave a cough of laughter. *You cannot help but remind me. His smile faded to a look of wistfulness.*

Accept my thanks, Rephanin. You have given me—much comfort.

Bereft of words, Rephanin watched him walk away, slowly this time, toward the army's camp. Ehranan paused and looked back, his blue eyes piercing Rephanin's soul. He smiled briefly, sadly, then went on.

Rephanin closed his eyes. Confused and conflicting feelings assailed him: desire, regret, sympathy, hope. After a long moment he shook himself, and slowly followed.

One must go on.

❈ Darkwood Hall ❈

Shalár peered at the map spread on her work table. If they marched swiftly—very swiftly—they would reach Woodrun in three nights. If her hunters could not capture the town at once, they would have to retreat and find shelter, and would be vulnerable to being hunted down and dragged out into the sun.

Shalár closed her eyes briefly at the surfacing of ancient memories of the Bitter Wars, of folk dragged from their homes in Ghlanhras into the poisonous light of day. Even centuries later she recalled the screams, the pleading that was wasted upon the unyielding ælven.

That must not happen to her people now. She had pledged to protect them, and that was one pledge she fully intended to keep.

So, the warriors must needs spend a third day sheltering in the forest, and be ready to sweep upon Woodrun at nightfall. They would then have a full night to subdue the town. That would be best.

She looked up at the hunters in the room, the best leaders she had. Torith, who had led all the hunts since their arrival and kept the pens in Ghlanhras well stocked with kobalen. Gavál, who had scouted several times to Woodrun and knew the forest trails as well as any. Gæleth, who had brought the second group of hunters to Ghlanhras.

None were strong leaders. Of all of them, Shalár trusted Torith the most, but she did not feel comfortable entrusting this venture to him.

She wished for Ciris, Yaras, or even Irith. Bold hunters, all, able to foresee danger and make intelligent choices on their own. They had been watchers for her in the Ebons, tracking the ælven and reporting to her, even going into ælven settlements at night to bring her information. She would have trusted any of them to lead this foray, but they were not here.

Ciris she had sent to Midrange. If he lived yet, he would be making his way back to Nightsand. Irith remained in that city, recovering from sun poisoning. Yaras she had made her steward in Nightsand; she knew he would not return to Ghlanhras. He preferred to remain in the west, with his family.

She looked at Torith. He was competent enough leading a hunt or handling the watchers on the city wall, but would he be a strong leader in a battle? She tried to remember where he had been, what he had done, during the taking of Ghlanhras. She recalled no great accomplishments.

"Are the hunters ready?"

He nodded. "I bade them to assemble at the gates after sundown. They should be gathering now."

"Have they all fed?"

Torith blinked. "I do not know, my lady Governor."

"Have you spoken to Wahral about sending kobalen along?"

"No, Bright Lady."

Shalár leaned back in her chair, resisting the urge to reprimand him. If he were to lead the advance against Woodrun she must not undermine the others' respect for him. She rubbed her forehead, where a slight ache had begun to tease her, then lifted the raven quill from her inkstand and drew a slip of paper toward her.

"Take this to the pens and give it to Wahral. Select thirty kobalen for the journey, and as many as twenty more for those who need to feed before setting out. Make haste, Torith. They must march tonight, as early as may be."

"Yes, my lady Governor." He bowed as he accepted her note, and hurried from the room.

She should have reminded him that he would need to assign hunters to watch the kobalen and move them along. They would not keep up with Clan Darkshore, but they would arrive at Woodrun by the time they were needed.

Too many details, and it was stifling in this crowded room. She stood up, and the hunters all drew back. For the briefest of moments she missed Ciris, whom she suspected of aspiring to take her place. She did not trust him in that respect, but she enjoyed his arrogance.

That was what she needed now. Someone with arrogance. This lot were sheep. Not a one of them could be counted on to be as ruthless as the capture of Woodrun would require.

She stepped to the curtained doorway of her bedchamber and pushed it aside. Her ælven attendant sat just within, whither she had retreated when the hunters began to arrive. Shalár met her startled glance.

"A robe. Something plain. I am going out."

The ælven rose and went to the wardrobe, her step lighter than usual. Her mood seemed to have improved of late, and Shalár wondered if she had made peace with her lot or was plotting something.

She returned at once with an open-fronted robe of black fleececod, somewhat heavier than most of Shalár's clothing. Shalár shrugged it on over the tunic and legs of scarlet silk she was wearing, not bothering with a sash. She left her chambers, followed in haste by her hunters.

Outside Darkwood Hall she felt the mist of a cold drizzle on her face, blown beneath the covered walk by a winter gust. She strode along the walk in the wake of hunters who were no doubt answering Torith's summons.

When she reached the unfinished inner court behind the gates, she found it nearly full of warriors, the leaf weights on the nets at their hips glinting in the dull night, an honored few bearing captured ælven swords. Reminded of the night her three hundreds had set out for Fireshore, she felt a swell of longing to go with them now.

If not for the child, I would go.

She clamped her teeth on the inside of her lip as her hand went to her belly. The child's safety could not be risked. She dared not lead this fight—and yet, perhaps she dared not let some other lead it.

She must take Woodrun now, secure it against attack. Doing so would have two benefits: it would give Ghlanhras a forward line of defense, and it would all but end the darkwood trade.

If Shalár controlled darkwood, she would have something to bargain with. Something with which to command the ælven's attention.

She looked at the darkwood wall that Kelev was building, and the pile of salvaged darkwood that remained to be added to it. Wet in the drizzle, like her black-clad warriors patiently waiting. They stood here because they had faith in *her.* They looked to her to lead them, and her heart ached to answer.

She closed her eyes, seeking the feather touch of her daughter's khi. It hovered at the back of her awareness, as ever, present but maddeningly out of her reach.

Child, I would not risk you, but nor can I risk three hundred hunters. Nor the failure of this venture. It must not fail.

A flutter answered, a stirring within her. At first she was uncertain whether it was movement of the tiny body growing inside her, or the soul that waited to enter it. A warmth then flooded her and she knew it was the soul.

Do what you must. Follow your path.

Shalár drew a deep breath and opened her eyes. The pale faces of her hunters were turned toward her. Her pack, watching for her command.

She turned and strode back toward the hall, leaving Gæleth and the others. On her way she met Torith hastening toward the gates.

"I have done as you commanded, my lady Governor. The kobalen will follow."

"Good. Choose ten to guard them. They will not keep up, but no matter."

"Yes, my lady."

She strode on, leaving him behind, feeling the slight bewilderment in his khi. Reaching Darkwood Hall, she skipped a step in her haste, but would not let herself run. She passed through the audience hall and sought her own chambers. The ælven looked up in surprise from straightening the maps Shalár had left on the work table.

"Roll those up and tie them."

Shalár went into the bedchamber, shrugged out of the robe, and stripped off her silks. Pausing, she smoothed her hands across her belly. Too early yet for the burden to show, but she felt its presence, a small glow within her.

I will take the best care of you I can manage, child.

As usual, she received no answer. Smiling nonetheless, she stepped to her wardrobe and pulled out a fresh tunic and legs, these of fleececod. She pulled them on and strode across the room to a chest that stood against the wall.

Above it hung the sword left behind by the Stonereach, a handsome piece, wrought with vines and the pommel a huge crystal, no doubt from Clerestone. She was saving this sword for her daughter. It was only fitting, for the blade had belonged to the child's sire.

Shalár touched the hilt, searching for a hint of his khi. Strong khi it had been, with its own distinctive tone. A whisper of pines and thin mountain air. She thought she felt it briefly, then her attendant intruded, holding aloft the roll of maps.

"Where shall I store these?"

"Put them on the bed and come here."

The ælven obeyed, glancing into the chest as Shalár raised its lid. Its contents were also bounty from the capture of Ghlanhras. The black dye had not completely taken, but it was black enough. The ælven's face showed confusion as she met Shalár's gaze.

Shalár smiled. "Come, you must have seen armor before. Now help me put it on."

✤ The Trade Road ✤

Turisan reined his mount to a walk, though his inclination was instead to urge it to gallop. Sensing his mood, the animal neighed a protest, and he stroked its neck to soothe it.

The riders followed his lead, and their horses blew and snorted as they fell to the pace that was their rest for the moment. At the next halt they would have to switch to their remounts, but Turisan thought they would manage one more round of trotting before then.

Always he looked ahead, toward Fireshore. The sight of the Varindel was what he hoped for, though it would set him a quandary. Eliani was riding along that river—she had left Bitterfield three days since, the morning he had left Riversease.

If he had not met Eliani by the time he reached the Varindel, duty would have him press onward. He clenched his teeth, wondering how long he might wait at the river before his command began to question the delay. Or should he send them on, and ride westward from there himself, toward Bitterfield?

His father would disapprove that, and he felt in his heart it would be wrong. But he and Eliani had sacrificed so much. Would Jharan begrudge them one day to meet and be together again?

He knew the answer. Not even one day—nor part of a day—could be spared from the push to reach Woodrun. The fate of Fireshore depended on his arriving there before the alben.

A flush of heat rose into his face. How could he even have considered failing in that duty?

The road ahead seemed to climb endlessly. No sign of trees that would mark a river. They had crossed no streams since the morning. If they did not find water soon, he would have to turn west to seek it.

He thought of asking Eliani's advice, but did not send the signal. She had not been on the road when she came north; she would have little help for him. Glancing westward, he saw that the column had left Great

Sleeper behind to the south. That white-shouldered mountain had taunted him for the last two days, reminding him of Eliani's sojourn there. A spark of annoyance rose in him at the thought, though she had proved to him that she had been true to him.

Sighing, he closed his eyes briefly. His moods were too volatile; he must quiet himself. Had he not lived a century and more without such emotional tempests?

Yes, without Eliani. And no, he did not wish to return to that lack of excitement. Nor could he, bound as they were.

"Lord Turisan?"

He looked at the rider who spoke, one of Eastfæld's captains. The rider nodded northward, and Turisan followed his gaze.

The horizon had not changed, but the air had. It held a spark of something different, a waver. Frowning, Turisan nudged his horse to a trot and rode ahead of the column, holding a hand in the air to signal they should not follow.

The steady rise of the road had leveled somewhat, though the change had been so gradual that he did not notice. Ahead stood two standing stones to either side of the road. At first he thought them conces, then he realized they were guideposts. As he drew abreast of them he inhaled.

The stones marked the edge of a cliff. The road turned sharply east and descended, switching back and forth on its way down until it disappeared into a forest of greenleaf that stretched as far as Turisan could see. His heart beat faster as he realized that somewhere beneath that tangle of green flowed the Varindel.

They had reached Fireshore.

Eliani bit her lip to keep from saying something sharp or stupid. She could scarcely think, so impatient was she to reach the trade road, but she managed to avoid tormenting her escort with her feelings. At least, she hoped she had.

Their road followed the Varindel, twining through the forest in a way that made riding faster than a walk impractical. Sunahran and the others chatted happily as the horses ambled along. Only Vanorin was as silent as Eliani herself. She did not care to think about why.

She had done nothing to hurt him, yet she knew that he would inevitably be hurt. She could not prevent it, nor ease it. He must cope, that was all. And while she wanted to offer him comfort, express her regrets, she knew that this would only increase his distress.

Her mount tossed its head. Eliani sympathized, and loosened her rein. The horse veered toward the riverbank, reaching for grass. She let it pull a mouthful, then nudged it onward.

Too early in the day to halt. The horses must graze, but they could do so come nightfall, while their riders made camp. Eliani looked over her shoulder, trying to judge how long she had until sunset.

Not another night.

Eliani?

Oh! You startled me.

Forgive me. I...we are at the Varindel.

Her heart swelled with excitement. Without thought, she leaned forward and her mount picked up a trot, then a lope.

Grinning, Eliani shifted her weight with each turn in the road. Her mount was nimble; she really should halt, but the joy of the ride and the unbearable thought of waiting any longer made her give up all proper ideas.

One querying shout followed her, then the thudding of hooves came after her. No use telling them to stay behind. Vanorin would insist on accompanying her, his endless fears for her safety his excuse.

Just as her horse's breathing began to labor and she thought she would have to stop, a lightening in the forest ahead made her catch her breath. The road straightened; the horse ran faster without her bidding.

She saw other horses lining the river-bank, many horses, their riders watching them drink. The way widened before her and spilled onto the trade road.

Standing in a pool of sunlight, holding his mount's reins and talking to two Ælvanens, he was there. Turisan.

Eliani halted, suddenly shy. This Turisan—how did he manage to look so elegant after traveling for days?—was little more than a stranger to her. Yes, they had shared a bed, once. Many nights ago. The thought did nothing to calm her.

He looked at her and smiled, causing her heart to thump wildly. She dismounted and stood holding her reins, frozen in doubt.

"Allow me, my lady."

Vanorin's voice made her turn. He stood beside her, offering with a gesture to take her horse. His face was stony and he did not meet her gaze.

Eliani swallowed and handed him the reins. "Thank you."

He bowed, then led the horse away. She watched, her heart aching for him.

What is this?

Startled, she turned to find Turisan beside her. No longer smiling; a slight frown creased his brow.

Vanorin has...developed a fondness for me.

So I gather.

I did not encourage it.

Turisan gazed at her for a long moment. "Let me introduce you to my captains."

She followed him, obediently greeting several people whose names did not catch in her memory. Her misery increased.

He was disappointed in her. Regretting their partnership, perhaps. She had done nothing wrong, but she had failed him nonetheless, somehow.

Did he think she had lied to him? Was his opinion of her that low?

One of the captains addressed her. "How many days are we from Woodrun, Lady Eliani?"

"Oh...four."

Turisan's eyes narrowed as he looked up the road. Too long; she knew that was what he was thinking. What they were all thinking.

Turisan shifted his gaze westward. The light was already becoming golden.

"Let us camp here the night, rest the horses well." He turned to Eliani. "This is the last river before Woodrun, yes?"

She nodded. "There are streams, but yes. The Lanarindel is at Woodrun."

"Very well."

The captains dispersed to settle their companies for the night. They were strung out along the river, many moving up the Bitterfield road in search of room for their horses. Not an ideal way to camp, but there were more than enough ælven to discourage any kobalen in the area from attacking.

Will you camp with me?

So formal. She met Turisan's gaze. *Of course, if you wish it.*

I do. Shall I send someone to fetch your packs?

No need. I can do it.

Instantly she felt this was the wrong answer. His very khi radiated disapproval. She drew a sharp breath.

Will you come with me?

Again, a long stare. *You wish me to?*

Of course, yes. Please.

They walked up the trade road in silence, following a company of Ælvanen who were looking for space along the river. Eliani realized she was digging her fingernails into her palms, and forced herself to relax.

Why was it so awkward now that they were together? They had talked comfortably at a distance for all of a season.

Guardians gazed at them curiously, even pausing as they made camp to watch Turisan and Eliani pass. The great mindspeakers. Eliani huffed a laugh.

What is funny?

Nothing. Turisan...

Yes?

Have I done something wrong?

She stopped, bracing herself for his answer. He turned to face her.

I was thinking that I had.

Eliani shook her head, bewildered. She saw a swallow move his throat.

I have failed you. If you must turn to others—

What? No!

Ulithan, and Vanorin as well. Why did you not tell me of that?

Feeling her cheeks burning, she lowered her gaze. *I hoped it would pass.*

What Vanorin feels is more than fondness, if I am not mistaken.

I did not....

She bit her lip, fighting tears. Heard him step closer, saw his hands held out. Slowly she placed hers into them. As his fingers gripped hers—so warm and her hands were cold—she closed her eyes.

You did not mean for it to happen.

No. And it hurts him, and I do not know what to do.

There is nothing you can do but let him go.

Dismiss him? That would hurt him even more! He is proud of his duty.

Then you are right, he must finish his task. When you are back in Alpinon, he will be free.

Eliani sighed. Alpinon was far from her thoughts just now.

You are fond of him as well.

Of course I am! I am fond of them all. After what we have been through together—

I meant no criticism.

She bit her lip, and said nothing for fear of saying something wrong. After a long moment, his grip on her hands loosened.

Forgive me, Eliani. This is harder for me than I thought it would be. Being apart, knowing you are with others—

I have kept my pledge.

I do not question that.

She felt him lean toward her and opened her eyes just as his lips brushed her brow, sending a tingle from her scalp down to her toes.

We have this night. Let us forget the rest until tomorrow. Shall I woo you again, my lady?

She gave a nervous laugh. *Ridiculous.*

She became aware of others watching. Pulling her hands out of Turisan's grasp, she started up the road again. Turisan walked beside her.

Ahead, she saw her escort grooming their mounts. Her own horse was there as well, drinking from the river. Its tack and her gear lay neatly piled beneath a tree. Vanorin's work, but he was nowhere in sight.

She nodded greeting to her escort, then found her saddle packs and slung them over her shoulder. Turisan waited on the road. On impulse, she beckoned to him.

"Turisan, have you met my escort? This is Sunahran, and Cærshari. Revani, who kindly loaned me these leathers, and Hathranen."

Turisan came forward. "Well met."

He clasped arms with each of them, smiling and paying them small compliments. He was much better at that than she.

"I will be in Turisan's camp, if you need me. We ride in the morning."

Sunahran nodded, and Cærshari flashed Eliani a grin. "Enjoy your rest!"

Turning away before they could see her blush, Eliani started back down the road. Silence fell between her and Turisan again. Too many others watching; heads turning as they walked to a camp made by Turisan's escort, twenty Southfæld guardians unknown to Eliani.

Only a few of them were in the camp. Turisan introduced them to Eliani, and she did her best to imitate his courtesy, though she felt awkward. They all sat around a campfire and shared a meal as evening fell. Others came and went, and one of the guardians produced a flute. The music was subdued—rather mournful—but it gave a sense of peace to the camp.

Eliani? Shall we walk?

She drew a breath. *Yes.*

They rose and quietly stepped away, the flute's music drifting after them. The forest here was open enough to walk through. They passed more campfires and were soon surrounded by trees and dusk, stars glinting now and then through the canopy. At length Turisan stopped and turned to Eliani, gently gathering her in his arms.

He smelled of horse and leather and himself—that smell that she had so longed for. She leaned against him, heart pounding. His fingers slid up the back of her neck to her scalp.

Your hair has grown.

Well, it has been a season.

Yes. Too long.

His kiss caught her by surprise, deep and intense, lighting fire in her loins. Their khi blended and her anxiety burned away, replaced by desire.

They had spent the night of their handfasting in the Star Tower at Hallowhall, surrounded by luxury. Now Turisan spread his cloak on the forest floor, a much humbler bed. Turning to her, he began working to unfasten her leathers.

She reached for his in turn, impatience making her fumble at the straps. His soft laughter tickled her ear.

We have all night.

He removed a bracer from her arm and kissed her wrist, and made a game of it, kissing whatever part of her he freed from the next garment. She did likewise, and by the time their clothes were gone they were deeply entwined in thought, beyond drawing back.

They slid into one another, sensations both familiar and new enthralling them. Turisan kept the pace slow, driving Eliani mad. Each shift, each touch sent responses echoing between them. They moved together toward a perfect height of ecstasy, so deeply lost within each other that the echoes rang again and again before subsiding slowly, leaving them spent.

Resting, they spoke in feelings, having abandoned words. Wellness, peace, agreement. Together, no outsiders, no distractions. They sought passion again, rested again, until the forest began to lighten with morning.

It was Turisan who first drew back into himself, not completely but enough to remember that self. Eliani reluctantly let him go, returning to awareness of herself as an individual. So lonely; she preferred to remain entwined, but Turisan thought something was important.

We must ride.

Yes.

I do not wish to say farewell, Eliani.

I am coming with you.

His concern and worry rippled through her. To shield herself she withdrew further.

Ehranan expects you.

I will go after we have reached Woodrun.

It is too dangerous.

I am not leaving you.

Eliani opened her eyes, inhaled deeply, relishing the smells of the forest and her partner, her love. At last she slid away from him and sat up, stretching her arms skyward. Her handfasting ribbons glinted softly, still tight on her forearm.

Not here, then. A relief; she had no desire to make a home in the wilds of Fireshore.

We are running out of possibilities. I hope we do not discover our home in Eastfæld.

Or the Steppes. Turisan rolled onto his side and ran his hand over her flesh, making her shiver.

Eliani—

Four days. It will make little difference to the army. They will reach Woodrun when they reach it, whether or not I am with them.

Uncertainty, then resignation. It was what he wanted, too. Selfish, yes. This bit of selfishness they would permit themselves.

If the alben are in Woodrun, you will ride south at once. Promise me.

I am a guardian—

Promise me.

Very well.

He kissed her again, long and slow, then withdrew completely at last, leaving only a thread of connection that neither was willing to release. They held it gently as they dressed each other, making ready to face the coming war.

Preview: *Eternal*

(coming in April 2012)

After the human race evolved the ælven went into hiding, still struggling against the alben, and now fighting to survive in a world that belonged more and more to humans.

= 1 =

I never should have let them talk me into giving blood.

It was almost eight and the donation center was getting ready to close. Still light outside, since it was late May, and the view from the center's picture windows of the Sandia Mountains east of Albuquerque was fantastic. All the couches faced those windows, for which I was thankful as I lay squeezing a little foam bar and contributing my pint.

I hated needles, and I didn't much care for the sight of blood even if it was in neat little plastic bags. I was pissed at myself for letting Len wheedle me into this. Ever since she switched to pre-med, she was nuts on this kind of thing.

She and her boyfriend Caeran had already finished donating and were over in the lounge area with the cookies and punch. So sue me, I bleed slow.

The technician came by and jiggled my little bags of blood. "Almost done," she said cheerily.

I didn't answer. I was working up to a first class sulk.

Ever since Len had hooked up with Caeran, I felt like a third wheel. Now that the semester was over they were heading up north to visit his family—tonight was our farewell fiesta—and I was looking at a boring, lonely summer.

I sighed and gazed out the window. The mountains were turning pink in the sunset, earning their name, "watermelon." Not as picturesque as the Sangre de Cristo mountains east of Santa Fe, named for the same reason but rather more graphically. Those Catholics.

My eye was caught by movement just outside in the parking lot. A man, I thought: tall and slender in a hooded sweatshirt, walking toward the side of the building. For an instant I thought it was Caeran, but I could hear his voice behind me, and he wasn't dressed like that.

The tech returned and declared me done. She removed the needle and made me hold my arm in the air for a minute, asked me if I felt dizzy, then wound some hot pink vet wrap around my arm and released me to the snacks.

I got up carefully, since I hadn't done this before. I'd heard of people passing out, but I just felt a little lightheaded, and even energized.

Len looked up and smiled as I made a beeline for the drinks. "Feeling OK?"

Ignoring her, I filled a paper cup with lemonade. It was bad, from a powdered mix. I chugged two cups.

"I'm always thirsty too," Len said. "I wish they'd have something besides all this sugar."

I glanced involuntarily at Caeran, who was munching an apple. Probably he'd brought it along. He was Mr. Healthy Eater, claimed he didn't like sweets. I could have hated him if only he wasn't so damned gorgeous. And nice. Disgustingly nice.

OK, I was jealous. Len had scored the best-looking guy on campus. I'd had some dates, but none of them came close to Caeran for all-around wonderfulness. I kept telling myself I'd find the right guy eventually, but it was hard not to wish I'd spotted Caeran first. Or rather, that he'd walked up to my station at the library desk instead of Len's.

"Movie starts in twenty minutes," Len said. "We'd better go."

She and Caeran headed for the door. I hung back to look through the cookies, grabbed the last packet of Oreos and shoved a Moon Pie into my pocket, then hurried after them.

The front parking lot had been full when we arrived, so we'd parked in the lot to the north. Now the center's lot was empty except for one car at the end of the row. The pavement radiated the day's heat.

I paused to open the Oreos and stuffed one into my mouth. As I looked up, I glimpsed the man I'd seen through the window standing by the blood red wall that surrounded the center.

He had long hair like Caeran's, and it was white even though he looked young. Goth, maybe? His clothes were black. Same lean bones, same high cheekbones as Caeran. I stood ogling him, then he looked at me and his nostrils flared.

Cold flooded my gut. Not a rational reaction; purely instinctive. My lizard brain knew he was a killer.

April 2012

Blood of the Kindred series

The Betrayal
Heart of the Exiled
Swords Over Fireshore

Immortal series

Immortal
Eternal

About the Author

Pati Nagle was born and raised in the mountains of northern New Mexico. An avid student of music, history, and humans in general, she loves the outdoors but hides from the sun.

She writes in a variety of genres, but is most often drawn to fantasy or (as P.G. Nagle) historical fiction. Her stories have appeared in *Asimov's Science Fiction*, the *Magazine of Fantasy & Science Fiction*, and in various other magazines and anthologies, including *Elf Magic*, which featured "Kind Hunter," the story that sparked the ælven world. Her Blood of the Kindred series includes *The Betrayal, Heart of the Exiled*, and *Swords Over Fireshore*. A contemporary series featuring the ælven began with *Immortal* and continues with *Eternal*.

Pati Nagle still lives in the mountains in New Mexico, with her husband and furry feline muse, where she loves to walk in the woods and look up at the stars.

www.patinagle.com
www.pgnagle.com

bookviewcafe.com

www.ingramcontent.com/pod-product-compliance
Lightning Source LLC
Chambersburg PA
CBHW022027260626

47156CB00017B/430